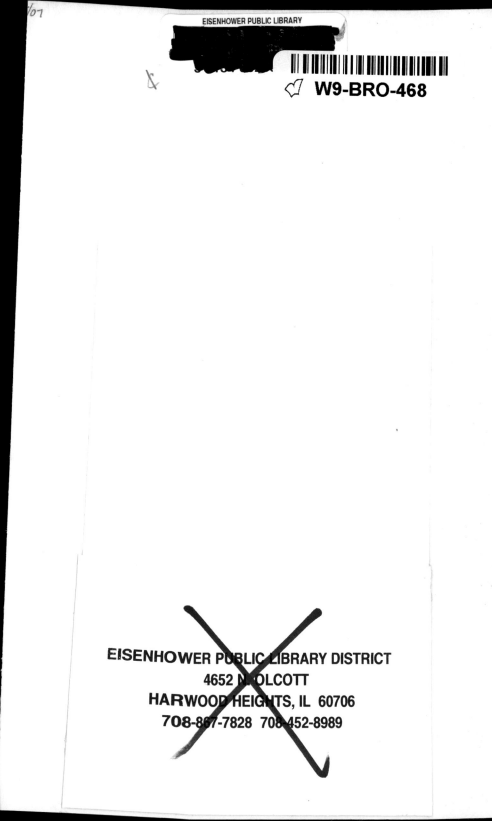

EISENHOWER PUBLIC LIBRARY

W9-BRO-468

EISENHOWER PUBLIC LIBRARY DISTRICT
4652 N. OLCOTT
HARWOOD HEIGHTS, IL 60706
708-867-7828 708-452-8989

CROSSFIRE

CROSSFIRE

P M Carlson

This first world edition published in Great Britain 2006 by
SEVERN HOUSE PUBLISHERS LTD of
9–15 High Street, Sutton, Surrey SM1 1DF.
This first world edition published in the USA 2006 by
SEVERN HOUSE PUBLISHERS INC of
595 Madison Avenue, New York, N.Y. 10022.

Copyright © 2006 by P. M. Carlson.

All rights reserved.
The moral right of the author has been asserted.

British Library Cataloguing in Publication Data

Carlson, P. M.
    Crossfire
    1. Hopkins, Marty (Fictitious character) - Fiction
    2. Police - Indiana - Fiction
    3. Detective and mystery stories
    I. Title
    813.5'4 [F]

    ISBN-13: 978-0-7278-6388-1
    ISBN-10: 0-7278-6388-6

In memory of my father and mother

Except where actual historical events and characters are being
described for the storyline of this novel, all situations in this
publication are fictitious and any resemblance to living persons
is purely coincidental.

All Severn House titles are printed on acid-free paper.

Typeset by Palimpsest Book Production Ltd.,
Grangemouth, Stirlingshire, Scotland.
Printed and bound in Great Britain by
MPG Books Ltd., Bodmin, Cornwall.

To make our weak hearts strong and brave,
Send the fire, send the fire!
To live a dying world to save,
Send the fire, send the fire!

William Booth (1829–1912)
Founder of the Salvation Army

In the bleak mid-winter
Frosty wind made moan,
Earth stood hard as iron,
Water like a stone;
Snow had fallen, snow on snow,
Snow on snow,
In the bleak mid-winter,
Long ago.

Christina Rossetti (1830–1894)

ACKNOWLEDGEMENTS

Many people generously shared their insight and expertise to make this novel possible. I especially want to thank Kay Williams, Robert Knightly, Al Ashforth, Theasa Tuohy, Jeanne Mackin, Emily Johnson, Linda Myers, Janis Kelly, Nicola Morris, Jane Crawford, Lisa Harris, Major David W Toumey, Mark Holton of Cornell Outdoor Education, Robin Coleman, Ryan Kinnally and Paul Wu of Mountain Edge Outfitters, Mike 'Motor' McElroy and, as always, Marvin Carlson. Any errors remaining are mine and not theirs.

One

Cold had shattered the night into crystals. Crystalline snow lay brittle as ground glass on leafless earth and branches. Crystalline stars pierced the black sky, except straight ahead to the north where a denser black loomed. Jagged stubs of broken bushes, sharp as diamonds, bit at her shins. Even her feet seemed crystallized, numb in her boots, as Deputy Martine LaForte Hopkins climbed up the ridge thinking about her warm bed miles away. Or better yet, Romey's bed.

Her shift was supposed to be over as of midnight, twenty minutes ago. But despite Marty's eight years on this job, her new boss, Sheriff Chuck Pierce, still doubted that a woman could cope and kept devising little tests. So messing up was not an option.

Half a mile behind her, on the icy mud of the access road, more trail than road really, her cruiser waited behind a Hoosier National Forest truck and a TV van. Ahead of her, where the frozen moon lit the wooded crest of the hill, she could see a pickup-sized Nichols County Fire Department truck with a triangular brush-breaker frame of heavy-duty steel bars jutting forward around its nose. Like a snowplow, it had crushed down the shrubs and saplings to make the trail she followed.

Marty paused, listened. A faint crackling noise, and male voices. She pushed past the brush-breaker truck, shone her flashlight into the shadows. The truck had stopped here because the hill plunged down so abruptly from this ridge. She remembered the map she'd looked at before starting the climb. Must be Little Deer Creek down there. A canvas hose, lying flat and unused, led from a reel on the brush-breaker truck down around a limestone outcrop. Marty followed it, skidding sometimes on the steep icy ground. Branches still snapped at her and now that she was no longer following the brush-breaker she had to raise her forearm to protect her face. An occasional

1

whiff of smoke put her in mind of the Fourth of July – barbecues, fireworks, and a big bonfire in the riverside park. Heckuva lot better weather than this, though.

As she rounded the limestone, she saw tree trunks illuminated in glowing orange light, then the bright glare of flames. A shack blazed on the far side of the little creek.

Three human silhouettes were standing to the right as she approached. One of them occasionally whacked at the branches behind him with a long axe. The other two were discussing whether this was national forest or private land. Obviously the main action was over and nobody had been hurt.

'Man, you guys pick weird places for your cookouts,' Marty called, following their tracks from one rock to another across the ice-bound creek.

'Hey, Marty,' said one of the silhouettes – Ray Bramer by his voice. 'You come to tell us a ghost story by the campfire?'

The flames had already awakened ghosts, a childhood memory of her mother's weeping face and a closed coffin. Marty said, 'Nah. I'm no fan of fires.'

'Amen,' said one of the guys with Bramer. Marty was close enough now that she could see him, an older guy wearing a Forest Service firefighting outfit, his skin glowing pink in the firelight. He pushed up his safety goggles to look at her and asked, 'You're sheriff's department?'

She nodded. 'Yeah. Deputy Marty Hopkins.'

'Smythe, Forest Service. You're the one Wes Cochran hired?'

Wes Cochran had hired a bunch of deputies while he was sheriff but she was the only woman. Marty said, 'Yep. Glad to meet you. So what've we got here?'

'Not much. Mostly over now, just lettin' it burn out. Hope you like your venison well done.'

'Venison?'

He gestured at the cabin. Its roof and narrow windows had collapsed and the thick plank walls were licked by flames, angrier inside than out. Where the door had been Marty could see a deer carcass just inside the threshhold, the flesh black and shriveled on to the bones. She asked, 'If that deer got in there, why didn't it get out?'

'One theory, it squeezed in through a window,' Ray Bramer

said. 'Door's gone now but it hadn't burned yet when we got here; big padlock on the outside, so it had to be a window. So maybe it knocked over the stove, then couldn't find the broken window to get out again.'

Marty said, 'Those windows look way too skinny even for a deer. I bet somebody killed it and dragged it into the cabin for safekeeping.'

Smythe nodded. 'That's the other theory. Deer season's over. Guy maybe locked it in to hide it from us rangers or from the coyotes, and forgot to douse his cookstove when he left.'

'Yeah, that's what I think too.' The third guy had stopped cutting brush at the sound of her voice and approached them. Marty couldn't remember his name but, like Ray Bramer, she'd seen him at other Nichols County fires. He added, 'The idiots had propane or somethin' stored in their cabin.'

Marty opened her mouth to ask about it, but Bramer did a palm-down gesture to quiet them both, nudged his chin a millimeter toward his right, and Marty realized that what she'd thought was the silhouette of a rock was in fact a crouched man holding – what? Ah, of course, a hand-held video camera. The guy stood up and said, 'Deputy Hopkins. I'm George Katz, WATH Indianapolis . . .'

'Yeah, hi, George; saw your van back on the access road. Didn't we talk a couple years ago?'

'Yeah, that tornado. You got any info about this fire for our viewers?'

She shrugged. 'I've been here what – thirty seconds?'

George said, 'What's all that about propane?'

Stan Smythe answered. 'Like we told you, they'll send investigators in the daylight and then we'll know what we've got. May be a while.'

George frowned. 'Can't you tell me anything? I mean, these are damned pretty pictures. But they probably won't get air time 'cause it's just someone's hunting cabin. Even propane could give me an angle. Hey, Marty, can you at least tell me whose cabin?'

'We'll find out. Check with me tomorrow, George,' Marty said.

He shrugged again. 'OK, but you know – yesterday's news.'

'We'll give you what we get. Tomorrow.'

'OK. Too cold tonight anyway. I'll just get a couple shots from over there and be off.' He walked past them along the creek toward the west and the stepping-stone crossing. Marty envied him, going home.

She glanced at the cabin. Sparks rose with the smoke billows and drifted away to the north. Not much wind: that was good. So was the fact that even this far away she could feel the warmth, welcome on this twelve-degree night. She turned to the firefighters. 'OK if I take a quick tour so I can make my report?'

Ray Bramer said, 'No problem unless the wind picks up.' He glanced at the TV reporter's retreating back, then his chin nudged toward the northeast, so she started around that way.

The firefighters had chopped a firebreak lane around the cabin, the brush tossed to the outer side, the tallest trees left standing with only a few low branches removed. She wished Ray Bramer had given her more than a chin-point to tell her what to look for, but it turned out to be obvious. She climbed the steep hillside behind the cabin, following the chopped lane over boulders and eroded roots, pulling herself along sometimes by grabbing branches or shoving against stones. She could see why George Katz hadn't come this way for his videotape. Clambering on these icy slopes with a camera wouldn't be fun.

But about a third of the way around the heavily trampled firebreak was a single line of footprints in the ice-crystal snow. They led away from the cabin along a narrow natural ledge.

One of the firefighters? She examined the trampled firebreak lane in the combined light of moon and flames, and soon she'd identified three different sizes of boots. But none had the same pattern as the prints that ran along the ledge.

This must be what Ray Bramer had wanted her to find. The deer hunter, probably, who'd taken his illegal trophy to the cabin, then forgotten to check for live embers in the grate before he locked up and left.

Even field-dressed, a deer was heavy. So broken twigs should show up somewhere around the cabin, and drag marks if he'd done it after the snow fell.

Marty moved on to look for them. She was north of the flaming cabin now, and even though there wasn't much wind she could see why the firefighters chose to wait on the other

4

side. The drifting smoke was pungent, made her hungry for that venison, set her coughing as she peered at the snow outside the firebreak to see if there were signs of where the hunter had come from. A puff of smoke brought a shower of embers with it. She looked sideways at the cabin to see where it had come from, watched in fascination as a section of plank wall buckled and fell. Through the flames and smoke she could make out a few shapes inside: a metal stove, the thick square posts of a bunk bed, and . . .

Jesus.

Bile rose in her throat, and dizziness, and behind her eyes the lid of that closed coffin began to open. She clenched her jaw and forced herself to move down toward the cabin until a blast of heat and sparks drove her back up again. But she knew what she'd seen in the flames, pinned to the bedpost by a two-foot blade.

Charred black, twisted, but human.

Two thirty a.m. and ex-sheriff Wes Cochran couldn't get to sleep. He'd assigned himself the four-to-midnight shift in his new job as head of security at the Asphodel Springs Resort, because half the guys working for him had teenagers and Wes thought fathers should be around for their teenagers. Doc had told him a different job would be good to reduce his stress, but being sheriff had been calm waters compared to juggling all this blood-pressure medication and arthritis stuff and now the damn prostate – nothing major wrong, Doc said, but it seemed like it kept Wes running to the head every half-hour. Talk about stress. At least when he was sheriff he'd had clear actions to take against the drunks and bad guys that were his main problems. But when your own body is the bad guy, what can you do?

The job at Asphodel Springs was stress-free, all right. Biggest event of the last three days had been chasing some snowmobilers off the golf course. But he had trouble getting to sleep these days. You'd think coming home at one a.m. a guy would be tired, but he found himself wide awake fretting about dumb stuff like his blood pressure or some blunder by the new sheriff Chuck Pierce or even his son Billy's long-ago death in a motorcycle accident. When he was sheriff, dealing with other people's problems had kept the rest in perspective.

He didn't want to bother Shirley with his thrashing. These days she kept busy as she always had, learning to cook new things for Wes, tasty despite Doc's restrictions, plus she was saving probably half the kids in Asia with all her church committees. She needed her sleep. So he got himself a glass of milk and went into the den, turned the TV on and muted it. Checked the sports channels, watched critically as they replayed some college basketballers in the last few minutes of a Big Ten contest. Man, he coulda done better than that in high school! They kept missing easy plays. Though the kid with black curly hair wasn't too bad. With a better coach, he might make pro.

The game ended and he channel-surfed, still on mute. Found the Indianapolis news and watched the pretty blonde newscaster for a moment. Her silent mouth moved, discussing something odd. Looked like a rite of some kind, people in robes shaking evergreen branches in the snow. In the upper corner the headline said: 'Solstice ritual in Bloomington'. Before he could click to the next channel the screen filled suddenly with bright flames and the corner headline switched to 'Breaking news – Nichols County.' Wes said, 'Damn,' and turned the sound on to hear the story, quickly cranking the volume down to a whisper. But there didn't seem to be any story yet, just those pretty pictures. Somebody's hunting cabin out on the edge of the Hoosier National Forest had caught fire. 'The sheriff's department is seeking the owner of the cabin,' the blonde said, and suddenly there was a shot of Marty Hopkins bundled up in her brown cold-weather uniform, strain around her pretty gray eyes but her voice calm and competent, saying, 'All these questions are under investigation, George. We hope to identify the victim soon.'

Victim?

Chuck Pierce had sent Hopkins out to a fire with a victim? After what had happened to her father?

Wes slammed his fist on to the sofa arm. Damn the man!

Rivers and creeks in limestone country wear away the rock, widen and deepen the channels, leaving hills and plateaus, bluffs and ridges high above. The White River carves the deepest, widest valley. Not far away Gordon's Creek has dug a narrower cut almost as deep. The two meander back and forth, and in Nichols County swing very close and run almost parallel for nearly a mile. The steep hill on the White River side rises hundreds of feet, then it's only a short way across to an even steeper cliff that plunges down to Gordon's Creek. Locals call it Demon Ridge.

A woman hiked along the high wooded ridge between the river and creek, her short cap of silver hair glinting in the cold dawn light. She moved easily, her steps sure on the familiar ground. This morning the wind was mild, closer to a sigh than to its usual moan. She came to the back door of a small shingled house that sheltered in a shallow depression among some twisted pines, and smiled to hear a voice as high and pure as a flute singing within. She bounced up the stairs and into the kitchen, where without removing her parka, she pulled a loaf of bread and some peanut butter from the cupboard. Her eyes shone with anticipation.

The song stopped and another woman entered the room, taller than the first but with the same silver hair. She leaned in the door jamb a moment, watching, then asked, 'What's up?'

The shorter woman glanced at her, said, 'Just getting something to leave out for the birds.'

The taller woman gazed at her a moment and then her eyes sparked too. 'Good, good!' she exclaimed, and seized the other by the hands. They spun in a quick exuberant dance around the worn linoleum.

A quarter to nine in Brooklyn. Liv Mann stood in her studio apartment with a swimsuit in each hand. Red tankini or green jungle-print one-piece? Elena preferred the jungle-print. What the hell, take them both; she planned to do a lot of swimming in Cancun. And hiking. And climbing ruins. All the stuff it was hard to find time for in her job. Including Elena. She pushed her curly black hair away from her eyes, and began riffling through her T-shirts. Better hurry. Damn airlines wanted you there so early, and with traffic and long check-in lines she should get out of here really soon. Elena had had to pull an all-nighter finishing a project at her computer graphics job in Jersey, and was probably already on her way to the airport.

Liv was small, serious, and well organized. She'd been

making herself a packing list for the past week whenever she had a few minutes to spare. In Brooklyn there were constant drug busts of small-time dealers on street corners, cases that had to be passed on by a Grand Jury before they could go to trial, and the District Attorney's office where she worked had a lot to do. Not that their efforts seemed to be deterring anybody. If they got one locked up the cops were back in a couple of months with a new guy they'd caught at the same corner. She'd complained to her dad about it a few years ago, not long before his death. 'It's like working in a meat-processing plant, Pops,' she'd told him. 'No matter how many dealers we jail, there are always more right behind them.'

Ronald Mann's sad blue eyes had peered over his half-spectacles at her. He'd worked years at the Telmeck Corporation designing municipal electrical systems, often for foreign governments, and she'd come to respect his knowledge of the world. 'Liv, honey, it's good money for guys with no other options.'

'C'mon! Most of them seem smart enough to hold a job.'

'They've got a job. It just happens to be illegal. And the risk means they get more money for it.'

'The risk of getting shot?' she asked dubiously. 'They've divvied up the territory. Not many turf wars these days. And cops don't shoot if they can help it.' Despite a few headline cases, most New York City cops used their guns only rarely. The chance of accidentally hitting a citizen was too high, and the paperwork could consume months of a guy's life.

Ronald Mann smiled at her. 'You're right; getting shot isn't likely. The big risk is getting jailed by hotshot lawyers like my daughter.'

'Wait a minute. You're saying it's my fault they get so much money?'

'Basic economics. Don't they teach you lawyers about the invisible hand? Everyone has his price.' He sounded bitter.

Liv shook her head. 'Never thought of jail being part of their job.'

'That's why they get the big bucks.' He'd stared into space a moment, then taken pity on her, patted her small tan hand with his big freckled one. 'Look, honey, we want to keep people from getting addicted, and until the lawmakers figure out a better way to do it, we have to do the best we can with this system. And you've told me that even these first months you've helped prosecute a couple of real bad guys. Getting them off the street even for a few years is worthwhile.'

Dammit, she missed her dad. Liv blinked the sting from her eyes and tried to think warm sunny thoughts about Cancun. Sunglasses, beach towel, hiking boots went into the suitcase. A long skirt for dancing in case they found a place to dance . . .

She glanced at the TV in the corner of her room. It had been giving the weather but was doing news now. A striking image of flames against snowy woods danced on the screen, one of those bits they put on because the images are good, not because it's of any use to the viewers. So what had caught her subconscious ear? The headline said 'Machete Killing' and the voice-over was saying now, 'Nichols County Sheriff's Department is investigating the death. We'll be back after these messages.'

Liv stared at the flames on the screen a moment. Nichols County? Machete? She hurried to her phone, got the number from Information.

A man answered. 'Sheriff's Department.'

Her hand tightened on the phone. 'I just saw on TV – I mean, is this the Nichols County where a guy got killed by a machete and a fire?'

'Yes, ma'am. Do you have information for us?'

The guy's accent clinched it more than his words, the same not-quite-southern drawl that her world-traveler dad used to slide into when he relaxed. Liv said, 'No, but can you tell me what happened?'

'I'm sorry, ma'am, it's still under investigation.'

Liv hung up, looked over her shoulder at her suitcase, then back at the phone. Elena would understand. Maybe. She dialed the travel agency. 'Lucy, I'm sorry, I've changed my mind. I know it'll cost me, but can you get me to Indiana today?'

Two

Morning: cold pale sun. Marty was on day shift today even though she hadn't gotten off work last night till five a.m. She'd grabbed an hour's nap and woken up to the sense of something wrong. The scene last night – no, more than that. Pounding like a drum.

Dammit, it *was* a drum! Loud chaotic music. She stomped downstairs and punched off the sound system on her way to glare at her daughter. 'What is that? I hated "Mmm-bop" but this is ridiculous!'

Chrissie had just turned thirteen, both pleased and embarrassed by the first hints of coming curves in her coltish body. She'd gotten her dark hair and deep brown eyes from Marty's ex-husband Brad, now off in Tennessee, her athleticism and curiosity from Marty, and her taste in music from her friends. She looked up from her cinnamon toast and said, 'Pearl Jam. You wouldn't understand. God, Mom, you look awful today!'

'Shut up. You're talking to a TV star,' grumped Marty, pouring herself a cup of coffee.

Chrissie jerked upright. 'TV?'

Aunt Vonnie, in her curlers and robe, plopped a plate of cinnamon toast in front of Marty and said to Chrissie, 'Yeah, your mom was up all night because some guy died in a fire.'

'Who was it?'

'Don't know yet,' Marty said.

'Which channel?'

Aunt Vonnie said, 'Melva called and said CNN picked it up.'

'Cool!' said Chrissie, while Marty groaned. That meant reporters would be lying in wait all day while the deputies tried to figure out what happened to the poor guy.

And sure enough, there they were as she dragged herself into headquarters, a small mob headed by Betty Burke from

10

the local paper. Deputy Grady Sims was at the dispatch desk, answering them in monosyllables while trying to do his job. Grady was a tall rangy guy who'd lost the use of his left arm in a shootout a couple years ago. He would've been eligible for disability but Wes Cochran, then sheriff, had kept him active on dispatch, knowing the guy needed to feel useful. The new sheriff, Pierce, grumbled about not having enough deputies and shot a glance at Sims occasionally when he said it, but knew that he'd never get reelected if he pushed Sims out. Plus the lanky deputy had patrolled Nichols County roads for years, and more recently than the new sheriff, so he knew a lot about the county troublemakers.

Marty looked around for Sheriff Pierce. But besides Sims, the only other official occupant of the office was young Deputy Howie Culp, also fending off reporters with enough success that they all pounced on Marty as she came in.

She shook her head. 'Sorry, guys, you know as much as I do. Sheriff Pierce'll be here soon – right, Grady?'

When Sims nodded, Marty turned back to the reporters and said, 'Hey, Betty, why don't you and your friends go talk to the fire department or the coroner, and come back in five?'

'But you were there.' Like all of them, Betty Burke was persistent.

'I was there for a little while, but I don't have the latest.' Marty put some steel into her voice. 'Try the fire department.'

Betty shrugged, said, 'Good idea,' and they left.

Marty tossed her coat and Stetson on to a peg and sat down at a computer to write her report. When the door closed behind the reporters she asked, 'Any ID yet?'

'The coroner's only now getting the body,' Howie Culp said. He jerked a thumb at his computer screen. 'But that blue pickup you guys found on the logging trail nearby just came back as registered to Robert Corson.'

Grady Sims looked around. 'That's Zill Corson! He and Don Foley have a hunting cabin out that way. I was wondering if that was the one.'

Don Foley had been a deputy sheriff too, retired from the department just last year. He'd hassled Marty the whole time they'd worked together because he thought it was a man's job.

Marty asked, 'Did you ask Foley about it yet?'

Sims said, 'Not yet.'

Howie Culp was frowning at the computer screen. 'How'd they get a nickname like Zill from Robert Corson?'

'Not from his Christian name,' Grady explained. 'From his size. Those Corsons are big guys. Foley told me when Zill was still a kid they called him Godzilla.'

Marty said, 'His brother is Jumbo Jim Corson, right?'

'Yeah, works at . . .'

Grady shut up because Sheriff Pierce was walking in the door. Not a tall guy but muscular, dignified in his uniform. His pale-blue eyes scanned the room as he said, 'Been talking to the coroner. That woman reporter Betty Burke said she was going to show up here.'

'Yes, sir, she was here,' Marty volunteered when the two men kept silent. 'She decided to check with the coroner and the fire department and come back in a few minutes.'

'I just came from the coroner,' Sheriff Pierce said. 'Hasn't started the autopsy yet. Do we have an ID on the pickup truck?'

Grady Sims said, 'Yes, sir. Belongs to Zill Corson.'

'Corson. The guy that works at Brock Lumber?'

Sims said, 'No, that's his brother Jimmy, sir. Zill works security for that used-car guy over in Evansville. And if I remember rightly, he and Don Foley own a hunting cabin out by the national forest.'

Sheriff Pierce snapped his fingers. 'That's it! That's where I met Zill Corson: he was with Don. I'll get the coroner to send the dental X-rays to Corson's dentist. Sims, find out who that is.'

'Yes, sir. Uh – should I find out Foley's dentist too?'

'Foley's? God, you're right; they could have gone out there together. What a shame.' Pierce, looking shaken, thought a moment. 'But there's only one body, and it's Corson's truck. Start with him.'

'Yes, sir.'

Pierce went on, 'The state crime-scene technicians are working the scene with the fire investigators and Deputy Mason. They'll give us updates, like Mason is checking that line of bootprints. His shift is over and he'll be back soon. Culp, you liaise with them.'

'Yes, sir. Um, the reporters are heading back here.' Howie gestured at the window behind him.

'Don't tell them anything till we hear from the dentist,' Pierce said. 'And even then we have to notify next of kin first.'

'Sir, even if the body isn't Zill's, he's involved,' Marty said. 'His pickup, maybe his cabin . . .'

'I know, Deputy.' Pierce gave her a chilly glance. 'Culp, you go find Don Foley. He'll know about the cabin and about Corson too. Marty, you go over to the courthouse and double-check that Foley and Corson own that particular cabin.'

'Yes, sir,' she said. Culp would get the credit if Foley gave him some good info, or if he found out Foley was missing. But after the grisly discovery last night she was just as glad to be assigned to the paperwork today.

She and Howie Culp got out just ahead of the return of Betty Burke and the other news hounds. Betty called, 'So, Marty, you got a lead?'

'Just checking who owns that cabin. Sheriff's back now; he's got the latest for you.' Marty escaped into her squad car. Howie was already revving his engine.

Nichols County records were filed in a big semi-basement room under the courthouse, guarded by high barred windows and by the tough woman who ruled the room. Despite her wrinkled face, Flo Duffy's hair was slinky, shoulder-length, and auburn-red this month. Her satiny tunic top was patterned with overlapping circles in shades of turquoise and silver.

'Hey, Flo, you look like a mermaid!' Marty said.

Flo rested her illegal Virginia Slim on her favorite ashtray. It faced away from the clients but Marty had glimpsed it once, shaped like a toilet seat with 'Shit happens' printed on the raised lid. 'Damn right!' Flo said. 'If you came to arrest me for smoking in a county building, you can't. That's just bubbles rising.'

Marty smiled. 'I can see that, Flo. Listen, I need your help finding out whose cabin burned last night.'

'Yeah, saw that on TV.' Flo fetched the county maps and Marty figured out exactly where the fire had been, a private plot of land next to the Hoosier National Forest. Twenty minutes later Flo had proved that, as Grady Sims had predicted, it was owned by Robert 'Zill' Corson and ex-deputy Donald Foley.

Marty was about to make copies for their files when her

radio came to life. 'Three-twenty-one,' said Grady Sims's tinny voice.

'Yeah, three-twenty-one here,' she replied.

'We got confirmation. Sheriff Pierce wants you to tell the next of kin.'

He hadn't mentioned names over the air. Seemed every day more people monitored the police bands. Marty said only, 'I'm on it,' and turned to Flo. 'Gotta go. Can you do these copies for us?'

Flo blew smoke at the ceiling. 'What's in it for me?'

'Hershey bar. Almonds, of course.'

Flo smiled a yellow smile. 'Done. That's what we mermaids come out of the water for. I'll send the copies to your office.'

'Thanks,' said Marty, already halfway out the door.

Marty hated next-of-kin assignments. So did everyone. But someone had to do it, and she was curious to see what Jimmy Corson had to say about his brother. So with both dread and anticipation, she headed for the lumber mill.

She didn't see Jumbo Jim often, occasionally at the 7-11 or the county fair. He'd been maybe three years ahead of her in grade school and they went to different churches. She remembered him being helpful a couple of years before when they'd been hunting for someone who'd killed a bank teller.

That time she'd spoken to him in the sawmill shed of Brock Lumber, but this time he wasn't there. She went into the showroom and saw him back in the paint section helping someone choose a color. She spoke quietly to his boss. 'Hi, Virgil. I need to have a private word with Jimmy Corson.'

'Sure, Marty, you can use my office if you want. I'll send him in. What's happening?'

'Sheriff Pierce thought he could help us with something we're working on,' she said evasively. She went into the office, windowless and lined with shelves holding cluttered cardboard file boxes, but boasting a new desktop computer on the battered oak desk.

In a moment Jimmy Corson came in and the room seemed to shrink. Football-player size and solid to begin with, the years were adding thickness to his big frame. But big as he was, he looked uneasy. Maybe it was her uniform; maybe he had an idea of what was coming. He said, 'How ya doing, Deputy, ma'am?'

Marty said, 'Jimmy, I'm afraid I've got some bad news. There was a hunting cabin burned down last night. On Little Deer Creek near the national forest.'

She paused but he didn't help her, just continued to watch her warily. She went on, 'Someone died in it. They just told me it was your brother Zill.'

'Zill.' His eyes closed a moment and she could see the strain of tamping down emotion. Finally he said hoarsely, 'It's gonna kill Momma.'

'Yeah. I'm sorry. We were hoping you could help us out with some things, Jimmy, you know, to spare her? We've got to file reports. Grady said it was Zill's cabin; is that right?'

'I guess so. Yeah.' As she'd hoped, the question brought him back to the present. 'Leastways, his and Don Foley's. Don retired; he's not with you guys any more.'

'OK, fine, we'll check with Don too. D'you know why Zill was out there last night?'

'No, I don't.'

'He didn't tell you stuff like that?'

'We don't see each other a lot. He works in Evansville. Worked,' he added, and cleared his throat.

She noted that down, asking, 'Whereabouts in Evansville?'

'Pinkett's Auto Mall. He does security.'

His voice was dull, but he was still with her. Marty asked, 'How long did he work there?'

Jimmy's brow furrowed. 'Lemme think. He graduated in sixty-eight, went in the Marines, stayed maybe six years. That's where he got to know Don Foley, 'cause they were both from this county even though Don was a sergeant already. Then Zill came out and started working security.'

'At Pinkett's?'

Jimmy shook his head. 'No, first he worked for an outfit that got contracts in a lot of different countries. Zill said he wanted to see the world. Nam gave him a taste for travel.'

She made a note. 'What was this company called?'

'Don't remember. Based in Texas, Zill said.'

'And they sent him to different countries, and then to Pinkett's?'

Jimmy was staring at the desktop but seemed to be seeing

the past. 'No, he got shot in the leg in Africa somewhere, guarding a storage yard for Chevron. His company paid to fix his leg but it wasn't usable for a long time so they laid him off anyway. By then he was ready to stay in the USA.'

'Yeah, I can see his point. So he got the job at Pinkett's on his own?'

'Pretty much. Took over a year for his leg to heal. That's when he started drinking. That's what happened, right? He was drunk and didn't notice the fire?'

He hadn't heard about the machete. Marty didn't have the heart to tell him just now. She said, 'Yeah, they tell me he was in no shape to react. Did you ever use the cabin that burned?'

'Every now and then. I don't hunt as much as Zill and Don but I helped them build it. I got a deal from Virgil for the lumber. Good solid cabin.'

Marty nodded. 'It was. Did they let other people use it too?'

'Sure, they took friends there sometimes.'

She hesitated, decided to ask. 'The firemen saw a padlock before the door burned down. Did they keep valuables in there?'

'Not usually. But he and Don had three or four pretty expensive rifles they left there sometimes. Virgil gave me a deal on the locks too – basic but high quality. Big padlock on the outside, bolts on the inside for when they were there, steel reinforcement bars.'

'What about the windows?'

'Skinny little slot windows. Nobody could get in there. A little five-year-old, maybe.'

But not a deer. Marty asked, 'Who had keys to the padlock?'

'Just the three of us, them and me – wait a minute.' Jimmy Corson emerged from his state of numbed automatic response, stared at her. 'You're saying the padlock was locked?'

Marty said gently, 'That's what they told me.'

'It was locked? And Zill was inside?'

'Yeah. That's why we want to find out who else might have been there. You got any ideas?'

He was frowning now, his eyes darting from the desk to her and back. 'I gotta think on this.'

'Did he mention anybody recently that he might be taking to the cabin?'

16

Jumbo Jim stared stubbornly at the desktop and repeated, 'I gotta think on this.'

What did he know? Marty could have pressed him but she didn't want to do that to a guy in pain. Worse, it might antagonize him, and she wanted to keep him on the team for later questions. So for now she backed off, saying, 'OK, let me know if anything more occurs to you. Right now, do you want me to help break it to your mother?'

A flash of pain crossed the big man's face, and he looked at her with almost childish relief. 'Yeah, Marty, I'd be right grateful if you'd come along.'

'OK, Jimmy.' She closed her notebook. 'I gotta make a call. Clear it with Virgil, and I'll meet you in the parking lot in five minutes to go tell her.'

He nodded mutely and they went out.

Three

Wes Cochran slid through the water, his eyes closed, his legs kicking lazily, his mind in a long-ago time. Summer in the quarry swimming-hole, he and his buddy Rusty LaForte and a few of the other guys, maybe Johnny or Corky or Mark, skinny-dipping to cool off after a strenuous basketball practice. Rusty was red-haired like his Irish mother, intense and humorous like his Frenchie dad. Also quick, pugnacious, and diabolically accurate on the basketball court. Wes was almost as quick and five inches taller, so he was the star and heavily guarded, but Rusty was the one who got the ball to him in the split-second he was in the clear.

They shared the turquoise waters of the swimming-hole with fish, frogs, and the skeletons of machinery. Stone company workers like Rusty's father had hammered open the earth with puffing steam channelers or jackhammers, sliced the limestone with powerful wire saws, hoisted away the huge blocks with derricks. The stone had been shipped off to build Rockefeller Center or the Pentagon or somebody's courthouse. When the men had hauled out all the usable stone they'd left the pit behind and moved on to the next quarry, first discarding their broken machines by dumping them into the water, then erecting a barbed-wire fence around the top to discourage swimmers. But of course nothing discouraged boys like Wes and Rusty, sixteen or seventeen years old and glowing with invulnerability, on the verge of winning the state championship and after that the world.

Wes rolled his head sideways to take a breath and the scene jerked back to the present in a puff of chlorine-reeking air. Not August, not the high-school team, not skinny-dipping in a quarry swimming-hole. Just old Wes Cochran, ex-basketball star, ex-Army, ex-sheriff, trying to keep his aging body in shape, dreaming of long-gone glory days as he swam laps at the Y on doctor's orders.

Well, on Shirley's orders. Doc had said join the gym, but Shirley knew him better, knew the machines would bore him silly. She'd told him to go swimming instead. 'That always made you happy,' she'd smiled, and it was true: in high school they'd courted too in those quarry pools. Rusty with his pretty dark-haired Marie, Wes with Shirley the cheerleader, sweet and slick as a fish in her red daisy-print swimsuit. No skinny-dipping for Shirley, who taught Sunday school to little kids at the Methodist Church. She'd only allowed a few kisses at first, though he'd always suspected that she knew in her heart about his lustful hours of Shirley fantasies after he'd dropped her off at her parents' trim house. And maybe she'd had a few fantasies of her own, judging from the enthusiasm of her response when they'd finally gotten engaged.

Of course then Nam happened, that waste of a war. Wes and Rusty and some others had been lucky: after a year in the jungle they'd been sent to finish their tours in Korea and they'd made it back home, heroes to most of the Nichols County folk though not to the hippies at the university up in Bloomington. But it didn't feel heroic inside, not when you'd lost buddies in those jungles. Shirley and Marie got back husbands who weren't at all what they'd sent to war. The shining boys of that invincible team had been shattered, turned into ordinary mortals except for nightmares worse than everyone else's.

Aah, quit whining, old man, Wes scolded himself. The past is past. Think of the future. This was a good-paying job, less stress, right? He climbed out of the water, hitched up his swim trunks. Maybe in May he'd go swimming in the quarries again on his days off. Now that he wasn't sheriff any more he didn't have to round up the trespassers like a good little public servant. Now he could become a trespasser himself. Even if the deputies came, Chuck Pierce wouldn't dare arrest him. Not if he ever wanted to be elected again, he wouldn't.

Wes picked up his towel and rubbed his face dry, headed for the lockers to put on his uniform. Odd to dress in blue instead of brown.

He was tying his shoelaces – something else that wasn't so easy now that his middle was thicker – when his cellphone rang. It was Hopkins – Rusty's daughter.

19

'Hey, Marty, how you doing?' he asked, glad she'd called, anxious too. Was she OK?

'Hi, Coach. We're off the record, right?'

'Sure.'

'You know about the fire?'

'Saw it on TV.' Saw it, and he'd been thinking about Rusty ever since. Had she?

Her voice sounded OK as she said, 'Got an ID on that guy who burned in the cabin. Turned out to be Zill Corson.'

'Zill. So the cabin was the one he and Don Foley built?'

'Yessir. And that's my question. I've talked to his brother Jumbo Jim, and in a minute I'm going with him to talk to his mother, but seems to me Foley could tell us more about the cabin – you know, who else had keys to it.'

'Didn't Jumbo Jim help build it?' Wes toweled off his neck, where water from his damp hair still trickled.

'Yeah, but he claims he didn't use it that much, and when I asked about keys he quit talking.'

'Interesting. And Chuck Pierce didn't send anyone to talk to Foley?'

'Yeah, but he just sent Howie Culp to talk to him, and—'

Wes saw where she was headed. He said firmly, 'Then Culp will talk to him, and he'll report back to the rest of you and you'll hear it then.'

'But Howie's so green!' she objected.

She was right. A couple years ago, in his second month on the job, Culp had mishandled a road stop of an armed suspect. It had set up Grady Sims for his injury and almost got Wes killed too. Wes said, 'We were all of us green once. Culp is a good man; he's learned a lot. And there's good reasons you shouldn't go after Don Foley.'

'I know.' She sounded – not angry, exactly, more like disgusted at the ways of men. 'Foley hates my guts. But isn't there some way I can change his attitude?'

'Nope.' She didn't know the half of what Wes had gone through, getting the other guys to accept her. Foley had been the worst but all the rest of them – even easygoing Grady Sims – had started out suspicious, even hostile. 'Look,' Wes had told them, drawing on all the authority he'd earned in years on the job, 'I've coached the Hopkins kid and I think she's got what it takes. And you know I play fair. If she falls down on the job, if she doesn't shoot straight on the range, if her arrests don't stand up in court, anything like that – out she goes. Same rules as you.' Looking back, Wes thought that might have been part of Foley's problem. He was terrific on the range but poor on the law, so that his arrests got thrown out several times. And here was this upstart female nailing everyone from drunks to murderers. But if he tried to pick holes in her performance people might notice that his was worse.

Still, there was enough grumbling among the troops that Wes sometimes wished he'd kept her on dispatch instead of bowing to her insistent demands to send her out on patrol. He sure wouldn't have done it for anyone but Rusty's kid.

Now he told her, 'Foley was always a stubborn guy. His worst quality but also his best. Once he had hold of something he wouldn't let go. Trust me, if he's on the sheriff's side on this, he'll do all he can to help.'

'Yeah,' she said eagerly, 'and he's got to want to find out who barbecued his friend, right?'

Wes frowned at the empty locker room. 'Right. But he may or may not want to help the sheriff's department get the glory. And if he thinks he can get you into trouble . . .'

She sighed. 'Yeah, like when we were working together. But towards the end he'd quit making up stories about me, so—'

'Not because he'd changed his mind, Hopkins. It was because I told him off when I found out some of the stuff he'd done.'

'You told him off?'

'And then some.'

'I see,' she said slowly. 'I didn't know that, Coach.'

'Let the guys handle him.'

'Yeah, but I'd hoped – oh, hell, you're right; I'll have to see what Howie can learn.'

'Course I'm right.'

'Yes, sir. Look, Jim is coming out now so I gotta go talk to Mrs Corson. But maybe I can come by later and ask you about Zill and his friends.'

'I probably can't add anything to what those other folks will tell you. But sure, come on by.'

They clicked off. Wes finished tying his shoelace and

21

wished he was still on the job. He'd heard about the machete, seen the TV fire, but when Hopkins said 'barbecued' it all came home to him. A shame to have an asshole like Chuck Pierce in charge. Pierce had worked a few murders long ago as a deputy under old Sheriff Cowgill, most of them sad endings to bar-room brawls. But he'd never yet been in charge of a murder investigation, and Hopkins was right: it was odd to send young Culp to talk to Foley. A better choice than Hopkins, of course, no matter what Hopkins thought, but Culp was too young. Personally, Wes would have sent Grady Sims, who could draw on years of working side by side with Foley.

Wasn't the first dumb decision Pierce had made. It still made Wes mad to think about the teen athletic program. After years of politicking Wes had finally got funds to get it started, give youngsters something to do besides get into trouble. And give them a positive experience with law enforcement. But it wasn't off the ground yet when Pierce took over and cancelled it, claiming the deputies should spend their time on fighting crime. Most likely arresting the same kids when they did get into trouble.

But Wes was off the job now. He should quit worrying about stuff he couldn't do anything about. He adjusted his blue necktie and headed out to make the rich skiers and vacationers from Chicago and Cincinnati feel secure at Asphodel Springs.

High above Indiana, the snowclouds were slowly moving east, and in their wake an Arctic high promised clear cold days before the next snow. And high above the snowclouds, a small, tan, dark-haired woman brooded out the window of a jet. Elena had been furious. 'Jesus, Livvy, we've been planning this Cancun thing for eight months!'

'I'll be there in a couple of days. But I've got to go to Indiana. Really. I'm not asking you to go,' Liv said.

'Damn right! No way I'm going to Indiana; I'm going to be on the plane to Cancun. And you should be too. I know you want justice and all that, but it's already been years. Why can't you let it go for a couple more weeks? Call them when you get back?'

Elena sounded so logical. The old despair crowded around

Liv's heart, and she had to fall back on the only thing she knew. 'I've got to go.'

'The cops won't tell you anything. They wouldn't tell you on Staten Island.'

'I got them to tell me more than they wanted to. Anyway, I've got my hiking shoes and swimsuits with me. Soon as I talk to them I'll head south.'

'Yeah, right. Why should I believe you this time?' But Liv heard, or hoped she'd heard, a softening in Elena's tone of voice.

Four

On the major highways and most streets in Dunning they'd spread salt, reducing yesterday's inch and a half of snow to wetness. But the hill roads of the county were still as white and icy as the stubbled fields around them. Marty followed Jumbo Jim's red pickup from the lumber mill as it wound southeast for eight slick miles. Finally he turned into an ice-and-gravel driveway that led to a barnyard with a trim red barn and a small neatly painted apple-green house. Marty had painted her own place a couple of years ago and appreciated the care that had gone into the job. A TV satellite dish perched on the snowy gable of the house. She parked her cruiser cautiously beside Jim's truck, hoping she wasn't messing up a hidden flowerbed.

By the time she got out of the cruiser Jim had already gone up on to the little white-framed porch. A gray-haired woman, her rawboned hulk unsoftened by her flowered housedress and pink sweater, loomed in the doorway. Marty saw that Jim would have to duck to go in. The woman didn't have to duck, but she didn't have a whole lot of clearance.

As she climbed the porch steps Marty realized that she'd seen the woman around, at the Rockland Mall and a couple of times at Reiner's Bakery, where Aunt Vonnie worked. Hi, Maudie, Aunt Vonnie had said, and asked her how her hens were doing. Marty took a deep breath, nodded a greeting.

'Hey, Momma; you know Deputy Hopkins, right?' Jim asked.

'Sure do. Marie LaForte's daughter. C'mon in, you two, before we all turn into eskimo pies.' But the tall woman's cheerful welcoming words were belied by the lines of anxiety around her dark eyes.

24

'Thanks, Miz Corson, it's cold, all right,' Marty said soberly as she went in, followed by Jim.

'You sit down, now, and I'll put the coffee on,' Maudie Corson suggested.

'That'd taste real good, thank you.' Marty had learned that it was usually quicker and kinder to let people do their usual hospitality tasks, partly to avoid arguments but mostly because it gave them a moment to prepare themselves for what was obviously not going to be a social call.

Marty took off her Stetson but not her coat and sat down in a stuffed chair. Jim walked around the room, finally sank uneasily into the sagging sofa. Like the chair, it was upholstered in a rust-and-blue plaid design, clean but dimmed by wear and partly obliterated by a handsome navy crocheted throw on the back of the sofa. There was an old TV with a beat-up rust-colored recliner aimed at it, a couple of framed family photos, a flowered bag of knitting or something next to the recliner, a coffee cup on the table next to it. It was all clean enough but not new, not near as spiffy as the paint job outside.

Maudie Corson returned, saying, 'There, that'll be ready in a minute.' She glanced at the recliner but elected instead to stay nearer the kitchen door and plopped her big frame on to the sofa next to her son.

Facing the two of them from her chair, Marty had the sense of being in the house of giants. She looked down at the hat she still held on her knees, rotated it in her hands. Get it over with, Hopkins. She looked up and said, 'We've got bad news, Miz Corson. There was a cabin that burned down last night up by the Hoosier National Forest.'

'The one on TV? Was it the one that belonged to you boys?' Maudie Corson turned to Jim, a mute appeal in her eyes: Let that be all it is; let that be the bad news.

Jim nodded and glanced at Marty with an appeal of his own. She steeled herself and said, 'Your son Robert was in the cabin. Zill. I'm real sorry, Miz Corson, but he didn't make it.'

'Oh, lord. Oh, lord, no!' Maudie Corson looked up in anguish at the ceiling. Then she bowed her head and covered her eyes with her hands, still wailing, 'No, no!'

Jim sat helplessly, obviously fighting to keep from joining

25

his mother in her sobs. Marty stood up, picked up the box of tissues on the table next to him, and shoved it into his hands. 'Jim, help her out.'

He grabbed the box gratefully and extended it to her. 'Here, Momma, here. Take it easy, Momma.'

'Oh, my baby! Bobby, Bobby! First they shoot him in the knee, and now they do this!' she cried and flung her lanky arms around Jim's neck. Marty patted her back.

'Take it easy, Momma. He didn't suffer, not much. It kind of snuck up on him.' Jim pushed the tissues at her again and this time she took one, dabbed at her eyes and cheeks. Marty stepped back toward the window, hoping that the first storm of weeping was over.

But Maudie's eye fell on the TV and she began to wail again. 'Oh, my baby! He got me that new satellite service. I told him, don't go up on the ladder with your bad leg! But he insisted, bless his heart!'

'Yeah, he took real good care of you, Momma,' Jim said. 'Helped me fix those steps too.'

'Yeah, and helped you paint the house,' Maudie sniffled. 'I'll never forget you two coming in to wash up that day; you were both green as Martians!' She gave a half-sob, half-chuckle.

Jim smiled back weakly. 'We were just horsing around.' But then she began blubbering again and his face began to crumple too.

There was nothing she could do for them except the little services to get them through the minutes. Marty slipped into the kitchen. No coffeemaker. The pot of coffee Maudie had started was sitting on an ancient stove. There was no spare money in this household. Human labor had provided the neat paint job and the nice crocheted sofa throw but couldn't mint the money to buy new appliances or sofas. Marty found the mugs, poured some coffee, and carried them out to the Corsons. 'Here you are,' she said. 'I'm sorry, I don't know if you like it with cream or sugar.'

'No, no, black's fine,' Maudie said automatically. She stared at the mug and it seemed to pull her back to the present moment. 'Oh, but Jim likes it with milk! And you, Marty honey, do you want milk? Or sugar?'

'Black's fine for me too. I'll get milk for Jim.' When she

returned Maudie had released Jim and was sipping from her mug. Marty put down the carton, said, 'Here you go, Jim,' and sat down again.

'Thanks.' He poured milk into his coffee.

Marty took out her notebook. 'Now, Miz Corson, I know it's hard. We have to make a few decisions soon. Dr Altmann is taking care of your son right now, and he'll want to know where you want him taken.'

'Taken?'

'Yes, ma'am – which funeral home.'

'Oh, funeral home. I guess Portman's, don't you think, Jim? Portman did a real nice funeral for your dad.'

'Yeah.'

Marty made a note. 'OK, I'll let Dr Altmann know. Jim, you can call Portman's, OK?'

'Sure.'

'Now, Miz Corson, Jim was just telling me how Zill was sent to work abroad and that's where he got shot in the leg.'

'That's right.' Maudie Corson snuffled and took another sip of coffee.

'And you said, first they shot his leg and now they do this. You mean his company?'

'They put him in danger!' Maudie said. Jim frowned and started to protest but his mother was off and running. 'They go into those foreign places, send the boys out to patrol and don't give them backup—'

'Momma, please; Marty doesn't need to know all that ancient history.'

'Didn't seem ancient to Bobby!' Maudie said indignantly. 'Last time he was here he was saying they were after him again! Wasn't his fault, he just followed their orders! He was a good boy.'

'Who was after him?' Marty asked.

'Momma . . .' Jim said.

'Jimmy, don't you even care that they got him killed? He should never have listened to that Bowers guy! Marine buddy, he said. From this county. On the football team, basketball too. And now look!'

'Dammit, Momma, we gotta earn a living! Bowers gave him a good tip. You think your van and your TV come free? Zill got good pay, good benefits and—'

'What good do benefits do him now?' Maudie began to sob again.

'Oh, Momma, for God's sake!'

Jim looked helplessly at Marty, who said gently, 'Jim, if they had something to do with him getting killed, we should check it out.'

He shook his head. 'But they didn't. Look, I didn't want to say this about my brother, but Momma, you know he only talked like that when he was drunk.'

'Drunk?' Maudie protested through her tissue. 'He wasn't drunk.'

Jim, clearly unconvinced, shook his head.

Marty asked, 'What company did he work for?'

'Pinkett's, like I told you,' said Jumbo Jim.

Maudie Corson shook her head. 'No, it was the other one he was talking about. The Texas one that sent him all over.'

'Momma, that was years ago!' Jim said. 'And they paid for his rehab. They were taking care of him, not trying to hurt him.'

It made sense to Marty. But Maudie Corson was stubborn. 'He was talking about Sergeant Bowers, so it had to be the Texas one.'

'What did he say about it?' Marty asked.

'He said Sarge was wrong, it was a bad idea. He said Spics never forget. Bobby, Bobby, what have they done?' Maudie Corson began sobbing again. Marty glanced at Jim, who gave her a baffled shrug.

'Miz Corson, do you remember the name of the company?' Marty asked, but the big woman was unreachable again. Marty closed her notebook and stood up. 'Jim?'

'Yeah?' He looked up at her, full of grief and anger at the world.

Marty said, 'I don't want to pester her now, but if either of you think of the name please let us know, OK? Or why he was talking about Spics?'

'Yeah.'

'And . . . well, now that you guys have been notified, the sheriff will probably give out Zill's name to the press. So you two should decide how you're going to deal with it.'

'Damn! Can't you keep it quiet?'

She said gently, 'You already told your boss, right? And

your mother will be telling her friends. And Zill's friends will be asking where he is. It's real hard to keep the press from finding out. But you can be a big help to your mother right now. A lot of things have to be done.'

Jim nodded slowly.

Marty suggested, 'Like maybe she has a friend you could call for her.'

'Yeah. I'll ask her,' he said.

'OK. And call us too if we can do anything. Goodbye, Miz Corson.'

Maudie Corson looked up at Marty, her bony face raw with weeping, and said distractedly, 'Goodbye, honey. Jimmy, get the door, OK?'

'No, no, you take care of your mother now. I'll let myself out.' Marty fastened her jacket and closed the door behind her.

Outside she replaced her Stetson, the cold air sharp in her nostrils. As she climbed into the cruiser she glanced back at the house with its carefully painted apple-green siding. 'You were both green as Martians,' Maudie had said, and Marty could almost see the two hulking brothers reverting to boyhood, splashing paint on each other, laughing together as they fixed up their mother's house.

There was love in that paint job.

She brushed a tear from her lashes.

When Marty pushed open the glass door of Dennis Rent-All, Romey Dennis was behind the counter. He was helping a customer; otherwise she might have thrown herself over the counter to hug him. Not for sex, not at the moment, but for comfort. With him she could go wild, yeah, but she could also find peace. She'd known Romey practically for ever. Childhood friends and teammates in Peewee Basketball, they'd both moved away from Nichols County in their early teens. She'd come back first, with baby Chrissie and her dying mother, to live with Aunt Vonnie. He'd spent a few years wandering the world before he returned three years ago and again became her buddy, and soon much more. He wanted to marry her, but Chrissie was still hurting from the divorce and Marty didn't want to rush her.

Today Romey was in his work clothes, jeans and a wine-red

polo shirt with the Dennis Rent-All logo. But she knew the feel of the muscles beneath that shirt, the taste of his skin. She smiled to herself. Nothing Peewee about him now.

His brandy-colored eyes lit up at the sight of her. 'Hey, Marty, be with you in a minute,' he said. 'Gotta write up this snowblower for Pete.'

'OK.' She took off her Stetson and glanced at the second man with the Rent-All logo on his shirt. Romey's Uncle Corky was tall as Romey, balding, no beard, but a similar crinkle around his eyes when he grinned. He was handing a receipt to a young woman in a pink parka. She held a fat blond toddler on her hip.

Corky asked her, 'You need help getting that clamshell on your car?'

'No thanks; Jase is out there waiting for us. He knows how to do it.'

Uncle Corky looked out the window and smiled. 'Sure does. He's got the thing up there already. Well, have a good trip now.' He crossed the room with them to hold the door, then came back with a critical look at Marty. 'Lady, you got a long face today.'

Marty shrugged. 'Kind of a sad case I'm working on.'

'Yeah, Wes tells me it gets bad sometimes. He also tells me you're real good at the job.' Uncle Corky patted her hand reassuringly.

Mention of Wes Cochran jogged her memory. 'Hey, you and Coach Cochran were on the same high-school team, right?'

'Just a year – my senior year; that was the only time we overlapped.'

'Was there a guy named Bowers too? On the championship team?'

Corky Dennis leaned back against the counter, crossed his arms. 'Bowers. Yeah, there was a Johnny Bowers graduated two years after me. Football player, basically. He played basketball too, but he wasn't near as good as Wes and your dad. None of us were.'

'Have you heard anything about him since?'

He frowned, clamping his lips together in thought, then said, 'He went into the Marines right after high school but I kinda lost track because I was Army. His family moved to Indy or someplace and he wasn't even here for vacations.'

The customer who'd returned the snowblower was leaving and Corky's eyes followed him out the door. 'You know who might know about him? Don Foley. He was probably Bowers' best friend.'

Don Foley. Marty kept the disappointment from her face. 'OK, somebody's already talking to Don so we'll hear about it. Thanks.'

Corky asked, 'How come you're interested in Bowers?'

Romey's warm hand slid around Marty's waist. She smiled up at him as he told his uncle, 'You know she won't answer questions like that, Uncle Corky.'

'Sure I'll answer,' Marty said, putting her hand over Romey's. 'I'll say: "His name came up in our investigation."'

'Same thing,' grumbled Uncle Corky. He looked out at a pickup pulling into the parking lot. 'Here comes Herb to return that big old table saw. He'll probably need some help.' He headed for the door.

Romey looked at her, asked, 'What's up?'

'I just had to tell someone her son was dead.'

'Bummer.' His beard brushed her forehead in a quick nuzzle, and in a moment he continued, 'When I was in Athens, I climbed up to the Acropolis where they say Athena hangs out to keep an eye on the city. And there are lots of statues of her as a warrior goddess up there in the museum. You know, helmet and spear and shield, defending the city, striking down the bad guys.'

Marty frowned at him suspiciously. 'Wonder Woman?'

'No, better. One of my favorites was a little wall carving. She's wearing her helmet and leaning on her spear, head bowed, and she seems very sad, mourning the ones who died.'

Marty nodded slowly. 'So even a goddess feels sad sometimes.'

'Yeah, but she was still holding the spear.'

'Yeah.'

He touched her nose, grinned. 'Tell you what: tonight I'll bring over some takeout for you and Chrissie and Vonnie. About six thirty, OK?' He gestured at the cross-country skis on the sporting-goods rack. 'I'll have those skis in the car if nobody rents them today. And maybe the sheriff won't call and you can see me home afterwards. And if that doesn't work out, hey, we've got for ever.'

'OK.' Marty smiled at him. Right after her divorce, his certainty that they belonged together had seemed presumptuous and unrealistic. But now, for ever with Romey sounded just about right.

Five

The sense of peace Romey had given her didn't last long. Back at the sheriff's parking lot, a square-built man limped toward her as she started from her cruiser toward the door. Don Foley.

She didn't slow down, said in her most neutral voice, 'Hey, Don, how's it going?'

'My buddy just got crisped, and you ask how it's going?'

She paused. 'Yeah, Grady said he was a friend of yours. I'm sorry.'

Don had a round face with a few more lines since he'd retired from the department but he seemed less flabby. Maybe he worked out more now, kept his weight down. He said, 'My buddy gets crisped and you're the one on TV.'

Marty looked closer. A whiff of alcohol, and as angry as she'd ever seen him. She said mildly, 'Luck of the draw, Don. Coulda been any one of us on that shift.'

'But it wasn't, was it? It was you.'

'Don, take it easy. We all want this killer caught.'

'That's what I want.' He pointed at himself, then stabbed his finger at her. 'What you want is the glory. Like last time, *USA Today*, "Beautiful Deputy Catches Rock Star's Killer".'

Why was he obsessing about that stupid long-ago headline? She repeated, 'Everyone wants to catch this killer. We've got no control over the media idiots. Deputy Culp talked to you, right?'

'That's between Howie Culp and me! You're not going to go weaseling it out of me! Getting free information!'

Jesus, his buddy dead and his main goal was still to keep her off the team! Furious, Marty forced her voice to remain mild. 'We only get information if people give it to us. And if we know what to ask them. Howie Culp didn't know yet to ask you about Sarge Bowers.'

For an instant Don Foley's small eyes widened in shock; then he turned his back and stalked away.

Damn. Coach Cochran was right: this guy was hopeless. She'd get no information there.

Of course she couldn't tell Sheriff Pierce directly to follow up with Foley about Sarge Bowers. The sheriff didn't hate her the way Foley did, but he always seemed suspicious, ready to turn down her suggestions. Better just slide the Bowers stuff into the report and hope Sheriff Pierce followed up.

It sure had been easier to work with Sheriff Cochran, who gave some weight to her suggestions.

She went into headquarters. The reporter Betty Burke was talking to Grady Sims but turned to her eagerly. 'Hi, Marty, anything new?'

'Not yet. Sheriff Pierce may be able to give you an ID soon. Grady, is he here?'

Sims shook his head. 'At the hospital. Back soon.'

Maybe Doc Altmann had completed the autopsy. Marty asked, 'Is Howie Culp around?'

'Did his interview this morning, out doing some follow-up now.'

So Foley must have told him something useful. About Bowers? She said to Grady, 'I'll try to catch the sheriff.'

Doc Altmann did autopsies now in a new section of Mercy Hospital, all silvery steel and glass. A tough-looking hospital security guy nodded her through the first set of double doors, although Marty thought the signs with precautions about AIDS and other horrible diseases probably kept more people out than the guard. She followed the sound of Doc Altmann's voice to the third metal door.

Even with top-of-the-line ventilation, the place smelled of formaldehyde. And today, of smoke. On a steel table on the far side of the room, a sheet hid a long object. Doc must have straightened those burned, bent arms and legs, Marty thought.

Hair frizzy as a Brillo pad as usual, Doc Altmann stood by a nearer table that held a collection of objects including some photos. He was indicating one of them. Sheriff Pierce watched, hands on hips and a skeptical look on his face, as Altmann spoke. 'You never know what the labs might find, Chuck. But I can tell you right now, from what was in your vic's lungs, it was the fire that killed him, not the machete.'

'But you said that big blade slashed right into him!'

'It did. Deep cut in the waist, blade stuck in that bedpost behind him.' He pointed at the photo. 'He may have been tied to the post too, see? Something funny about his wrists. My guess is that the buckle we found on the floor was from a belt that bound his arms to the post. Basically he sat there slashed and bleeding while the fire cranked up all around him and finally killed him. Now, maybe he was drunk or sedated and didn't feel a thing. Won't know that until we get the lab analyses.'

'So that cut didn't kill him.' The glaring fluorescents made the sheriff look even paler than usual as he studied the photo.

'No, the blade missed the vital organs. It would have taken hours for him to bleed to death. If there was no fire, if he had a phone, if help got there quick enough – well, he'd be lying in a different wing of this hospital today with a sore middle and a fair chance of recovery.'

The sheriff shook his silver-blond head and turned to Marty. 'What're you doing here?'

'Just reporting in, sir, on the next-of-kin notification.'

'OK, be with you in a minute,' and turning back to Altmann, 'So you can tell me if he was drunk or not?'

'That'll be in the lab report too,' said Doc. 'Maybe.'

Marty edged closer to where she could see the photo, but there was nothing new in it. Even with the shifting clouds of smoke and showers of sparks, she'd seen the bent and twisted body shown in the photo, the projecting hilt of the machete. There was less smoke in the photo but the rest was the same. Nothing in that charred body to connect it to the big guy who'd helped his brother paint his mother's house.

Beside the photo were some blackened objects. Marty saw the belt buckle Doc had mentioned. Also some sooty coins, a piece of charcoal that might once have been a wallet, and two knives – a hunter's gutting knife and a small smoky Swiss Army knife. There was also a three-inch shape that looked like a partially melted rat. Marty bent to peer at it.

'Back off, Hopkins; don't contaminate the evidence,' growled the sheriff.

Marty backed off and Doc Altmann's spectacled glance flicked from her to the sheriff before he said, 'Yeah, you're right, that's the only thing in his pockets you wouldn't expect.

Little ceramic critter, came through the fire with no problems except the smoke.'

So that was its real shape. Didn't look like any Indiana animal. Rats had blunter noses and longer, thinner tails. If it wasn't so black it might look like a crude little armadillo.

Sheriff Pierce asked, 'What the hell is it?'

Doc Altmann shrugged. 'Animal of some kind, a souvenir or keepsake. Maybe his girlfriend gave it to him, or maybe it's a good-luck charm.'

Sheriff Pierce snorted. 'If so, it didn't work.'

Marty was inspecting the last object on the table, the machete. The blade had connected to a wood or leather handle which was mostly burned away, only the metal connecting spike remaining. The blade had some charred smears but was in fair shape, relatively clean because it had been sheathed in the body and the bedpost, protected from the heaviest smoke. It was sharpened all the way around the curved tip. Marty could make out a design on the flat metal, maybe some incised letters. Doc Altmann was watching her but had apparently processed the fact that Marty wasn't getting the same respect from Pierce that she used to get from Cochran, because he addressed the sheriff. 'Yeah, Chuck, you're right to ask about that machete,' he said, even though Pierce hadn't said a word about it. 'Possibly handmade, definitely not from the USA. I'm going to take it to a guy at IU who knows about knives. Ep Waldheim. Military history.'

'Good idea.' Pierce seemed excited at the thought of calling in an expert. 'How long'll it take him to report?'

'Aah, you know these pointy-head IU guys. But I'll try to hurry him up.'

'Anything else we should know?'

'Not till the lab reports come. Maybe tomorrow.'

'OK, thanks. C'mon, Hopkins; tell me about the next of kin on our way to the car.'

As they walked back through the glass-and-steel halls, Marty reported on her interviews with Jumbo Jim and Maudie Corson. 'Miz Corson started blaming some company Zill used to work for. Friend of his named Sarge Bowers got him the job.'

'Bowers?'

'Real name Johnny. Probably from this county originally. They were in the Marines together, Miz Corson said.'

36

'Why did she think this company was to blame?'

'She said Zill had been complaining about it recently.'

He pushed open the door to the parking lot where their cruisers waited and asked, 'What did Jim Corson say about it?'

'He thought it was hogwash, but . . .'

'Then it probably is hogwash. The mother's hysterical, poor gal.'

Marty said evenly, 'The brother was broken up too, but he said he'd try to remember who else had keys to that cabin padlock.'

'Keys? Jesus, yes, the lock was outside, wasn't it? Even if he'd gotten himself untied he couldn't of gotten out.'

'No, sir, he couldn't.'

Sheriff Pierce was shaking his head as they reached the parked cruisers. 'Tie him there, slash him, lock him in, set the fire – we're dealing with one mean bastard here.'

'Yes, sir. What do you want me to do next? Follow up on the keys?'

'Nah, right now I need someone to check out a stolen vehicle out on the Milo Road. And when you've got their info, come back and do your paperwork.'

'Paperwork?'

'On the scene last night. The fire and everything. I gotta deal with the press now so we'll meet at the end of the shift. I want everyone's input then. So be sure your report's ready.'

'Yes, sir.' Frustrated, Marty turned on her heel and got into her cruiser. Not the way Coach Cochran had run things when he was sheriff. The first hours were the most important, he'd always said, when people's memories were freshest and the bad guys hadn't yet figured out a quiet way to leave town.

He had already left town, but he hadn't driven far. There was still work to do here to balance the equation. With luck, he could do one today or tomorrow, another next week. The preparation was important. The preparation was what balanced the accounts. It was dangerous, of course, to do two more in the same state. But he'd known for years it would come to this, and had made himself strong and invisible to all but his friends. That part of the preparation was done.

He'd been born for this job. My *chaski*, she'd called him

all those years ago, and she'd been right. *Chaskis* were the Inca messengers, but they were more than that. They were accountants, bookkeepers even though the books were kept on knotted strings, and they ran and climbed from one end of the empire to another. So it was important now to stay fit, to get in his daily run. He reached a snow-sparkled hill and followed the trail up from the river. Seven miles so far, body working harmoniously, breath light in the icy air. Like his fellow *chaskis*, his home was in the Pacific mountains, far above this gullied flatland, and he trained by rock-climbing or ice-climbing or running marathons in the high rare air. These lowland workouts were not as effective but he didn't want to lose his edge if he could help it.

He'd been up late, keeping an eye on Zill's pyre for a while. Zill Corson was a big strong guy and even with a couple of drinks hadn't needed much help slinging that deer carcass into the cabin. So he'd worried a little that Zill would break away, die of the wounds instead of the fire. But the bonds had held. He'd watched through binoculars while the snow sifted down and the flames writhed like snakes and the screams faded, and was about to leave when the first firemen arrived. He'd waited then, watching. The firemen chopped brush to form a firebreak, pointed through the collapsed door at the venison, greeted the TV cameraman. Nice pictures the guy got. He'd seen them on the TV at the diner this morning. The firemen had decided not to use their pumps in the frozen creek but to let the fire burn itself out. One of the firefighters was a parks guy, probably didn't care about the cabin, just didn't want it to set the forest on fire.

A forest fire, now – that would be glorious, wouldn't it? Like that battle of the two gods, the one god flaming up to the heavens, the other raining down from above. Water disappearing into steam, flames succumbing to water, everything consumed or drowned. Zeroed out. Equation solved. Glorious.

A boyhood memory stirred. Wasn't there a hymn like that? 'Adore and tremble, for our God is a consuming fire!' But he wasn't big on boyhood memories. Until he'd met her in those mountains, he'd had no purpose, no life. Like being outside a window looking in.

Last night was better. Eventually the sheriff's deputy had come. No one to worry about; a woman, in fact. She'd spotted

38

Zill's body, started things in motion sooner than he'd expected, so he'd left. But that was no problem; his plans were always flexible. And what could they do? Law enforcement in this state was no great shakes. He'd outsmarted a lot more sophisticated departments than this one.

Twelve miles would be enough today. He could take the shortcut back down to his camp. Then he could turn his mind to the preparation of the victim. This next one should be easy. But the one after would be hard to reach and more risky; it would take some thought.

He looked up at the evergreens, jagged against the pearly sky, paused when he spotted the landmark limestone outcropping ahead where the shortcut led back downhill. As he buckled his harness, he noticed a pinecone on the icy trail before him, and picked it up. Its segments lined up in rows that curved away from the center stem. Fibonacci spirals. Nature was beautiful, obeying precise rules from the tiniest molecules to the vast reaches of space. It was humans who upset the equation. But he would put his part of it right.

The *chaski* reached the top of the limestone outcropping. There was already protective webbing around a tree. He pulled a rope from his belt, clipped it to webbing and harness, added a prusik knot, and swung down off the lip of the rockface. Strong and fit, he slid smoothly down the rope, focused, balanced, ready.

Six

The so-called stolen-vehicle case that the sheriff had asked her to check turned out to be a waste of time. Grizzled fifty-year-old Joe Ferro lived out near the hospital. He told Marty that he'd heard a noise yesterday afternoon from the direction of his detached garage and had seen an SUV that looked like his rolling away down the street. He hadn't called the sheriff because his seventeen-year-old niece had keys and borrowed it sometimes, so he figured it was her, plus he was in the middle of watching a hockey game. But she hadn't asked permission this time and when he finally phoned her to complain this morning before school, she swore she hadn't taken it. Ferro wanted to know who did.

'So, Mr Ferro, can you describe the SUV so we know what to look for?' Marty asked.

'Oh, you don't have to look for it, it's in the garage.' He waved at the shed-like building at the end of the driveway.

'I see,' Marty said neutrally. 'And your niece convinced you she didn't borrow it yesterday?'

Ferro looked at the floor, rubbed his ear. 'Hell, what'm I supposed to say? I want to believe her. But if she didn't, that means somebody else did.'

Marty checked the vehicle, but there were no signs of forced entry. So maybe the kid had taken it and lied, or maybe Uncle Joe had seen another car and jumped to conclusions, and his car had been in the garage all along.

Either way, he was wasting her time when all the deputies should be working on poor Zill Corson's murder.

She started the cruiser and headed for her next assignment, the paperwork. Mostly a waste of time too, but at least this paperwork had to do with the murder.

When she got to headquarters, angular Grady Sims was alone at the dispatch desk. 'Where'd everybody go?' she asked.

'Accident out on the Bloomington highway. Three vehicles.'

'Casualties?'

He gave his one-shouldered shrug. 'Nobody killed. One of the passengers has a concussion; they took her to the hospital. Aside from that, just bruises all around. And crumpled cars.'

'What was it? Ice?'

'Yeah, they said it was a slippery turn and somebody over-corrected.'

'So who's there? Mason?'

'Yeah, and the sheriff. And the reporters went with them.' Anticipating her next question, he added, 'Sheriff just called; they don't need anyone else.'

'OK.' She hung up her coat and Stetson, dropped her notepad by her computer, then turned back to Grady. 'Wanna take five? I'll do dispatch for you.'

'Yeah, thanks, Marty.' Grady pushed himself up one-armed, limped toward the restroom. He'd received a commendation for his bravery in the shoot-out that had cost him his arm. The bad guy had received a chewed-up face and torso from Wes Cochran's shotgun blast, plus a life sentence from the Feds.

Grady had a life sentence too, living with his useless arm and painful spine.

She fielded a couple of calls, someone reporting a cow dead and frozen beside the Milo Road, and a guy who thought his fifty-year-old girlfriend had run off. Marty explained that adults could go where they wanted and they couldn't be arrested unless they actually broke the law. The caller swore at her and slammed down the phone.

'Our grateful public,' she muttered.

'Hey, you think you got an earful, he woulda really blistered me.' Grady was back, grinned at her. 'You females get protected from a lot of language.'

'Maybe from some of it.' The guy who'd just cussed her was mad at all females but Grady was mostly right. Coach Cochran had always said she was good at talking down belligerent drunks partly because most of them didn't see her as a threat, saw her more as a sympathetic listener to what-ever grievance they thought they had. It gave her an edge, and she used it, but even if they forgot she carried a gun, she never did.

OK, Hopkins, quit procrastinating. Paperwork time. She

returned to her desk, flipped to the right screen on the computer, pulled out her scribbled notes. She'd stopped about halfway through the crime-scene part of her report. She'd written about spotting the body in the flames. Left out the wave of nausea, the battle to shut out the image of her father's coffin, her mother's tearful face. In the next paragraph she'd described running back to ask the firemen to help secure the scene, then climbing the hill until she could use her radio to get help. Now she typed in that she'd warned off the WATH reporter who'd snuck up behind her to eavesdrop, but she decided to leave out the fact that she'd had to trade him a one-minute interview in exchange for him clearing out. That was the TV interview that had upset Foley so much. Next she'd gone back down to track the single line of footprints in the snow, found that they led from the burning cabin to an evergreen grove and a logging trail where a blue pickup truck was parked. Zill's truck, she knew now.

Then she had to write that the footprints had disappeared. No one in the truck. But no more footprints.

She closed her eyes an instant, trying to recreate the scene in her mind. Gun drawn, she'd checked inside the truck, under the seat, in the truckbed. On top, streaks of snow, no prints. Underneath she'd even checked to see if someone was clinging to the truck's underbelly. Then, with her flashlight, looked at every inch of ground.

Same result. No one in the truck, on the truck, under the truck. But also no footprints leading away.

Plus there hadn't been any tiretracks to show that Zill's truck had been moved after the snow started. Or that any other vehicle had been there.

After a while she'd given up, slung some crime-scene tape around the area. The only thing she'd figured out was that there was a surprisingly good view of the burning cabin from the truck cab. Someone could have sat in the truck and watched the flames. Arsonists liked to do that, liked to watch their handiwork, according to an Indianapolis arson detective who'd given them a training lecture once. He'd said you always should keep track of the helpful citizens who hovered around a fire. Most of them were the good guys they claimed to be, but in that haystack of helpful citizens you often found the needle you were looking for, if you found him at all.

But there were no helpful citizens to hide among in that remote forest, only firemen and a TV reporter. So it looked as though the arsonist had decided to watch from the truck. In the truck he was invisible in the dark, because not much moonlight penetrated the overhanging evergreens, but he'd had a good view of the burning cabin through the treetrunks.

In daylight, though, someone might have spotted the truck. Plus there'd been no attempt to hide those footprints in the snow. The killer had meant for them to find the truck, Marty was sure. But better not write that down. Sheriff Pierce had snapped at her a couple of times for what he called speculation.

When Wes Cochran was sheriff, he'd listened.

She got back to the report. Typed in that she'd gone back down to the cabin – jaw clenched, willing her father to stay quiet in her mind, but she didn't type that – and completed the tour that she'd cut short when she'd first seen the body. Sure enough, on the far side she'd found a line of broken brush and twigs. Someone had dragged something heavy – a body? – toward the cabin. No footprints or drag marks in the snow, so this trail was from before the snowfall. All the same she'd stayed well to one side, just in case there was something useful under the snow. She'd followed the broken brush uphill a quarter-mile to a clearing. Coyote pawprints paralleled the track too, headed down toward the cabin.

In the clearing, there had been blood on the moonlit snow. Had the victim been slashed here? Doc Altmann said he'd been alive when the cabin burned. She was confused for a moment until she realized that this must be where they'd field-dressed the deer before the snow fell. They'd left the warm entrails behind in a pile that melted the snow as it fell. Judging from the pawprints a lot of forest scavengers had been attracted, not just coyotes but also foxes and coons. The pile had been consumed or dragged off by the time Marty arrived, leaving only a bare spot of earth and some bloody snow.

So it was the deer carcass they'd dragged to the cabin before snow fell.

She swung the flashlight around to see if there was a hunter's tree stand or other signs of where they'd waited for their game, but realized that it was too dark for an efficient search. Maybe in the daylight the crime-scene technicians would find something – spent shells or candy wrappers – to show where the hunters had waited, maybe provide a clue to the identity of the killer.

That was it for the crime-scene portion of her report. She turned to the interviews, summarized her talks with Jumbo Jim and Maudie Corson.

Leaning back from the computer a moment, she stretched her arms. Much as she hated writing reports, it did sometimes bring up good questions. Like, Zill's mother had said he'd been nervous for a couple of weeks. What light did that throw on the crime scene? On the guy who'd left the scene after snowfall?

Well, if Zill had had the feeling someone was after him, he wouldn't have gone hunting with just anyone, would he? It had to be a trusted friend.

Or relative.

Of course he might have gone alone, thinking he could escape his troubles in the woods, and the other guy found him there. But Zill would have to be pretty dumb to hide all alone in a cabin half the county knew he owned. He was safer sticking with people. So he'd probably ask a buddy, someone he trusted.

OK, suppose Zill and this trusted buddy had tracked and killed a deer, field-gutted it, hauled it a quarter-mile down to the cabin, all before the snow fell. Maybe they'd shared a meal or a drink. Then the trusted buddy had put his plan into effect, which ended with big strong Zill bound to the thick bedpost and slashed by the machete. Still alive, Doc Altmann had said. Conscious? No way to know. If so, in pain. Plus he'd had to watch his trusted buddy pouring accelerant around, lighting a fire, backing out the door and locking the padlock.

Could it have been just a couple of guys drinking to celebrate killing the deer, then an argument gone bad? That didn't seem right. Zill was a powerful guy, experienced in working security. The buddy must have had a plan.

Zill's mother thought he'd been nervous. So maybe he'd noticed some of the planning. Still, it looked like he'd trusted the hunting buddy. Why else would the big guy go deep into the woods with him?

Well, suppose Zill didn't trust him. Maybe he knew his buddy was out to get him and it was Zill who'd planned to

44

take his buddy into the forest to kill him. But somehow the buddy had turned Zill's plan against him.

Possible.

She thumbed back through her notes. Pulled over the map Flo had sent clipped to the copy of the cabin's title of ownership. She waited for Grady to finish soothing someone whose cat was missing before saying, 'Grady?'

'Yeah?'

'Why would a couple of hunters put a deer inside their cabin?'

'I been wondering that too.'

'They field-dressed it, so they must have wanted the meat. Then they dragged it straight down to the cabin. Quarter-mile maybe. But they could have got their truck closer than that on the same logging road they were parked on.'

Grady frowned. 'My guess is they wanted to spend another day hunting. Didn't want to drive back that night.'

'But my dad used to say you gotta cool the meat fast, right? The cabin was warm, and the outdoors was a nice big refrigerator last night. The Forest Service guy at the scene said they were hiding it from the rangers. But why couldn't they hide it in the pickup overnight?'

'Naw, if the rangers spotted a pickup they'd check it out. And they can tell a deer even if you wrap it up in . . .'

Grady stopped talking as Sheriff Pierce burst through the door. When he saw Marty he charged over to her desk. 'Why the hell were you interrogating Don Foley?'

Startled, she stared up at his angry face. 'Sir, I wasn't! In the parking lot he—'

'He said you were asking him about the case!'

She'd scrambled to her feet so she wouldn't have to bend her head back so far to see him. 'Sir, Mr Foley came over to me in the parking lot. He was upset because Mr Corson was his friend.'

'Doesn't mean you should be questioning him, Hopkins!'

'No, sir, I wasn't questioning him. Only question I asked was to check if Deputy Culp had been able to talk to him yet.'

'He said you were trying to pry information from him.'

'That was not my intention, sir.'

'I don't give a damn what you say your intention was! Leave Don Foley alone!'

'Yessir.' Her eyes shifted to the door that was opening behind him. He glanced back, saw Betty Burke the reporter coming in.

Pierce looked back at Marty and then at her computer screen, and said in a more civilized tone, 'Finish your report, now.'

'Yes, sir.' She sat down again.

'And then you're outta here. Go get some rest. You've been up all night. What can I do for you, Betty?' He turned to the reporter.

Simmering, Marty forced herself to look over her report. Damn Foley! And damn the sheriff for listening to him. She did her best to stow her anger, fixed some typos, but she couldn't focus enough to make any more changes. She printed out a copy.

Howie Culp came in, hung up his Stetson. Sheriff Pierce asked, 'Culp, good. Get your report ready; we'll be talking about it.'

'Yes, sir.' Howie sat down at a computer.

Sheriff Pierce looked at Marty, then back at Culp. 'Howie, I want you in charge of this investigation when I'm not around. You keep track of where everyone is, what the crime scene technicians tell us, and so forth.'

'Yes, sir.' Howie glanced uncomfortably at Marty.

Pierce continued, 'I'll be back in twenty minutes. Want to get Betty squared away with the state troopers about that accident.' He checked his watch. 'Howie, I know it'll mean overtime but wait for me here. I want to talk about the Corson murder. Hopkins, you go on home.'

Howie said, 'Yes, sir,' and after a moment Marty said it too.

Her shift, like Howie's, was over in five minutes. As soon as the door closed behind Betty Burke and the sheriff, she typed a quick note about the non-theft of Ferro's vehicle, left it on her desk, and went to the restroom.

Three minutes later, angry tears dried and hair brushed, she came out, put on her coat and Stetson, and dropped her printout about Zill Corson's death on Howie's desk. Fumbling for the sunglasses in her pocket, she walked out the door.

A dark-haired young woman was climbing the steps. She wore a well-cut black coat and trousers and a long scarf in several shades of green mohair wound around her throat.

She said in an East Coast accent, 'Excuse me, Deputy, is this where I can talk to someone about the man who died in that fire?'

For an instant Marty's gaze met dark eyes as intelligent as her own. But she said only, 'Talk to Deputy Culp,' and started down the steps.

The woman called after her, 'But weren't you the one at the scene last night?'

'My shift's over,' Marty said, sliding on her sunglasses before she looked back and repeated more gently, 'Talk to Deputy Culp.'

Seven

No welcome-to-our-fair-city from that one! Liv Mann looked after the woman deputy for a second, watched her get into a cruiser and go screeching off. Then she turned back, smoothed her travel-rumpled coat, opened the door.

On one side of the big room, doors. One marked 'Sheriff Charles Pierce'. Also a restroom, and a big door reinforced with steel. Probably led back to the jail – she'd seen barred windows from outside. Beat-up old desks lined two walls, separated from the rest of the room by a low-gated oak barrier. Only one deputy back there, a young brown-haired man typing industriously at a computer.

In the center of the room, straight ahead, was a higher desk and phone console. Behind it sat a skinny older guy in a headset. He said, 'Yes, ma'am, can I help you?'

At least that woman deputy had given her a name. Liv said, 'May I speak to Deputy Culp?'

The headset guy looked at the younger man. 'Deputy Culp? Can you talk to the lady?'

'Yeah, gimme a minute here.' The young guy looked over his shoulder, waved an arm at the bench next to the front door. 'Sit down, I'll be with you in a minute.'

They all had accents like her dad's. Liv unwound her scarf and unbuttoned her wool coat, but decided that sitting would make them think there was no hurry. Instead she walked over to the bulletin board. The same FBI set of most-wanted faces that she knew from Brooklyn looked out at her, along with some locals, mostly failure-to-appears on drunk-driving or forged-check charges. There were homier postings too: a scribbled note about a rifle for sale, another asking for volunteers for a security detail at a talent show at a place called the Rockland Mall.

Deputy Culp didn't take long, soon stood up with a glance

at his watch and opened the gate in the barrier. 'C'mon in, have a seat right here.' He indicated a scuffed metal chair next to his desk. He had broad shoulders, close-set blue eyes, and dark-brown hair cut a little longer than most cops, maybe to distract from ears that stuck out like sugarbowl handles. 'What can we do for you, ma'am?'

'I work in the District Attorney's office in Brooklyn.'

'Brooklyn? That little town up in Morgan County?'

'Sorry. Brooklyn, New York.' Liv could almost hear her dad chuckling at her that time she hadn't been able to find the newspaper article she was hunting for in *The New York Times* index. Turned out it had appeared in the *Los Angeles Times*. 'You New Yorkers are so provincial,' her father had teased. 'The only *Times* is *The New York Times*, the only Brooklyn is a New York borough.'

Deputy Culp asked, 'What can we do for your District Attorney?'

An awkward question for this unofficial visit. Liv said, 'We know of another case where a man was cut with a machete and burned to death. I hoped we could share information.'

'This was in Brooklyn?' He was taking notes.

'A different part of New York City. Staten Island. It happened at a city landfill.'

'I see. Recently?'

'Four years ago.'

'Four years ago, in New York, a man was cut and burned to death,' Culp repeated, rubbing his ear as though trying to tame its sugarbowl attitude. 'But the way I hear it, that kind of thing happens pretty often in New York City.'

'But he was my father!' Liv blurted.

'I see. I'm sorry, ma'am.' There seemed to be genuine sympathy in Culp's face. But he'd stopped taking notes.

Liv leaned forward. 'See, my father was raised here in Nichols County. So I thought . . .'

A wintry breeze ruffled her hair and Culp waved to someone coming in. 'Hey, Ken!'

'Hey, Howie. Hey, Grady, is the sheriff here?'

The skinny guy at the dispatch desk answered, 'Back any minute.'

A woman in a khaki-colored polo shirt opened the big metal-reinforced door. Jail matron, maybe. 'I brought doughnuts,

49

guys. Oh, sorry, ma'am.' She glanced at Liv with curiosity, then greeted another deputy coming in. 'Hi, Fred. How's Ellie Ann?'

'Gettin' there. Hey, Grady, anything I oughta know?'

Culp looked back at Liv. 'Sorry, ma'am, shift change. Could I have your name, please?'

'Oh. Right. I'm Olivia Mann.' She spelled it for him. 'And my father was Ronald Mann.'

'OK.' He scribbled it down as he asked, 'Where can we reach you?'

'I'm at the Limestone Motel.'

'OK. Phone?'

She recited her cellphone number and added, 'Did the machete come from South America?'

'I'm sorry, Miz Mann, this case is still under investigation.' He glanced at her, must have seen something in her face, because he added, 'You know how it is, if you work for a DA.'

She did know. When cops were groping to make sense of a crime they didn't talk to outsiders. Not even the DA's office, in fact, unless they were afraid they'd blow the case by an inadmissable search or something and wanted to do it by the book. And once her office got it, they too kept as much to themselves as they legally could. Still, she'd hoped that face to face someone would bend a little and tell her something. She said, 'Yes, but it could be a good idea just to check, to see if there are similarities.'

'Yes, ma'am. I'll suggest that to the sheriff.'

'Suggest what to the sheriff?' Another cold breeze on her neck announced a new arrival. Liv turned to see a pale, handsome, middle-aged man undoing his coat.

Must be the sheriff because Deputy Culp had jumped to his feet. 'Sir, Miz Mann here says her father was also cut and burned four years ago. In New York City.'

'Ma'am, I'm sorry.' There was sympathy in the sheriff's face.

Liv stood up too. 'Thank you, Sheriff Pierce. I think when you check into it you'll find the cases are related, because—'

'Thank you, ma'am, for coming forward. Now right now we have an important meeting. Culp, you've got a number where we can get back to her, right?'

'Yes, sir.'

'We'll be in touch, ma'am. Culp and the rest of you – into my office. We got a lot to talk about.'

All the deputies followed him in, except for the one who'd replaced the skinny guy at the dispatch desk and was talking to someone on the phone about a dangerous ice condition somewhere.

Slowly, Liv wound her scarf around her neck. For this brush-off she'd given up Cancun? She could almost hear Elena, half angry, half amused, 'So next time listen to me!'

There was a printout on Culp's desk. She tried to read it upside down as she buttoned her coat. It had to be about this case, because the top page described the cabin fire and listed the firefighters present at the scene when the writer of the report arrived. The writer – there it was. Submitted by Deputy Martine Hopkins.

Must be the woman deputy who'd been in such a damn hurry, the one who'd been on TV.

Liv tried to figure out how to see the next page of the report without alerting the deputy at the dispatch desk. But the sheriff's office door opened, Culp popped out, grabbed the report, and asked, 'Miz Mann, d'you need directions somewhere?'

'It's OK, I was just buttoning my coat.'

But as she left the desk area she had a thought. 'Deputy . . . Sims?' she said, reading the name card on the dispatch desk.

'Naw, I just haven't changed the card yet,' said the new guy in the headset. 'I'm Walker.'

'Glad to meet you, Deputy Walker.' She smiled at him. 'Can you tell me how to get to Holtsclaw Road?'

'Sure thing. Go around the courthouse square here, then east on Twelfth Street, OK?'

'OK.'

'Keep going straight and pretty soon you get to the highway. Turn north, go maybe five miles. Holtsclaw comes in on the right.'

'Thanks.'

Liv went out into the cold, climbed into the bright-red Escort she'd rented at the airport, turned the ignition to get the heater going, but didn't move. She pulled out her Palm Pilot and entered the names she'd just learned: Deputies Culp and Hopkins, and the firefighters that had been on the page of the report she'd seen – Bramer and Smythe.

She checked her messages. One from Elena, en route to Cancun. 'Call me tonight.' Could mean anything.

Then, still not sure she wanted to do it, Liv checked another entry. Yes, there it was, 3006 Holtsclaw Road: her dad's old friend Mark Lugano. Wife's name Arlene. It had been a long time since she'd seen the Luganos, even though as a child she'd visited them often with her father. They'd lived in Connecticut then, not too far from the Manns' house on Staten Island. She remembered a big yard, lots of trees, a separate room for a library, trips to a nearby riding academy where they'd gone horseback riding. That had impressed her at ten. Still did. But when Lugano retired he'd moved back to this county. By then Liv was in college but her dad had come out here to visit them a time or two, and they'd gone back east to see him. Then seven years ago her dad had quit visiting, though he'd said nothing about a falling-out. And when he'd died, they didn't come to the funeral, but they did send Liv a nice condolence note.

Still, a pretty fragile connection. She hadn't really planned to look them up – maybe a phone call after she'd accomplished her first priority: finding out what she could about this second murder so like her father's. But now she was wondering if Mark Lugano could give her a tip about how to break through the wall of silence the sheriff and his deputies had erected.

Wouldn't hurt to knock on the Luganos' door. She adjusted the heater and turned the Escort toward the courthouse square. Nice-looking little courthouse, made of big blocks of pale stone, adorned with columns and simple carving along the roofline and around the tall windows. The four streets that formed the square around it boasted lamp poles with white bell-shaped holiday decorations.

Why the hell wouldn't her father visit this place? Looked like a postcard for the American heartland. Women in pink or turquoise, even a few flowered parkas, walked around with kids or with each other. A variety of stores lined the square, mostly small: Edna's Cafe, Soup & Sprouts, Dawn's Unisex Salon. A florist, clothes for kids, clothes for women; the

Sportswoman and a place called Hot Couture, even though the clothes in the window were far from daring. Demure Couture would be a better name, Liv thought. The two larger stores were a Ben Franklin and a national drugstore that took up half of one side of the square. Beyond it was a shoestore, then a small bakery, and . . .

Coming out of the bakery, in lively conversation with a teen-aged girl, was the woman deputy who'd written that report.

Liv spotted the cruiser nose-out by the courthouse, found a parking space three slots away, jumped out of her car. The deputy – no sunglasses now – was smiling as the girl grace-fully shoe-glided across a big ice patch on the sidewalk. As the deputy turned to the cruiser to unlock it, Liv hurried around the nose of the vehicle and said, 'Deputy Hopkins.'

'Yeah?' The warmth and liveliness disappeared, was replaced by the intelligent but noncommital cop-face she'd worn before.

Liv said, 'Sorry to bother you. I spoke to Deputy Culp, like you said, but—'

'Good. Then you know everything we can say at this point.'

Liv stood her ground. 'Yeah, I know it's under investiga-tion, but you were there at the beginning. You saw the body. See, I know a case just like it. Machete, fire.'

A spark of curiosity flared in those gray eyes but Deputy Hopkins said, 'Look, I'm seriously off-duty. Did you tell Deputy Culp about this other case?'

Liv didn't answer directly, said, 'The sheriff came in and interrupted us because they had to have a meeting.'

Deputy Hopkins, jaw clenched, opened the cruiser door and flipped the switch so the girl could get in the other side. She said, 'You're a citizen, ma'am; you can talk directly to the sheriff.'

Odd comment. Liv remembered the report on Culp's desk, the fact that Hopkins had left at the end of the shift but Culp had been called into the meeting, and asked, 'What do you mean? The sheriff doesn't want a woman on an important case? Damn, it's the same for women cops in New York City.'

Deputy Hopkins already had one foot inside the cruiser. Now she paused. 'How come you know about New York City cops?'

Liv said, 'I'm Olivia Mann. I'm an ADA in Brooklyn so I

talk to cops a lot. Men and women. Seventy-five percent of the guys think women shouldn't be in uniform.'

'Then you've got the picture, except here it's more like ninety percent. Tell your boss if he wants to compare cases he'd be better off waiting until the county prosecuting attorney here has it. Sit down, Chrissie, we're about done,' she added to the girl, who had popped out of the cruiser again.

Liv said, 'My boss didn't send me. See, my dad grew up in this county. Ronald Mann. And it was my dad who was murdered. Machete, fire.'

'Your dad.' The gray eyes darkened and she studied Liv a moment. Then she shook her head, muttered, 'Shoot. I'm sorry,' and before Liv could say a word she whipped into the cruiser and pulled out while her door was still closing. Stunned, Liv looked after her.

Ten feet down the street the cruiser stopped, waited for a car to pass, then reversed and stopped again in front of her. The window rolled open and Deputy Hopkins said, 'Listen up, Ms Mann, here's an example why I can't help you. One of the ninety percent here who doesn't want women on the job is an ex-deputy named Don Foley, used to make my life miserable. He's retired now. Foley was a friend of the dead guy. Today he comes up to me in the parking lot and starts yelling at me. And the sheriff assumes I was doing an un-authorized interview and chews me out. So that's why I'm telling people who come up to me in parking lots to talk to Deputy Culp or the sheriff or the Prosecuting Attorney. And that's what I'm telling you. D'you understand?'

'I think I do, Deputy Hopkins. Thank you for explaining.'

The sunglasses went back on, the window rolled up, and the cruiser rolled away. Liv added the name 'Don Foley' to her Palm Pilot, stared at it a moment, then headed for the store misleadingly named Hot Couture.

Eight

Marty parked in the fire lane at the Rockland Mall and followed her daughter inside. Bob Rueger, the Arizona-based developer of the mall, had semi-promised Nichols County a big new super-mall on a proposed major Indianapolis-to-Evanston highway. When the highway was rerouted to another county, he'd pulled out of the deal, but added a new Food Court to the Rockland Mall as a sort of consolation prize. It was a big circular structure tacked on to the central angle of the two-armed mall. A two-story-high steel framework supported walls and roof of glass. Marty liked it when the sky was blue, but it was gloomy now with snow covering the glass. Or maybe it was her own mood, frustrated because the murder was cruel and baffling, frustrated because she kept flashing on her father's coffin, frustrated because the sheriff wasn't letting her do much on it.

Beside her Chrissie craned her neck, looking for her friend. Ringing the big room were assorted fast-food counters. The main part of the arena was filled with tables occupied at this after-school hour by teenagers as well as the usual retired folks. In the center, a round raised stage with an upright piano and microphones was sometimes used for live music concerts or talent shows. Right now the music was piped-in easy-listening instrumentals.

'There she is!' Chrissie exclaimed, and ran toward her best friend Janie Tippett, who was sitting with a Coke at a table not far from the Chicken Delight booth.

Marty spotted a curly strawberry-blonde head. Janie's mother, Carolee Tippett, worked early shift at the hospital so she had afternoons off. She was walking toward the girls holding a coffee in her plump freckled hand. As Marty approached, the recorded music stopped and a plinky banjo was heard. Marty looked over her shoulder at the stage.

55

Two clowns had appeared, wearing orange polka-dots and little bowler hats that sat precariously atop bright-green fright-wigs. They wore whiteface with big painted staring eyes and grins so wide they reminded Marty of death's-heads. One clown had hopped up to sit on the piano and was strumming a small banjo-type instrument. They opened with a parody version of a popular rock song about lost love and a cruel wind. 'The wind with ice on its breath,' sang the banjo player in a strong soprano. The other clown was beating time on a little hand drum while miming a stronger and stronger wind, eventually losing the drum and taking a couple of spectacular pratfalls in the pretend gale. Even the teens in the audience were won over despite themselves, clapping and laughing when the bowler hat went flying but landed magically on the clown's head at the end of a fall.

Next the clown pulled something with bright stripes from a pocket, fastened it to one side of the stage, and tugged at it while backing across the platform. A paper arc unfolded, seven feet high at its peak and striped in bright colors. The banjo-strummer shifted to 'Somewhere over the rainbow'.

'Looks like Stanni and Eunie have a new act,' Marty said to Carolee.

'Yeah.' Carolee smiled at her, then at the clowns. 'Who says you can't teach an old dog new tricks?'

'Those sisters have been around a long time, all right,' Marty said. 'I remember them at birthday parties when I was a kid.'

'How old do you suppose they are? Been a long time since I could do those flips. Course, Stanni still teaches gymnastics. Where did she go? All I see is her hat on the piano.' Carolee lifted her coffee for another sip, then exclaimed, 'Oh, look!' The rest of the audience was exclaiming too, because as Eunie, the singing clown, came to the second repetition of 'bluebirds fly', a figure in blue with feathers on its arms and a yellow beak jutting from its face came soaring above the heads of the crowd and over the paper rainbow.

Marty looked up, saw rigging firmly fastened to the steel beams above. The bluebird-clown turned aerial somersaults and waved its wings in time to the music. At the end, the bird landed on the stage and took off its beaked mask to reveal the painted grin of Stanni the clown, while Eunie sang the last mournful 'why can't I?'.

They got a big hand and both used their bowler hats to collect coins from the crowd sitting at the tables and standing in lines at the booths. Carolee Tippett turned to Marty. 'You need Chrissie home any special time?'

'Aunt Vonnie and I should both be back by six, so any time after that. Janie can come for dinner if you want.'

'Only if she's got her homework done. See you later, Marty.'

'Thanks, Carolee.'

Marty started back to the cruiser, but paused to drop a dollar in a bowler hat as it passed nearby. 'Hey, Stanni, I like your new act.'

'Thanks, Marty,' said Stanni from behind her mask, and bounced on to collect from the next table.

Liv Mann came out of the Hot Couture store with her black pantsuit packed into a big plastic bag and wearing her new clothes. Pink jeans, pink-and-green flowered sweater under her new lime-green parka and lime-green woolly hat. Elena would laugh. She loved costumes, sometimes brought home a forties gown or a French beret so she could take photos of Liv. But this stuff was the opposite of glamorous.

She tossed the plastic bag into her trunk, started the heater and opened her map of Dunning and Nichols County. After a few moments, she found the street on the outskirts of town, and started toward it.

It was a neighborhood of little one-story frame houses, painted white or pastel colors with contrasting trim, probably inexpensive here though in Brooklyn they'd have cost hundreds of thousands. Except for some evergreen foundation plantings, the yards sat flat and cold under an inch of snow.

Don Foley's house was a buckskin-tan color with brown doors and woodwork. Liv parked the red Escort in the blacktop drive and followed a narrow cement walk to the front door. Up close she could see that the trim needed repainting. She pushed the doorbell. Inside the house, a dog barked at the buzzing noise. A big dog.

Liv waited. A cold breeze huffed up the street, rattling the bare branches of trees and bushes.

She buzzed again, and again was answered by the dog. But this time she heard uneven footsteps and a moment later the door was opened by a round-faced man in a white shirt and suit trousers. He looked her over with some suspicion, said, 'Yes, miss?'

'Mr Foley? My name is Olivia Mann.' She tried to sound feminine and prim. 'I talked to Deputy Culp, and heard you were a friend of that poor man who died. And my poor father died the same way.' She let her lower lip tremble a little. 'I just wanted to, you know, talk about it a little bit.'

His suspicious eyes had softened. 'Yeah, honey, I'm sorry about your loss.'

Was that a whiff of alcohol? She asked cautiously, 'D'you think you could maybe talk to me a few minutes?'

He glanced at his watch. 'Right now I gotta go visit the Corsons. My friend's family. But tell you what, tomorrow morning I can meet you if you come back then.'

'Oh, thanks, Mr Foley! Nine o'clock?' When he nodded she said, 'See you then. Thanks!'

Well, a half-victory, she thought on her way back to the car. She'd wanted to talk right now, but no sense pushing too hard and antagonizing the guy. Morning might be better anyway if he'd been drinking. She'd call the Luganos, see if they could tell her anything.

Arlene Lugano answered the phone and sounded delighted. 'Why, Liv, honey, of course! You come over right now. It's been way too long!'

Feeling welcome for the first time, Liv backed out of Don Foley's drive and turned the Escort toward Holtsclaw Road.

Wes Cochran was picking up a few logs from the snow-covered woodpile stacked against his garage when the cruiser pulled into his driveway. He paused, said, 'Hey, Marty,' as she got out. She looked tired, he thought.

'Hi, Coach. Got a minute?' Her breath puffed white in the chilly air.

'Yeah, don't have to be at work for another hour. Come on in and help me lay a fire. Shirley's out at some church committee meeting and I wanted to have it going for her when she gets back.'

'Sure thing.'

58

He maneuvered the bundle inside while she held the storm door for him, and after they'd hung their coats on the pegs he threw the logs into the limestone fireplace and lit the kindling, then rocked back on his haunches and looked at her. She was brushing away snow that had fallen from the logs on to Shirley's green carpet, a little worry line between her brows. He said, 'You told me you had some questions.'

'Yes, sir, lots.'

'About what?'

She shrugged. 'About the crime scene. About the victim's motives. About the victim's background. About what's eating Sheriff Pierce.'

Wes wanted to offer to punch him out, but instead shook his head. 'On the last one, it's really between you and him, Hopkins.'

'Yes, sir; he's the boss. I know.'

'And for the rest, I already told you, I don't think I can help much there either. Didn't know Zill Corson except to say howdy. And I didn't see the crime scene. But hell, let's sit down.'

He pushed himself up from the rug and settled into his recliner while Marty pulled a side chair closer to the fireplace, saying, 'Two things about the crime scene. See, they shot a deer, field-gutted it, and dragged it a quarter-mile to the cabin, even though they could of parked their pickup on that logging trail a lot closer to where they killed it. Plus keeping it in that heated cabin would spoil the meat, right? So the ranger at the scene said maybe they wanted to stay awhile and were afraid they'd get caught if they stored it in the truck. Grady said that's probably right.'

'Yeah, maybe they thought one night wouldn't hurt,' Wes said dubiously.

He didn't think she looked satisfied either, but she said, 'Yeah,' and went on, 'OK, second thing about the crime scene was, no footprints going in so they got there before the snow fell, but there was one set of footprints in the snow leading away from the cabin to the truck.'

'Whose footprints?'

'Don't know yet. But somebody cut Zill, set him and the cabin on fire, and was gone when we got there. And somebody went from the cabin to the pickup, driver's door. Then the prints disappear.'

'Probably walked down the logging road. Or was there snow on it too?'

'Lots of snow. No footprints of any kind leading away from that pickup. I searched the truck top to bottom, nobody there.'

Wes frowned at her. 'Must have missed him somehow in the dark.'

Marty nodded. 'Yeah. But how? When the sheriff brought the guys to relieve me I asked Bobby Mason to check in the daylight, and he said there was still nothing there except that set of footprints going to the truck, and of course mine, both directions.'

Wes thought a second, shook his head. 'See, I told you I wouldn't be much help. What're your questions about Zill?'

'Zill. OK, his mother thought lately he was worried about something. She said he mentioned that security company he used to work for abroad. Couldn't remember the name. His brother didn't see how that company could be the problem. But anyway, some guy named Bowers got him that job. Sarge Bowers. Real name maybe Johnny Bowers. He was from here, they said.'

Wes nodded. 'I remember Johnny Bowers. He was a couple years ahead of me in high school. Mostly a football player, but tall enough for basketball too.'

'What kind of guy was he?'

Wes stared at the flames, remembering. 'We were all jocks on that team, OK? Your dad, me, all of us. Some of us smarter than others. You know Mark Lugano, goes to the Catholic church? Bright guy, went on to get a business degree, made big bucks and retired back to this county a few years back. Well, I remember the first year I played, Johnny Bowers was about to flunk math. Mark had to tutor him to get his grades up so he wouldn't be kicked off the team.'

'Corky Dennis said he went into the Marines.'

'Yeah, the Marines were a good fit for Johnny. Tough, big, disciplined. Better than your dad on that.' A memory nudged him: Rusty's grinning face as he held out a bottle of whiskey he'd sneaked from his father the night before a game. Next day Wes, playing through a roaring headache, had scored only half the points he usually did, and from then on he'd limited himself to beer. Not Rusty.

Marty was smiling. 'Yeah, you're always complaining about how he corrupted you.'

'Not complaining. What're friends for?' Wes said lightly.

She got back to business. 'D'you know why Bowers left the Marines?'

'Don Foley told me he and Bowers both got disgusted with the military when we pulled out of Viet Nam. Don got himself hired as deputy here, Cowgill was sheriff then, and Bowers musta gone into private security about the same time. Mid-seventies.'

'Zill was younger than Bowers,' Marty said. 'His mother thought they met in the Marines, and then, when Bowers switched to private security, he followed. Jumbo Jim said Zill liked the job partly for the travel, at least until he got wounded in Africa somewhere. Is Bowers still with the same company?'

Wes shrugged. 'Don't know. He's a couple years older than I am, so they probably aren't sending him to do the heavy lifting these days. Seem to recall Don saying he lived in Indy now. But those private companies get big money, they can offer good retirement benefits. Could be Bowers is living happily on some tropical island.' He looked hard at Marty. 'Don Foley has probably told all this to Howie Culp.'

'Yes, sir. Nobody's told me, though. Not yet.' Wes felt his fist clenching at Chuck Pierce's stupidity, made himself relax. She added, 'One last question. Do you remember a guy called Ronald Mann?'

'Mann.' Wes frowned. 'I know the name.'

'He grew up here. Went east somewhere to work. He died four years ago from a machete followed by a fire.'

'He what?' Wes straightened up.

Her gray eyes were troubled. 'His daughter is some kind of ADA in New York City and flew out to talk to us when she heard how Zill died. But the sheriff hasn't talked to her.'

'I might not talk to her either,' Wes said sharply, standing up and heading for the kitchen. 'But I'd sure as hell listen to her.'

'Yes, sir.'

She followed him through the kitchen, out to the cold, empty garage. He switched on the light, squatted down by the storage case in the corner, found the books he was looking for. He stood up again with a grunt. 'Let's go back to the light,' he said.

61

Nine

The *chaski* had had his binoculars on the house for half an hour, but the only interesting thing that had happened was when blonde Arlene had come out the front door to sprinkle salt on the front walk. It was a big house, silvery-gray limestone like the cliff where he crouched on a ledge. Even the graceful columns on the long front porch were carved from stone. There was a semicircular drive and a half-acre snow-covered lawn sweeping down to the roadside evergreen hedge and the stone gateposts. A new house, but built with a nod toward the old days.

The luxurious grounds complicated things, especially with the snow. Bad enough to have to worry about the electric fence hidden in the hedges. *Chaskis* were messengers as well as accountants, and the problem here was how to get a message in without leaving footprints or, worse, being seen. The Indy apartment had been easy, and Corson's trailer a piece of cake to warn. But here, the most important of them all, it was frustrating to have all that snowy expanse like a moat around a castle.

He had to get to Indy soon to meet an old friend in a bar, and if the friend was feeling down about his life he'd buy him a few drinks and help him to bed. Just like Zill. But first he wanted to find the solution for this place. He could shoot the message through a window. But ballistics were very scientific these days, and these Hoosiers in the hills were damn good shots themselves: even a stupid deputy could probably figure out trajectories. Might be better to wait until they drove out in their fancy BMW and parked it somewhere. But it was always more effective to get it right in the house – that really got them sweating.

Hey, what was this? Something happening at last. A red car coming slowly along the road, and yes, turning in at the stone gateposts. The *chaski* swung his binoculars quickly to look at the front windows of the house. Yes, a flicker of a curtain. They knew someone was in the drive. Sensors, probably, in those gateposts.

He looked back at the red car, which was stopping by the newly salted walkway. Ford Escort, he saw. Short person getting out, dark-haired female. Green parka, green-striped fuzzy scarf. She pulled off a green hat and shook her head. Lots of black curls. Wait a minute. Something familiar about the way she moved. She was looking around. He kept the glasses on her and when she glanced toward the cliff where he crouched, he was sure.

Ronnie Mann's daughter. He'd seen her often enough over the years. What the hell was she doing so far from home? Kids usually weren't all that close to their parents' friends. Hadn't heard this girl was any different.

Had she noticed what Ronnie Mann and Zill Corson had in common?

Must have! And just by showing up, she'd solved the *chaski*'s problem. He could get on with his work. He smiled, turned to the cliff behind him, sighted on its little edges and eroded pockets, and skillfully climbed back to the woods where he'd left his truck.

Funny to think she would fire the warning shot for him.

'Why, Liv, honey, it's so good to see you again! What in the world brings you to Indiana?' Liv was enveloped in a big hug but Arlene Lugano didn't stop talking. 'Let me take your coat. Isn't it cold? You should come back in the spring, when the redbuds and dogwoods are out; it's just beautiful riding the trails then. Now, we have coffee ready for you, or would you rather have a cocktail? You sweet thing, it's so good to see you!'

Liv smiled at her bubbly hostess. Arlene was short, about Liv's height, and as she put Liv's coat in the closet Liv noticed she had a few more pounds and a few more wrinkles than the last time she'd seen her. But the wavy blonde hair and the outgoing personality were the same. When she paused for breath Liv said, 'It's great to see you, and I'd love a cup of coffee.'

Arlene caught Liv's hand in hers the way she'd done when

Liv was ten. 'Well then, come on in and sit by the fire.' Through an arch behind the tiled foyer there was a big living room with a fire in the limestone fireplace and a couple of leather-covered sofas. A big window looked out on snowy fields and a backing of woods. But Arlene was leading her past the archway, and also past the next room, a big dining room with the same view.

'What a great view! Is that your barn too?' Liv said as they passed.

'Oh, yes, and our woods.' The next room was a family room that opened to a big cheery kitchen. Here the fireplace was brick with a white-painted mantel. Above it was a reproduction of a famous Madonna painting, the Madonna smiling happily at the child. Maybe Leonardo. Elena would know. This was Arlene's part of the house, clearly. The big front rooms announced wealth and success; this one was friendlier. Arlene released Liv's hand and waved toward the floral-print sofa and the round oak table and chairs. 'Have a seat, honey. Cream and sugar?'

'Black's fine.' Liv pulled up a chair to the oak table near the fireplace. 'That fire feels good.'

At the counter in the kitchen, Arlene poured coffee from an espresso machine and brought in two little sunflower-painted cups, placing them on the table with an uncharacteristically anxious look at a door that led beyond the family room. 'Mark, honey? Are you back?' she called through it. 'Liv Mann is here. Shall I pour you some coffee?'

'Sure.' Mark Lugano opened the door, a tall rugged man, still lean but with less hair and more sorrowful eyes than Liv remembered. He smiled when he saw her, though, and as she rose to meet him he strode in and seized both her hands. 'Good to see you! Getting all those bad guys in Brooklyn locked up?'

'I'm sure trying, Mr Lugano.'

Arlene joined them with the third cup of coffee. 'What's this "Mister" stuff? You're all grown up now, Liv honey; call us Mark and Arlene.'

'Thanks, Arlene.' As they sat down Liv went on, 'You've got a nice place here. You must be enjoying retirement. Or would you like to be back in the thick of things?'

Mark smiled and shrugged.

Arlene said, 'Sure, we're enjoying it. We didn't have room for horses in Connecticut, and here we are, three hunters to ride plus three thoroughbred brood mares. Did you know this was bluegrass country too? We're real close to Kentucky so we can send our yearlings to the sales there. You've got to see them, honey! I remember how much you used to like going to the riding stables in Connecticut.'

'Yeah, that was fun,' Liv agreed. 'I still ride when I can.'

Arlene went on, 'And the other thing is, it's like really coming home after all those years in Connecticut, because we have so many friends here from when we were young.'

Liv nodded but kept her eyes on Mark. Something about his smile hadn't rung true. Bitterness or despair or something flavored the friendliness. After a second he became aware of her gaze and echoed Arlene: 'Yeah, from when we were young. Those were the days.'

'Mark wants to be young again,' Arlene said with a little laugh. 'I suppose that's the only problem with seeing our old friends now. I look at Shirley Cochran's gray hair and, much as I love her, I'm reminded that I can't do those cheerleader jumps any more.'

'Well, I hope when I'm your age I have half as much to show for my life,' Liv said.

Mark's eyes closed but Arlene beamed. 'Thanks, honey. How long are you planning on staying? You've got to stay with us! We have room.'

'Thanks, Mrs – Arlene. I'm not real clear on my plans yet. Actually, I had a couple of questions for you.'

'Sure. Fire away,' Mark said easily, but if he'd been a witness in a courtroom Liv would have thought he'd tensed a little.

She glanced at Arlene, then back at Mark, and said bluntly, 'This guy Corson who just got killed. It was a lot like how my dad died.'

Arlene exclaimed, 'Oh, honey! It wasn't! Or – I guess I see what you mean, but this was a cabin fire, his own cabin. It's not the same.'

Liv said, 'There was a machete.' She looked silently at Mark until he said, 'Yeah, I noticed that too. But Arlene's right: there are so many differences, it has to be a horrible coincidence.'

'They both grew up in this county. Like you,' Liv insisted.

Mark said, 'We didn't know this man – what's his name, Corson? I doubt if your dad ever heard of him either. There are so many differences, the similarities are just coincidence.'

No way, Liv thought, but aloud said only, 'What kind of differences? All I know is the little snippet on CNN.'

Mark shook his head. 'Liv, it can't be good for you to be obsessing about this.'

'But if I don't follow up it will be worse,' Liv said earnestly. 'It's – Look, I know you were his friend. But I'm his daughter, and I owe it to Pops. The Staten Island cops worked hard on his case. My work brings me in contact with law enforcement a lot, and I know those cops did all the right things. But they never found the guy who did it.'

Mark said, 'The cops here may not find this guy either. You're setting yourself up for disappointment.'

'But I have to check, or I couldn't live with myself!'

Arlene had been uncharacteristically quiet, but now she said, 'Liv, I can see how you'd feel that way. But really, we don't know that much. Just what we saw in the paper today.'

'The paper. Do you still have it?' Liv asked eagerly.

'Sure. I'll fetch it.'

When Arlene had left, Liv said to Mark, 'I'm sorry, I know Pops was your friend and it was a loss for you too.'

'Yeah, it sure was,' Mark said, and cleared his throat. 'I don't much like to think about it.'

'I know. I guess we have different ways of dealing with it.' Was that all it was? She looked at the handsome man staring gloomily at his coffee and added, 'See, my job is all to do with justice, trying to make sure murderers and drug dealers and rapists are taken off the streets. So this is – I mean, I'd miss Pops just as much no matter how he died. But on top of all the grief, this is almost like a personal insult that the justice system hasn't caught the guy. D'you see?'

'Yeah. Yeah, little Liv, I see.' His dark eyes flicked up to meet hers and she was surprised to see how tormented they were.

Arlene returned and put the paper on the table in front of Liv. 'Here you are, honey. But I don't think anyone knows much yet.'

Liv took the paper eagerly. It was front-page news – Betty Burke was the byline, and Liv made a mental note of the name. There was a photo of the charred remnants of the cabin, a long description of the scene of the fire, quotes from the firemen. 'Goin' pretty good when we got here, no way we could've saved him,' one of them had told the reporter. 'It was too hot to go in and anyway it looked like nobody was in there, so we followed procedures to contain the fire. Then when the wall fell Deputy Hopkins saw there was a victim inside.'

The last column was a much shorter story, with a photo of the handsome pale sheriff who'd sent her packing. 'Fire Victim Identified', said the headline, and the story explained, 'As we went to press, Sheriff Charles Pierce announced that the identity of the victim of the cabin fire has been confirmed as Robert (Zill) Corson, one of the owners of the cabin. "We're going all out to catch this criminal," Sheriff Pierce told us. "We've developed some important leads. But anyone with information about this situation can help by calling us."'

Liv was beginning to get a picture of this sheriff, eager for publicity but insecure, threatened by capable women, not as bright as he ought to be to lead a team of crime fighters. Or maybe he was, Liv self-corrected. She was taking Deputy Hopkins's word for it. Of course there was a lot of real harassment but Liv knew from experience that sometimes women complained of unfair treatment although careful investigation found no hardships that men in the same job didn't suffer. Tomorrow she'd be talking to the ex-deputy Foley, apparently the victim's friend and Hopkins's enemy. She'd see if he was as bad as she'd said. He'd been polite enough at his door.

She glanced back at the longer article, skimmed it again. Something not quite right – what? It wouldn't come.

She looked up to find both Luganos watching her. She flicked Pierce's photo with her fingernail and asked, 'Is Pierce a good sheriff?'

Mark shrugged, and Arlene explained, 'We don't know much about this sheriff. We knew the one who retired last year, Wes Cochran. Mark was on the high-school basketball team with him. And his wife Shirley and I were both cheerleaders!' She smiled proudly at her husband.

Arlene was still the right type but Liv was amused at the thought of dignified Mark Lugano jumping around in shorts.

She said, 'Really? Pops only mentioned knowing you in the math club.'

Mark nodded. 'Yeah, Ronnie didn't go out for sports. Closest thing was some kind of folk-dancing club, I think.'

Liv said, 'Right! He told me he learned more Spanish from those songs than he did in Spanish class.'

Mark smiled. 'He probably did. Language teachers in this county weren't the best. But when we were that age, I think our real motive was to meet girls. That's half the reason I was on the team, right, Arlene?' He patted her hand. 'I wanted to meet those cute cheerleaders.'

Arlene laughed. 'Only half the reason? What was the other half?'

'Wanted to get into a good school,' Mark said. 'Just like Ronnie. All those activities count. Make the college think you're a well-rounded person.'

'Yeah, still works that way,' Liv said, and pulled the conversation back. 'So you didn't know this guy Charles Pierce back then?'

'We've met him since, just casually, but he wasn't around in those days. Where's he from, Arlene?'

'Somebody told me Kokomo. We'd left Nichols County by the time he moved here.'

Liv said, 'I stopped by the sheriff's office to tell them about how Pops died. I thought they'd want to, you know, at least check. But they wouldn't tell me anything, not even if they're going to do anything about it.'

'Well, they don't talk much while they're investigating,' Mark said. 'I remember Wes Cochran shutting people up a couple times when they asked about cases, and he often complained about being badgered by reporters. Said it got in the way of the investigation.'

'Yeah,' said Liv glumly, 'but I really think it would help if they looked at my father's murder too.'

Arlene winced at the word 'murder', and Mark looked uncomfortable and said, 'It won't help if it's just a coincidence. What could this fellow Corson have to do with your dad?'

'Yeah, OK.' He was right, she had no idea. No wonder he wasn't eager to get involved. Liv changed the subject. 'I hope I'm not talking out of turn here, but I wondered – I mean,

68

Pops came out here to visit you a couple times, and then just quit. He never seemed mad at you or anything, but I wondered what happened.'

'Oh, honey, you're not thinking we had a fight or something?' Arlene seemed distressed. 'No, of course not! He just took it into his head not to visit Indiana any more. We kept asking but he always had an excuse.'

Liv said, 'I'm glad you didn't have a fight, but why wouldn't he want to visit?'

'All he said was, he didn't enjoy traveling any more. I wondered if maybe it was arthritis or, you know, something physical like that.'

'Yeah, maybe that was it,' Liv said, giving up for the moment. She didn't want to alienate the only friendly faces she'd seen here. Maybe they didn't know anything, and if they did she needed more ammunition to break down their defenses. So she said, 'I hate to ask you to go out in the cold, but I really would love to see your horses.'

Arlene's face lit up and she bounced to her feet, and Liv knew she'd said the right thing.

Ten

Wes pulled a little folding table to where he and Marty could both see the books and opened the first: Nichols County High School, 1960. The senior photos were first. 'There's Johnny,' Wes said, and Marty leaned forward to study Johnny Bowers' photo. Broad jaw, close-set eyes, crew-cut hair.

'Looks like a Marine already,' she said.

He paged ahead but she stopped him at the Ds, squinted a moment at Corky Dennis without comment. Wes looked too. Family resemblance to his nephew Romey, especially that grin. Marty and Romey seemed more than buddies these days. He started to make a joke but when he glanced at her he saw she was now looking at the next page. He followed her gaze, saw young Don Foley's round face.

'He looks nervous,' Marty said.

Wes said, 'Don never had a lot going for him. Marines trained him well and he got to be a good shot, but he was never leadership material. Even before he bent himself out of shape over a female deputy, it never crossed my mind to put him in charge of anything important.'

She nodded.

He flipped on a few pages, stopped to point out Mark Lugano.

She inspected the handsome dark-haired youth. 'You said he was on the team too?'

'Yeah. He, Johnny and Corky were seniors, graduated at the end of the year. Your dad and I were only sophomores but they put us in the starting line-up right away.'

'So we should talk to Mark Lugano too, if we're trying to find out where Bowers is.'

'Yeah.' Wes turned the page to where the Ms began, said, 'Oh yeah, I remember the guy now. One of the brains.'

'Who? Oh, Ronald Mann?' Marty leaned forward, inspected the little photo. Light-colored hair, strong bones, horn-rimmed glasses. 'What do you mean, one of the brains?'

'Ronnie used to hang out with Mark when Mark wasn't being a jock with us. Math Club or something.' He thumbed to the back pages where Activities were listed. 'Yeah, there they are, with Mr Fischer.'

Six students and a paunchy teacher with a bow tie stood in front of a big sign saying 'NCHS Math Club'. Handsome Mark Lugano was listed as President in the caption, Ronald Mann as Vice-President, a youth named Sullivan as Secretary-Treasurer. Pointing at each, Wes said, 'Sullivan sells insurance now. The squinty-eyed one is McGabben – studied accounting, I heard. Poor old Schiff didn't make it back from Nam. Breen moved away; don't know what happened to him.'

'All boys,' Marty observed.

'Yeah, math was supposed to be for boys,' Wes said. 'Couldn't prove it by me.'

She picked up one of the later yearbooks, flipped through it. This was the year of the big championship and there was a whole spread on the basketball team, including some action photos of a young, fit Wes and teammates. She paused. 'Oh, look, there's Dad!'

The photo showed Rusty LaForte leaping high to block a throw by a much taller Bloomington North player. She added, 'Dad really was good, huh? Wasn't just a coach's trick?'

He raised his eyebrows. 'Coach's trick?'

'When you coached us in peewee basketball. You didn't just tell me I had good genes to get me to play harder?'

'You know he was good, Marty; he helped me coach you guys whenever he could get a Saturday off.'

'Yeah, but was he good for real? On this famous championship team?'

'Absolutely. Fact is, he was quickest and smartest of all of us. But I was taller so we worked out plays where he fed me the ball and I dropped it in.' She still gazed at the photo, and after a moment he added, 'You OK?'

She stirred, glanced at him. 'Yeah. It's just odd to see him there, like frozen in the middle of a jump. And he's younger than I am. He doesn't know what's going to happen. It's years before I'll be born. More years before he dies in a burning car.'

Wes said slowly, 'I don't much like playing what-ifs. But I think if he'd known all that stuff, and had the choice of staying in that moment or moving ahead, he would have moved on. For you.'

She made an effort, shook off her moodiness. 'Not for me. He used to tell me I was a real headache.'

'From day one!' Wes smiled, grateful for the lighter tone. 'I went with him to the hospital right after you were born, and you already had lungs. When they handed you to him, you let out a holler like to split both our heads open. Your ma was laughing at us.'

She grinned too, then glanced toward the kitchen as the outside door closed. 'Hoo, it's like an icebox out there!' called Shirley. She came into the living room, pink from the cold, pulling a fuzzy hat from her crisp silver curls. 'Why, hi, Marty! It's a treat to see you. And what a nice fire!' She leaned down to give Wes a peck on the cheek, glanced at the yearbooks. 'What're you two dredging up from the old days?'

'Just heard that another Nichols County High graduate died in a fire.' He pointed at the book with the Math Club photo. 'D'you remember Ronald Mann?'

Shirley inspected the page. 'Arlene Lugano mentioned that Ronnie died a few years ago, but didn't say how. She said it really hit Mark hard. Got so depressed she was afraid he was thinking of jumping off a cliff or something.' She shook her head sadly. 'It's a shame how many people die in fires. Ronnie Mann, Zill Corson. Rusty in a way.' She put a sympathetic hand on Marty's shoulder. 'The Lanza family last year on the south side of town. Oh, and a while ago, that girl who wanted to be a nun – May, wasn't that her name? One of the Gordon sisters. The missionary school where she was teaching burned down.'

Wes could see the sorrow in Marty's eyes and decided to change the subject for her sake and maybe his own. He took the later yearbook from her hands and flipped to a page near the back. 'Look at this cute gal strutting her stuff, Marty.'

Marty looked, and grinned. Eight cheerleaders in formation smiled at the camera. In the front row, kneeling in a saucy hands-on-hips pose, was young Shirley Cochran.

'Oh, you!' Shirley swatted Wes on the forehead with the

woolly hat she'd just removed. 'I'm going to hang up my coat.'

'And I'd better get mine on,' Wes said, standing up. 'Gotta get to work.'

Marty stood up too. 'Thanks for the help, Coach.'

'Sure,' he said. 'Do you want me to have, um, a word with Chuck Pierce?'

She paused, gestured at the photos of Wes's high-school glory, said slowly, 'It'd be like hitting the guy with a lightning bolt from on high, don't you think? Everybody knows you're the best, Coach. He's a mere mortal. That may be his problem.'

He hadn't thought of it that way but she might be right. One arm in his coat, he met her gray eyes. 'Well, let me know if I can help.'

Liv was enjoying being back on horseback even though her new pink jeans weren't broken in yet and her boots were for hiking instead of riding. The snowy woods were beautiful, and the Luganos seemed relaxed and happy despite the chilly air.

'I remember Don Foley a little bit,' Arlene said in answer to Liv's question. 'Kind of a round face, always showed up at the pre-game rallies. But I never knew him. Freshman when I was a senior, I think. Do you remember him, Mark?'

'Not really. The guys on the team, the guys in math class, the pretty gals – those I remember. Shall we show Liv the hill trail? It's spectacular in winter. You can see a long way with the leaves fallen. And the one down by the creek gets cold faster.'

'Maybe with the snow we should wait on the hill,' Arlene said.

'In the Andes we rode in a lot worse conditions than this,' Mark said.

'All right, honey,' Arlene said. 'Cricket's raring to go.'

Liv's horse, a dark gray named Blueberry, also seemed happy to be moving. They paused on the top of a low knoll where Mark pointed out the edges of their property. 'Our place used to be the old Gordon farm,' Mark explained. 'Big place. After the old man died the family kept it a while but they decided to sell most of it about the time I decided to move back, so it worked out well.' He pointed. 'On the north it butts against that patch of forest – see it? On the south it runs all the way to a creek under that limestone bluff.'

'How far away is that?' Liv asked.

'Close to a mile away from the barn. And the rear border is hard to see, back there in the hills and woods.'

Looking around, Liv said, 'Arlene's right: I have to come back in the spring. I want to see all those redbuds in bloom.'

'Honey, come stay with us tonight! We'd love it,' Arlene said.

'Can't get packed that fast,' Liv told her. 'Plus they made me pay for tonight.'

'Tomorrow, then. We see you so seldom! And – I promise you can go riding again.'

Liv said, 'Deal!'

They rode back across the snowy pastureland toward the barn, blazing red in the slanted late-afternoon sun.

The Limestone Motel tried to counter its hard, grey name with floral curtains, carpets and bedspreads. Liv got out of her new pink and green things, pulled the blankets up to her chin, and called Cancun.

Elena didn't swear at her this time. 'Hey, Livvy, how's Indiana?'

'Snowy. Met a bunch of deputies who won't tell me much. But I've got a couple of good leads for tomorrow. How's Cancun?'

'Mmm.' Liv could almost see strong lithe Elena stretching in her deck chair. 'It's warm. Full of nice brown Mariah Carey types almost as pretty as you, all wanting to serve me. Best thing about them is, they're here.'

'I'll be on a plane fast as I can,' Liv said wistfully.

'You better be. I need you to translate all the sweet Spanish things those Mariahs are telling me.'

Liv laughed. 'They're just asking you if you need more towels.'

'Hey, until you get here my imagination will run wild,' Elena said, and added more seriously, 'Good luck, love.'

Pushing midnight, Marty and Romey stood on the Dennis Rent-All cross-country skis, looking at the grapevines in a south-facing field he'd planted near his not-quite-finished house in the woods. Far down the slope, the White River gleamed in the silent shifting moonlight.

'Pretty night,' Marty said, leaning her ski poles against a tree and flexing her cramped fingers.

'Yeah.' Romey glanced at her. 'So what's up? You were real quiet at dinner. I know it's hard to get a word in with Chrissie these days, but it's more than that, isn't it?'

Marty nodded. 'Yeah, it's this murder. I was asking Coach about the victim's background, and he got out his yearbooks, and there was a picture of my dad there. D'you remember him, Romey?'

'Sure. He and Coach used to show us plays. Didn't help a lot because the only one on our team quick enough to copy them was you.'

'Was he happy?'

'Why are you asking me?'

'You were a little older than I was. You're a male.'

Romey thought a moment. 'You know, those guys who came back from the war – Coach too – it's like it never lets them go completely. They make good lives and really appreciate the good stuff, but the memories are always there.' He glanced at her. 'Doesn't always have to be a war.'

'Yeah. Like if your dad burns up when you're twelve.'

He took her hand. 'Yeah, like that.'

'Those memories come back – I mean, this guy died in a fire too.'

'Does it make you want to quit the case?'

'No! It makes it more important. More frustrating when I'm still so much in the dark.' He nodded, and after a moment she went on. 'It was strange looking at that picture of my dad, like he was frozen there in that glorious moment and didn't know what was coming. But Coach said even if he'd had the choice to stay there or go on, he would have gone on. For me, he said.'

Romey said firmly, 'Yeah, for you, but also for himself. Because it's bad to stay frozen. Even in a happy moment, it's bad to stay frozen.'

That was true. She nodded slowly.

Over her head a branch shivered. Her breath caught as a silent shadow flew across the moonlit clouds, then plunged. A tiny squeak, then all was silent again. Marty whispered, 'Wow.'

Romey squeezed her hand. After a moment he said, 'Owls

are at home with death, aren't they? With death, and night –
and yet they soar like angels. The darkness has meaning to
them. Maybe that's why we think they're wise.'

Marty thought about it a moment. 'But it's still dark.'

'Of course. And you're still wise. Of course.'

'Yeah, sure.' She made circles of her thumbs and forefin-
gers, held them to her eyes like spectacles.

He grinned at her. 'Tell me, O wise one, if a hot shower
and a hot rum punch in front of the fire sounds good to you.'

'Sounds better than good.' She retrieved her ski poles.
'Sounds hot.'

It was.

Eleven

Sagging snow clouds drooped across the morning sky, although to the west there were a few pale gleams of timid blue. Snow still covered the fields and, driving down a hill on her way to work, Marty felt the cruiser skid a little on a refrozen patch of ice.

Back in her own bed last night she'd slept OK until daybreak, when she'd been visited for the first time in months by the staring eyes and accusing hand of a man she'd had to kill a few years ago. It was probably Zill's death that had awakened that old nightmare. Zill, or the Pearl Jam music her daughter now used as a wake-up. *Can't see*, the young man howled, *I just stare*. Marty shuddered. Chrissie was barely thirteen. It was going to be a long few years.

At the morning briefing, Chuck Pierce asked Howie Culp to bring the day shift up to date on what they had on the Corson murder. Marty listened avidly. Much of what Howie said had been drawn from her report, but he did have some new information. He'd looked at the spare room Zill slept in when he visited his mother, and reported nothing much there – extra shirts and pajamas mostly. 'Miz Corson said most nights Zill stayed near Evansville with a guy name of Lewis,' Howie explained. 'This guy has a two-bedroom trailer, and his wife took the kids and ran off, so Zill helped him with the payments and used the kids' bedroom. I've been in touch with Vanderburgh County. They're going to search the trailer there and talk to Lewis for us. Other thing is, I talked to Don Foley about the cabin. He said they didn't use it much after deer season ends. He said he had a drink with Zill last week, but Zill didn't say anything about going to the cabin. Don thought he did seem jumpy about something.'

He stopped, and Marty asked, 'Did Foley know why he was jumpy?'

Howie shrugged. 'He said Zill was pretty drunk. He said he was mostly reliving some old war stories.'

'Did he say what they were?'

Culp reddened a little. 'Foley said I was never in combat, I couldn't understand.'

Marty had more questions but Chuck Pierce said, 'Yeah, looks like Zill didn't see it coming. Went to the cabin without even telling Don Foley or his brother Jim, and got a nasty surprise. Now, what's the deal with these footprints?' He glanced briefly at Marty but said, 'Mason, you checked them in the daylight; what'd it look like?'

Bobby Mason said, 'There was that one line of footprints headed away from the cabin. The state crime-scene technicians say they don't belong to Zill – too small. Trail disappears up by Zill's truck.'

'And did you see Hopkins's footprints?'

'Yes, sir, going and coming, over to the side. I walked on top of her prints to keep from contaminating—'

'That's good, unless Hopkins was walking on top of the return path.'

Pierce thought she was a rookie. Marty began, 'Sir, I didn't see—'

Pierce nodded patiently. 'We know it was dark, Hopkins. I've asked the crime-scene technicians to check out both trails. See, I figure the killer maybe left something in the truck, went there to fetch it, came back to the cabin, then eventually walked away down the creek to wherever he left his own vehicle. Anyway, Culp, you liaise with the state crime-scene technicians, get them to check the banks of the creek for his trail. And get Vanderburgh County to talk to Corson's employers – whatchamacallit, Pinkett's – and check back with Foley to see if he's remembered any more. Mason, check with Doc Altmann to see if he has any more results from the autopsy and get them to Culp or me. Adams, I want you on this armed robbery at the convenience store. Hopkins, you do background checks on the people Zill Corson knew, but if Culp or Adams needs backup, you do it.'

As he went on with the assignments, Marty was relieved. OK, she'd rather be on the front lines interviewing Zill's friends or looking again at those damned disappearing footprints, but she wasn't off the case. And checking 'background' she might be able to ask some interesting questions.

She sat down at her computer and began.

Liv stood on the porch of the buckskin-tan house smiling timidly and shaking her head. 'Oh, thank you, Mr Foley; maybe we could go to a coffee shop or something?'

She was trying out a good-girl act, on the theory that if Don Foley really was as bad as Deputy Hopkins claimed, he'd have only two categories of women – demure good girls and brazen sluts – and would be upset by strong professional women like her or like Hopkins who didn't fit into either of his pigeonholes. Lawyers always had to role-play a bit for judge and jury, and she figured that with Foley – maybe with most of these Midwesterners – she'd get farther if she dressed the way most women dressed here and said what most women would say. Certainly her black jacket and New York power image hadn't got anyone to open up yesterday. She'd see what pink jeans could do.

It was working so far. A good girl wouldn't go into a strange man's house, even if the man was her father's generation, and Foley seemed fine with her refusal to come in. He said, 'We can go out to the Country Griddle.'

'Can you lead the way? I'll just follow your car.'

The Country Griddle was in a brand-new strip mall not far from town. Foley gestured her into a booth already set with blue-flowered paper placemats as he called to the waitress, 'Two coffees, Karen, and some cinnamon rolls.' He hung up Liv's parka next to his own before he sat down across from her. He wasn't in a suit today, just jeans and a plaid flannel shirt. He frowned a little and said, 'Olivia, you're not from around here.'

'No, I was raised in the East. But my dad was from this county. Ronald Mann.'

'Ronald Mann.' Don Foley squinted for a moment at the blue-checked shade on the wall lamp that lit their booth, then said, 'Ronnie Mann! He was in my high-school class!'

Bullseye! Liv didn't have to fake her delight as she exclaimed, 'You knew him! That's wonderful!'

'I didn't know him real well, but – oh, yeah, thanks, Karen.' Foley nodded as the waitress set down their mugs of coffee

79

and a basket of fragrant breakfast rolls. When she'd gone he went on, 'Ronnie Mann. Yeah, he was friends with that Italian guy. Mark Lugano, on the basketball team. Here, have one!' He nudged the basket toward her. 'Karen makes the best cinnamon rolls in the county.'

'Thanks.'

'See, both Lugano and your father went east to college, and I kind of lost track.'

Liv said, 'Dad kept up with Mr Lugano for a while. Do you know him?'

Foley slathered butter on his roll. 'Nah, he was always on the fast track. He's a rich guy now. Came back to live in this county but sticks with the rich businessmen.'

There was a trace of bitterness in Foley's tone and Liv had a sudden vision of an ungifted pimply high-schooler jealous of the talented few who made the team, got the grades, attracted the girls, made the money. And today he still thought they were snooty bastards. Liv was glad she hadn't babbled on about knowing the Luganos. Instead she said, 'Yeah, he made a lot more money than my father did,' and bit into her roll. 'Hey, this is good,' she added.

'Told you. Do you still have folks here?'

'No, Dad's parents died a while ago. I was still in grade school. And my mother's not from here. Dad said once the Luganos still have relatives around here; maybe that's why they moved back.'

'Yeah, I heard his wife's mother is still alive. Nursing home or something.'

'Yeah.' Liv sipped at her coffee, plunged ahead. 'So anyway, my dad was murdered. Cut with a machete and burned, and they never found who did it, and when I heard about Mr Corson I thought there might be some connection.'

Foley frowned. 'Don't see how.'

Machete! Fire! Nichols County! Liv wanted to shout. Instead she sighed. 'Yeah, I don't see how either. But they said you were a deputy sheriff, so I thought you'd be the one to ask.'

'Well, I'm helping the sheriff,' Foley said cautiously. 'He's a good man.'

'Oh, yes, of course, Mr Foley! I didn't mean – see, I don't really understand what's going on, and I thought you could kind of explain it to me.'

'Well, sure, in a general way,' he said, warming up again.

'That would be wonderful!' Liv said, but she wanted more so she took a gamble and added, 'I knew she was wrong.'

'Who?' He took a drink of coffee.

'That woman deputy. She said you were retired and couldn't help much.'

His mug hit the table harder than necessary as he put it down. 'She said that?'

'Well, I don't think she understood that you have a lot of advantages here. You were Mr Corson's friend, and it turns out you even knew my father!'

'Lotta things that one doesn't understand.'

He was scowling and Liv decided Deputy Hopkins had read him right. She said, 'Yeah, well, the guy was your friend, not hers. But I was wondering: do you know if Mr Corson knew my father?'

'Probably not. Zill was younger than us. Signed up for the Marines in sixty-eight. That's where I got to know him. I was already doing my second tour and here was this recruit from my home county. So I sort of gave him a hand.'

'Yeah, that was good,' Liv said. 'See, I'm wondering why Mr Corson died the same way my dad died, pretty much. I mean, if he didn't know many people the same age as my father.'

'Yeah. I wondered that too. I mean, coincidences happen, but . . .' Foley turned his mug in his hands, frowning, then said, 'You know, this is weird; Zill did ask about one person when I saw him last week. Your father's friend, that rich b— You know, Mark Lugano.'

'He asked about Mark Lugano? Mr Corson did?'

'Yeah, see, Zill hasn't been living in the county the last few years, since he got the job in Evansville. Comes here a lot on his days off to see his ma and brother. But most nights he stays with a buddy near Evansville. Kinda cramped – that's why he loved to visit the cabin. He . . .' Don Foley paused for a moment and stared at the lampshade, jaw working, and Liv realized that he was hiding real grief.

She tried to fill the gap, saying, 'Yeah, right now I have a real small apartment, and it's good to get away when I can. Beach, woods, whatever.'

Foley cleared his throat. 'Yeah, the woods are great. That's why I went in with him for this cabin. I like to get out of town too.'

'Yeah.' She drained her coffee cup, asked, 'So what else did Mr Corson talk about when you saw him last week?'

'Oh, you know. Old times and such.'

'Stuff he'd seen overseas? That's what my dad talked about when he'd had a few beers.'

'Yeah.' Foley was staring at the lampshade again. 'Kept coming back to talk about some village he'd seen. There was a fire.'

'Were you there too?' she asked gently.

Foley shrugged. 'Probably. We saw plenty of villages in Nam. Plenty of fires too. But he didn't say which village, he was pretty far . . .' He stopped talking, picked up the one remaining cinnamon roll.

Liv said, 'What did he want to know about Mr Lugano?'

'Nothing. He'd just heard he moved back. And I said, yeah, he bought the old Gordon place a few years ago, fixed it up. Zill was mad he hadn't heard about it yet.'

'Why would that upset him?'

'Yeah, I said, you didn't even know the guy, did you? And he said no, but Sarge had mentioned him.'

'Sarge?'

'Friend of ours, lives in Indianapolis.'

Liv frowned. 'So he was mad because someone in Indianapolis knew more than he did?'

'Yeah, I asked him, I said, what's it to you? And he said, nothing, just seems I never hear about things. Hey, we better get going. Unless you want another cup of coffee?'

'No, but thanks. Here.' She put a five on the table.

'No, honey, this is on me.'

'But . . .'

When he pushed the bill back across the table, she gave in, saying, 'Thanks, Mr Foley! And thanks for talking to me about this. Maybe we'll figure out the connection between your friend and my dad. Anyway, it's good to talk to you.'

'Yeah, maybe we'll think of something.'

'If you do, can you call me? Here.' She scribbled her cell number on a corner of the blue-flowered placemat and tore it off for him, then stood and smiled her best good-girl smile.

'And thanks. I know my father is sitting up there smiling because you're helping me out.'

But as she left, she had the feeling her dad was really shaking his head at her in amused reproach.

Twelve

Marty had found a website for Zill's employer, Pinkett's Auto Mall, ninety-five percent about their terrific values in pre-owned cars but also including the boss's name, William F. Pinkett, and an address, so she copied that for their files. She also found William F. Pinkett's home address in Evansville, and while she was in the directories she checked out Sergeant John Bowers. Yep, there he was, on Bybee Street in Indianapolis. After a moment's thought, she checked the Brooklyn District Attorney's office. A phone call confirmed that Olivia Mann worked there, 'but she's on vacation this week'. She also looked up Ronald Mann, but except for a brief death notice in the Purdue alumni magazine, no details given, there was nothing online.

Most of the deputies had left, but Howie Culp was still at his desk. He and Sheriff Pierce were talking quietly. After a few minutes Pierce clapped Howie on the shoulder and said, 'OK, give my regards to the Vanderburgh County fellas,' and went into his office.

Marty picked up the addresses she'd found and took them over to Howie. 'This Evansville address is Zill's boss, if you need it while you're there, and this guy Bowers on Bybee Street in Indianapolis is Zill's friend. He's the one who got him the earlier job, the one he had before Pinkett's. Has his mother remembered the name of that company?'

'No, she was still broken up,' Howie admitted. 'She remembered his friend Lewis, and she showed me to the room Zill used, but then she started blubbering and wasn't much help. So I didn't even ask.'

'Yeah, she was that way when I did the next-of-kin notification. Up and down. Maybe we can find out from his brother, or from Bowers in Indianapolis.'

'Yeah. Anyway, the sheriff wants me to start with Evansville.

I'm supposed to see if I can go along with the Vanderburgh County guys to talk to Lewis.'

'Good idea . . .' Marty paused and looked around at the sound of an agitated voice.

A young man had come in and was talking to Grady Sims. 'No, no. Right!' he was saying.

Grady was frowning. 'Look, Ali, there's nobody here named Doak.'

The newcomer was in his twenties, five-ten, curly black hair and brown skin. He said, 'No, no. Doak Toralt Mahn.'

Grady said, 'Mahn? Nobody named Mahn either.'

'Right? Please, right?' He was carrying a long cardboard box and the index finger of his free hand made little circles in the air. He didn't look crazy to Marty. She decided he was saying 'write', not 'right'. Probably wanted to spell out the name Grady couldn't understand.

Sheriff Pierce came out of his office and asked, 'What's going on?'

Grady said, 'This is Ali Handro. Says he wants to see someone named Mahn or Doak or something.'

'Write, please?' said the young man.

Chuck Pierce muttered 'A-rabs', and walked toward them. 'Now, son, where you from?'

The front door opened and Liv Mann came in as the young man answered, 'Bloom-een-tawn. Wall Dime. For Doak Toralt Mahn. Machete.'

'Jesus!' Chuck Pierce yelled. 'Get that box, someone; he's got a machete in it!' The young man's big dark eyes widened at the sight of three service revolvers suddenly trained on him.

Marty vaulted over a chair and grabbed the arm holding the long box. She saw Liv Mann dive to safety under a desk. 'Take it easy, sir,' Marty said to the young man, and then to the others, 'It's OK.' She kept herself between him and the guns.

Howie Culp moved up next to her, gun still drawn. Sheriff Pierce yelled, 'Get the damn box away! The backpack too!'

The young man was hugging the box, looking terrified. Marty said quietly to Howie, 'It's OK; this guy is helping Doc Altmann.'

Howie looked confused. 'Altmann?'

Pierce said, 'Get the weapon away from him!'

85

The young man said, 'Paper. Sign paper. Doaktor Altmahn.'

Marty said, 'Howie, he's from the weapons expert at IU. He's returning the machete to Altmann.'

Howie finally understood, looked around at Sheriff Pierce. 'Sir, he's returning the machete to us. He needs a chain-of-custody signature before he can give it to us.'

Marty added, 'It's from the IU weapons expert. Waldheim.'

The young man nodded eagerly. 'Wall Dime, yes!'

Sheriff Pierce holstered his gun and said gruffly, 'Look, son, why didn't you just tell us? Hopkins, you take him over to Altmann at Mercy Hospital. And while you're there, ask Doc why the hell he doesn't use UPS like everyone else.'

'Yes, sir,' Marty said, and grabbed her coat and Stetson. 'Come on, sir; we'll go to Doctor Altmann.'

'Tank you. Tank you,' the young man said politely, turning to nod at all of them, and she got him out the door and gestured to her cruiser. He added, 'Sorry. Eeng-lees not good.'

'Yeah. What's your name again? Ali?'

'No, no. Alejandro Gallegos.'

Ali Handro. A-rabs. It'd be funny if it hadn't almost got him killed.

An eager voice said, 'You need a translator?' and Marty saw that Liv Mann had followed them out.

Marty said, 'Great idea, but I'm not authorized to hire one. And the sheriff – well, I'd wait before offering your services.'

Liv said, 'Yeah, he looked embarrassed. You may have saved Alejandro's life in there.'

Marty secretly agreed, but said, 'Wouldn't have gone that far. So you speak Spanish?'

'Sure, my mother's from Ecuador.'

Alejandro exclaimed, '*Tu madre es ecuatoriana? Yo tambien vivo en Ecuador!*' He added to Marty, 'I from Ecuador too.'

Marty looked at the machete box, remembered the smoky blade with the inscription. She asked, 'Why did Waldheim send you?'

'Am writing master's tee-sis about eendeegenous weapons in Ecuador.'

'Ecuadorean weapons? Is the machete from Ecuador?'

'*Sí, señora.* Yes.'

Liv had tensed and Marty looked at her sharply. 'Your dad's death too?'

'Yes. Machete from Ecuador. I thought it was because of my mother.'

Damn! Marty wanted to sit them both down and hear everything about Ecuador. But she was straitjacketed by her assignment. She said to Liv, 'I'm authorized to get background but this seems more than that. Talk to Deputy Culp, OK? Better hurry; he's about to leave for Evansville. If he doesn't have time for everything, you can tell me later for background. Right now I have to get Mr Gallegos to Doc Altmann.'

Liv's lips pressed together in frustration, but she turned obediently back to the sheriff's office.

In the cruiser, Alejandro Gallegos proved to be a bright young man once Marty got used to his accent. 'I born in mountains. An-dees,' he explained. 'My eschool very little, no Eeng-lees. Teacher good but no Eeng-lees.'

Marty made the turn on to State 860. 'So how did you get into Indiana University?'

'*Primero*, first, I go to university in Ecuador.' Now that he wasn't clutching the box, his hands were lively, filling in for words he didn't have. 'In Quito. You know Quito?'

'I've heard of it, yeah.'

'I estudy engineer and metals. Learn to read Eeng-lees, not espeak very much. I want to estudy in United Estates for good engineer university and for learn better Eeng-lees.'

'I see. How long have you been here in the US?'

He held up one brown finger. 'One semester. In tee-sis I will estudy metal in weapons. Professor Wall Dime say I talk to Doaktor Altmahn because dees machete from my country.'

'Interesting. OK, here we are.' They pulled into the parking lot of Mercy Hospital, and Marty waited with him in the lobby a few minutes while they found Doc Altmann on his rounds. A call came in from Grady on her shoulder radio, saying they'd just heard from Deputy Roy Adams, who was investigating the robbery at the 7-11. 'Adams says the perp was Todd Seifert. He's going to bring him in but wants backup.'

The Seifert boys were chronic troublemakers. She asked, 'Where is Todd – his ma's house?'

'Yeah, you know where it is?'

'Sure do. Tell Adams I'm almost finished here. I see Doc Altmann coming right now.'

Doc looked rushed, but he beamed when Marty explained,

'Professor Waldheim sent Alejandro with the machete because he's an expert in Ecuadorean weapons.'

'Plees to meet you,' Alejandro said.

'*Mucho gusto*,' said Doc.

'*Habla usted español?*' Alejandro asked.

'*Un poquito*,' Doc admitted. 'But I tell you what, I'll speak English and you speak Spanish and we'll see how far we get.'

Alejandro nodded and Marty said, 'I'm supposed to bring him back too but I just got a call. Why don't you give our dispatcher a ring when you're ready?'

Altmann nodded, saying to Alejandro, 'Let's go down the hall where we can put the thing on a table. It's a special machete?'

'*Sí, es un machete de cazador.*'

'*Cazador*. Hunter?'

'*Sí, señor.*'

Marty left them to it and went back to her vehicle. She turned toward the Seifert place on Milo Road. Roy Adams's cruiser waited half a block away.

The sad thing about the Seiferts was that everyone had seen this coming. The father had done some jail time and run off years ago, the mother was alcoholic – neglectful, not violent – and Todd and the middle brother soon had long juvie records. Once Child Protection had tried to take the boys away, but by the time they'd sent their investigator, Mrs Seifert was temporarily sober and the boys knew all the right answers to give. At age twenty Todd was an old hand already at getting arrested, knew not to run or resist. And when he came out to meet them on the front porch before they were out of their cruisers, Marty glanced at Roy Adams and they both shrugged. Roy didn't have a search warrant yet, and no one in that savvy houschold would give them permission to come in. By the time they came back with a warrant to look for the gun, the two younger boys would have hidden it somewhere else.

They brought Todd Seifert to the lockup and Marty left Adams to organize the questioning. As she came through the door from the jail into the dispatch room, Sheriff Pierce called her into his office, leaned back in his chair. 'So, what did Altmann have to say about the machete?'

'All they said while I was there was the machete was from South America. Ecuador. They said it was a hunter's machete.'

'Nasty-looking thing.' Frowning, the sheriff smoothed back his short white hair. 'Well, I guess we're marking time until the state crime technicians give us a report, or until Culp gets back with word from Evansville. You keep working on background.'

'Yes, sir. I'll see if I can find any other South American connections.'

'Yeah.' He rocked forward to rest his elbows on the desk. 'You know that pushy young woman – Olivia something? She was telling Culp about South America. Maybe we should get back and check her story.'

'Yes, sir; I'll give her a call. For background. And do you want me to take a run out to Brock Lumber? I could ask Jimmy Corson if his brother was ever in South America.'

'Wouldn't hurt. And hey, ask him what he knows about this guy Lewis that Zill stayed with. Culp will be getting the Evansville angle but might as well double-check.'

'Yes, sir.' Marty left before he could change his mind.

Liv Mann didn't answer her phone so Marty left a message and headed for Brock Lumber. She had to wait a few minutes while Jumbo Jim finished loading a truckload of framing lumber and roofing for a farmer whose tractor-shed roof had collapsed. 'He's gonna have a cold job of it,' Jim said, his own breath puffing white as he effortlessly tossed the two-by-six beams into the truckbed.

Marty nodded, and when at last the loaded truck pulled out they stepped out of the wind into the shelter of the big lumber warehouse.

He filled her in on his brother's friend Lewis. 'He was one of Zill's drinking buddies. They got to know each other at some bar in Evansville. I met him a couple of times. Lewis was OK.'

'Even when he'd been drinking?'

Jim shrugged. 'He was OK. His wife didn't like it; he slapped her around a couple of times and she left. But he never bothered Zill or me.'

Marty wasn't surprised. Zill probably weighed twice what the wife did, and most of it muscle. She asked, 'Did Zill and Lewis ever, you know, have words? Sometimes when you live in the same place you get on each other's nerves.'

'Not really. They were both ex-Marines, knew how to stay

outta the other guy's face. Zill was late with the rent once, got chewed out, but you can understand that.'

'Yeah.' Marty flexed her fingers, cold from holding the pencil over her notepad. 'The other thing I wanted to ask was, did Zill ever work in South America?'

'Long time ago,' Jim said. 'They sent him to Brazil, and to another country down there too, up in the mountains.'

'Ecuador?' Marty asked.

'Ecuador! Yeah, that's it. He was impressed by those mountains.'

Marty felt the familiar adrenalin rush as another piece fell into place. 'Who sent him?'

'That company. Been trying to think of the name. Something like Coyote Security.'

She wrote down 'Coyote Security' with a question mark and asked, 'Did he have any problems there?'

Jim pursed his lips thinking, shrugged. 'Got a digestion problem a couple of times, he said.'

'How about problems at work?'

'He never talked about work. Security, you know – have to keep your mouth shut just like the military. But if he had any trouble, it didn't interfere with enjoying the mountains. Had some terrific pictures.'

'Pictures. Could we have a look at them?'

A flash of pain crossed Jumbo Jim's face as he shook his head. 'See, when he moved into Lewis's trailer he took the rest of his stuff to the cabin because there wasn't much room.'

Shoot, Marty thought, all up in flames. But as she drove back she wondered if Zill might have sent letters or photos to his mother too. When Marty had been at Maudie Corson's place her task was to notify her of her son's death and Maudie had been too devastated to give a lot of information. A few hours later Howie Culp had talked to her, but he'd been focused on Zill's more recent job at Pinkett's, plus he said Maudie was still broken up and unable to answer questions. But somebody should go ask if she had any photos.

Back at her computer, Marty looked up Ecuador, but it was a complex country. She needed more to narrow the search. Jim was right, though: those mountains were amazing. She wondered if Romey had been there on his travels.

She tried again to reach Liv Mann, but she still wasn't

90

picking up. Maybe she'd told Howie something before she left and Marty would hear about it when he got back. She typed a quick report on what Jim had just told her, made copies for Howie and for the sheriff, looked around for something to do. To kill time she checked the day's police bulletins from across the state to see if Nichols County could help with anyone else's problems. There was the usual list of crimes and emergencies, blocked roads and suicides and fires and stolen vehicles, stretching from Gary to Evansville, from Fort Wayne to Terre Haute. She was skimming down the Indianapolis list when something made her eyes jerk back and she focused on an address: Bybee Road. And it was a fire! No further details – well, it had only been reported this morning.

She called Indianapolis, eventually was put through to the office of Detective Lyons, the investigator in charge. The officer who answered said, 'Sorry, Lyons is still at the scene.'

'Do you have a victim?'

'Three. It was an apartment house and not everybody got out.'

'Damn. Have you ID'd them yet?'

'Still working on that.'

'OK. If one of them's a male, late fifties, named John Bowers, will you call Sheriff Pierce in Nichols County?'

'B-O-W-E-R-S?'

'That's right. And – well, it'll probably be obvious, but keep your eyes open for a machete too.'

'Jesus, is this connected to that cabin fire you had?'

Marty said grimly, 'That's exactly what we're wondering.'

Thirteen

Deputy Culp had been in a hurry to go somewhere, so Liv only had time to tell him that her father had been to Ecuador and had been killed with an Ecuadorean machete. He seemed interested but had to rush away, though he did stick his head in the sheriff's door before he left. She waited a few minutes but no one came out to get more details. She went out to the car, bowed her head against the wheel, felt the darkness oozing up.

Elena, sympathetic and practical, had asked her, What's it like? Drowning?

No, Liv had told her, worse, it's thicker than water.

Oh – like blood?

Liv had flashed on an image of her mother with a machete, said, No no, it's black. Thick.

Yuck, Elena had said with a comforting hug; does anything help?

And she'd replied, Sometimes hiking, swimming. Action.

So act. Liv dragged herself out of the car, furiously kicked icicles from her wheelwells until she was panting, and drove to Mercy Hospital. She lurked in the lobby until she saw Alejandro come out with a frizzy-haired doctor.

'Thanks for the information,' the doctor was saying. 'I'll call the deputy to come take you back to your car.'

Liv strode over to them and said to Alejandro, '*Si quieres acompañarme, tengo mi auto aquí.*'

'*Pues sí, gracias,*' Alejandro answered.

The doctor seemed to follow and said, 'Good, your friend can give you a ride. Nice to meet you, Alejandro,' and disappeared back into the hospital halls.

She drove him back to the courthouse square where he'd left his car. On the way he told her about his graduate work at Indiana University, and she explained about her father's death. Alejandro was both sympathetic and intrigued. When they reached the square, she said in Spanish, 'You probably want to get back to Bloomington for lunch, but do you have time for a cup of coffee with me? I want to hear more about the machete.'

'*Por supuesto* – of course,' he said.

The Salvation Army band was standing on the square playing a hymn: 'Send the fire, send the fire, to burn up every trace of sin!'

Liv shuddered and pointed at a diner named Edna's. 'Do you like pies?'

'American pies, *muy bueno*,' Alejandro agreed. They slid into the green plastic-upholstered booth. Liv was still full of the cinnamon rolls she'd had with Don Foley so she asked for coffee only, but Alejandro ordered cherry pie as well from the red-haired, gum-chewing waitress, giving her a dazzling Latino smile. She preened a little and twinkled at him as she left.

Liv was checking her cellphone messages. Arlene Lugano could wait, but she returned the other call. 'What can I do for you, Deputy Hopkins?'

The deputy explained, 'The sheriff wants me to get some background on Ecuador, so I'd like to talk to you.'

'Yeah, definitely, just a sec.' She cupped a hand over her cellphone and spoke to Alejandro in Spanish. 'The woman deputy wants to ask about Ecuador. Do you want to talk to her too?'

'Yes, but I have to get back to Bloomington soon.'

Liv spoke into her phone. 'If you can come to Edna's on the square right now, Alejandro Gallegos is here with me. He can probably tell you a lot about Ecuador too, but he has to leave soon.'

'Oh, I thought he was still with the coroner. See you in five minutes,' said Deputy Hopkins.

Liv pocketed her phone and told Alejandro in Spanish, 'She'll be here soon. So where do you come from in Ecuador?'

She heard about his village, about going to university in Quito. The red-haired waitress returned with the pie and coffee. Alejandro said, 'Tank you,' with another big smile and then switched back to Spanish to ask Liv, 'Was your mother born in Quito?'

93

'Yes, and she lives there now with her family. I don't see her much because I'm working in Brooklyn.'

She was still explaining about being an ADA when Deputy Hopkins dropped her Stetson on to the white plastic table top and slid into the booth beside Alejandro.

'Hi,' she said. 'Could you guys speak English for a few minutes?'

'Sure,' Liv said. 'What can we tell you?'

Deputy Hopkins looked thoughtful as she shrugged out of her winter jacket and said, 'First, Mr Gallegos, is the machete definitely from Ecuador?'

'Yes. Not low country. From mountains.' His fingers walked up to a point above his head.

Like the other deputies Liv had spoken to, Hopkins wore a brown shirt with khaki-colored epaulets and gold cloth stars on the sleeves, in addition to her badge. Her gray eyes as she looked at Liv were frankly curious, a nice change from the blank, forbidding cop stare she'd given Liv before. 'You said the machete in your father's case was from Ecuador, and you thought it was because of your mother. How come?'

'She's from Ecuador too. Raised in Quito.'

Liv was trying to stay relaxed, but the deputy seemed to have the radar good cops and lawyers have and pursued it. 'But your father was from here. How did they meet?'

'He was sent down there by his company,' Liv said.

Deputy Hopkins's gaze sharpened. 'What company?'

'An engineering firm called Telmeck. They build electrical plants, phone interchanges, stuff like that. Basic infrastructure, my father said. Do a lot of business overseas.'

Alejandro was interested too. He asked, 'You fa-ter was engineer?'

Liv said, 'Yeah, in those days I guess there weren't enough Ecuadorean engineers. So the Ecuadorean government hired US companies to do the work.'

'Plenty engineers in Ecuador,' Alejandro objected gently. 'But US companies – how you say? – consultant, dey told de government to hire US engineer companies.'

'Well, yeah, you're right,' Liv said. 'A friend of my dad's worked for a consulting firm that did economic forecasts. That was the company that the Ecuadorean government brought in first. And they figured out that Ecuador would develop faster if they built power plants and so forth, and my father's friend recommended Telmeck as good people to design the plants and supervise the construction. That's why my father was down there. He met my mother at a party, I think at the US embassy in Quito. Her father's a newscaster for one of the two largest radio stations. TV now too.'

Alejandro looked intrigued and broke into Spanish. '*Cómo se llama, tu abuelo?*'

'His name is Carreras.'

'*Sí, lo he visto!* Sorry,' he turned to the deputy with his big Latino smile. 'I see him on TV.'

Deputy Hopkins smiled too, but turned back to Liv. 'So we've got your mother living down there, your father goes down for Telmeck to build a power station in Quito, and—'

'No, not in Quito; the job involved a dam up in – wait, sorry, I'm mixing up two projects. The second job was the dam in the mountains. This first one was smaller, just a sub-station on the outskirts of Quito.'

Deputy Hopkins was taking notes. 'OK, there were two jobs. When were they?'

'The first one, the substation, would have been in the late sixties. That's when he met my mother. Later Ecuador invited Telmeck back for the bigger job, 1979, 1980 – I was about ten and we were living in the US so I could go to school, but I remember spending two whole summer vacations in Ecuador.' She frowned, chasing a memory. 'There were some problems – not while my mother and I were there, later – and I never really understood. But I remember my father had to stay on longer than expected.'

The deputy's gray eyes were still intent on her. 'Engineering problems?'

Liv answered, 'No, political. But I don't know exactly what. I was just a kid. There was a new president or something who didn't like the plans.'

'Roldós,' said Alejandro. 'Was elected President of Ecuador in 1979.'

'Yeah, that sounds right,' Liv said. 'I've heard my mother and grandfather talking about him. But I didn't pay much attention. I wasn't that interested in Ecuadorean politics.'

Alejandro looked sad. 'Americans never interested.'

Liv said defensively, 'Hey, it's hard enough keeping track

95

of our US politicians. They decide stuff that affects our lives.'

Alejandro's eyes flashed and he answered rapidly in Spanish, the fingers of both hands stabbing at his chest. Then he noticed Deputy Hopkins and said, 'Sorry.'

She asked, 'What did you say? All I understood was Texaco.'

'Say dat –' He paused, frowned, gave up. 'Liv, pleass translate.'

Liv was trying to fit his comments into what she'd heard at her grandparents' house. She said slowly, 'He said US politicians decide stuff that affects Ecuadoreans too. He said Ecuadoreans don't get to vote for the people who make those decisions. He said President Roldós tried to stand up to Texaco, and that's why he was killed.'

Deputy Hopkins was frowning. 'That sounds crazy. A president was killed?'

Alejandro shrugged. 'Maybe crazy. But in my country, dey believe eet. Roldós try to estop Texaco, and so – how you say?' His finger circled above his head.

Part of that long-ago conversation came back to Liv. 'Helicopter,' she said. 'Roldós's helicopter crashed.'

'Yes,' Alejandro said, his circling hand plunging to slap the table top. 'De newspapers say, CIA.' He shrugged, smiled his winning smile at both of them. 'Many years ago. Me, only twelve years, don't know. But in my country, dey believe.'

Deputy Hopkins nodded slowly, her gray eyes thoughtful, and Liv knew suddenly that other things in the investigation fit with this bit of history, and her heart lurched with hope. Would she finally learn something about her father's death? But the deputy went back to her first question. 'Mr Gallegos, can you tell me any more about the machete Dr Altmann gave you?'

'In report explain everyting. Is hunter's machete, not very wide blade. Writing on blade say Cuenca area.'

The deputy looked at Liv. 'And yours? Was it similar?'

'Not exactly. There was no writing on the blade. They knew it was from Ecuador because of something about the handle. Alejandro, could I show you the photos? They're back in my room.'

'Yes, want to see dem. But have to go back. Class in Bloom-in-ton now.'

'I could drive them to Bloomington to show you tomorrow.'
'No, no. Long trip for you.' His expressive brown hands indicated her, then himself. 'Better I come here. Like to drive. Like American cherry pie. Eleven thirty o'clock OK?'
'Eleven thirty's fine. Right here,' Liv said, and added, '*Muchas gracias.*'
'*Hasta mañana.*' He zipped up his parka and Deputy Hopkins slid out of the booth to let him escape. Alejandro smiled, shook hands with both of them, and went out.

Fourteen

Marty watched Alejandro leave Edna's Diner, his dark silhouette turning gray as the steamed-up glass door closed behind him. She was remembering Maudie Corson's words, quoting her son: 'Spics never forget,' and Alejandro certainly remembered that helicopter crash. But that was a presidential death, like Kennedy's. She was investigating a humbler crime.

Marty looked down at Liv, still seated in the booth in her pink-and-green sweater, and said, 'I have a few more questions for you.'

Liv spread her hands in an of-course gesture. 'Hey, that's why I'm here.'

Marty looked around for the red-haired waitress and called, 'Hey, Kelli, let's have some more coffee over here.'

'Be right there.' And she was, almost as soon as Marty was seated again. As she poured their coffee, she said, 'Hey, Marty, how come you chased off our handsome Latin lover?' and winked at Liv.

'He's a cutie, isn't he?' Marty smiled up at Kelli as she turned away, then glanced across at Liv. The young lawyer's light tan skin and mass of black curls hinted at her Latina background. Marty hoped she could tell her something useful.

Liv said, 'You're looking at me the way I look at witnesses: *Where are they coming from? What do they really want? Can I trust them?*'

She was exactly on target and Marty had to smile. 'Good questions. Wanna answer them?'

'What I want is to find out who killed my father. And until these last five minutes, your department was giving me the runaround. So that's the other part of where I'm coming from.'

She was right, but departmental loyalty made Marty say,

'Yeah, sorry about that; we're following up on a bunch of things. But how about your last question? Can I trust you?'

'Of course. Just give me a chance! And, um – can I trust you?'

The words were soft, but the dark eyes blazing into Marty's demanded truth. She said, 'Yes, you can. But remember I'm on a team with slightly different priorities. Number one being Zill Corson, right now.' Liv nodded her understanding, and Marty went on, 'What did Don Foley tell you about him?'

There was delight in Liv's grin. 'So you did sic me on him!'

Marty smiled back but wagged a finger at her. 'In fact, I told you to contact Deputy Culp or the sheriff or the District Attorney. Let's be clear on that.'

'Oh, right,' Liv said, still grinning. 'Those were your exact words.'

Marty put down her pencil. 'So off the record, what'd he tell you?'

Liv got serious too. 'He told me he was working with the sheriff, so I stayed away from crime-scene questions. Figured you guys would be getting that stuff anyway. I looked for similarities to what happened to my father. But Mr Foley didn't know much. Zill Corson never mentioned my dad to him, and Pops never mentioned Corson to me. So I don't think they knew each other. But my father was edgy for a while before it happened. Mr Foley said Corson was too.'

Marty asked eagerly, 'Did Foley say why Zill was nervous?'

'I wish.' Liv shook her head. 'He didn't know, or wasn't telling. He did say Mr Corson got upset recently when he found out that Mark Lugano had moved back to Nichols County.'

'Mark Lugano? The rich guy?'

'Yeah.'

Marty said, 'Lugano went to high school here. And he was in the math club with your father, right?'

Liv's dark eyes widened. 'Jesus, how'd you find that out?'

'Talked to some of their classmates. But how did Zill Corson know Lugano? Zill's younger. Must have met him after he moved back.'

Liv shrugged. 'Maybe. Mr Foley never heard Mr Corson mention Mark before. And Mark said he didn't know Mr Corson.'

She'd called him Mark. Marty said, 'You've already seen the Luganos, then. Family friend? Kept in touch with your father?'

'Exactly. We used to visit back and forth when we all lived in the New York area.'

'But he denies knowing Zill Corson.'

'And so does Arlene. His wife.' Liv pushed back a black curl that had fallen across her forehead. 'Mr Foley seemed to think Mark was stuck-up. Hangs out with rich businessmen, he said. Zill Corson hung out with regular guys like Foley.'

Marty nodded. Even in small counties, class differences kept people apart. 'But you said Zill found out recently that he'd moved back and got upset for some reason. Did Foley say why?'

Liv frowned. 'It was odd because the way Mr Foley tells it, it didn't have much to do with the Luganos. More a matter of being mad because he was out of the loop. He found out from a friend who doesn't even live in this county.'

'Did Foley tell you the friend's name?'

'He just said Sarge.'

Sarge Bowers again! Marty asked, 'Did he say anything about Sarge? How Zill knew him? Anything?'

Liv was shaking her head. 'Nothing. Just that he lives in Indianapolis. I thought maybe – well, if he's nicknamed Sarge, and both Mr Foley and Mr Corson were Marines . . .'

'Yeah.' Marty gnawed at the problem a moment. So Sarge Bowers had belatedly told his Marine buddy Zill that Lugano was back in Nichols County, and Zill was upset by the news, or by the fact that Sarge had heard it first. And now one and possibly both of them had burned to death. She asked, 'What else did Foley say?'

Liv shrugged. 'That was it.'

'OK.' Marty picked up her pencil. 'Tell me about your father's edginess. What set it off?'

'I don't know. I went home at Christmas – I was in college, must have been, let's see, 1989 – and Pops was kind of distracted and gloomy. And that same year he got a card from the Luganos asking him to come visit here. I noticed it and, you know, thinking to cheer him up, I asked him if he was going to visit Indiana. And there was this instant of, like, terror in his eyes before he covered it up and said no, he didn't like to travel that far in winter.'

'What did your mother think? You must have asked her.'

'No.' Liv picked up her coffee mug with both hands and studied it. 'She wasn't there. My parents were separated.'

Liv's hands were tense on her cup and Marty knew suddenly that there was something important here, about the case or at least about this witness. An Ecuadorean mother, a bad marriage . . . Marty asked, 'This was 1989, you say. Had they separated recently?'

'No, she walked out years before this happened. She went back to live with her family in Ecuador. I was fifteen – must have been 1985. Pops wasn't killed until ninety-two.'

Still that unwillingness to meet Marty's gaze. Marty was remembering Maudie Corson's words, quoting her son: 'Spics never forget.'

She waited a moment and Liv burst out, 'Look, the Staten Island police thought that too! Decided it might be a hit man hired by my mother or by her family. And they checked, they really did, and couldn't find anything.'

Marty asked, 'And did you believe them?'

Liv shook her curls violently. 'I didn't know what to think! First I was just stunned. Then the Ecuador connection came up and – well, it's true I was angry when she left us.'

There were tears in the young lawyer's eyes. Marty had been through a divorce, had watched her bright loving daughter getting torn apart emotionally, lashing out at both of them. She stifled an urge to give Liv a comforting hug, instead asked gently, 'She just walked out? What happened?'

Liv seemed to sense the sympathy and went on more calmly, 'I don't know what happened. Pops was such a decent guy, never violent. Neither one of them had a drinking problem, nothing. He got a little moody sometimes, but nothing major. And Mama used to be a sunny person, smiled a lot. I really think for fifteen years she was happy.'

'And you were too?'

'Yeah. I mean, I bitched a little, felt put-upon having a foreign mother – you know how teenagers are. You've got a kid, right?'

'Yeah. Anything goes wrong in her life, it's always my fault.' Marty grinned ruefully.

'Yeah. But my friends liked my mother; some said they'd be happy to trade with me, and most of the time I knew they were right. I knew in my heart that things were pretty good. And then, bang! She started screaming at my father. That seemed so unfair, he was kind of down anyway that week. Then she came to me, said we were both going to go live in Ecuador.' Liv grabbed a tissue from her bag, dabbed at her eyes.

Marty asked softly, 'Did she say why?'

'She said she couldn't live with my father any more. And I said, then she couldn't live with me either, 'cause I sure as hell wasn't going to leave him and my friends! And I thought that would make her stay.' Liv's voice had become husky and she bowed her head. Marty sensed the unhealed wound, the teenage hurt and astonishment and despair when her mother left anyway. She reached across the table to put a sympathetic hand on the weeping woman's arm.

Kelli started toward them to help but Marty shook her head at the waitress.

Slowly Liv came back from the past, became aware of Marty's concern. She blew her nose, sat up straighter. 'Sorry. It got worse.'

'How?'

She looked across the room at the steamy windows that gave on to the square. 'She wouldn't come back. Pops tried to talk to her, I know, and he made me go visit her in Quito a couple of times, but she wouldn't explain to me. Said it was my father's business. And when I asked him he just shrugged and looked sad. First I figured maybe he'd had an affair or something but I can't really believe that. He loved her, I know it. They were Catholics – you know: no divorce. But it was more than that. Even after she left, he didn't – see, I'd pop in unexpectedly sometimes for a weekend home with him if a case got delayed or something, and I never saw any signs of a girlfriend in all those years.' She caught Marty's flicker of doubt and leaned forward to make her point. 'No boyfriends either, if that's what you're thinking! It was my mother's picture on his nightstand till the day he died. And his will gave a third to me, a third to her, and a third to the Catholic Church in Ecuador.'

'So when you say it got worse, you mean she wouldn't come back?'

'Yeah, partly, and partly . . .' She was twisting her tissue tightly in her hands. 'Well, see, the reason the Staten Island police were checking her was because when Pops was killed I blamed her. Not at first, but as soon as I heard the machete was from Ecuador, I was all over them, telling them it had to be her doing. And I haven't been to see her since. Can't get it out of my head that somehow she's behind it. Except – well, I still remember that look of terror when I suggested to Pops that he might come out here to Indiana to visit Mark and Arlene. And when CNN said this guy had died the same way, and in Indiana, I thought – I mean, I hoped maybe she hadn't . . .' She leaned back in her seat. 'I don't know what I thought. But I had to come.'

Marty's heart went out to her. A father's death was bad enough; thinking your mother had done it would make it unbearable. Liv had lost both parents. She said, 'Yeah, I understand.'

'Don't give me that! Nobody can understand!' Liv grabbed a fresh tissue.

Marty almost protested, Hey, give me a chance, my dad burned up too. Instead she took a deep breath, reminded herself that she hadn't yet checked out Liv's story, and got back on track. 'Did Deputy Culp have time to get the name of the Staten Island cop who worked on the case?'

Liv seemed ready to be businesslike too. She said, 'No, but the guy's name is Detective Giuseppe Bruno. His buddies call him The Juice.' She punched something into her little palm organizer and read off the detective's contact numbers.

Marty wrote them all down. 'I'll do what I can,' she said cautiously. 'What can you tell me about Mark Lugano?'

Liv said, 'You seem to know the basics about him so I'll cut to the chase: yeah, he did a project in Ecuador too. But not while my father was there.'

Marty looked at her sharply. 'Lugano worked for Telmeck too?'

Liv shook her head. 'No. His company did economic forecasting. Much more abstract stuff. But he and my father steered work to each other. Like if Pops was building a phone system in, say, Honduras and heard a rumor that the Hondurans were interested in developing their hydropower, he'd tell Mark so his company could contact the Honduran government, maybe land the contract to crunch the numbers. And if Mark's numbers said it was a good idea to build a dam, he might tell them Telmeck was the perfect company to actually build the thing.'

'I see. And was he the one who told Ecuador to hire Telmeck for the projects your father worked on there?'

'Not the first one. I think he did the forecast for the second one, the dam in the mountains. But he'd moved on to Indonesia or somewhere by the time my father was doing the work.'

'I see. Now, you said they were friends. But your father seemed frightened at the thought of visiting him.'

Liv's nose wrinkled as she thought. 'No, it wasn't visiting Mark that was the problem,' she said. 'It was visiting Indiana that scared him. And now it seems Pops was right. Not that staying away saved him.' She dabbed at her eyes again.

'Yeah.' Marty flipped through her notes. 'Oh, I wanted to ask: back when your mother left, you said your father was already feeling down. Do you remember why?'

'Some guy he'd known had died in Ohio. Pops called him Gene but I never knew his last name. Not a close friend. D'you mean . . .' An instant of hope flared in her dark eyes, then faded as she shook her head. 'No, he didn't die in a fire. He was shot during a robbery.'

'I see. Any other thoughts that could help us?'

'I think you hit them all. And then some,' Liv said.

'OK. The only other thing was, you told Alejandro you had photos of the machete. If they're handy, could I have a look?'

'They're back in my motel room. I can bring them by tomorrow on the way to see Alejandro.'

'Good.' Marty stood up, waved a couple of ones at Kelli and put them on the table as the waitress approached, then stuck out her hand to shake Liv's. 'It was good to talk to you. Very helpful.'

'I'm glad. Keep me posted.'

'I'll do my best,' Marty promised, and headed for the door, eager to find out if Indianapolis had called to say if Sarge Bowers had died in that fire or not, if Mark Lugano could tell her anything about his friend's death, if Detective Giuseppe Bruno on Staten Island could fill in some gaps. Liv had given her a lot to check out.

As she reached the door she heard Liv murmuring a question and Kelli's cheerful response, 'Oh, yeah, Marty's a good deputy. You know that rock star who died in the tornado here? She figured that one out.'

Looked like Liv was doing some checking too.

Fifteen

The *chaski* sat in his borrowed Honda munching a peanut-butter sandwich and frowning at Edna's Diner. Hard to see in: the windows were steamed up. But here came the woman deputy. She was the same one he'd seen at the pyre, he was sure. Where was Ronnie Mann's daughter? They must have been talking all this time.

He watched the deputy stride along the sidewalk to the corner of the courthouse square, turn left. Going back to the sheriff's office, no doubt, just half a block away. How much was the Mann kid able to tell her? A lot about her father's death. And they could compare it to Zill's death. Would that be enough? They were studying the machete too. He couldn't let them stop him, now that he was so close.

But how could they stop him? Even if they guessed who he was – and they couldn't – they wouldn't know where to look for him.

Unless they also figured out who was next. Put some kind of protection into place. Some kind of trap.

The Salvation Army started to sing something wimpy about a lamb. He preferred the one they'd been singing earlier: 'To make our weak hearts strong and brave, send the fire! To live, a dying world to save, send the fire!'

He glanced again at the corner where the woman deputy had disappeared, toyed with the idea of meeting her casually, asking her about the fire. But even the dumbest cops these days knew better than to talk much about their investigations. No, that wouldn't solve anything.

Ronnie Mann's daughter, though, she'd know what kind of questions the cops were asking. And she'd know what her friends the Luganos were thinking. A mine of information there.

The *chaski* nodded to himself, thinking, Yes, little Miss Mann, it's time we had a nice long talk. In private.

As Marty climbed the steps of the station, a swirl of people burst out the door and she stepped aside. Sheriff Pierce, excitement flashing in his blue eyes, was fastening his jacket as he ran down the steps while telling Betty Burke and some of her fellow reporters that, yes, there was a new lead. 'Can't give you details yet, but they've done some good police work in Indianapolis and I'm off to consult with them and check the new evidence.'

Betty asked, 'Does that mean Nichols County can breathe easy? The killer has moved on to another location?'

'Like I say, I can't give details yet, but we're getting close to this guy.' The sheriff paused a moment at his cruiser door and favored the *News* photographer with a confident smile.

It was clear to Marty that he wasn't going to give her any additional instructions, so she went on inside and paused by the dispatcher's desk. 'Hey, Grady.'

'Hey.'

She waved her hand at the door. 'Does all that mean that Sarge Bowers died in a fire with a machete?'

'Yup.'

'Ecuadorean machete?'

'Didn't say. Some Naptown detective named Lyons called, said Sergeant John Bowers had died in similar circumstances to Robert Corson and could he speak to the sheriff. Couple minutes later, the boss was out the door.'

'Well, I'm glad he's on it.' About time, she added to herself, shedding her coat and hat.

As she passed his desk Grady murmured, 'Lemme run something by you. About that cabin.'

'Yeah?' Grady wasn't the brightest and was shy about offering ideas, but he had solid practical sense, and it was usually wise to listen to him.

He said, 'That deer carcass. In the door, right? Where the firemen would see him first if they thought about going in?'

'Yeah. It was pretty obvious.'

Grady said, 'It would account for the smell.'

Marty remembered the jokes about well-done venison, remembered the barbecue smell of the smoke, from the deer

107

and . . . 'Oh God!' She clapped a hand over her mouth and nose, mumbled, 'Zill was part of that smell!'

Grady glanced nervously at Roy Adams, reading a legal paper at his desk, and muttered, 'Firemen woulda noticed. So he used the deer.'

'Grady, you gotta be right!' Marty enthused. 'Roy, Grady's solved this part! No wonder the guy went to all the trouble of getting the deer inside. The firemen would have been in there maybe saving Zill's life if they'd investigated the smell! Tell Howie or the sheriff – that's good thinking!'

Grady looked pleased. Roy Adams gave Grady a thumbs-up.

Marty headed for her computer and asked Adams, 'How's the Seifert thing coming?'

He pointed at the paper. 'Just got the warrant to look for the gun he used in the hold-up. I got Judge Relling to sign it for the whole property, not just the house, because I figure they tucked the gun away outdoors somewhere. But with the snow I've got a chance of finding some footprints, so I'll start outside.'

'Good idea. I was thinking: when the Seiferts stole those tools a couple years ago, they brought them in from the back of the property. The Fricks' place on State Eight-Sixty – you know it? The Frick barnyard lane goes almost up to the Seifert fence.'

Adams looked up appreciatively. 'Good tip, Marty. I was trying to figure out a way to use the warrant without coming up their driveway and tipping them off.'

'You got enough help for the search?'

'Yeah, I'm going to take Phil along.' Phil Vogler was an ex-football player, a rookie hired when Foley retired. Adams stood up and reached for his coat.

'Good luck.' Marty plunked herself down in front of her computer. What next?

She thought about the picture of Johnny Bowers in the year-book, the square-jawed youngster soon to be a Marine, and wished she'd pushed to contact him sooner. Would it have saved him?

Coach Cochran always said, forget the what-ifs, go from where you are. Sheriff Pierce was working on the Bowers angle now, so she should cross that off. But she still felt sad.

She thought over what Liv had told her and decided to start with the Staten Island police. Detective Giuseppe Bruno was away from his desk, but she left a request for him to get back to her about the Ronald Mann murder.

She looked up Mark Lugano's phone number, but hesitated. The man led a quiet life here, didn't interest himself in politics or business or even Kiwanis. Charities, yes. Soon after he moved back, Wes and Shirley Cochran had worked with him on a fundraiser for the hospital. And Wes had told her that Lugano was a member of the local Catholic church. Aside from that she knew almost nothing about him. Except that he was rich, and deputies always had to be careful when interviewing rich guys. Even just for background on the Ronald Mann case, it would be a bad idea to talk to him without clearing it first with Sheriff Pierce.

Who'd be in Indianapolis for hours.

She sighed. What else counted as background? She thumbed through her notes.

Ecuador. But she'd done what she could on that for the time being. She wanted to check with Liv's mother but not until she had Staten Island's take on the situation.

On the next page of her notes, she paused. There was that one detail: what Liv had said about her father being upset by the death of the Ohio guy. But she really didn't know enough to follow up. She had a state, a year, and it was a murder and robbery, so there would be information somewhere. But how to find it? Ohio was a big state, and all she had was a first name. Not even that – a nickname. Plus the connection to the case was so thin – just that Ronald Mann had known him, and had later been murdered in a different way, in a different place. Anybody in law enforcement would just laugh at her if she asked them to invest hours of work looking through old files for so little cause.

What else?

Fires, she thought suddenly, nudged by Grady's insight about the burned deer. This murderer knew fires. She should check fires that looked accidental too. And probably were accidental, but if even one was connected . . .

Nichols County had a good list of recent fires in the computer files. Not many deaths, thank goodness. The last fatality before Zill was over a year before, a bad one, the

Lanza family house. She pulled up the record. Yeah, the whole family had died. The father worked a forklift at a building-supply store and did too much drinking during his time off, and smoked. His body had been found near the charred remains of the kitchen table in their small one-story frame house. The investigator said the fire had started in the floor under the man's chair. There were two empty bourbon bottles nearby, and an ashtray, though the fire had destroyed any remnants of cigarettes.

Neighbors had noticed when the fire burned through the back wall of the kitchen and the firemen had responded quickly to put it out. But two kids who'd been sleeping in the back bedroom were already dead from the fumes when they rushed them out, and the wife in the next room was in a coma. She'd died too after a few hours in the hospital.

Marty looked at the interviews. Lanza had hardly even been out of the state, according to his best friend. She wrote down the friend's name – Davis – to double-check about Ecuador, but she was already convinced that this fire was exactly what it looked like, a tragic accident.

For the four years before that, Nichols County had been lucky. Two or three buildings were destroyed by fires almost every year, but no fatalities, just several burns and some smoke-inhalation cases that the hospital took care of quickly. Plus there was no mention of Ecuador or of machetes in any of the cases.

Earlier than 1990 there was nothing in the database. Marty sighed. The older records sat in files in the basement, waiting for transfer into the computer. They were filed chronologically, but she didn't know what fire she wanted, or even what year.

Time to check with an expert. Marty pulled on her coat. 'Hey, Grady, I'm going to have to turn off my radio for half an hour. I'm checking something at the library.'

'Sure thing,' he said.

Wes Cochran had grabbed some lunch at the Soup 'n' Sprouts because they had a good chili even if there wasn't any meat in it, and Shirley and the doctor told him to lay off real food. He was on the square because he wanted to get some kind of Valentine's pin for Shirley, and old man Culler was reliable.

110

Probably some of the jewelers at the mall were reliable too, but he'd worked near the square for a long time and these were the merchants he knew.

He came to the curb and waited to cross because a Honda was pulling out from a parking space in front of him. The driver was wearing dark glasses and seemed focused on a red Escort that was passing. He looked familiar, somehow. Wes frowned a little, trying to place him, but with the dark glasses it was hard to tell. The Honda rolled away after the Escort, and Wes shrugged and headed for Culler's.

Joanne Quick was a tall, trim, broad-shouldered woman a little older than Marty, maybe forty. She was in the reference section when Marty arrived, helping a white-haired man find something in a journal. *Consumer Reports*, looked like. Joanne's dark hair was caught back at the nape of her neck, her smile was friendly, and today she wore navy trousers and turtleneck under a soft turquoise tweed jacket. Joanne had two passions. One was finding information, which made her the darling of local amateur genealogists and of serious high-school students. The other, not so relevant to Marty just now, was diving. There were rumors that in college Joanne had come within a few points of qualifying for the US Olympic team. She and her husband, also a diver, still drove to IU a few times a week to practice on the high board.

Her husband worked as a funeral director, and Joanne had confided to Marty once that she'd long since OD'd on jokes about 'the Quick and the dead'. She got her white-haired patron settled, then crossed to where Marty stood by the reference desk. 'Hi, Marty. Can we help you today?'

'Hope so. I'm looking for a couple of things. First, anything you can find on a murder that happened during a robbery in Ohio in 1985. Only other bit of information I have is the victim's first name: Gene. Eugene, I guess.'

Joanne frowned. 'Not enough. If you had a last name . . .'

'My source was sure she never knew the last name. No way to get a list of robbery-murders?'

'Well, we can get summary statistics of violent crimes, but – hey, wait, maybe we can get some info from the Ohio newspaper indexes. Let me take a look at the NewsBank index. And Lathrop's.'

111

There was a sparkle in Joanne's eye now. She was striding over to a shelf, her soft jacket flaring in the breeze. She took down a bright-blue volume and a dull-green one, thumbing through. The expression on her face was familiar to Marty. Where had she seen it recently? Intense, focused. As though she was thinking about her next dive from the high board. And then it came to Marty: the expression on her father's face in the yearbook photo of the championship game.

'Got it!' said Joanne after a few minutes of scribbling notes. 'That is, I've got the first step. I know the papers we should check. But somebody in Ohio will have to do the checking because no library in Indiana has them. So it may take a few days. I'll call my friend Meg in Columbus.'

'Will she charge anything?' Marty asked anxiously.

'No. She was my roommate sophomore year, plus she owes me for a couple hours I spent doing some work for one of her genealogy researchers.' Joanne smiled kindly at Marty. 'Now, what was your second thing?'

'Nichols County fires in the 1980s, especially if somebody died.'

'Fires. Newspaper articles OK for that too? *Nichols County News*?'

'Yeah, that'd be great. Once I have a name I can check our own files for details but our old files aren't indexed yet by type of incident.'

'I see. Fires are easy. I'll bring the references right out.'

In five minutes she'd set Marty up with a machine at the end of the row of microfilm readers, and handed her a spool of the 1980 *Nichols County News* and a set of page references to articles about fires.

It was kind of weird scrolling through those papers. Marty felt her own history breathing through the pages.

The early part of the eighties seemed distant because she hadn't been in Nichols County. Her mother had moved to Monroe County shortly after her father died, so in 1980 Marty was graduating from high school in Bloomington and starting college at Indiana University, working at odd jobs to earn her tuition, meeting handsome Brad Hopkins at an Elvis-themed dance party, marrying him hastily in 1983 because Chrissie was on the way and he was full of beautiful dreams about the luxurious life their child would lead once he hit the big

112

time. Then came two years of growing up. Her mother got cancer and moved back to her Nichols County house because she needed her sister Vonnie, and Marty came to realize that Brad was a long way from his goals, that most of the time the only income they had was what Marty earned from her entry-level job at IU Security, and that Chrissie's future was in her hands. On trips back to Nichols County Marty had been focused on those personal problems. Even though Aunt Vonnie had told her about some of the stories she was reading now in the *Nichols County News*, they seemed second-hand and far away. Joanne Quick had found references to five articles about fire fatalities in those early years, but Marty didn't remember any of them. Looked like two were about the same victim and one was about a schoolteacher who hadn't even died in Nichols County. No machetes or even knives were mentioned in the articles.

1986: a big year for Marty, filled with low points and high points. That's when she gave up the Bloomington apartment and, Chrissie in her arms, moved to her dying mother's house in Nichols County. It was to help her mother, yes, and to save money, but also to give her talented husband a hand up, to let him go to a bigger city to look for his big break. Also, she was determined to get a decent job. Marty had gone to see her dead father's best friend Sheriff Cochran. Coach Cochran, looking at her IU Security credentials and remembering her toughness on the basketball court, had agreed to try her out as a jail matron.

And hey, there were two fire fatalities that year, just after she arrived. A bar called the Sandman had burned up, two customers found too late to save. She remembered going past the smoking shell of the building shortly afterwards, remembered the acrid smell of melted plastic and charred wood. Just off the square it had been, on the lot where the Denton brothers built a new law office a year later. She wrote down the names of the two deceased Sandman customers.

The next year, 1987, she'd gotten Wes to move her from jail duty to the dispatch desk. Her recollections of the cases that marched through the pages of the *News* were clearer, not because she'd investigated them but because she'd sent other deputies to work them. But no one had died in a fire in 1987.

1988 and '89 were her first years on patrol. It'd been like

113

pulling teeth to get Coach Cochran to move her into a cruiser, and even when he did it took a while for the others to take her seriously. Don Foley never did. But her memories of the most run-of-the-mill DWIs and forged-check cases still glowed with that first excitement and adrenalin surge of being a real patrol officer.

No fire fatalities in 1988, but in 1989 she remembered the fire that had killed crotchety bald Charley Laine who lived alone in an old house with old wiring.

Marty looked at her watch. Oops, the half-hour she'd promised Grady had stretched past forty-five minutes. She copied the articles to look at later.

'Joanne, this is a wonderful help,' she said, returning the spools of microfilm. 'Give me a call if your friend finds anything on that Ohio murder. And thanks.'

'It's a pleasure,' said the tall librarian, and remembering the intense expression on Joanne's face when she'd found the trail to follow, Marty knew she was telling the simple truth.

Sixteen

Back at the office, Marty helped a rookie named Neal to process a forged-check complaint they'd received, then Grady Sims told her nothing much was happening so she might as well take her lunch break. She got a tuna sandwich from the machine in the back room and headed for Reiner's Bakery to cadge a piece of peanut-butter pie from Aunt Vonnie.

'So, are you coming home before the church supper tonight?' Aunt Vonnie asked, handing over a plate of pie and a hot coffee.

The three tiny tables were taken, so Marty put the coffee on the counter and leaned against the wall. 'That's the plan. Romey said he'd stop by and we could all go together.'

Aunt Vonnie looked at her shrewdly. 'Sometimes I think Romey Dennis is courting Chrissie and me instead of you.'

Marty smiled. 'Let me know if he makes any progress, you old flirt.' Aunt Vonnie's retort was cut off by a customer coming in for cookies. But as Marty munched her pie, she realized how much Romey had worked his way into all their lives. Aunt Vonnie liked him because she knew his Uncle Corky, had known his parents while they were still alive. Chrissie was warier but seemed happy to listen to his stories.

Marty was only halfway through her pie when her radio squawked, 'Three-twenty-one!'

'Twee-twimmy-um,' she responded, trying to swallow.

'Call for you,' Grady's voice said. 'From Staten Island. Says he'll only be at that number for twenty minutes.'

'See you in five.' Marty left her pie and waved at Aunt Vonnie as she ran out the door.

'Bruno,' said a gravelly voice when she dialed the number Grady gave her.

'Deputy Hopkins here, Nichols County, Indiana. We hear you had a case four years ago that might—'

'Yeah, your message said it was about the Ronald Mann thing,' growled the voice. 'One of my guys saw something yesterday on CNN. Fire and machete, right? That's why you're calling?'

'Yes, sir. Plus Ronald Mann grew up right here in this county.'

'Huh! I don't think we had that.'

'Plus it turns out the machete here comes from Ecuador. Our victim, Corson, worked there once.'

Bruno whistled. 'OK, here's a secure site where you can e-mail the stuff to me.' He gave her an address.

'Got it. Can you send us your case records?'

'Yes, ma'am, but I'll have to fax them. We're behind on getting our old cases digital.'

'I know what you mean.' She gave their fax number and added, 'Could I ask a couple of questions?'

'Fire away.'

'Did Ronald Mann have any dealings with our vic? Robert Corson, nickname Zill?'

'Don't think he was ever mentioned.'

'How about a guy named Bowers? Ex-Marine, Sergeant John Bowers.'

'Don't remember that name either. But it's been four years. Who's this Bowers?'

'Bowers was a friend of Corson's, and he died in an apartment fire in Indianapolis this morning. They say there was a machete.'

'Son of a gun. You didn't tell the FBI, did you?'

'No, sir, I'm just a deputy. My boss is in Indianapolis now, getting the details on the Bowers death. It'll be his decision.'

'Yeah.' Bruno seemed resigned. 'We'll have to call them, but it always takes a while to get the Feds up to speed.'

'Yes, sir, that's been our experience too. Another question. Ronald Mann's daughter Olivia gave us your name. Did you find her reliable?'

'Ah, yes; little Liv left a message for me this morning to get in touch with you.' Bruno's growly voice sounded almost fond. 'She's smart and accurate and I'm warning you, she won't let it go if she thinks you should be chasing down a clue for her. Only thing . . .' There was a pause and Marty imagined a furrowed brow while he thought things over before he continued, 'Did you find a connection between your vic and Liv's mother who ran off to Ecuador?'

'Only just learned about it, so we haven't had a chance to look yet, but it sure looks like there's an Ecuador connection. Did you talk to the mother?'

'Yeah, early on. She came to the funeral. Nice-looking woman name of Luisa. She seemed broken up about the death. I did the routine interview, but she said she didn't know much, they'd been separated several years and she'd gone back to her people.'

'I know you're faxing me the official version, but what was your gut reaction about whether she was telling the truth?'

'Gut reaction.' Again the gravelly voice paused; again Marty could almost see the thoughtful frown. 'The grief was real, OK? She had feelings for the guy. Only glitch was when I asked her if her husband had any enemies in Ecuador. She said no, not any more. I asked, so they talked it over and ended up friends? And she said no, they died long ago. See, I didn't know yet there was an Ecuador connection. So I moved on.'

'Did you ask her about the machete?'

'Only in passing. I mean, they use the things down in Latin America but up here there are plenty of guys who get one for show or for a souvenir or something, because they look cool.'

'Yeah.' Marty flashed on the machete in the side of Zill's kinked, charred remains. Didn't look cool at all.

Bruno went on, 'She said she didn't know about any machete and I wasn't getting any vibes from her so I didn't push it. By the time the lab analyst said it was from Ecuador it was a week later and Luisa Mann was already back in her country.'

'You called her, of course.'

'Yeah, even before little Liv came steaming back into the office, saying it had to be her mother's fault. I told her I'd already been in touch with Luisa.'

'And?'

'And Luisa had seemed surprised, but it's hard to tell on the phone. She still had no idea who it could be. The whole conversation will be in the stuff I fax you. Also a lotta stuff about Luisa and her family from the Ecuador police.'

'So back to gut feelings. Early on, like at the funeral, did Liv seem angry at her mother?'

'Nowhere near as angry as later. But she wasn't friendly either. I get the feeling she blamed her mother for walking out. A couple of times I saw Luisa try to comfort her when she was crying and both times Liv turned away from her.'

'I see,' Marty said. So far it jibed with what Liv had told her. 'OK, I'll send you what we've got. Um . . . the guy in charge of the Indianapolis case is named Lyons.' She read off the contact number.

'OK, got it. You can look for my fax within the hour.'

'Good, thanks.'

'This is a real break, Deputy Hopkins. Sure hope we can clear this thing without too much interference from the Feds. That's one mean bastard took out Ronald Mann.'

'You said it.'

Marty found the Corson file in her computer, attached it to a message to Bruno, then hesitated. Should she wait to check with Chuck Pierce? She was saved when Howie Culp came in, looking frazzled.

'Hey, Howie,' she said. 'What's the word from Evansville?'

'Nothin' much. Zill only kept a couple of things in that trailer.' Howie tossed an evidence bag on his desk, stared at it gloomily while he took off his coat. 'But hey, we got clear evidence that the guy shaved.'

Grady Sims chuckled, then said, 'Sheriff's off to Indy.'

'Yeah, he gave me a call,' Howie said, tossing the coat on to a hook. 'Told me some friend of Zill's died in a fire up there.' He looked at Marty. 'Sheriff said the cops there were sharp, got the connection to Zill real quick. I'm wondering if you had anything to do with it.'

Marty met his eyes, saw suspicion lurking there. Howie wanted to catch this killer, she knew, and he also wanted to win points with his boss the sheriff. Didn't want another deputy grabbing the credit. She said, 'That address I gave you for Zill's friend Bowers turned up on a list of fires in Indy, so I called to see if Bowers was involved. They hadn't ID'd him yet so it gave them something to check.'

'I see.'

'And I got something else coming in for you. I called to see if the Staten Island cop who worked the murder of Liv Mann's father could give us some background.'

'Oh yeah. She said it was a fire and machete with him too.

So you got background.' He stared at her a moment, then suddenly relaxed a little. 'So what'd he say?'

Relieved to be back on the team, Marty reported, 'His name's Detective Bruno. Not much new on the phone but he's sending us his case file. It'll be coming in on the fax any minute. He wanted us to send along what we have on Zill. Do you want me to do that?'

Howie said, 'Sure, if he's sending us his file. Always better to work together. Hey, is that it now?' The fax machine had started to clatter.

'Could be.' Marty turned back to her computer, hit the 'send' button and Bruno had his material. She stood up. 'I want to finish the background stuff on fires in Nichols County. So I'll go look at the files in the basement unless you guys think of something better for me to do.'

'Hey, this is interesting.' Howie was reading the first pages from Bruno's fax. 'Yeah, Marty, go ahead.'

'OK. Want me to take Zill's shaving cream down to the evidence room?'

'Yeah, thanks. Hey, this guy's wife ran off and went to Ecuador!'

Marty went down to the basement, glancing into the clear-plastic evidence bag in the elevator. Not much: two neckties, his Pinkett's badge, a cleaner's receipt for a uniform, a length of twine with knots in it, and of course the shaving supplies. She signed it into the secure room, and then headed for the file room a couple of doors down the hall.

They hadn't been in the new building all that long but the file cabinets were the old battered ones trucked over from their previous home three blocks away. They smelled ancient even in the new room. Marty pulled out the six articles she'd copied at the library. Number one, 1980, a Mrs Roche had been deep-frying doughnuts when the big pot of oil over-heated and flamed, and she'd tried to put it out with a splash of water. The house had been saved except for the kitchen, but the woman had died. Not immediately, two weeks later in an Indianapolis burn unit. Nasty way to go.

The official file didn't add anything to the newspaper article. On to number two, also 1980. The article she'd copied was about May Gordon, the schoolteacher who'd died in a fire down in Peru. There was a photo of a slim, pretty young woman with a wild mop of curls that belied her prim dress. She was hovering over five Indian-looking kids with a warm smile. But there was nothing about her here in the departmental files, because the fire hadn't been in this county. South America was interesting, though, even if it wasn't Ecuador. She made a note of the next of kin's address, on Ridge Road, and moved on to number three: 1983, a guy named Moody, smoking in his bedroom. Their file added only that the idiot had barely escaped with his life three years before, identical circumstances of smoking in his bedroom. Number four was Amelia Barber, aged twelve, who died on the Fourth of July of 1984 in the fire her brother started when he set off fireworks on their deck. The rest of the family escaped.

Next were the two guys who'd died in the Sandman Bar fire in 1986. The sheriff's file added a couple of things: that the fire had started in built-up grease in the chimney, and that one of them had been a Marine. That might be worth following up. She made another note.

And finally there was Charley Laine, the last fire fatality of 1986. She looked through his file but she'd remembered correctly: an electrical malfunction.

She closed the 1989 drawer, then looked irresolutely at a much older file, 1975. She'd been twelve, and suddenly a gaping hole had been torn in her life. She'd cut out all the newspaper articles about her father's death and practically memorized them. She'd asked Coach Cochran about it a few times. But she'd never looked at the official report.

'LaForte, Christopher', said the label. It wasn't very thick. She looked at the first page. Wes Cochran had been first on the scene. Deputy Cochran back then, under Sheriff Cowgill. A short report. The next page was in Grady Sims's handwriting. Made sense, because you wouldn't assign someone to investigate his best friend's death once you found out who had died.

She looked back at Wes's incident report. Her father's El Camino pickup had crashed on a curve of the main highway from Bloomington. She'd visited the place before, still couldn't pass it without a sense of sorrow. Her father had been at a bar not far from the Terre Haute highway, up near the county line, and was headed back home toward Dunning. He'd taken

120

the curve too wide, hit a tree. He was still in the car when it burst into flames.

Three motorists had passed – well, maybe more, but at eleven thirty at night there wouldn't be heavy traffic, and most of what there was would be hurrying home or off to work a midnight shift somewhere. Still, three motorists had taken the trouble to call in. No cellphones in those days: they all had to locate a phone booth, pull over and stop, make the call. So there was a delay of a few minutes before the first call came in.

Wes Cochran had been on patrol back in Dunning and made good time to the scene, six minutes from the first call. His report was facts-only: time, place, vehicle (sixty-eight El Camino), incident (hit tree, caught fire, no apparent survivors). The Nichols County Fire Department had arrived two minutes after Cochran, managed to extinguish the flames, and half an hour later they were cutting away the metal so they could get the body out. They took it to the Shady Rest funeral home because the funeral director there was also the county coroner in those days.

There was a sketch map. Coach had drawn it very carefully, showing the bend in the highway, several trees, the fatal one clear because the outline of the nose of the truck was mashed in around it. He'd shown the exact angle of the vehicle, the skid marks leading to it. Coach hadn't made any comments. But, staring at the diagram, Marty could see that her father must have been going way too fast. Well, he always liked speed.

Marty swallowed and looked at Grady Sims's reports, equally terse. And the autopsy report: cause of death, asphyxiation from smoke inhalation. Also noted were multiple fractures including a fractured skull. Probably unconscious before death. Marty breathed a prayer of thanks for that. Blood alcohol level was .11. Too high, but not off the charts.

The victim was identified from dental work as Christopher 'Rusty' LaForte, Grady Sims had written. The El Camino was identified as LaForte's.

Grady had interviewed Marty's mother, Marie LaForte. Apparently Wes had been along but didn't say much. Grady reported Marie was weeping but at the end of the interview said, 'Write this down. Rusty wasn't that drunk. He called me before he left the bar, said he'd be late because he had to tell Wes that Walt bought guns from the gunshop burglar, then hung up. You gotta check it out.'

What was that about? Marty stared at the words. Who was Walt? She'd have to ask.

At the back of the folder was a large envelope. Photos, no doubt. The only photo she'd ever seen was one published with a newspaper article, taken the next day as men struggled to get the blackened El Camino on to a truck for transport to the dump. Marty hesitated, pulled out the first photo. Retched. Slid it back in.

Still saw it in her mind.

Coach Cochran might have taken the photo. The camera had been somewhere in front of the driver's side of the vehicle. The fire was going strong by the rear wheel and inside the car, but hadn't yet moved to the motor area. The photo showed how the passenger-side fender had caved in and the hood had buckled from the impact. The shattered windshield revealed the blaze within as well as the silhouette crumpled over the steering wheel.

Marty retched again, dropped the folder into its place in the 1975 file, shoved the drawer home, and ran upstairs without waiting for the elevator.

Seventeen

Liv was headed for the public library to read old newspapers from her dad's days in high school, but she paused in the library parking lot before getting out of the car and took out her cellphone. She returned the call from Arlene Lugano, who wanted to invite her to come soon, for dinner and if possible before. 'Mark's feeling down today,' she told Liv. 'It'll be so good to have you staying with us.'

'I've got stuff to do, but dinner's fine,' Liv said. She'd packed her things already, checked out and left her bags in the motel office. 'Is Mark sick or anything?'

'No, you know how men are. Moody.'

Liv watched a man get out of a Honda and go into the library as she said, 'Maybe we can go on another ride. Mark seemed to enjoy the horses yesterday.'

'He does. The sun sets a little after five, you remember from yesterday. But if you don't get here in time we can go out tomorrow morning.'

'That'll be great. See you soon!'

In the library, for one shocked delighted instant she thought she saw Elena. But the dark-haired librarian who came to help her find the microfilms was too tall and didn't have the right crooked grin. Liv felt hollow as she sat down to scroll through the old newspapers. They were disappointing too: no references to Pops. Mark Lugano, yes, because he'd been on the basketball team. Maybe she should go to the high school and see if they had any records of her father.

The door to the basement stairs slammed behind Marty. The image of her father in the burning El Camino still throbbed in her mind. She took a shaky breath, started to open the door into the big dispatch room.

There were a couple of citizens talking to Grady, and Betty

123

Burke from the *News* was waiting near the front door. Marty couldn't face a reporter right now. She turned back, went into the jail door instead, told Barbara, the corrections officer on duty, that she wanted to go out the back way.

'You feeling sick?' Barbara inspected Marty as she heaved herself up from her desk. She was a tall, wide, deceptively soft-looking brunette who was the unofficial champion arm-wrestler in the department.

'Just avoiding reporters. Got a job to do,' Marty said.

Barbara didn't seem convinced and said, 'Well, honey, you look like you seen a ghost. Take care,' as she let her out. Marty slid into her cruiser, rubbed her temples, then pulled out her copy of the newspaper article to check the address and headed out of town.

Driving relaxed her a little, and as she approached the city limits she radioed back to dispatch. 'Three-twenty-one. I'm going to talk to someone on Ridge Road. Shouldn't take long.'

Grady acknowledged and she turned on to the highway.

The soft droopy clouds of the morning had blown away, but higher, harder ones remained. Against the steely sky everything looked jagged and sharp and colorless: gray barns and fenceposts, white fields. Even the cedars and pines looked black instead of green, shivering in the cold wind.

The photo of the burning El Camino kept poking at Marty's mind, but she ignored it, focusing on the landscape, on the crackly voices on the radio. Here came Deputy Neal, calling in a fender-bender south of town. A few minutes later Roy Adams reported that he and Phil Vogler were heading back to the station. He sounded happy, so they'd probably located the gun Todd Seifert had used in that hold-up.

She was on County Road 870, heading through patchy woods and limestone roadcuts down to the flat half-mile of flood plain near where Gordon Creek joined the White River to roll on west to the Wabash. She crossed the wooden truss bridge over the creek, but Ridge Road was on this side of the river, so at the Y intersection she turned away from the big highway bridge and went east along the riverbank until the road began to climb again through the cold ice-spangled hills.

The penny dropped. Ridge Road. Next of kin Constancia Gordon and Eunice Ann Gordon. The schoolteacher who'd died in Peru had been the sister of Stanni and Eunie, the

124

clowns she'd watched yesterday at the Rockland Mall.

Marty had never been to their place, but she'd heard they lived up on Demon Ridge. When she turned off the county road on to Ridge Road, it got a lot steeper, angling up three switchbacks to the top. She was glad to find it passable. Nobody had plowed, but that brisk wind had swept the road mostly clear.

At the top, Marty understood why someone might want to live here. The views were amazing: miles of wooded hills, and through the tree trunks on the right side there were occasional glimpses of the wide meandering White River far below. On the left you could see across to the steep hills of the far wall of the Gordon Creek gorge. The creek itself was invisible in the depths of the chasm.

Ahead of her, the ridge widened out a little and she saw the house on the creek side of the road, nestled in a shallow natural depression. It had stained-brown shingled walls and eaves jigsawed into complicated curvy shapes. Parking was along the road. She pulled up behind an orange minivan with a green-haired clown face painted on each door.

When she got out, a wind gust hit her hard in the face and she had to grab for her Stetson. The wind whistled through the trees, complicated as a musical chord. There were footprints in the snow leading down from the Land Rover to a back porch and beyond, but also to a front porch which was nearer. Besides being cupped in the natural depression, the house was also sheltered by tall yews that cut the force of the ridge-top blasts. About as snug as you could get up here. When she reached the porch Marty realized that part of the wind-song really was music, a voice singing high and mournful as a flute inside the house. Eunie practicing. She waited for the end of a phrase before knocking, and the music stopped. In a moment Eunie opened the door, her curious expression replaced by puzzlement when she saw Marty's uniform.

'Hi, Ms Gordon. I'm Deputy Hopkins. Marty Hopkins.'

'Oh, yes, of course, come in! Um, Marty LaForte, you were?' Eunie seemed bashful and uncertain.

'That's right. I saw you just yesterday out at the Rockland Mall. Nice show.'

'Thanks.' Eunie gave her a shy smile. Out of her clown make-up she was a handsome forty-something woman, nice

125

bone structure, trim figure, big sad eyes, short gray hair. She was wearing a Nordic sweater in a complicated pattern of blue and white. 'Um, Stanni's just out feeding the birds, she'll be back any minute.'

'Good. It'd be good to talk to both of you.'

Eunie gestured with the banjo she still held toward the living room. 'Want to sit down? We have some coffee hot.'

'This won't take long, but hey, I'd love some coffee. Black,' Marty told her. 'That wind is so cold.'

'Sure is. There, sit on the sofa, I'll be right back.' She disappeared.

Marty glanced around the living room as she entered. On the right wall, the sofa was an orangey-tweed Scandinavian type with scuffed teak arms. Straight ahead on the far wall was a fireplace flanked by bookcases. Two photos sat on the mantel. As she crossed the room she saw that one was of Stanni and Eunie in performance, Stanni doing a high kick, Eunie playing that banjo, both riveting with their grotesque painted grins and fright wigs topped with the goofy little hats.

The other photo was of three little girls in overalls, standing in front of this very house, big snaggle-toothed grins. There was a postcard propped behind the frame, majestic mountains against a blue sky. Marty turned it over: 'Feb. 4, 1980. Dear Sis 1 and Sis 2, kids are doing great! Working hard on the alphabet, & my Hoosier buddy got us medicine for the dysentery. Took a trip to the Puyango petrified forest down in the valley – they loved it. Yes, Santo Tomas is the address, quicker than going through the office in Lima. We're going to do a play! love, Sis 3.'

Feeling sad, Marty tucked the card back where she'd found it and continued her tour of the room. The front window wall had a straight-back chair and music stand surrounded by piles of sheet music that probably had overflowed from the nearby bookcase. On the other side of the window, a spinet piano took up the rest of the wall.

No TV. Against the fourth wall there was an upholstered chair that matched the sofa, next to the door where she'd entered, and another bookcase. On top of the bookcase was a big aquarium. Wait, no – despite a large pan of water it was not an aquarium. It was a terrarium, fitted with branches and potted plants beside the water. A few live crickets crawled on the terrarium floor but she couldn't see anything else. Unless . . . up on that branch behind some leaves there was a long green tendril, thin as a whip. Marty moved sideways to see it better, spotted a wise round golden eye looking back at her. A snake!

She peered at it with interest. One advantage of being a tomboy good enough to play boys' basketball was learning about interesting stuff boys liked, like snakes. She'd gotten intrigued, even did a sixth-grade science project about them. Her then-teammate Romey had helped her catch a young blacksnake for her report. She smiled at the memory of crouching one morning by the rockpile where they'd seen it, silent together, scarcely breathing, until the snake came out like a spirit from the netherworld looking for the sun. She'd hooked it with a straightened coathanger and dropped it into the sack Romey held for her.

The snake in the terrarium wasn't a blacksnake. It was leaf-green with a paler belly, over two feet long and very thin. The scales were dimensional, neatly defined, not smooth the way they'd been on her blacksnake.

'You like Pythia?' Eunie asked, coming back in.

'Yeah, she's pretty.' Marty turned to Eunie. 'I had a blacksnake for a couple of weeks when I was a kid, but it turned out I had to feed him mice and I was no good at catching them. So I let him go again. Pythia eats crickets, I guess.'

'Yes, you can buy boxes of live crickets so you don't have to catch them.' Eunie smiled and handed her a hot mug of coffee.

Marty nodded her thanks and took a sip before she said, 'Actually I came to ask about your sister.'

'Like I said, Stanni'll be back any minute.'

'Yeah, but I mean your other sister. May.'

'May!' Eunie's startled eyes glanced toward the mantel photo, then at Marty. 'But she – I mean – '

'She died years ago!' Stanni came in dusting snow from her gloves, still wearing her parka. She was a little shorter than Eunie, more muscular.

'Yes, I'm sorry, I know that,' Marty said. 'I wondered if you could tell me something about what happened. The newspaper said she was down in Peru.'

Eunie's big sad eyes jerked toward Stanni, who said, 'Yes.

May decided to become a nun, and her order did a lot of missionary work. Schools, hospitals, that sort of thing. But why are you asking us now?'

Marty took a sip of her coffee. They were all still standing up. She said, 'We're trying to get a list of Nichols County people who died in fires in the last fifteen years or so. Most of the cases are in our files but not May because she wasn't in this county. So this is just to complete our files.'

'I see. Probably has to do with that fellow who died in the cabin fire, right? Well, we can tell you about May but we don't know much about what happened down in South America. Wanna hang up your coat?' Stanni opened the door of the entry closet to hang up her parka. Marty caught a glimpse inside of orange polka-dot clown suits hanging among the coats.

'No, this won't take long, really,' Marty said. 'I just need a couple of details.'

Stanni closed the door again, turned back. 'So, what details do you need?'

Marty put down her mug next to the terrarium and pulled out her notepad. 'OK. How old was she when she died?'

Stanni looked at Eunie. 'Thirty-two? She graduated high school – what, two years after you?'

'One year. I was class of sixty-four, she was sixty-five.'

'Yeah. And she decided to become an Ursuline nun. Went down to Mary Mount in Kentucky. They wouldn't take her at first, made her go to college and get her teaching degree, made sure she had a vocation.'

'What's that exactly?' Marty asked.

'Deep spiritual commitment,' Eunie explained.

'Yeah, they want to make sure you won't wimp out,' Stanni said. 'No danger of that with May. She was tough and committed. She may have looked like a little dandelion, skinny and innocent and all that curly hair, but she never would take no for an answer.'

'She had a run-in with your momma once,' Eunie said slyly.

Marty was astonished. 'My mother? Really?'

Eunie smiled. 'You wouldn't remember, you were a baby, and May was still in high school. Real pretty – the boys liked her a lot but she wouldn't give them the time of day. Even in grade school she was talking about being a nun.'

'A teaching nun. She always loved kids,' Stanni said.

Eunie nodded. 'Anyway, your Aunt Vonnie had to be at work before four so your parents got May to babysit after school until dinnertime, when your mom got back from her job at the hospital. And May was good, very responsible, until she lost her head about this lieutenant stationed over at the Naval Ammunition Center.'

'Way too old for her, and no sense,' Stanni snorted.

Eunie said, 'He came to visit her while she was babysitting you. And she let him in. Your momma got back a few minutes early and caught them cuddling on the sofa, and she just hit the ceiling. Fired her. Said May was totally out of line. Said her baby – you – deserved watchful care and respect.'

Marty shook her head in wonder. 'She never told me that story.'

'Well, your mom was right,' Stanni said. 'Later May broke up with the Navy guy, but I think when they heard about him, that's when the Ursulines got suspicious of her vocation. But the vocation was real. The Navy guy was just hormones or something, not serious. So May was twenty-three or twenty-four when they let her take her vows.'

'This is the early seventies, right?' Marty said. 'And she died in 1980.'

Eunie's lip trembled a little. 'Yes, she'd only been in Santo Tomas a few months, but they'd sent her other places before.'

'That's right.' Stanni was looking at Eunie with concern. 'First Mexico – she learned most of her Spanish there; then Peru.'

'OK,' Marty said, noting it down. 'So how did she die?'

Eunie gave a little sniffle, and Marty reached out to touch her sleeve. 'I'm sorry to be bringing this up again.'

Stanni said briskly, 'The school burned down and she and some of the kids were in it. Didn't the newspaper say that?'

'Yes.' That image of her father was flickering at the edge of Marty's consciousness again. She plowed ahead. 'So May couldn't get out in time? Didn't they have a fire alarm?'

'Wouldn't have helped,' Eunie sobbed.

Stanni went to her sister and put her arms around her. She gave Marty a resentful look and said, 'It was a wooden building. The fire started after school from an explosion. May knew there were kids still inside and rushed back to help them. They tried to stop her but she ran inside. Burned with them.'

Eunie's hands were over her face and she leaned on her sister, making a high keening sound. In Marty's head her cry merged with the sobs and wails of her mother, of herself, when her father had died. The swarm of sounds and images threatened to suffocate her. But there was something she had to ask, something they'd said. She hacked through the memories and looked at her notes. 'Explosion?' she asked.

'Probably the stove,' Stanni snapped. 'Dammit, you're upsetting my sister. Me too. Don't you have enough details now for your damn records?'

Marty wrote down 'stove', looked up and met Stanni's angry gaze. 'I'm really sorry,' she said. 'This job can be a bitch. I'll let myself out.'

Eighteen

Wes Cochran, in the navy-blue Asphodel Springs Security uniform that didn't seem right even after two months, had been called by Amber at the desk to deal with a Mrs Harkett, a guest who was part of a bird-watchers' group out of Chicago. She seemed less worried about birds than about her diamond necklace. 'This place is so far from the police!' she wailed, a gesture of her thin wrinkled arm taking in most of the resort grounds. 'What if a burglar breaks in?'

'Not gonna happen,' Wes said soothingly. He thought about mentioning that Chicago had a whole lot more burglars per square mile than Nichols County, but then she'd probably have the heebie-jeebies when she got back home too. He explained, 'We patrol the grounds regularly and the staff and guests know to call us if they see anything odd happening. And management here has invested in the best safe in the business.'

'But this was my grandmother's necklace!' She clutched the velvet case to her thin chest, her heavily mascaraed eyes blinking rapidly in her distress.

Wes decided that her problem had more to do with loneliness than burglary. 'Y'know what, Mrs Harkett, let's take your necklace right over there to the desk, and Amber and I will personally lock it away in that high-tech safe for you.' He took her gently by the elbow. 'And then we'll go right through those glass doors over there to the Palm Court and Jimmy will serve you the cocktail of your choice. And pretty soon the rest of your group will be downstairs, and your grandma's necklace will be snug as a bug the whole time.'

Back in his office after turning the Harkett woman over to Jimmy and his Martinis, Wes saw a message on his cell-phone to call Bob Rueger. Interesting. Rueger was the multi-millionaire owner of a bunch of malls, including the Rockland

Mall right here in Nichols County. He lived in Arizona but had Indiana roots, and even though he'd recently decided against expanding the Rockland Mall he kept it up well. Wes had met him a couple of times in connection with a case three or four years ago, a square-built graying man, full of enthusiasm.

A secretary answered Wes's call but he was on hold only a second before he heard Rueger's voice.

'Wes Cochran! Good to hear your voice.' He sounded just as vibrant as last time.

'Sure. What can I do for you?'

'A lot. I just heard you'd decided to go into private security work.'

'Uh-huh.'

'And I wanted you to consider working with me.'

'Well, thanks, sir, but I got a good job – you probably heard.'

'Yeah. Asphodel Springs, great place. My malls don't have palm trees and golf courses, so I know I'd have to pay you a little more.'

Wes frowned. 'I thought you had a good security team in place.'

'At Rockland that's true, and I want to keep it that way. Larry's a good man. Look, here's the deal. I got an opening at Saguaro in Arizona. A lot bigger than Rockland, triple the acreage, five anchors, big sports complex too.'

'But no palm trees?'

Rueger laughed and Wes could almost see him – not a tall man but with outsize energy, practically bursting from his shirt. 'No trees period! But we got a nice big cactus by the main door, and a waterfall in the rotunda. Anyway, I haven't mentioned this to Larry 'cause I wanted to give you the choice. Arizona if you want the challenge and don't mind moving. Or, if you want to stay in your county, you can have Rockland and I'll move Larry to Arizona.'

Wes stared out the window at his view of the opposite yellow-brick wing and the wintry grounds beyond. 'Well, sir, I appreciate the offer, but—'

'Stop!' Rueger said. 'Don't say yes or no yet. I'll call you in a couple days. And you tell me what you'd need from me to take the job, and I'll tell you if I can give it to you. OK?'

132

'OK.' Wes couldn't see much reason to work for Rueger, but he ought to run the offer past Shirley.

Rueger said, 'Great! Must take some getting used to, going private after being one of the chief elected leaders for so long. I'll be in touch.'

Wes hung up and shook his head. He should be flattered to have a multimillionaire personally calling to ask for his services. And it was true: the work Rueger was offering would be more varied and, dammit, more useful than dealing with Mrs Harkett's worries or shooing snowmobilers back on to their trails. But he didn't want to go to Arizona, and Shirley wouldn't either. Too many roots here, too many friends, too many memories. He flashed on his son's gravestone in the hillside cemetery.

He wouldn't have to move if he worked at Rockland. But Rueger had put his finger on the problem there. Wes had been one of the most powerful men in Nichols County, elected and reelected by the voters to run an important and complicated department. And now he was just a working stiff like everyone else.

He didn't want to see his friends looking at him every day as a has-been. The best thing about Asphodel Springs, Wes admitted to himself, was that most of the guests were strangers. Of course that was the worst thing too.

The *chaski* had followed Ronnie Mann's daughter into the library. Amazing hair the kid had – brought back memories. While she worked at a microfilm reader, he'd read Indianapolis newspapers nearby, his gray knit cap pulled low. There was one small notice in the bottom corner of the City section of the largest paper about a fire on Bybee Street. The others had nothing.

When the Mann kid left he followed, but casually. He pretended to check his watch, returned his paper to the right slot, walked past the counter where she'd left the boxes. They held microfilms of old Nichols County newspapers, from her father's high-school years. So she was still fishing. He went out, pausing to look at the New Acquisitions shelves, a man in no special hurry. And he didn't have to hurry. She was still sitting in her little red Escort in the parking lot, talking on her cellphone. He drove out of the parking lot and around the

133

block, pausing where he could see the intersection. Pretty soon the Escort came out and turned south. She drove to a small shopping mall. It looked brand-new except for a massive jagged stump at the corner of the parking lot. Must have been some storm that took down that tree.

The Mann girl was going into a diner called the Country Griddle. He changed jackets and put on a Pacers cap in place of his gray knit one before he followed her in.

In the cruiser driving back from Demon Ridge, Marty decided to ask Grady Sims about the 'Walt' her mother had mentioned in that long-ago interview after her dad's death, but she got back to the station only a few minutes after Sheriff Pierce and things were busy. Three reporters and three deputies plus Barbara the corrections officer crowded around the sheriff. He nodded, signed a paper for Barbara, then said, 'Sorry, ladies and gentlemen of the press. I'll have to see you folks later. Deputy Culp here is right, we need a meeting.'

Howie Culp spotted Marty hanging up her coat. He hesitated, licked his lips, then blurted, 'Um, sir, it'd be good to have Hopkins there too.'

Sheriff Pierce looked around, saw her, and surprised her by nodding. 'Good idea. Hopkins, you come along, and Mason. Sims, hold the calls. If anything comes up send Neal out.'

'Yessir.'

Marty followed the others into the sheriff's office. Big map of the county on the wall, pictures of his wife Abby and grown daughters on the same battered gray desk that Coach Cochran had used all those years, and probably Sheriff Cowgill before him. Pierce perched on the edge of the desk; the rest of them leaned against the wall. He said, 'OK, I'm going to bring you up to date on Bowers first. The guy was an ex-Marine, a sergeant, served the same time as Zill Corson. So there's one connection. Another thing, there was a machete. Doesn't look much like the one we found with Corson but Indianapolis is checking to see if it's from Ecuador. If so that connects to the guy in New York too. Indianapolis is also trying to find out if Bowers ever worked down there. Hopkins, you told me before I left that Jumbo Jim Corson said his brother Zill had worked there.'

134

'Yes, sir; he said the security company that Sarge Bowers got him into sent him down.'

'Yeah. OK, Culp, what'd you find out in Evansville?'

Howie shuffled the papers he was holding, glanced at one. 'Not a lot, sir. Zill stayed with that guy Lewis but they weren't real close friends – met each other at some bar after working at Pinkett's. It was mutual convenience to share that trailer. And Zill didn't keep much stuff there. Lewis was a Marine too, so there's that connection. But he says he's never been to Ecuador, and I'm thinking your Ecuador thing is more interesting.'

'You know for sure he hasn't been to Ecuador?'

'The Vanderburgh County guys ran a background check; nothing contradicts him. Only thing in their records was some complaints from his wife.'

Pierce nodded, his light blue eyes sober. 'Hopkins, you get any background on Ecuador?'

'Yes, sir, a little. I followed up with Liv Mann and Alejandro Gallegos. Mostly historical; I'll write it up for you. Two things. One, Mark Lugano's an old friend of Ronald Mann. He might be able to tell us more about his work in Ecuador than Liv, because she was pretty young, doesn't remember much. But I didn't want to talk to Mr Lugano without checking with you.'

'Good,' Pierce said. 'I'll talk to him myself. What was the other thing?'

'I got the name of the cop in New York who worked Ronald Mann's murder. Detective Bruno. He just faxed us his material.' She gestured at the papers Howie Culp was holding.

'Good. What does it say?'

The pale eyes shifted to Howie, who said, 'Mann's wife was from Ecuador, and when they separated she went back there. Good interviews with her. But I don't see connections to anyone besides her husband.'

'Of course that's all they knew to ask about,' Pierce said.

'Yes, sir. Detective Bruno added a note that he was going to call her when he got our material. Also, he sent crime-scene descriptions. It happened on a big landfill they've got there. Apparently the ground was too messed up to take good tire-tread impressions, so they didn't get much; but there was a machete from Ecuador. Ronald Mann was tied up and cut with the machete, then set on fire.'

'Damn!' Pierce shook his head. 'Hopkins, any other background stuff?'

'I've been checking Nichols County fire fatalities. Went back fifteen years, even checked out a schoolteacher who died back in 1980 because it happened in South America. But it was Peru, not Ecuador.'

'Yeah, too long ago too. Anything else?'

'Not yet, sir.' She decided not to say anything about the death of the Ohio guy, an even flimsier connection than May Gordon's death.

'I got something else, sir.' Howie pulled out a short report from his papers. 'We got some preliminary notes a few minutes ago on the cabin-fire scene from the state evidence technicians.'

'Anything new there?' Pierce asked eagerly.

Howie shook his head. 'Not as much as I hoped. It's pretty much what Hopkins and Mason reported. The state guys confirm that accelerant was used, and there were signs on the bedpost that he'd been strapped to it.'

'Did they make any progress on those footprints?'

'They've got the brand of the boots: Bighorn. They, um, checked out the creek but didn't find any footprints, upstream or down. They think maybe the guy went to Zill's truck to watch the fire; it's pretty clear he got in, but after that – well, they say they're working on it.'

'Not the creek?' Pierce frowned. 'Dammit, he can't vanish into thin air!'

Marty closed her eyes, picturing the scene again. Cold dappled moonlight on the snow, evergreens, those damn footprints leading up to the driver's door, her yellow flashlight beam methodically swinging back and forth over Zill's truck, under it, all around it. Something tickled at her mind. 'Sir?'

'Yeah, Hopkins?'

'I was just thinking: there were little streaks of snow on top of the truck. Not a layer. Right, Bobby?'

Bobby Mason shrugged. 'Yeah, fell from the branches.'

Marty said, 'Right! I figured it was parked under those evergreens so no snow could fall directly on the truck. And like Bobby said, a few branches dumped their snow on it. But the ground under those same trees was more evenly covered.'

Mason was nodding thoughtfully and she was encouraged to

136

go on. 'So I'm wondering now if the guy swept off the top of the truck. So he wouldn't leave footprints when he jumped into the trees.'

'The trees?' Pierce looked suspicious. 'But you said there was some snow on the top, wherever it came from, and no footprints in it.'

'Yes, sir.' She could almost see it now. 'He climbs out of the driver's door on to the roof of the truck. He sweeps the roof bare. He jumps into the trees. And maybe that's what shakes the branches so they dump snow on to the roof. Meanwhile he's going away from branch to branch.'

'We're dealing with an apeman now?' Pierce said, but when the others snickered he raised a hand. 'Look, don't laugh yet; if the creek idea isn't working out we have to check out the far-fetched ideas too. Culp, get back to the state evidence guys, tell them to look—'

The phone shrilled. Pierce frowned at it. 'Dammit, I told Grady no calls!'

Marty glanced at Bobby Mason, and he said what they were both thinking. 'Sir, maybe it's an emergency.'

Pierce picked up, said curtly, 'Yeah?' and then his shoulders sagged. 'Send them in.' He hung up, looked at his assembled team, sighed. 'FBI,' he said. 'You guys go do your jobs. I'll handle them.'

The deputies filed out as two men came in, a square shrewd-eyed black man and a short man with pale skin and dark hair and features so neat they looked painted on. He looked at Marty. 'Deputy Hopkins?'

'Yes, sir, Agent Jessup, how you doing?'

Sheriff Pierce said, 'I'm Sheriff Pierce. Come in, Agent Jessup. You know Hopkins?'

Jessup nodded. 'Yes, she was very helpful on that Klan case a few years ago.'

'Well, no Klan connection with this one,' the sheriff said, closing the door with a sour look at Marty.

Whatever points she'd gained with her apeman theory had probably been wiped out by that compliment from the FBI. Thank God her shift was over soon.

Nineteen

Liv sat down in a booth in the Country Griddle. There were only a few other customers there midafternoon, a group of three guys working on someone's roof and complaining about the snow, a couple of solitary white-haired guys nursing their coffees. Foley came in soon, trying to hide his limp, and she jumped up to be polite. 'Hi, Mr Foley!'

'How you doing?' He hung up his jacket next to Liv's.

'I'm fine. How about you?'

The waitress – Karen, according to her name tag – arrived and they ordered coffee. 'Cinnamon rolls?' Foley asked Liv while Karen poured.

She looked at Karen and smiled. 'They're delicious. But I already ate too many this morning.'

'Yeah, I'll have some tomorrow,' Foley said. When Karen had gone he asked Liv, 'So what's up?'

'Well, see, I wanted to compare notes, because that Deputy Hopkins had some more questions for me.'

'Huh. What kind of questions?' Foley had tensed a little.

'She was interested in Ecuador.' He didn't respond, and she added, 'You know, South America. My father did a job there. Did anyone ask you about Ecuador?'

A man in a Pacers cap and sunglasses came in to sit at the counter and Foley's eyes followed though they seemed far away. 'South America? Yeah, Deputy Culp called up. Wanted to know about the time Zill was in South America. Mighta been Ecuador.'

'Your friend was down there too?'

'Yeah, some kind of security project for Armadillo. He and Bowers were down there. What's wrong?'

Liv realized she'd frozen in surprise. She made herself shake her head in confusion. 'I don't know. It's another connection, isn't it? Working in South America?'

'Yeah. I'm thinking now some wetback type maybe knew both of them. Followed them up here, tracked them down.'

'But why?'

Foley shrugged. 'Probably about some woman. Revenge thing.'

'Not my father!' Liv was genuinely outraged but managed to stay in her demure role as she added, 'My father was a good man, Mr Foley! He would never offend a woman!'

He looked uncomfortable. 'Yeah, sorry, I didn't mean it was true. These Spics, you know, they blow things up, won't let go even if they're wrong.'

'Yeah, I see,' Liv said, although she wanted to throw her coffee in his face. 'Did Deputy Culp think the killer is a South American?'

'He wasn't saying, but he mentioned one had been hanging around. You better watch out, now; never know what those wetbacks'll do next.'

'Yes, sir, I will.' Liv wondered if that meant Alejandro was a suspect now. 'Did Deputy Culp say anything else?'

'That was about it. You got any idea what Hopkins was after?'

'Just the South American thing. I guess Deputy Culp told her about it.'

'Yeah, she's a pushy one,' Foley said. 'Always trying to get hold of cases so she gets the credit. Problem is, her schemes get in the way of the real law enforcement. You watch out for her too,' he added severely.

'Yes, sir, I'll remember. I'll call you again if something comes up.' Liv stood up.

'OK. See you.'

From the counter the *chaski* had a sideways view of the booth where Ronnie Mann's daughter had been. This guy she called Mr Foley was faintly familiar. Older than she was. Round face. Who was he? Not a relative, because her father hadn't had any relatives here for quite a few years, and hadn't visited them often even when they were all alive. Was Foley her father's friend? He looked to be from that era. The *chaski* didn't remember him, but he was a pretty average-looking guy. Could be she'd found his name in those old newspaper microfilms she was looking at. Or maybe he was a friend of Lugano's – though he didn't look like it. Even in his country clothes Mark Lugano always looked rich: suede jackets, fancy wristwatch. Classier even than Ronnie Mann had been. Funny, though, how Ronnie's daughter was dressing down now – cheap pink jeans and sweater. If she'd cut her hair, she'd look almost girl-next-door.

Foley wasn't dressing down. He was the genuine article. That flannel shirt had been through many washes; his boots were worn and probably resoled. He signalled the waitress and the *chaski* heard him order a sandwich and pie, so the *chaski* asked for more coffee.

Then he called for his check, but didn't pay until he saw Foley receive his. He went to the men's room to give Foley time to get to his car before he followed him.

To his surprise, Foley was still standing in the vestibule next to the coin-operated newspaper-vending boxes. He'd bought a copy of the Indianapolis paper and was staring at the little article in the corner of the front page, muttering, 'Fuck. Fuck.'

'Hey, buddy, you OK?' asked the *chaski*, curious.

Foley looked up, through him rather than at him. 'Yeah, fine.'

'You sure?'

Foley seemed to pull himself together, said gruffly, 'Yeah, sure; just found out a guy I knew died in a fire.'

'Huh,' said the *chaski*. He looked at the paper, wondering who Foley was, how he'd known Sarge, how Ronnie Mann's daughter had found him. He said, 'Hell of a thing. Wasn't there another one?'

'Yeah, he was . . .' Terror flashed across Foley's face before he could hide it, and the *chaski* knew he was thinking, *Two of my friends have burned; am I next?*

Better change the subject – didn't want to look too curious. He said, 'In Fort Wayne there was something on TV, that lady deputy?'

He'd meant only to establish that he was an outsider, but from the sudden anger in Foley's glare he knew he'd hit pay dirt.

Foley said, 'Yeah, if she could she'd be announcing this one too.'

'You know her? She was kinda cute.'

140

'You wouldn't think cute if you worked with her. Used to be the boss's pet. Always getting special treatment.'

O-K, thought the *chaski*; get off the topic now – this guy's a deputy, or ex-deputy. He said, 'Yeah, women don't play by the rules. In Terre Haute I heard of a lady reporter who used to bribe kids to steal things so she could get the story first.'

'Yeah, exactly!' Foley nodded at him grimly, then glanced back at the paper. 'Well, gotta check this out.'

'Yeah. Sorry about your friend,' said the *chaski*, and left.

By the time Liv got her suitcase to the Luganos' place, the sun was a dull orange glow in the western clouds and there wasn't time for a horseback ride. Arlene sent Mark and Liv out to help the groom, a sturdy gray-haired woman named Carrie. They didn't talk much as they led the animals from the darkening paddock into the bright, well-kept stable, sweet-smelling from the clean straw on the floor. The five horses, two of them swollen in pregnancy, were glossy and alert, swiveling their ears and flaring their nostrils at Liv. Blueberry looked her over with a wise sideways glance before dipping his head for his oats. 'He remembers you,' Carrie said, and Liv was ridiculously pleased.

When they got back to the house, Mark poured Liv a glass of Chardonnay. Soon Arlene bounced into the living room to announce that the roast chicken was done. She served it at the fireside table in the room with the bright colors and the happy Madonna, accompanied by sweet potatoes and peas and some kind of fruit relish. Liv was hungrier than she'd thought and laid into it with gusto. 'Haven't eaten like this since Thanksgiving,' she told Arlene.

'Oh, it's nothing that fancy,' Arlene said, glowing with pleasure. 'Did you have Thanksgiving with your mother?'

It hadn't been so noticeable while they were working in the stables, but Mark had been withdrawn and monosyllabic all evening, his handsome face a mask except for occasional warm smiles. But now he looked up and said, 'They don't usually celebrate Thanksgiving in Ecuador.'

'You're right, they don't,' Liv said, and because more seemed expected, 'A friend invited me to have dinner with her family on Long Island.' Elena's family, tense as usual, really trying to make her feel welcome, hiding their unhappiness that Liv wasn't a man. Pops hadn't lived long enough to meet Elena. He'd given Liv a hug when she first came out to him – sad and worried but a hug, even though he was a Catholic. Tough to be family sometimes.

Liv brought herself back to the conversation. Arlene was saying, 'That's nice.' But Mark was still looking at her and Liv decided to forge ahead while she had his attention.

'I haven't seen much of my mother the last few years,' she said. 'After Dad died – well, see, the machete was from Ecuador.'

Arlene winced and Mark leaned back in his chair, horrified realization creeping into his eyes. 'You don't mean you blamed Luisa!'

'Oh, no, I'm sure . . .' Arlene began.

But she trailed off because Liv was nodding, saying, 'Of course I suspected her. The police were checking her out too. Found nothing.' She narrowed her eyes, trying to read Mark's reaction, and went on, 'It's awful to say this, but I'm almost glad poor Mr Corson died the way he did.'

Mark said, 'Because he's got no connection to your mother.'

'Right, no connection with my mother. Mark, how is he connected to my father?'

He shook his head, looked down at his plate. 'I don't know. I never met him.'

Arlene was looking anxiously back and forth at them. 'Look, people, let's talk about something else at dinnertime, OK? Liv, unless you want seconds, I have a real Hoosier dessert for you. Have you ever had Indiana persimmon pudding?'

Mark had retreated into his own thoughts again, and yet Liv felt she had gained ground, cracked his facade a little. She'd learned that he'd never suspected her mother. Why not? What did he know? Maybe she could get him to tell her. For now she said cheerfully to Arlene, 'Dad talked about persimmon pudding, but I've never tasted it and I'd love to. Here, let me help you clear the table.'

Twenty

There was no Hoosier persimmon pudding at the Cedars of Lebanon Methodist Church pot-luck church supper. German potato salad, yes, and Tex-Mex chili. At least the people were pure Hoosier. They stood up to hear Pastor Kemble say grace and to sing a hymn to the all-victorious Lord: 'Strike with the hammer of Thy Word, And break these hearts of stone.' Then they swooped down on the casseroles, filling their plates before sitting down at the long tables set up in the basement fellowship hall.

Whenever she could Marty attended the church supper, for professional reasons as well as social ones. For years she'd watched Sheriff Cochran work the room, picking up all kinds of useful information, often learning about problems soon enough to head them off with a quiet word to the right dog owner or skateboarding teenager. Sheriff Pierce wasn't as good at it yet, but this evening she'd seen him talking to Pastor Kemble and Greta Sadler from the Chamber of Commerce and even old deaf Herb Frick, so he was learning the usefulness of it too. Marty usually kept her ears open, but tonight she was still edgy about that photo of her father and wanted most to talk to her own Aunt Vonnie.

Wasn't going to be easy. Aunt Vonnie, her face creased now but her hair just as blonde and wavy as the day she had first peroxided it, was seated on Marty's right, gossiping with her friend Melva Dodd two seats down. Janie Tippett was on Marty's left, and across from them Chrissie, in a downy blue sweater her father had given her, was telling them about the new science teacher she had this term. 'She's like, you've got to do four projects and learn to write like a scientist. I mean, who wants to write like a scientist? And four projects! Can you think of four things that aren't boring?'

'I can't even think of one,' Janie said.

Romey Dennis was sitting next to Chrissie, listening attentively. He'd chosen Clara Johnson's beef stew tonight, rich and tender and with a secret ingredient. Some thought it might be raisins but Romey claimed it was something less Methodist and more alcoholic.

'Well, maybe fossils?' Chrissie's words were mumbled around a mouthful of macaroni and cheese. Besides that her plate held three Jell-O salads and a corn muffin. 'Fossils are cool. But most science is boring.'

'How about snakes?' Marty asked, and Romey flicked a smile at her. He remembered her blacksnake too.

'Eww!' Janie exclaimed. 'They're slimy and awful!'

'No, slugs are slimy, not snakes,' Marty said. 'Snakes are nice and dry.'

'Unless they're swimming,' Romey offered.

'Snakes can swim?' Chrissie asked.

'Some can,' Romey said.

Marty mused, 'Don't know how they do it with no hands or feet.'

'Yeah.' Chrissie's dark eyes sparked with interest. She took another bite of macaroni and thought about snakes swimming. Marty noticed Aunt Vonnie's friend Melva excusing herself to go refill her iced tea.

Janie was ready to change the subject. 'Hey, Chrissie, you know that Pearl Jam line: "Can't see, I can only stare?"'

Chrissie rolled her eyes. 'In "Alive"? You mean "just" – "just stare".'

Marty left the girls to work out what their raucous heroes were saying and nudged Aunt Vonnie. 'Got a question.'

'Mm?' Aunt Vonnie had chosen chicken fricassee tonight.

Marty's hands tensed on her glass of tea. 'I was, um, looking at some old files today and ran across the one about Dad's accident.'

Aunt Vonnie frowned, but she was still chewing and couldn't voice her skepticism that Marty just happened to run across it. Romey didn't say anything, but he was watching Marty too.

She made her fingers relax and went on, 'I wanted to ask about something Mama said. She told them Dad had called her that night and said Walt had evidence about the stolen guns. Who's Walt?'

Aunt Vonnie took a swallow of iced tea. 'Walt Seifert. Turned out he had evidence because he'd stolen them.'

'Walt Seifert? Todd Seifert's father?'

'That's the one. Always a no-good.'

'So Dad was going to give evidence against him?'

Aunt Vonnie looked at her, exasperated. 'Course not! They'd been drinking together at that bar. Buddies, you know? Marie said your father told her someone else stole the guns and his good buddy Walt bought a couple. But it turned out it was Walt who did it. Went to jail for stealing those guns, got out and spent a few years drinking and loafing around, then ran off and left Sue with the boys and a drinking problem of her own.'

Chrissie said, 'Cody Seifert drinks too,' and casually popped some corn muffin into her mouth while watching bright-eyed to see if she'd shocked the adults.

But Marty already knew about Cody, had picked him up three years ago lying blind drunk in the middle of a road. His two older brothers weren't quite as drunk and were watching over him, sort of, trying to figure out what to do. She said, 'It's a real bad situation there. How old is Cody now? Twelve?'

'Yeah, but he's like two years behind us in school because he got held back a year.'

'Well, steer clear of him and his brothers. And his friends,' Marty said.

'OK,' said Chrissie slowly.

Too slowly. Marty's radar went on alert. 'What's the problem?'

'Nothing.'

Marty looked at Janie, who fidgeted and finally said, 'See, his brother Damon is so cute. Looks like Eddie Vedder.'

Like who? was obviously the wrong answer. Romey stepped in to save her. 'You're right, he does, Janie. He knows it too: the hair, the chains, the torn jeans. You think when his voice changes he'll be able to sing like Vedder too?'

'That creep Damon? No way!' Chrissie was indignant. 'Nobody can sing like Eddie!'

Problem solved, for the next few days anyway. Marty's eyes roved over the hall to see if Coach was around. Might be working today. She saw Shirley Cochran alone – if being

145

with half a dozen friends counted as alone. Marty said, 'Be right back,' and went to talk to Shirley.

'Hi, Marty honey, how are things?'

'Fine, thanks, Mrs Cochran. I thought of another question for Coach. Is he working tonight?'

'Yes, he is.'

Fran Russell, sitting next to Shirley, said lightly, 'He's always working.'

But Shirley looked uncharacteristically serious and Marty asked quietly, 'How is the new job working out? He never complains to me.'

'He doesn't complain much,' Shirley admitted. 'But you know that fellow Rueger? Owns Rockland Mall? Wes says he called to offer him a security job, but I could tell he thought he'd be bored. He misses being sheriff.'

'He was the best,' Marty said, and Fran nodded vigorously.

Shirley looked across at Sheriff Pierce, who was talking to Pastor Kemble. 'You know what bothered him most? When Chuck Pierce cancelled that youth program. Wes knew there would be a lot of changes. But he'd just got the funding for that program. He was thinking of it like sort of a legacy.'

'Yeah, it was a really good idea,' Marty said. 'Aunt Vonnie and I were just talking about the Seifert boys. Todd's in jail again, you know. And I wonder, if they could have met someone like Coach, if maybe things would have turned out better for them.'

Fran Russell frowned in skepticism, but Shirley nodded. 'Yeah, that's the way Wes looked at it. Can't save them all, but some kids can use a second chance. And he thought of it as a way to remember our Billy too.'

'Yeah, it was a good idea,' Marty said. 'Maybe someday some other group will fund it. Anyway, tell him I'll be looking for him tomorrow.'

Arlene took a plate decorated with a strawberry vine from Liv, scraped it, put it in her dishwasher. 'Mark says I should get a full-time maid,' she said, 'but now that the kids are grown, what would I do? And I have to admit, I enjoy taking care of my things.'

Liv fetched her another plate. 'They're lovely,' she said.

146

'How about Mark? Does he mind being retired? He seemed to like the horses, but he was pretty quiet.' And he'd gone off for a solitary walk after dinner.

Arlene shook her head. 'I don't know, honey. He seemed happy to retire. On the other hand, he had a real bad reaction to your father's death. I mean, of course he would, but he was so blue I called the priest to talk to him. Since then it's kind of up and down with him. One day I found him staring at a little string with knots in it, tears running down his cheeks. Just a grimy little string!'

Liv paused an instant, remembering that after Pops died, while she was cleaning out his clothes, she'd noticed in his bathrobe pocket a little gray string with knots in it.

Arlene went on, 'Anyway, I think seeing you will help. We all have happy memories of those days in Connecticut.'

'Yeah, we do. Do you mean Mark was, like, suicidal?' Liv handed her the dessert plates.

'Oh, I don't know how serious he was. He'd have times he seemed to think he was to blame for the problems of the entire world. Father Como helped him, I think. It's true, we all have crosses to bear in this life.'

'That's true.' Liv was remembering her own reactions to Pops's murder. Not exactly suicidal, except for those moments of drowning in the black ooze. And there were moments of scarlet anger at his murderer. And moments of guilt when she found herself enjoying the spring breezes or watching the Times Square ball drop when he'd never ever do it again.

But not the guilt Arlene had just described. Sometimes Pops had been really down, those last years. No spoken threats of suicide, but really blue. What had Arlene just said about Mark? Seemed to think he was to blame for the problems of the entire world? Liv wondered if Pops had felt like that.

They got the dishwasher started and Liv went to the spacious bedroom they'd given her. She tried to call Elena on her cellphone but apparently out here in the country she couldn't get through. So she asked Arlene's permission and called on the Luganos' land line to give Elena the number. 'Just for emergencies. Can't really talk on their line,' she said. 'I'll call tomorrow from downtown.'

'We'll be climbing those Maya temples tomorrow,' Elena said.

'Damn. Well, I'll figure out a way to call tomorrow night.'
Liv hung up, irritated, wondering why the hell she'd come.

Wes was taking off his jacket after his evening check of the Asphodel Springs Resort boundary fence when his phone rang.

'Hi, Champ.'

'Hi, Shirl. Thought you were at the church supper.'

'Just got back. I've been thinking about Bob Rueger's offer.'

'The one you said you wouldn't accept for a zillion dollars?'

'That was Arizona. I'm talking about Rockland, right here.'

Wes rubbed the back of his neck. 'Seems to me Asphodel Springs is just as good.'

'Not if you get Rueger to fund a youth program.'

'What?'

'He could get those old airport buildings next to the mall cheap, I bet. Remodel them into the Billy Cochran Memorial Gym. And if you run the program it'll be terrific.'

'Christ, Shirl, you do want a zillion dollars!'

Shirley laughed. 'I'm not saying he'll give it to you. But you're worth it. And you know we need that youth program.'

He was silent. The Billy Cochran Memorial Gym. Goddamn.

She said, 'You weren't going to take the job anyway, the way it was. So ask him to add on enough to make it worthwhile. What've you got to lose?'

'Shirl, honey, you are one nutty lady.'

'Love you too, Champ. Promise me you'll ask.'

He hesitated, realized that his head was reluctant but his gut was delighted at the idea. 'I'll give it a shot,' he promised.

Romey had driven them to the church supper in his Taurus and took them back afterwards. As he helped carry in Aunt Vonnie's picnic basket, now holding the soiled dishes, he asked Aunt Vonnie, 'OK if I borrow Marty for a few minutes?'

'Go right ahead,' Aunt Vonnie smiled. She'd never gotten along with Brad but she liked Romey, a local boy even if he

148

had been around the world. She added, 'But get her back in time to write some checks. Heat bill's due day after tomorrow.'

'Oh, right,' Marty said. 'And the credit card's due soon too. OK, I won't be long.'

She got back into the Taurus, looked across the dark fields. No moon tonight, the clouds were still up there. 'What are we doing?' she asked him.

'Got a question for you.' He turned the ignition and drove a quarter-mile toward Dunning, pulling off the road where they were out of sight of Marty's house but could see the lights of the town glimmering through the bare branches. He left the heater running.

'So what's up?' she asked.

'I was wondering what was in that file that makes you so tense.'

Marty winced. 'Nothing. I don't want to talk about it.'

'I know. You don't even want to think about it. You're spending half your energy right now keeping it away.'

Dammit, sometimes he knew her too well. She said angrily, 'So don't make it harder for me!'

'It's hard. Like that song Chrissie and Janie were arguing about. All that pain in it. About a guy whose father died when he was thirteen.'

'You're kidding! I never really listened.'

'The young guy wonders if he deserves to die because he can't or shouldn't replace his father. Wanna hear a story?'

'You and your stories!' She watched a pickup climb the hill from Dunning and pass them. The photo kept nudging at her mind. She said, 'Yeah, tell me.'

'You've heard of Medusa?'

'Yeah – too ugly to look at. Snakes for hair.'

'Y'know, I always thought that could have been attractive. Depends on how she styled them.'

A laugh escaped Marty and she punched him in the arm. He patted her fist and went on, 'Anyway, point is, she was turning all these guys to stone, so a hero-type decided to kill her. But he had a problem. He had to look at her to aim the blow, but if he looked at her he'd turn to stone too. So he asked Athena for help. The babe who hangs out in the Acropolis?'

'Yeah, guarding people.'

149

'Yeah. She gave him a shiny shield, and told him to use it like a rear-view mirror. That way he could back up and slice off Medusa's head without looking at her directly. But the other interesting thing is what happened to the head.'

'What happened?'

'Athena put it on her own personal shield. So its power was channelled to help people.'

'Cool.' His hand was still on her fist. She turned her hand palm-up to lace her fingers through his and said, 'OK, listen up, rear-view mirror. There was a photo. Black-and-white official photo, taken early on while the fire was mostly in the rear.' Tears were starting down her face but it didn't matter. 'And my dad was slumped over the wheel. Unconscious from the impact. Or already dead, I don't know – the flames had just broken into the passenger compartment behind him. But that wasn't – I mean, I've imagined worse scenes for him.' She had to stop.

Romey squeezed her hand and in a moment asked, 'What was it, then?'

'I don't know. Something about that El Camino. He was obsessed with it, always tinkering. Washed it every weekend, remember? And I was so proud when he let me help him wax it. I knew every inch of that damn vehicle. And seeing that photo – I guess I never thought about the El Camino. Just made it all fresh. That front fender I'd polished was buckled up all the way to the passenger windshield, flames coming out the back corner of the truckbed – wait a minute.' She paused, staring through tears at the faraway lights of cars at a traffic light in the town but seeing the photo in her mind. 'Couldn't have happened the way they say.'

'What do you mean?'

'OK, this part is probably right: he's going too fast, can't make the curve, goes tearing into the ditch.' She used her free hand to demonstrate in the dashboard light. 'He's correcting, turning the wheel hard to get back on the road, still going sixty or whatever, front fender smashes into the tree.' Her fingertips touched the gear shift and she curled her fingers to show the crumpling.

Romey shook his head. 'So what's the problem?'

'The fire started in the back. That's where the fuel tank was, between the back wheels. But there was nothing for the back to hit, except . . .' She jerked upright. 'Romey, there were little holes!'

He was frowning. 'Little holes? What does that mean?'

'It means – well, maybe there's another explanation. But I think it means someone was shooting at him, and got the gas tank, and that's what knocked him off the road. Damn, I got a lot to ask Coach about!'

Twenty-One

The Arctic air was centered over Indiana now, cold but bringing bright-blue skies for the day, though more snow was promised for tomorrow. Marty hadn't slept well, jolting awake frequently, her mind wheeling from memories of the El Camino to images of the burning cabin – was that only two nights ago? She was almost glad for the wake-up screech of Pearl Jam claiming to still be alive. At the station, the morning briefing was quick because Sheriff Pierce wanted to get on the road quickly. 'I'm going to speak to Mark Lugano,' he said. 'Culp, I want you to talk to Maudie Corson again. Push her a little about the South American thing.'

Marty said, 'Sir, I was wondering if Zill sent his mother any postcards or photos from South America. Might help us figure out where he was.'

'Yeah, ask about that, Culp,' the sheriff agreed. 'If you get anything, check with Detective Lyons in Indianapolis. See if it fits with what he's learning about Sarge Bowers. Mason, I want you to talk to the state evidence technicians. If they haven't come up with another answer, find out if there's any support for the idea of our perp getting away through the trees.'

'Yes, sir.'

'Neal, you stand by to cover any calls that Grady gets. Hopkins.' He paused, looked at her. 'I want you to stay on background for Corson.'

'Yes, sir.' Not unexpected, but she was disappointed even so.

Howie Culp cleared his throat. 'Sir?'

'Yeah?'

'What's the FBI doing?'

Pierce said, 'They're in Indianapolis, checking first with Lyons about the Bowers case. Agent Jessup said next he'd go interview Jumbo Jim and Maudie Corson, and his partner will liaise with the state evidence technicians. So you guys better get there first. Go!'

'Yessir!' The deputies scattered.

There were two messages waiting for Marty at her desk. The first was from Joanne Quick, the librarian. 'Oh, hi, Marty,' she said when Marty returned the call. 'I got in early today and there was a fax waiting for me from my friend Meg. The one in Ohio? She found three different Eugenes that year who were killed.'

Maybe one was the man Liv Mann's father had known. Marty said, 'That was speedy!'

'Yeah, Meg's good. But the fax machine isn't. The print is pretty faint. Don't know if I can fax them again.'

'Oh, don't bother; I should be able to pick them up in a few minutes.'

Marty also returned the other call, from Liv Mann. 'Hi, it's Deputy Hopkins. You've got a new phone number.'

'Yeah, I'm at the Luganos. My cellphone doesn't work from here.' Her voice rose a little to call, 'Just a sec, Arlene, let me get rid of this call.' Much lower, she said, 'Hope you're the right person to talk to, because I've only got a minute. We're about to go horseback riding. Anyway, this is from our unofficial source. Your guy Zill Corson used to work for a company called Armadillo.'

'Armad— Jesus!'

Liv picked up on the excitement in Marty's voice. She said, 'Did Corson have one too? A little ceramic armadillo in his pocket? Like my dad?'

Like her dad. Marty said, 'Thanks, I gotta pass this on right now. Um, better tell Mark Lugano that the sheriff is on his way over to ask a few questions.'

'Oh.' Surprise in her voice. 'OK, 'bye.'

Marty hung up and ran out coatless to the parking lot, the icy air nipping her nose and fingers. Sheriff Pierce was talking through the window of Howie Culp's cruiser. Marty said, 'Sir, excuse me.'

'Yeah? What is it, Hopkins?'

Marty didn't want to talk about sources, so she said only, 'Just got a call about the security company Zill used to work for—'

'Pinkett's?'

'No, the one before. It was called Armadillo.'

Sheriff Pierce stared at her, brows rising as he made the connection. Howie Culp was saying, 'Yeah, that's right. Don Foley called me back last night with that name. Haven't had a chance yet to – what?'

Both Marty and Sheriff Pierce were staring at him. The sheriff said, 'You knew it was called Armadillo?'

'Yeah, Armadillo Security. He said last night he'd just remembered the name.'

Chuck Pierce muttered something under his breath. Teeth starting to chatter, Marty said, 'Sir, something else. Liv Mann just called. Said her father's body was found with a little ceramic armadillo in his pocket.'

'Jesus! Just like Zill! But . . .'

'Yeah,' Marty said. 'A big but. Ronald Mann never worked for Armadillo Security. Um . . . that's all I've got, sir.'

'Go see what background you can find on Armadillo, Hopkins. Don't call them; I'll do it when I get back from Lugano's.' The sheriff's voice was tight and he was glaring at Howie Culp.

As she climbed the steps to the station, Marty wondered how Howie had missed the connection last night when Foley had told him. She looked at the official file and saw the problem. Dr Altmann had listed the contents of Zill's pockets, but with his usual scientific caution had described the armadillo only as a 'ceramic animal, 2½ inches long'. She and Sheriff Pierce had seen the thing, but if they'd only read Doc's description they might not have made the connection either.

At her computer again, she looked up Armadillo Security. They had a website but it wasn't very informative: Security and Threat Assessment, Security Operations, US or International. There was a 'Contact Us' e-mail and phone number. She thought a moment. She didn't have any first-hand knowledge of security companies but she knew people who knew: Coach Cochran, who'd said that they made lots of money and could pay for pensions; Jumbo Jim Corson, who'd said they paid for Zill's medical.

And Jumbo Jim had also said he didn't know much about Zill's job. Zill 'never talked about work. Have to keep your mouth shut just like the military.'

Yeah, Sheriff Pierce was right: he'd better be the one to call Armadillo. A mere deputy wouldn't have a chance. She wrote down the contact numbers and a note, 'Should we pass this on to the FBI?' and left it for the sheriff.

Then she stood up, stretched, reached for her coat. 'Hey, Grady, gotta pick up some background stuff at the library,' she said. 'I'll be back in ten minutes.'

'OK.'

At the door, she hesitated. Deputy Neal had just left his desk and headed for the men's room. There was no one else around. She approached the tall dispatch desk and said, 'Grady, I got a question.'

'Yeah?' He looked at her kindly. Grady had been one of the first to accept her as a teammate on the job.

She said, 'You investigated that crash that killed my dad.'

He gave her an uneasy glance. 'Yeah, a long time ago.'

'I know. Aunt Vonnie said my dad called my mother from the bar that night. And my mother said he was going to talk to Wes Cochran about some weapons Walt Seifert had.'

Looking thoughtful, Grady pushed back from the desk with his good arm. His movement was stiffer since he'd been wounded but he was still lean, still angular as a derrick. 'Yeah, that sounds right. Walt went to jail for stealing guns from that shop out on the Terre Haute highway.'

'But Aunt Vonnie said my dad's story was that Walt didn't steal them.'

'Yeah, well . . .' Grady looked uncomfortable. 'See, that was what Walt said, and maybe your dad bought it, but a jury convicted Walt.'

Marty heard the unsaid *Your dad bought the story because he was drunk.* She asked evenly, 'What was Walt's story exactly?'

'Oh, hell, Marty, I don't remember! I wasn't in charge of that investigation. I was barely past the rookie stage, so with something like a major robbery Cowgill would give it to someone senior, or do it himself. Even the crash – I think he only put me on it because Cochran was too close to your father to be, you know, objective.' He was still uncomfortable.

'Yeah, that makes sense,' Marty said. 'In the crash investigation, did you figure out how my dad's vehicle got those shots in the back fender?'

155

'No, when I told . . .' Grady stopped, frowned. 'Did Vonnie know that too? Cowgill said it was probably old damage so not to put it in the report. Didn't want to make it harder for Marie.'

'You went along with that?' She wanted to shake Grady, sweet easygoing Grady, never wanting to make trouble unless ordered to.

'Hey, Cowgill was the sheriff, plus it was open and shut that the crash and fire was – you know.'

'Yeah, I know.' Deputy Neal was coming out of the men's room, so she shifted a little. 'Do you remember if Walt Seifert had a lawyer?'

'Yeah, court-appointed. Had a jury trial. What was that guy's name? Died a few years ago – oh, call coming in.'

Grady turned to his switchboard in relief, and Marty gave up for the moment. 'See you in ten,' she said, and went out into the bright cold.

She'd call Coach Cochran, maybe have lunch. Even though Cowgill had taken him off the case, he may have wondered about the damage to the rear of the El Camino. And he was her dad's friend. He would have thought about it more than Grady.

From the Luganos' glassed-in side porch Liv could see the three horses in the paddock, stamping and puffing steamy breath. She felt like stamping and puffing too, impatient for the ride, impatient to hear what the sheriff had to say. She unzipped her new lime-green parka, which was a lot better for a cold ride than her black New York coat. Mark and Arlene also wore their warm jackets. They had riding boots too. Liv wished she'd known to bring hers. Well, she'd ridden in hiking boots before.

Next to her Mark stood gazing gloomily at the horses. When she'd told them the sheriff was on his way, he'd said, 'Let's go riding anyway! He can come back later.'

But Arlene had said, 'Oh, let's get it over with. Shouldn't take that long,' and it was so obviously the right answer that he'd shrugged and led the way to the paddock, where they'd given the horses to Carrie to unsaddle.

Now he turned to look out the front of the porch as the cruiser came slowly up the driveway and stopped. The sheriff got out and Arlene opened the door of the porch to wave at him. 'Sheriff Pierce! Around here.'

He nodded and walked the short distance to the porch. 'Hello, Miz Lugano, Mr Lugano, Miz Mann. I'm Sheriff Pierce – guess you know that. Hey, nice-looking horses you got back there!' He cast an admiring glance through the glass.

Mark was wearing a friendly smile, no trace now of the slumped shoulders of a moment ago. 'Yes, we were about to go for a ride when we saw you coming,' he said.

'Well, I'll try to keep this as short as I can,' said Pierce. 'It might take a few minutes because I want to talk to you separately. The two of you, not Miz Mann, because we've already spoken to her.'

No, no! I want to hear! Liv thought. Mark, still friendly, still alert, said, 'Well, if it's about Mr Corson's death it won't take long. We didn't know him at all.'

'I'm sure, sir, but we have some other questions. Now, if the ladies will excuse us?'

'Oh, that's all right, we can wait here,' Arlene said, moving protectively toward her husband.

Mark smiled down at her, put his hands on her shoulders, said, 'Sheriff Pierce wants to talk to us one at a time. As you say, let's get it over with.' He gave her a tiny push toward the kitchen door.

'Are you sure?' Arlene was clearly surprised that she wasn't welcome.

The two men stood smiling at her, unmoving. Damn, Liv thought, it's hopeless; I'll have to grill Mark about it later. 'Let's go, Arlene.' Liv tugged at her elbow and pulled her through the door.

Once in the living room, Liv knelt to adjust her boot as the door closed slowly behind her. She heard the sheriff ask, 'Now, Mr Lugano, I apologize for bothering you but we're trying to get information about a few things. Have you heard of a man named John Bowers?'

'I knew a Johnny Bowers in high school, and later . . .' Mark replied.

The door clicked shut and Liv couldn't hear any more. Frustrated, she stood and followed Arlene toward the kitchen. Who was Johnny Bowers? But she couldn't think because Arlene was full of irritating complaints. 'It's such a shame for you to be missing your ride! And what does all this have to do with Mark and me?' she wailed.

Liv tried to keep her temper. 'Maybe nothing, but we should help them if we can. I really want to find out who killed my father.'

'Oh, yes, honey, of course,' Arlene said. She looked back at the porch door, and Liv saw fear in her face. 'What could Mark know? Why is he so upset?'

'He hasn't told me,' Liv almost snapped. She wanted to hear what Mark was telling the sheriff. Shut out again. The thick blackness was beginning to rise. She said, 'Arlene, could you let me take a quick ride on my own? The sheriff said he didn't want to talk to me and I'm really itching to do it.'

'Won't you get lost on the trails?'

'Your trails are well marked, Arlene.' Liv took a deep breath, tried not to let her desperation into her voice. 'See, the problem is, if I'm going to get any riding in, it has to be now. I have an appointment in town at eleven thirty. How about I meet you back here at ten? Then if the sheriff is finished we can at least have a short ride together.' And maybe Mark would tell her what it was about.

'Sure, honey.' Arlene smiled at her, but Liv was already half out the kitchen door.

Twenty-Two

Wes Cochran replaced the receiver and walked across the dining room to lean in the door of the kitchen. 'Rueger said yes.'

Shirley turned wide-eyed from the cupboard where she'd been stowing her just-washed rosebud-pattern breakfast dishes. 'Yes? Just like that?'

'Course not – plenty of ifs. Like he said not to breathe a word until he'd closed on the airfield property. That goes for you too.'

'That's great!' Shirley stood there beaming at him.

'I'd be three-quarter-time security, one-quarter running the youth sports program. See, Rueger thinks what we need here is not just a youth program, but a whole sports complex including a youth program. He wants to build a pretty big one – indoor track, gymnastics, weight room, and basketball court. Pool to come later. Rockland Sports Center, he'll call it. And I said, not good enough.'

'What?' Shirley looked amazed.

Wes still felt amazed himself. 'I told him, wait a minute, my wife wants the basketball court named in memory of our son. And he said, the Billy Cochran Gym in the Rockland Sports Center.' He grinned at her. 'I'm supposed to check and see if you'll accept that.'

She skipped across the kitchen to give him a big hug. Rosy-cheeked Shirley was as pink and white as her kitchen, dressed today in a white turtleneck and a jacket of a funny warm pink the color of a puppy's tongue. She probably called it geranium or hibiscus or something. Even after thirty-some years of marriage he'd never mastered the lingo. But he knew she meant it when she said, 'I accept! But do you?'

'Aah, nothing to accept yet. May all fall through. But if he

159

gets his act together I'll do it. It'd be great to be working with kids again – having a job that makes a difference.'

'Champ, you're a – a – champ!' She kissed him, then looked at her watch. Today she was going to a state-wide church conference on hunger in Africa. 'Hey, I gotta go try to make a difference too. Laurie's going to be here in a couple minutes to take me to Indianapolis. Could you put away those yearbooks before you go out? I better go freshen up.' She disappeared down the hall.

'OK,' Wes said to her retreating pink back. He started for the living room but paused to answer the phone. 'Cochran.'

'Hi, Coach, it's Marty.' He heard a rumbling in the background.

'How's it going?' he asked.

'You heard about Bowers.'

'Yeah.'

'FBI's here now, you know how it goes. But I wondered if I could see you during my lunch break.' There was a honk and a grinding of gears. She must be crossing the square.

He said, 'Sure. I'll meet you noonish. Soup & Sprouts – I get points with Shirley if I go there. Is this about Bowers?'

'Not Bowers. My father.'

He frowned. 'What do you mean?'

'My mother said he was rushing to see you that night because he wanted to tell you about Walt Seifert. What was he going to tell you?'

'I don't know, Marty. It didn't happen. Why are you bringing this up now?'

'There were holes in the back fender. I gotta go; see you at the Sprouts.'

Wes hung up slowly. What was she talking about? He'd spent half his life trying to forget that crash. It was loony to dredge it up again. He wished he hadn't promised to meet her about this.

Wes went to the little table by the fireplace to get the yearbooks. The top book was still open to the Bs because Johnny Bowers' death had been on the news last night. He looked again at the young soon-to-be Marine, flipped back to the sports pages where Bowers appeared in the team photo. Johnny had changed from a real Marine into a soldier-for-hire for that security company. Had he felt the same kind of frustration

Wes had at Asphodel Springs? Nah, must have been different, he decided. From what he heard, the overseas assignments were sometimes exciting, gunfights every now and then, so you'd get your adrenalin fix instead of a steady diet of Mrs Harkett-type problems.

God, he hoped this Rueger job would work out.

Mark Lugano was in the team photo too, young and handsome, preparing to go out into the world and get rich. Chuck Pierce must have spoken to him by now, must have asked him about Bowers. Mark had known Ronnie Mann too, in the math club. Wes flipped a few pages and looked at that photo again. Yes, there they were, the brains of the class, Mark and Ronnie and the others—

A horn sounded outside and Shirley rushed by in her pink jacket, pausing only to give him a peck on the cheek. 'See you tonight, Champ,' she called as she put on her coat.

''Bye, Shirl.' He glanced at her with an automatic smile, but his mind was still on that photo.

McGabben. It had been funny little Wink McGabben he'd seen yesterday in that Honda on the square. Wink McGabben, his squint hidden by the dark glasses.

What the hell was McGabben doing back in town?

Blueberry seemed happy to be moving at last, his head high and his step springy as he left the paddock. Nice horses the Luganos had. Liv decided that if she ever made any money at the law game she'd give a pass to the limos and yachts, go for horses instead. Blueberry's breath puffed white in the morning sunlight and Liv tried to settle into the rhythm of his walk. She really wanted to be running, something more strenuous, to keep the blackness away. It was so frustrating to have this lead about Johnny Bowers dangled before her, and then be shut out by the sheriff. Who was Bowers? Mark had known him in high school. Had her father known him too? She couldn't remember him ever being mentioned. Would Mark tell her why the sheriff was asking about Bowers? If not, maybe after she spoke to Alejandro she should stop at the high school, see if they had any records of the years when her father and Bowers had been there.

And Mark. Mark had been there too. He knew something,

she was sure. About Corson's death? Corson had been a younger man but he'd lived in this county, had probably gone to that high school. But Mark and her father had left the county right after high school. He claimed he didn't know Corson. But he had known Bowers, and maybe Bowers had stayed in the county and had a connection to Corson. Damn, this was all so vague.

At the corner of the paddock several trails angled away. She chose one that led toward the limestone bluff Mark had shown her yesterday, where he said a creek marked the edge of his property, and turned Blueberry's head that way.

Mark knew something, about Corson or about Bowers, or something. Arlene was worried about him, about his dark mood recently. Did Arlene know whatever it was? Liv wondered if it had to do with Ecuador. Mark had been there, but not the same time as her father, and not with the deep connection her father had gained with his Ecuadorian wife. But he'd been her father's friend, and maybe her father had confided in him.

Dammit, so many questions! But now the trail required her attention. The footing was sometimes icy, though the frozen ground had been blown bare in many places. The trail was descending a hill now, the woods around them a black tangle of trunks and branches that rattled in the wind. The trail was steeper than the one they'd ridden yesterday, so Liv stayed alert for signs that Blueberry was having trouble. The big gray horse seemed confident, though. He turned a corner and followed the trail down. It was probably taking them down to the creek. Mark and Arlene had kept the trail free of brush. Must be nice here by the little creek in the summer.

The cliff of smoke-gray limestone was on her right now, maybe fifty yards away, and she realized that it was much higher than she'd thought because yesterday she'd seen only the part above the trees and hadn't realized how far down the creek was. The trail made another switchback so the bluff was now on her left, and soon they were following the creek. It was small, flowing slowly between icy edges, and curving in a long scalloped arc. On this side there was a flat area, a tiny flood plain filled with brush and scrub trees at the foot of the wooded hill she'd just descended. On the other side the cliff rose more abruptly from the edge of the water. In a couple of places tumbled rocks showed where the creek had undermined the stone.

She had ridden about a quarter of a mile when Blueberry's ears swiveled and he raised his head and snorted, looking across the creek, just as something landed on the trail. Liv pulled up, scanning the opposite bank. A voice said, 'Sorry, you startled me. I dropped my water bottle.'

She hadn't been looking up far enough. She saw him then: a man wearing gray and khaki clothes standing about forty feet up the cliffside. 'God, how'd you get up there?' Liv asked, scanning the blank cliff. 'Oh, are you a rock climber?'

'Yeah, sorry I scared your horse.'

His accent was local, friendly, like her father's. She said, 'Oh, he's fine. You're going to need your water.' As she dismounted to get it, Liv remembered her lesson on the gym climbing wall in Brooklyn. She'd enjoyed that strenuous afternoon. She knotted Blueberry's reins around a slender tree and picked up the bottle, then squinted up at the man again and called, 'D'you want to throw down a rope or something so you can pull it up?'

He was already pushing his rope into a couple of those spring-loaded D-shaped clips – what had the guy at the gym called them? Beaners or something – that were tied to attachments behind him in the cliffside. He answered, 'Oh, I'll come fetch it. This is an easy climb, won't take a minute.' He tossed down the ends of the rope and a moment later he was rappelling smoothly down the limestone, landing lightly on the narrow bank across the creek. Liv found herself watching hungrily, as though her muscles were jealous of his.

'Looks like fun,' she said. 'Only climbing I've ever done is on a wall in a New York City gym.'

He was pulling gloves on over his white-taped hands. 'New York? I've taught climbing there.' His face was weathered and she realized he was older than she thought – fifties maybe, though he moved like a young guy. He was wearing gray-tinted glasses. Behind them he seemed to be squinting, reassessing his opinion of her. He asked almost shyly, 'Do you want to try it here? It's a whole different experience in the wild.'

It was tempting. Liv hesitated, and he added, 'My name is Gabby.'

'I'm Liv. I've got to meet some friends . . .' She looked at her watch. It had taken Blueberry only ten minutes to get here. She still had an hour to kill. 'Hey, I've got a few minutes. Let me give it a try.' Elena would be amazed. Liv patted her jacket to make sure her own water bottle was there, found a couple of stepping stones in the creek, and took Gabby's bottle across to him.

Joanne Quick had paper-clipped the faxes together for Marty. There were copies of three newspaper articles and two obituaries, and Joanne was right: they were all faint, barely legible in places. The photo that accompanied one article was just a gray smear. 'This'll take a while. I'll read them in the office,' Marty told Joanne. 'But while I'm here, I wonder if you have some good maps of South America.'

'Natch.' Joanne was wearing an orangey plaid jacket today. She led Marty to the oversize reference books and pulled one out. 'Here you are. Oh, wait – this one is more up-to-date.'

Marty carried the two big volumes to the nearest library table and opened the newer one. OK, here was Peru. She pulled out her notepad: May Gordon got her mail in Lima or Santo Tomas. Lima was pretty obvious, but Santo Tomas she couldn't find. Wasn't in the index. What was the name of that petrified forest May had taken the children to see? Marty looked at her notes again. Puyango. No town but the index had a Puyango river, up in the north of Peru, Pacific side of the mountains. It ran into the Zarumilla and, sure enough, there was the petrified forest, near the junction. Why wasn't it in the index? There was a dotted line along the Zarumilla. That meant it was part of the border between Peru and . . .

Oh, shit, Ecuador.

The damn petrified forest was in Ecuador! Marty turned the page of the atlas to the Ecuador map and found the index. Puyango was a river, yes, and a petrified forest, and even a town in Ecuador. What about Santo Tomas? No, still not in the index.

Marty still had the copy of the newspaper article with the photo of May Gordon and the kids. She pulled it out. Joanne's microfilm printer was a lot better at photos than her fax machine. You could see May's wild mop of corkscrew curls, her melting smile, and you could see a road making switchbacks up a hillside behind her to the left. Definitely in the mountains.

Marty turned back to the Ecuador map. It showed hills on both sides of the Puyango, steeper on the southeast side as they worked their way up to the Andes. Some towns there, a tributary river called La Joya, a big lake with the same name. The river ran through it. That gave her an idea.

She opened the older atlas, checked the date: 1965, OK. She opened to Ecuador, found the petrified forest again. No lake in this old atlas. Just the La Joya river and on its banks, yes, several towns not shown in the newer atlas. Not shown because they no longer existed. They were under water. Someone had built a dam.

One of the towns was called Santo Tomas.

In Ecuador, not Peru.

Damn – she had to talk to Liv again, and Alejandro, and especially to those Gordon sisters.

'You better take this,' Gabby said, unbuckling the harness and slipping it off. He'd already removed the rappel hardware and clipped it on to his shoulder sling. 'I can belay you from my belt if I anchor myself to this bush.'

Liv took the harness and stepped into the leg loops. She exclaimed, 'Oh, God, I've just got hiking boots! I need shoes like yours. Better not do this.'

Gabby shrugged. 'I learned to climb in boots. And this rock is nice and dry because it's a ridge – not much water to seep out and freeze. Easy.'

'Maybe to you,' Liv said, eyeing the cliffside dubiously. 'Well, at least I've got rubber soles, sort of.' She buckled the harness around her waist.

Gabby said, 'Double back the end to lock the buckle.'

'Oh, right! The instructor at the gym told us that about fifteen times. There's some kind of alphabetical safety list, right?'

Gabby nodded. 'Anchor – done. Belay –' He showed her that he'd threaded the rope through the simple locking slide device. 'Carabiners – they're on your harness correctly. Always check to be sure they're locked. Doubling back your buckle is D.'

'E is the eight-knot, right?' Liv said. 'But I've forgotten how to do it.'

Gabby showed her how to make the figure eight, handed her the end of the rope. 'Pass it through your waist and leg loops both – that's right. Now follow the figure eight around with the end of the rope so the knot is doubled – right.'

Liv fussed with the rope loops for a moment, making sure they lay neatly before tightening the knot, and Gabby nodded his approval as he pulled a roll of surgical tape from his jacket pocket. 'Now let's tape your hands because you've got to grip hard and this rock can take off skin like a cheese grater.' He taped around her knuckles, between her fingers, ending with a spiral down to her wrist and back. 'OK. You're ready.'

Liv looked around. Behind her the creek burbled quietly between its icy edges. On the far side Blueberry stood waiting contentedly by the woods where branches made black patterns against the snow. Ahead of her the limestone rose, a symphony of grays from smoky to tawny, only the faraway top lit by the slanting morning sun. She felt a pulse of adrenalin. But when she scanned the nearby surface for holds she saw only a couple of good ones.

Gabby cleared his throat. 'Save you a little time,' he said. 'My advice would be to do the first ten feet over here to the left. Then you've got a couple of good holds – see that little ledge? – to take you sideways over next to where the rope is hanging. The next twenty feet are straightforward, you'll see.'

She moved left, saw the vertical crack in the rock he was talking about, little protuberances and pockets of erosion to the right of the crack. Looked good. She said, 'OK. And the anchor up there for the rope is good?'

'Two solid anchors. Both bombproof.'

'And you're ready to belay?' She glanced back at Gabby to make sure.

'You're on belay.'

'Here I go.'

'Climb away, Liv.'

Twenty-Three

Back at the office, Marty phoned the Gordon sisters. 'I don't think it'll take long,' she said.

Stanni said warily, 'Sure, but we have a gig in Evansville this afternoon. Have to leave before noon to set up.'

'No problem. I'll be there soon,' Marty promised.

She called Liv and Alejandro, but neither one was picking up so she left messages that she wanted to talk to them and started gathering what she'd need to talk to the Gordons. She checked to be sure the newspaper photo of May Gordon was still folded in her notepad, and tucked in the photocopies of the two Ecuador maps that she'd obtained at the library. Oh, there were the faxes from Ohio. She'd almost forgotten them. Better get them out of the way first. Marty set to work deciphering the faint print.

She began with the news articles about Ohio murders in 1985, the three who might be the 'Gene' Liv's father had mentioned. Eugene Elkins, age forty-one, had been shot in his Toledo apartment in the course of a robbery. Elkins had been a paramedic for the Toledo police. The second man, Eugene Richards, fifty-seven, had been a math teacher at a Zanesville high school. He'd recently bought a new car and was sitting late at night at a traffic light when a car thief jumped in, shoved him out the driver's door, and took off. Richards had been run over by a semi while crawling toward the shoulder. The third, Eugene Washington, sixteen, had been shot in what seemed to be a tough neighborhood of Cleveland. Didn't really fit what Liv had said because there was no robbery, plus he was really young.

Elkins was closest to Ronald Mann's age. Marty looked at his obituary.

Born in Akron. He was a Marine, discharged 1972. At the time he was killed he'd been a paramedic with the Toledo PD for three years – that meant he started in 1982. There was nothing about the ten years in between. She studied the faint numerals in the fax but she hadn't misread the dates. The '7' in 1972 was pretty clear and the 'three' was spelled out. Elkins had been survived by a wife, two sons, and a mother and sister still in Akron. That was it.

She turned from the obituary to the news article about Elkins's death. No clue there about the missing ten years. Quote from a fellow paramedic saying Gene was a good hard-working guy. Quote from a Toledo police detective named Becker saying they were following up on some leads.

Marty looked up the number, called the Toledo police. A helpful officer told her, 'No detectives named Becker, only a lab technician.'

'Probably not him. Can you connect me with anyone who was on the job in 1985? Homicide or robbery?'

'Yeah, let's see – Detective Knauer should be in today.'

In a moment another voice came on, saying, 'Knauer.'

'Detective Knauer, this is Deputy Hopkins, Nichols County, Indiana. We're working a homicide that maybe connects to an old homicide case in Toledo. I believe Detective Becker worked it.'

'Becker retired a couple years ago.'

'Yes, sir. This case was a murder and robbery, one of your paramedics. Guy named Eugene Elkins.'

'Gene Elkins! Didn't work on it directly but I remember that case 'cause, you know, he was one of ours. So was the rookie.'

'The rookie?'

'Young beat cop. Looks like he met the bad guy leaving, wounded so bad he died a week later.'

'Is the case still open?'

'Yeah, never caught the bastard.'

'Did Mr Elkins have any Indiana connections?'

'Who knows? He was Ohio born and bred.'

'Was there any sign of arson?'

Knauer sounded dubious. 'I could check the files, but nobody mentioned arson.'

'Yeah, and Mr Elkins was shot – is that right?' This was sounding less and less likely.

Knauer said, 'Yeah, the guy used one of Gene's revolvers.

Gene had quite a collection of weapons and one of them was fired, wiped clean and left in Gene's hand. Pretty clumsy attempt to fake suicide. Powder burns were all wrong.'

No fire, no known Nichols County connection. Dead end. But he'd brought up a new question. 'So Gene Elkins collected guns? But he was a paramedic.'

'He'd been a Marine and worked security before he came to Toledo.'

The missing ten years. She asked, 'Security? Was it for a company called Armadillo?'

'Damn! That sounds right but I better look in the file for you,' Knauer said. 'I asked Gene once why with his background he wasn't on a SWAT team or something, but he said he was tired of the shooting side, wanted to save lives, so he'd trained to be a paramedic. But he kept his weapons collection. Guns from all over the world, big knives.'

Marty's knuckles were white, gripping the receiver. 'Big knives?'

'Yeah, machetes mostly, like the one he used on the rookie. You know, we couldn't figure it out because the guns were worth more, but that's all the perp took. Not all of Gene's collection. Just the machetes.'

The route Gabby recommended was basically a vertical crack in the cliff, maybe an inch wide. Liv placed the inside edge of her left boot on a low horizontal wrinkle in the rock, eyed the waist-high bump that would be the foothold for her right foot, then jammed her left hand into the crack as high as she could and reached for an eroded pocket in the limestone with her right. For a moment she froze there, clinging spider-like to the rock face, too aware of the icy ground three feet below her. What next?

Gabby's reassuring voice said, 'Remember, a tripod is very stable. Shift your weight smoothly.'

OK. Both hands braced, she took her weight on her right foot, lifted her left from the low foothold and crammed the toe into an irregularity in the vertical crack a little below her left hand, then slid the hand higher in the crack. Ouch – there was the cheese-grater effect Gabby mentioned. Didn't matter: now she could reach up to a tiny ledge with her right hand. Shift weight to her left foot in the crack, bring right foot up

169

to the pocket where her hand had been. Solid. And there was the next foothold on the left, suddenly clear to her. She was completely focused, her muscles straining, her eyes searching for the next hold. As she moved, everything – the chilly air, the frozen rocks below, the scraped skin on her fingers, the safety rope that stayed just short of taut – all faded into background, and the whole bright universe condensed to this beautiful rock, these smooth instinctive moves, this vivid moment. Only later did she realize she had been completely happy.

Wes knew that Sheriff Pierce would get defensive if he asked to see the departmental files, so he went instead to the county prosecuting attorney's office.

Art Pfann had worked with him for years, on some pretty hairy cases, and didn't give him any static about looking up the old court records. 'No problem,' Art said in his booming courtroom voice, and asked his secretary to send Steven in before turning back to Wes. 'You're looking good, Cochran.'

'Younger every day,' Wes said. Way too soon to tell Art the hopeful news he'd had from Rueger. 'The records I'm after are about Walt Seifert.'

'That was before my time, but we never throw anything away,' Art told him. A young blond man came in the door. Art said, 'Wes, this is Steven Haven, intern from IU. Steven, Wes Cochran was one terrific sheriff. Give him anything he wants, starting with the Walt Seifert records from . . .' Art frowned, looked at Wes. 'Seventies, right?'

Wes nodded. 'Yeah, the crime was 1975, took a while to get it to court. Trial probably 1977.'

Young Steven was efficient and within minutes had Wes sitting in a vacant conference room with the Seifert file in front of him.

The facts were straightforward. A gun shop on the highway to Terre Haute had been burglarized one night and a number of precision handguns plus four machine guns had been taken. The robber knew his weapons: he'd taken the most expensive and ignored the run-of-the-mill. Possibly because the owner had cleaned out the cash register before closing, no money had been taken.

The robbery was discovered late that night by a state cop who'd stopped at the 7-11 next door for coffee and realized

170

an Uzi he'd admired in the window was no longer there. Peering in the front window with his flashlight, he'd seen broken glass in display cases in the room behind. He'd called the owner, put out a bulletin.

And – this part wasn't in Art Pfann's files – Wes, a deputy back then and on duty that night, had heard the bulletin. He'd mentioned it casually to his friend Rusty LaForte when he ran into him at old man Terry's service station. An hour and a half later he'd received a garbled call from Rusty, who thought he'd seen the robber or something. And fifteen minutes after that, dispatch had sent Wes to the scene of a crash-and-burn that he still couldn't bear to think about.

He looked back at the file notes. When news of the robbery hit the local radio the next day, a man came forward who'd been at the Shamrock bar, also on the Terre Haute highway. He said he'd seen Walt Seifert come in and sit next to Rusty LaForte. They talked a few minutes and the witness thought he saw a gun on the table. Shortly afterward Rusty had gone out to the parking lot, but returned almost immediately, made a couple of phone calls, and left.

One phone call was to his wife Marie, saying he'd be a little late getting home, he was going to tell the sheriff that Walt Seifert had found the gun-shop robber. The other was the garbled call Wes remembered.

The evidence against Walt was clear: he had two guns from the burglary – serial numbers proved that. According to the prosecutor's file, Walt claimed that he'd pulled into the Shamrock's parking lot the same time as a young guy in a black Camaro. Walt had paused to admire it. Pretty soon the guy – whose name was Hardy, Walt said – offered him a couple of guns cheap because he needed cash, and Walt thought it was such a good deal he couldn't pass it up. He paid Hardy and went into the bar, and even though he'd been sworn to secrecy he couldn't help bragging to his friend Rusty.

But there had been problems. The Hardy guy had never come into the bar, Walt hadn't mentioned him to anyone else until he was arrested, and by then Rusty was dead and couldn't confirm or deny Walt's account. Sheriff Cowgill had checked out black Camaros but couldn't find one owned by a Hardy.

Walt's two weapons had some fingerprints on them, Walt's and the gunshop owner's plus two prints they couldn't identify, though they'd checked them against everyone in the Shamrock and every Hardy in the files. Also, they couldn't find the other stolen weapons even though they searched Walt Seifert's place thoroughly and questioned all his friends.

Wes looked around the book-lined room. Young Steven was taking notes from a fat law book at the far end of the conference table and pointed the way to the restroom when he asked. Damn prostate.

When Wes returned, he read about Walt Seifert's court-appointed attorney, old man Goodell, who'd died a few years ago. Wes remembered vaguely in those bleak days after Rusty's death that Goodell had asked him about the phone call, but Rusty hadn't said anything that would help Walt Seifert, hadn't mentioned Hardy, just rambled on excitedly about seeing the gun burglar. Goodell hadn't called Wes or Marie LaForte to testify about what Rusty said. Probably would have been thrown out anyway as hearsay. Goodell had asked for a couple of delays and the then-prosecuting attorney hadn't opposed them because, according to internal memos in the file, he was still hoping that more solid evidence could be found. Seifert was out on bail and they even detailed a guy to follow him around for a while, but he'd come up only with a list of odd jobs Walt had gotten, bars he'd gone to, friends they'd already questioned.

A couple of weapons finally turned up in Indianapolis, used in a hold-up by criminals known to be connected to the Klan, but they couldn't get evidence linking those weapons or those people to Walt Seifert. So the prosecutor finally went with receiving stolen goods, also a Class D felony and in any case all he could prove, even though the internal memos indicated he still thought Walt was the burglar.

Wes shifted uneasily in his seat. He hadn't known Walt Seifert very well but to his mind Walt didn't have the brains to pull off a major burglary and get the goods to the Klan undetected, especially since the stolen guns had been reported so promptly.

There were photos in the back of the file, prosecutor's exhibits. Photos of the gun shop. Photos of the stolen guns, of the serial numbers. Defense exhibits too: photos of the unidentified fingerprints, clear ones, middle finger and partial index. Photos of the bar parking lot. Photo of—

172

Damn. Wes swallowed, looked away, once again feeling the shock of seeing Rusty's burning El Camino, of trying to believe that if he took a photo it would show something else, prove his eyes wrong. It didn't.

But what was it Marty had said? Something about holes in the back fender? He sort of remembered. He forced his eyes back to the photo and it came back to him. He covered up the forward part of the car with a sheet of paper so he didn't have to look at Rusty. Blond Steven still sat at the end of the table. 'Hey, son, you got a magnifying glass?'

'Yes, sir.' Steven jumped up and was back a moment later.

In the photo flames were already coming out of the back fender area of the El Camino, but something else was clear under magnification: a set of dark holes on the silver fender around the wheel well, as though someone who knew the location of the El Camino fuel tank was using it for target practice.

Someone who knew cars. Knew Nichols County but was coming from Terre Haute. Someone connected to the Klan. Someone named Hardy . . .

'Damn,' said Wes, surging to his feet and heading out to talk to Art Pfann. Over his shoulder he said to Steven, 'Keep this file handy, son; we're going to need it again soon.'

Twenty-Four

The *chaski* thought Ronnie Mann's girl looked exhilarated up there at treetop level. She'd made it all the way to the eighteen-inch ledge where he'd been when he tossed down the water bottle, and she'd only had one scare, when she was crossing horizontally from the crack in the rock where she'd started up to the knobs and pockets ten feet to the right that formed a natural ladder to the ledge. He'd kept her snug and safe with the toprope. Now she was sitting securely on the ledge, panting as she followed his patient instructions from below: first, check the solidity of the chocks he'd placed in the rock to act as anchors; next, make sure the straps of webbing weren't frayed; then check that the 'biners were still locked; then tie herself into the anchors before removing the safety rope from her waist.

At first, he'd planned only a quick conversation down by the creek to check on Mark's state of mind and find out a little about the investigation. But she was taking so enthusiastically to climbing he wondered now if he should keep her a while. Might make Mark pay attention at last.

'Gabby, am I supposed to belay you now?' she called.

'Nah, I forgot to give you an ATC. Belaying gear. I'll show you how when I'm up there.' He hated having amateurs on belay; it was worse than nothing. He brushed away their footprints from the snow, though the wind was picking up, soon would smooth the snow. He scanned the rock to remind himself of what was there and swarmed up it in a minute.

'If you're trying to impress me, you did,' the girl said. He liked her bright expression and her mop of curls, so much like . . . Damn.

'Put your hat on,' he told her. 'You don't want to freeze.'

She obeyed, saying, 'Must have taken you a while to get so good.'

'Yeah, I've been climbing quite a few years,' the *chaski* said.

'I can see why. This is great.' The girl – Liv; that's what they called her – looked out across the sea of bare treetops punctuated by evergreens, and beyond to the snowy hills and Arctic-blue sky. From here you couldn't see the barn and house, so it seemed isolated.

The *chaski* said, 'You said you were from New York.' He started straightening out the rope, coiling it neatly on the ledge. 'How come you're here in Indiana?'

'Visiting some friends of my father's,' she said. 'What are you doing with the rope?'

'Making sure there aren't any knots. The time to discover problems is not in the middle of a pitch when you're trying to set gear in the rock with one hand.'

'Pitch?'

'Segment of a climb. We just did one pitch. One short pitch.'

'Cool.'

'Why friends of your father? You must have friends of your own.'

'Oh, sure, but – see, my father died a few years ago, and I hadn't seen these people for a really long time. How do these work?' She poked at the anchors he'd set.

He lifted one out and liked the way her eyes widened at how easy it was to jiggle it out. He showed it to her, a brightly colored wedge-shape threaded with sturdy cable. 'This thing is called a nut or a chock. You find a crack or a pocket in the rock, ideally one that's wider at the back than the front, definitely one that narrows as it goes down. You find the right size nut –' he grabbed the bunch he'd hung on his belt, showed her how to measure them against the crack – 'push it in up here, pull it down until it's secure, clip your rope into the 'biner, and you're all set.'

'You did that with one hand.'

'Got to. Most of the time you're hanging on with your other hand. Hey, sorry to hear about your father. Did he live around here, like his friends?'

'Only when he was a kid. What about you, Gabby? Are you from here?'

'I live out west.'

175

'But you know the rock so well!'

The *chaski* shrugged, warmed by her enthusiasm. 'Any good climber could figure out this cliff pretty quickly. I've done a lot of climbs. Rockies, Andes, Himalayas.'

'Andes?'

'Couple times. You ever been there?' He was pleased she'd picked up on it but stayed casual, squatted down to check his 'biners.

She explained, 'I've been in those mountains. Awesome.'

She sat down, blue-jeaned legs dangling over the edge. None of the ooh-this-is-so-scary he'd expected. Definitely a cut above most of his climbing students. Ronnie Mann didn't deserve this peach of a daughter. He said, 'Yeah, the Andes are amazing. What were you doing there?'

'Oh . . . family. My mom is from South America, so before I started working in Brooklyn I spent a lot of vacations there. God, this rock is cold!' She stood up again.

'I've got an insulated pad if you want.' She shook her head and he went on, 'What did your dad do?'

'Engineer. How about you?'

'Bookkeeper; how's that for boring?'

'Hey, it depends. I've run into a couple of very creative bookkeepers in the Brooklyn courts. They both went to jail.'

'Huh. Corporate accountants?'

She was looking at him oddly and he realized he was staring at her. He looked down at the 'biners again and she said, 'Yeah. They created exactly the account books their bosses told them to create.'

He nodded, said bitterly, 'Just doing their jobs, they thought. Blinded themselves to what was actually happening.'

'Sounds right,' she said. 'They went along, didn't blow the whistle.'

'Or quit if they couldn't blow the whistle. That's what I did: I quit. I work for the government now.' Why was he telling her this? He had to get back on track. Find out about Mark, about the investigation.

But she was asking, 'Why couldn't you blow the whistle?'

'It's complicated. It'd take me all day. So how did your father die?'

'I really don't like to remember that.'

She sounded uneasy now. He'd better change the subject.

He said, 'OK, we're about ready to go down. Did you do rappelling in your class?'

'No, we didn't get that far.'

'OK, in that case we should go on to that next ledge. See it? Wider than this one, and if I remember correctly there's a kind of stepped route down to your horse. It's a short pitch up to that ledge but good practice.'

She looked up. 'Let's do it.'

The *chaski* was pleased. On the next ledge he'd have as long as he needed.

Marty finished talking to the Toledo detective about Gene Elkins and hung up. Two desks away Howie Culp was also on the phone, to Indianapolis. 'Yes, sir; Corson sent his mother a couple photos someone took of him. He's standing on a mountain trail. Postmark was Cuenca, Ecuador . . . No, Detective Lyons, I can't tell from the photo.'

Marty scribbled a note. 'Machetes stolen in 1985 from Toledo, Ohio murder victim. Ronald Mann connection? Armadillo connection?' She slid it on to his desk.

Howie continued talking to Lyons. 'Yes, the dates Corson worked for Armadillo were 1978 to 1985 . . . I see. So they overlapped.' He paused, listening, noticed Marty's note, stiffened. 'Sir? Sir, excuse me, sorry to interrupt, but something just came in maybe connecting the machetes to Armadillo and to the Staten Island vic.' There was a bark at the other end and Howie said, 'Yes, sir; I'll let you talk to Deputy Hopkins,' and handed her the phone.

'What've we got, Hopkins?' Lyons demanded.

Marty said, 'We just now tracked down a friend of Ronald Mann. The Staten Island victim. This friend, named Elkins, was killed in Toledo in 1985. Shot, no obvious fire.'

'Eighty-five was a while ago. And the wrong MO.'

'Yes, sir. It turns out this guy worked for Armadillo Security until 1982 . . .'

'When did he start?'

'Don't know yet, but Detective Knauer in Toledo is looking up the details.' She noticed that Howie was taking notes too.

Lyons said, 'OK. Now what was Culp telling me about machetes?'

'Elkins collected machetes. He was shot in his apartment and the only things missing were the machetes.'

'Son of a bitch. Do they match the machete you've got?'

'Don't know, sir. Detective Knauer will be sending us the details. I told him you and Detective Bruno were working on it too.'

'What's his number?'

She read it off to him. He thanked her and rang off. Marty turned to see Sheriff Pierce taking off his coat.

'What's up?' he asked.

'Possible new victim. I mean, it was a while ago,' Howie said. Pierce jerked his head toward his office and they followed him in and told him about Gene Elkins and his machetes.

'No fire?' Pierce asked.

'Detective Knauer is checking the files but he didn't remember mention of it. And Elkins was shot; none of the others were.'

Pierce frowned. 'Strange. It's like it's related but not really. And all so long ago. We better keep in touch with this Detective Knauer.'

'Yes, sir,' Howie said. 'Did Mr Lugano help?'

'He was real cooperative but doesn't know much,' Sheriff Pierce reported. 'He's upset by the whole thing, of course. He knew Ronald Mann pretty well. Knew Bowers slightly back in high school but hasn't seen him since. Didn't know Corson at all. I'll call him and ask about this Elkins guy.'

Marty glanced at her watch. She should leave before long to catch the Gordon sisters, but she had another question. 'Sir, did Mr Lugano say anything about the projects Ronald Mann did in Ecuador?'

'Not really. See, the way it worked was, he'd talk to those foreign governments and he'd do economic research for them, tell them if they needed a power plant or something, and he'd tell them who did the kind of work they needed done. He said Mann worked for a good engineering company so he recommended it for the Ecuador project and a bunch of others too.' He shrugged. 'The Ecuador thing was a hydroelectric dam but he said it was like a dozen dams he'd recommended in different countries, and Mann's outfit had built five of them. Nothing special.'

'I see,' said Marty. Still, it was a dam.

Agent Jessup came in the door. Pierce said quickly, 'OK. I'll take care of Jessup and call Lugano about this Elkins thing. You two keep at it.'

Marty went back to her desk to collect the things she needed to talk to Eunie and Stanni: the information on the dam, the clipping with the photo of May in the mountains; but Pierce interrupted her to come in and explain the details of the Elkins connection to Jessup. Marty couldn't decide if that was a compliment or not.

Liv scanned the cliff, eager to be climbing again. Elena had been so pleased to be climbing those Maya temples, she was really going to love this.

Liv could see how Gabby the bookkeeper got his nickname. You'd think that a guy who chose to spend so many hours alone in the rocks would be more reserved. But maybe he was like her, someone who enjoyed people and conversation and yet felt the tug of nature – the friendly alien spirit of a horse, the eternal splendor of this beautiful stone. She was a little uneasy about how intense he'd become for a moment there when she mentioned bookkeepers who'd broken the law for their employers, but she could avoid that subject and he was a damn good climbing teacher. It was great that she'd get to do another climb – another pitch, she corrected herself – before starting down. Gabby was right: this wild rock was very different from the wall in the gym. That had been fun, and she'd learned good stuff, but with something humans had made you kind of expected to be able to climb it. Here the fissures and edges had been carved by faceless time with no regard for human abilities, so there were no guarantees. Instead there was a fierce joy in every tiny success as she matched her strength and spirit and skill against the ancient rock.

Gabby was all business when climbing. 'I'll take the lead across here,' he explained. 'I'm going to put in a couple of chocks for protection as I go, and clip the rope to them with 'biners. So if I fall I won't fall. You'll belay me, stop the rope with the ATC, and I'll just hang from the last protection I put in. Then I can climb back to where I wanted to be and move on.'

'But you weigh more than I do.'

'Your harness is anchored to the rock. The pull goes to the ATC on your harness, through the harness, to the anchors. The cliff holds the weight. Your harness is in the middle and it may move you a few inches as my weight hits the system. But you're not holding my weight; you're just keeping the brake on.'

'OK.' Nervously, she checked the neat coil of rope next to her on the ledge – the way it ran through the ATC, the carabiners that locked her to the anchor chocks. 'You won't really fall, will you?'

'Probably not, but be ready. Left hand feeds out the rope to me so I can keep climbing, right hand lets the rope move through the ATC as the left hand feeds, but it's always ready to brake. Right hand never ever leaves the rope.'

'And to brake I pull it sideways.'

'Sideways or back. Ninety degree angle or better. Climbing,' he said, and looked back. 'You're supposed to confirm by saying "Climb away" if you're ready.'

Liv took a deep breath. 'Climb away, Gabby.'

She fed out the rope and watched intently as he climbed across, some of the edges hard to see from here. He set chocks with one hand, sometimes holding the rope in his teeth until he was ready to push it one-handed through the gate of the carabiner. Soon he was across, the rope miraculously threaded through three carabiners in a straight line from her to him. He called back instructions about how to tie herself to the rope for her climb, how to unclip from the anchor hardware.

And then she was climbing. As she passed each chock he'd set, she had to remove her safety rope from it so she could move on. She'd paid close attention to his holds as he set them, and even one-handed, the first two clips weren't bad. She blessed the clever person who had invented carabiners, with the C-hook shape that closed to a secure D with an easy-to-open spring-loaded gate. Even one-handed, she was able to hold the gates open with one finger while pushing the rope out with another. In between the clips, the climb was glorious, a blissful focused flow across the smoke-colored rock.

The third clip was more difficult because she wasn't as tall as Gabby, and had to stretch to remove the rope. Muscles straining, focused on the little gate, she reached high – and her toe slipped off the nubbin where she'd placed it and she fell.

Except she didn't fall. The very rope she was trying to unclip caught her, and she found herself dangling in her harness next to the rock face, safe but astonished. She said, 'Oops. Any suggestions?'

'You're doing good. Next time keep part of your focus on your footholds.'

She took a deep breath, pulled herself up on the rope until she could get her right foot on the same edge as before and her left on that slippery nubbin. Strange – now that she'd fallen and was OK, she felt freer, less tense. The protection worked! But she was definitely going to get shoes like Gabby's for next time.

She looked across the eight feet to where Gabby stood, holding the rope wound through the belay device – ATC, he called it – then looked back up. If she slipped again after she'd unclipped the rope she'd fall farther, eight feet instead of two, and swing sideways until she was hanging under Gabby. But she could take that and anyway there was no choice, she had to keep going. This time she focused on her holds as well as on the gate above, and after four tries she finally got the rope out so she could move across those last few feet to the ledge. Gasping with exertion, she pulled herself up on to it, like getting out of a pool.

'Good job,' Gabby said. 'You're a natural, Liv.'

She was breathing so hard she couldn't answer, could only smile her thanks. She thought there was real admiration in his voice.

He said, 'Maybe it's that exposure to the Andes.'

'Maybe, or –' she panted – 'maybe it's in the genes.'

'How do you mean?'

'My mother has some Inca blood.'

'Huh.' Gabby nodded thoughtfully, then asked, 'These people you're visiting, your father's friends – have they been to the Andes too?'

This was a much wider ledge than the first – maybe four feet wide here, tapering to nothing thirty feet away. She found an anchor nut with a sturdy strap of webbing near the back of the ledge, and clipped her harness to it before removing the rope. 'Yeah, but not as long as my parents.'

'He's an engineer like your father?'

'No, he's an economist. Worked with numbers, like you.'

'What part of the Andes? Ecuador?'

She looked at him with interest, but his gray-tinted glasses were aimed down at the rope he was coiling. She said, 'Yeah. Is that where you were?'

'For a little while,' he said, so tightly that another chime of unease rang in her chest. But it subsided when he added, 'Great climbs there. Chimborazo.'

'When I get some more practice maybe I should go back there,' Liv said.

'You'd like it. You need a few extra days to get used to the altitude first.'

Liv wondered if Gabby had known Corson. She said, 'I hear that fellow who died in the fire was in Ecuador for a while. D'you suppose he did any climbing?'

She had his attention now. He asked, 'What was his name?'

'Robert Corson. Funny nickname – Zill or something.'

Gabby shook his head slowly. 'He wasn't climbing while I was there. Not Chimborazo, anyway.'

'Maybe he wasn't a climber. They just said he worked there.'

'Who said it? The papers? I must have missed it.'

'The sheriff's department asked me a few questions about Ecuador when they found out I'd been there.' She saw that he was frowning and added, 'But I don't think I helped them much. I didn't know him or anything.'

'Yeah. What else did they ask you?'

'Not much,' Liv said. 'Didn't they talk to you?'

'No, why would they?'

'You've been to Ecuador too.'

'So is the sheriff talking to your father's friends too?'

'Yeah.' Liv glanced at her watch. 'But they must be finished talking by now so I better get back to meet them. Where's that descent you mentioned?'

He stood up, gestured toward the narrow end of the ledge thirty feet away. 'It's a little farther than I remembered, maybe forty feet past the end. See that big vertical crack in the rock? Chimney, we call it, a couple of feet wide. Easy way down. But we'll have to climb across to it.'

Liv stood up in her tethered harness and peered where he

was pointing. There was a dribble of ice down the rock face and beyond it she could make out a vertical gash in the rock. Because she was looking at the rock she didn't see exactly what happened, just heard Gabby say, 'Oh shit.'

'What?' She turned back, saw him staring down the cliffside.

'Didn't mean to teach you this the hard way,' he muttered. 'Always keep your rope clipped to something. Be right back.' Then he was running along the ledge to the end, pausing to look up at the cliffside, then grabbing holds, moving up smoothly.

Liv peered down to see what the problem was, and saw their rope sprawled bright on the snowy creekside about six stories down. 'Shit!' she said, and looked back for Gabby. He had paused to insert a chock in the cliffside and was clipping some kind of double loop of webbing to it – oh! It was like a miniature four-rung ladder. He stretched to get his toe up into it, climbed up to a hold in the rock for his right foot, then leaned down to pull out the little temporary ladder. A moment later, he'd disappeared over the top lip of the bluff.

And Liv, astonished, was alone on the cliff.

Without a rope.

Twenty-Five

Prosecuting Attorney Pfann was in conference for the next hour. Frustrated, Wes shrugged into his sheepskin jacket and went out to the square. He knew his sense of urgency was personal, that a short delay after all these years didn't make any difference. The guy was dead. But damn, think of the good folks who'd be alive today if they'd caught that young gun burglar back in seventy-five!

Don't play what-ifs, he reminded himself. That way lay pointless guilt, because how could he have known Rusty was right? Rusty was drunk. Legally drunk. And Walt Seifert was no innocent babe. Sheriff Cowgill and the prosecuting attorney had reason to suspect him.

Marie had known. She'd been wise enough to know there was truth in Rusty, even drunk. But none of them had taken her seriously, not even Wes. They figured she was just being the loyal wife. Dammit, thought Wes, he should have listened to her.

Habit had directed his steps toward the corner of the square leading to the sheriff's office. Realizing where he was, he was about to turn back when he saw a familiar figure emerging with Sheriff Pierce. It was short slick-haired Agent Jessup of the FBI. Well, well, just the man he needed. Wes stuck his hands in his jacket pockets and ambled casually toward them.

They were turning toward the parking area and didn't see him for a moment. Jessup's inkstroke brows were frowning, his tinny voice stammering with excitement. 'I'll g-get back to you about the Elkins machetes. G-good work, Sheriff.'

Chuck Pierce said, 'Doc Altmann found some kind of machete expert at IU but he's a foreigner – doesn't speak two words of English. Might want to get a translator. If we—' He broke off as he spotted Wes, said stiffly, 'Well, Cochran, how you doing?'

Wes gave him his friendliest nod. 'Fine, Chuck. I just got a tip I wanted to pass on to you and Agent Jessup.'

Jessup had turned back and looked up at Wes. Things hadn't been all sweetness and light when he and Wes had worked together, but they'd got their man. He asked warily, 'Hello, Cochran. What kind of a tip?'

'Don't worry, you can take your time; it's nothing current. But back in olden times there was a gun-shop burglary. We never got the burglar because we couldn't match the fingerprints. But thinking over that case I reckon there's a real good chance you've got a match now. Same file we worked on last time we met.'

'That K-klan case?' Jessup's eyes brightened.

'Yep. Sheriff Pierce will show you when y'all have a minute. The prints'll be on the stolen guns Walt Seifert went to jail for, Chuck. Back in the seventies.'

'Pretty old case,' said Pierce shortly. His blue eyes were ice-cold, but Wes knew he was burned.

Jessup was getting into his vehicle. He said, 'Old case, but it was a b-big one,' and Wes knew he'd won. Jessup would make Pierce give him those prints.

'See you, Agent Jessup,' Wes said. The little man nodded and drove out of the parking lot.

Marty was coming down the steps, heading for her cruiser. She'd probably been waiting for the Feds to leave. She looked uneasily at Wes, said, 'Hello, sir.'

Pierce was still fuming. 'Where you going, Hopkins?'

'I need to follow up on one of those background cases, sir.'

'Leave it. Go back and finish your report,' he snapped.

She looked at the ground, said, 'Yes, sir,' and turned to start back up the steps.

Wes was furious that Pierce would humiliate her in front of him just to score a point and did what he'd vowed not to. 'Christ, Chuck, you've got a major case on your hands and you're tying down your best talent!'

A spark of alarm lit Pierce's eyes but he said coldly, 'Talent won't do us any good if she doesn't report.'

What an asshole. 'Hopkins, why the hell don't you quit?' Wes said to her back. 'Come work for me. I can guarantee you a job with more money and better hours. We'll see how well he can do without you.'

Hopkins turned back slowly. Standing on the second step she was a little taller than Wes. She glanced from one man to the other as though realizing that this wasn't about her, that she'd been caught in the crossfire. The gray eyes she turned on Wes were very sad but her voice was firm. 'You've done a whole lot for me, sir, and I appreciate the offer. But I'm on Sheriff Pierce's team now. And I'm going to play my position.'

She turned and walked back into the station.

It was worse than fouling out, it was like getting suspended from the game for life. Especially when he saw the startled triumph in Chuck Pierce's pale eyes.

Wes strode away without saying goodbye, because if Pierce had said anything back he would have punched him out.

Mid-morning in limestone country in January. Blue sky, icy wind blowing across ridges and hills and through hollows, sculpting the snow into drifts in places, baring the rock in others. Fires burned against the cold, mostly in stoves and furnaces and fireplaces. The cold sun glittered on rock and snow, on cedars and bare maples, on hedges and highways and rural roads. It shone on a short, strong, grieving man who called himself the *chaski* and, as he collected fresh gear, hoped his message would be heard at last. It shone on Liv Mann, huddling cold on a cliff, waiting for a rope. It shone on Wes Cochran, furious at ungrateful Marty Hopkins and at himself, driving aimlessly around town until he'd pushed his anger aside enough to remember he wanted to ask Mark Lugano about why McGabben was back in town.

It shone on Marty Hopkins, who was finally on the way to the Gordon sisters' home on the ridge. She was wearing sunglasses against the glare and to hide her tears. What the hell did Coach think he was doing? He'd found her the damn job, taught her to do it well, taught her to love it, and then . . .

Dammit, he'd probably never forgive her.

And Sheriff Pierce would keep bumbling along, listening to idiots like Don Foley about how she couldn't do the job . . .

Shoot, she was in no shape to do an interview. Coffee – maybe that would steady her nerves. She'd turned from State 37 on to the county road that led toward Demon Ridge. Not many cars on the side roads this morning, just her and a dark-green Crown Vic back there. She pulled in at Reba Brinson's, the last place to get coffee for miles. It was officially a gift store that advertised 'Hoosier Memories' on the highway she'd just left, but Reba always kept a pot hot.

'Black to go, Reba,' Marty told her, and wandered down the aisle looking at the stock. Today there were signs attached to heart-shaped balloons in the middle of the store. 'Don't Forget Your Valentine,' they said. Not a bad idea. Think happy thoughts.

Reba sold earrings, but Chrissie had gotten real particular lately, wanted to pick them herself. The small music section here had no Pearl Jam. Could all that drumming and shouting really be about the grief of surviving? Anyway, a gift certificate at the mall music store would make more sense for Chrissie. But there in Reba's party supplies were some silly hats, and one of them she just had to get for Romey in honor of his new vineyard – a victor's crown of plastic grape leaves with little purple bunches of grapes. And Aunt Vonnie had just broken her favorite salt shaker, a milkmaid design. These shakers weren't as well made but they were the figures of a little chef and waiter, good for someone who worked at Reiner's Bakery . . .

'Hey, Marty, don't let it get cold,' Reba called.

Marty paid for her coffee and gifts and, trying not to think about Coach Cochran, headed for Demon Ridge.

Wes, his thoughts still circling resentfully around Marty's ingratitude, drove up the curve of Mark and Arlene's driveway. As he slammed his door he took a deep breath to clear his head, focused on the house, one of his favorites. Beautiful limestone, rough silvery grain for the walls, smooth and creamy for the porch columns and lintels. Looked like a showcase demonstrating why Indiana limestone was the prettiest as well as the best damn building material in the nation. And even though the big house was up-to-date and gracious, it sat on its knoll like royalty.

A lot like Mark, Wes thought – approachable guy, but never any doubt he was the smartest and richest in the room.

Bob Rueger was a money guy too, but he'd made his bucks in construction. Wes thought he'd be OK to work with, if this project panned out. He was energetic, hungry, explosive in his ambitions. Very different style from Lugano. Even in high school, Mark had had a sort of dignity, friendly and distant all at once. No wonder he'd made it big dealing with foreign governments, like a diplomat for his company instead of a salesman. Wes couldn't imagine either of those guys succeeding in the other's field.

Arlene answered the door when he rang and clapped her hands. 'Why Wes! What a nice surprise! We haven't seen you since the harvest festival!'

Wes made an effort, said, 'Shame on you, Arlene! Don't remind me of that. Mark hit the target first try and I got dunked in with the apples!'

Arlene giggled, delighted. 'He said he had to buy a ticket just so he could dunk Cochran! But I noticed, when you got out of that tub, somehow a lot of water splashed on Mark.'

'Served him right too. But hey, we were glad to get the donation for the Cancer Society. Worth a dunking.' He smiled down at her, noticed a little tightness around her eyes and remembered what Shirley had said about Mark's moodiness. 'Arlene, is everything OK?'

'Oh, yes, I'm sure it is. Can I take your coat?'

'Nah, thanks, this won't take long.'

'Well, come on to the kitchen; at least have a coffee while I fetch Mark.'

He followed her past the fancy rooms where they gave parties for dozens of friends or to raise funds for charity groups. Not so many parties these last few months, he realized. Maybe Shirley was right.

Arlene poured him a cup, but as she handed it to him paused to frown past him. 'Now what is he doing out there?' He turned and followed her gaze.

Mark Lugano was pacing around the paddock out there, shoulders slumped in his suede outdoor jacket, hands in pockets, eyes on the ground. Arlene said, 'I'll go get him,' and opened a door. Through it Wes could see into the cavernous four-car garage, one BMW looking small in the space. Arlene was disappearing through a back door, shrugging into a jacket as she went. Wes put his coffee on a shelf and followed her out.

Mark saw them, seemed to straighten his shoulders with

effort as he walked toward the paddock gate to meet them. 'Wes Cochran!' he exclaimed cheerily enough. 'I'm honored. Two sheriffs in one day!'

Arlene laughed. 'That's true. Mark, why are you out here?'

'Trying to figure out why Liv isn't back.' He was serious again.

'Oh, she'll be back soon,' Arlene said. Her words were soothing, but Wes could see that tenseness around her eyes again.

Mark said, 'Wes, what can we do for you?'

'Just a quick question. Yesterday I was crossing the square and saw a guy in a Honda. It was Wink McGabben.'

'McGabben?' Mark looked confused.

'Honey, you remember Wink!' Arlene said. 'One of your accountants when we were starting out. He went to high school here, didn't he?'

Mark nodded without expression, but Wes had an idea that the machinery was working again, that this development fit with something Mark knew. He said nothing, so Wes asked, 'Yeah, you guys were both in the high-school math club, weren't you?'

Mark nodded. 'That's right.'

'You didn't know he was in town?'

'No. Haven't heard from him for years. Are you sure it was him? We've all changed a lot.' Mark was obviously interested.

Wes said firmly, 'I'm sure. Look, Mark, in my business we have to make IDs from lousy pictures all the time. We learn to look at features that don't change. Ears, bone structure, et cetera. So even if people grow beards or put on wigs we can spot them.' He grinned at Arlene. 'Besides, I cheated, I looked him up in our old yearbook.'

Mark looked startled, but Arlene smiled back. 'It'd be fun to see some people from back then. If I see Wink, I'll ask him over.'

Mark seemed miles away, so Wes said smoothly, 'Maybe he was just passing through – that's why he didn't look us up. Now, Mark, what's this about Liv Mann being missing?'

Arlene explained, 'We were going riding, and the sheriff – the other sheriff – came by to talk. But he'd already spoken to her and didn't seem to want her around, and she was so eager to go riding. Anyway, I told her to go ahead.'

189

'I see.'

Mark said, 'She told Arlene she'd go ride a little while and be back to meet us in an hour and a half so we could all have a short ride together. But she hasn't come back.' His worried brown eyes swept over the hills.

'Which way did she go?' Wes asked.

'All the trails start from there.' Mark's black suede glove pointed at a corner of the paddock. 'But you can go anywhere.' He swept his arm to encompass every direction except the road.

'We didn't see her leave; we were talking to the sheriff,' Arlene explained.

'Tell you what,' Wes said. 'Arlene, you go back, in case she finds a way to call. Mark, how about we two hike over and look at the beginning of those trails, see if we can make a guess about which one she took?'

'Sounds good,' Mark said, and Arlene nodded slowly.

As they went out the paddock gate Wes realized with surprise that he'd made the plan and Mark was following it, instead of vice versa. The guy must really be in a state.

Liv pulled her parka collar higher, hugged herself, and wished Gabby would show up. Even though the sun was now slanting on to her ledge, it was cold. The wind was definitely picking up.

After her first panic she'd talked herself into some patience. Gabby was a competent guy; he'd belayed her skillfully as she climbed, kept her safe. She'd had some uneasy feelings about him, but not in terms of climbing, only because his reaction to some of the conversation was so oddly intense.

Still, it was frustrating not knowing what he was doing. How hard was it for him to get down there to retrieve their rope? She didn't know. She personally would find getting down at least as hard as climbing up, even retracing her steps, and without instructions, without even a safety rope – no thanks. She'd thought about following him but, even if she had the skill, she didn't have the gear for that. Gabby, good as he was, had used the aid of that little ladder thing. And why had he gone up anyway? She thought he'd said they were going sideways to that vertical gash in the rock – chimney, he'd called it – and then down to where Blueberry still waited.

Not that she could see Blueberry any more. The bulge in

the cliff hid him. Liv took a step to the end of her tether strap toward the edge of the ledge so she could look down. No, not quite. Maybe someone taller could lean out a little further and see him. At least it looked like some sun was reaching him too.

On the other hand, their rope still sprawled where it had fallen, but the wind was blowing snow over it. So Blueberry was probably in the wind.

So was she. She shivered and moved back to the slight shelter provided by the cliff wall.

Where was Gabby? Had he fallen? He'd been gone half an hour now.

Of course, it wasn't as though he was going to the corner store to pick up a six-pack. In this strange world, where the quickest way down might be up, she had to give him time.

She made sure her cap was pulled all the way down against the wind and hugged herself again.

Twenty-Six

Marty got out of the cruiser, paused for a moment to look back down Ridge Road. Nothing. As she'd turned for the second switchback down there, she thought she'd seen that dark-green Crown Vic again, turning up the road. Still, other people probably had business on this road from time to time. There were only about three houses on it, the other two past the Gordon sisters' place where Ridge Road finally left the ridge top and eased its way down toward the valley on a long trajectory that wasn't as steep. Marty didn't see the green vehicle, though. She was probably imagining things, still rattled because of that scene with Coach.

Don't think about that, Hopkins. She turned firmly to the little jigsaw-decorated house. The van with the clown faces painted on its doors was parked on the lawn today near the front door. Footprints in the snow led from the front door to the back of the vehicle. They'd probably been loading it up with banjos or paper rainbows or whatever they needed this afternoon in Evansville for their gig there.

When she knocked, Eunie opened the door as before and said almost shyly, 'Oh, hi, Marty; come on in, please, if you want. Stanni said you'd be here, um, but . . .'

Today Eunie wasn't wearing a Nordic sweater. She was all in white – long leggings and a T-shirt, kind of like long johns, and big woolly socks halfway up her calves. It made her look unprotected and vulnerable.

Marty said, 'Yeah, sorry; I had to make a stop. I know you have to leave soon. Shouldn't take long.'

'Oh, um, OK.' But Eunie still looked anxious and Marty remembered how she'd lost it last time, wailing at the thought of her lost sister. It had been the question about the fire that had really set her off, and Marty sympathized completely. Thinking of her dad in that El Camino . . .

Dammit, she had so many questions for Coach about that. She blocked her thoughts from going that way and asked, 'Where's Stanni?'

'Oh, she just went out back; she'll be here in a minute – here she is.'

'Hi, Marty.' Stanni closed the kitchen door behind her and crossed to the entry hall where Marty and Eunie still stood. 'Just feeding the birds. Look, we gotta run; might be better if you came back later.' She took off her boots and parka, then her snow pants. Like Eunie, she was dressed in white long johns.

'Really, shouldn't take long,' Marty said. 'I just wanted to know where May was working at the time she died.'

'Little village in the Andes, like we said,' Stanni said brusquely. She pointed with her chin at the clown suits, two orange polka-dot and one bluebird, spread out on the sofa. Eunie hurried over and began to put one of them on.

'Yeah, I was wondering if the village was in Peru or Ecuador,' Marty said, following in step with Stanni.

Stanni hesitated just for a breath and Eunie's big eyes looked at her sister. There was a rustle from the terrarium next to Marty, a flash of green as Pythia the snake slid up her branch. Crossing to the sofa too, Stanni said, 'I think officially it was Ecuador. But May said down there in the mountains it's arbitrary. It's like hiking the Appalachian Trail, trying to figure out if you're in Tennessee or North Carolina.'

'Yeah, I see what you mean,' Marty said. 'Now, you said this mountain village, wherever it was, was called Santo Tomas?'

'That's right.' Stanni was pulling on her clown suit. Eunie was already closing up the front of hers. It had big orange pompoms arranged like buttons but it actually closed with Velcro.

Marty said, 'See, my problem is, I found Santo Tomas on an old map. In Ecuador, like you say. But it's not on newer maps because somebody built a dam across the river and turned it into a lake. Santo Tomas is under water now.'

The two sisters were staring at her and Marty knew she was on to something. Stanni cleared her throat. 'Yeah, guess it's all gone now.'

'Did May say anything about the dam project? Like who was doing it?'

She waited them out. Finally Stanni muttered, 'It was a government project. Ecuador government.'

'Makes sense,' Marty said, and thinking out loud, 'So they probably were moving the people out of Santo Tomas about the time May was there. Did she say what the villagers thought about the project?'

Eunie pinned a big white paper napkin under her chin. 'May said they didn't like it. They were losing their homes.' She went to the mirror over the fireplace and began smearing white make-up on to her face and neck.

'Boy, I'd hate losing my home too,' Marty said. 'But I guess if it's the government there's no stopping them.'

'You can say that again!' Stanni said. She was pinning on a napkin too.

'Didn't the government pay them? Or give them another place to live?'

'Much higher up in the mountains. Too cold and rocky to grow a lot of their crops,' Eunie said. Stanni took the powder box from her with a frown.

Marty asked, 'So May was teaching kids who were about to lose their homes. Didn't she try to talk to people about it?'

Stanni was powdering over the white paint over her face. 'Of course not. The Ursulines told her if she got involved they'd all get kicked out. She had no connection with the project except for feeling sorry for the kids.' Stanni picked up the greasepaint pencils and began drawing a grotesque grinning mouth from cheekbone to cheekbone.

Eunie had left the mirror and was leaning over the sofa. Stanni joined her sister. Speaking to their backs, Marty said, 'So May had no connection to the dam. And the explosion that started the fire had no connection either?'

Eunie gave a little sob. Back still to Marty, Stanni grabbed her sister's elbow and said, 'No connection. We have to go. Goodbye.'

Marty said, 'But . . .'

The two sisters turned to face her, but they weren't Eunie and Stanni any more; they were grotesquely grinning clowns with painted eyes and wild green hair. One clown did a little dance step and the other began to sing a hit rock song in a

194

piercing soprano, 'Baby, love is so warm, / But it freezes too, / And all I can feel is the wind of death, / The wind with ice on its breath.' The powerful voice filled the little room, made it vibrate, and Marty took an involuntary step back.

'Goodbye, Deputy Hopkins,' said Stanni's voice from one of the clowns.

Marty was all out of questions. She said, 'Um, yeah, goodbye; I'll be in touch,' and went out. When she reached her cruiser she glanced back. The sisters had put on parkas over the polka-dots and were locking their door.

Marty drove down Ridge Road, negotiating the switchbacks and pondering what she'd learned. The sisters had kept quiet about the dam until she pressed them. They knew more than they were telling, but she didn't know what to ask next.

Both times she'd come, Stanni had claimed to be feeding the birds. Odd.

That story was worth a few minutes of time. When Marty hit the county road at the bottom of the hill she didn't turn toward Evansville; she turned back toward Dunning. Around the first curve she K-turned and pulled on to the shoulder facing the Ridge Road intersection. Her cruiser was mostly hidden from the road by a thicket of tall bushes, but she was able to watch the intersection through the bare branches. Soon the van with the clown faces appeared and drove off the other way toward Evansville.

Marty waited for them to disappear and was about to pull out to go back up to their house when another car nosed out of Ridge Road and turned her way. A dark-green Crown Vic. She frowned as it passed and noted the license number as it disappeared around the next curve behind her. Then she headed back up the switchbacks.

Wes looked at the trail junction: lots of hoofprints but mostly old, frozen into the mud, because the wind had blown the recent snow away. 'Where'd you ride yesterday?' he asked Mark.

'Toward the knoll.' He pointed.

Wes looked around. 'Does this route go toward the cliff?' That looked like the most interesting direction. When Mark nodded, he headed out. Not much snow had stuck to the first wind-swept thirty yards of the trail, but when it eased around a sheltering rise in the ground towards the woods, the prints were clear. 'Where does this trail end up?' he asked.

Mark pointed. 'It goes down to the creek, pretty steep, then follows along it for a while, loops back through the woods and joins the middle trail for the last quarter-mile back.'

'How long does it take to ride?'

'Hour and a half for the whole thing, if you're not in a hurry.'

'You say the steep part is at the beginning?'

'That's right. You're thinking if she had trouble, that's where it would be?' His brown eyes, squinting against the snow glare, were troubled.

Wes shrugged. 'You know the trail. But with the snow and all, my guess is that's where a horse might slip. Wanna go look at the steep part?'

'Yeah, let's.' Mark seemed pleased to have a task. 'God, I feel responsible for Liv. Such a bright kid, and we pretty much taught her to ride when her family visited us back in Connecticut.'

'Yeah, someone was telling me that her father was Ronnie Mann.'

'That's right. A friend. Friends' kids are – you know, special.'

'Mm,' Wes said. Special, yeah; you break your neck trying to help them and they turn around and bite you.

They were heading into the woods now, bare branches on trees and underbrush making black scribbles across the snow and sky. Wes got back to the question. 'Course I'm not on this case, but I still hear things. Like, Ronnie Mann died the same way Zill Corson died.'

'True.' Mark's voice was tight.

Wes glanced at him. His old teammate's lips were clamped, fighting emotion. Wes pushed a little more. 'Is that why his daughter's here? Because she wants to find out about the Corson murder?'

'She thinks there's a connection, and, well, Ronnie was her father.' Still that tight voice.

'Yeah, I know how it is. You try to do them a favor but it's really for their dad.'

'Yeah, exactly! You can feel so damn guilty. And maybe you are.'

'Just for surviving, you mean.'

Mark shrugged. 'Sometimes that. Sometimes more.'

Wes thought about how he hadn't followed up on those bullet holes in Rusty's car. 'Yeah, maybe so. Some things in your life you wish you could do over.'

Mark said mildly, as though remarking on the weather, 'It's like your soul is burning already, and you aren't in hell yet.'

Whoa! This must be the mood Arlene and Shirley had talked about. Wes said cautiously, 'We do the best we can. Sometimes it doesn't turn out right. Hey, this is beautiful country here. Used to be old man Gordon's farm, right?'

'Yeah. Back in Connecticut I got a tip it was available. Not cheap, but I wasn't out to screw the family.'

'Man, this is getting steeper here.'

'Won't get a lot worse than this. Zigzags down this hill then levels off by the creek.'

'Well, the horse made it this far,' Wes said, looking at the steady hoofprints on a sheltered patch of snow ahead. 'Guess I can too.'

They tramped on down together, old teammates on a new mission, and yet Wes was troubled by the despair distracting his companion. He said, 'It's hard to cope with a buddy dying. You keep thinking, What if?' Mark said nothing, and when Wes glanced at him he saw he was blinking his eyes against the threat of tears. Time to change the subject. Get off Ronnie Mann and find out why mention of McGabben had made Mark so thoughtful. Wes said, 'I'm trying to remember what Wink McGabben was like. He wasn't on the basketball team like you and me. I remember him swimming, though. Pretty fast for a small guy.'

A little faraway smile played at the corners of Mark's mouth. 'Yeah, he was really athletic despite his size. You'd look at him, short and with that squint, but in PE he was always first up the bars or the ropes. Too bad for him we didn't have gymnastics in those days.'

'Yeah. Course it was math that paid off for both of you.'

'Hey, man, you did OK with your state championship!' Mark grinned and elbowed Wes. 'Nobody can get elected the way a hoop star can. Admit it, that was half your appeal.'

'Sure, first election,' Wes said. 'But second and third and fourth – that's 'cause I did a good job.'

'Not denying that,' Mark said.

'And,' Wes went on, 'all those years sheriffing gives a guy a sense of when somebody's sidestepping a question. Tell me about McGabben after high school.'

Mark adjusted his collar against the wind. 'Not much to tell. I was an economist working my way up the ladder at BB. Bielefeld Burke. Some of us kept up a little, mostly Christmas cards. You got some.'

'Yup.'

'So when Wink got out of the army—'

'Army? Was he in Nam?'

'No, they kept him stateside. He was with the quartermaster, some kind of bookkeeping. Anyway, he got out, wrote me that he was an accountant and did I know of any jobs, so I got him in with BB. He was good – seemed to like the job.'

'Accounting?'

'Hey, I know it's supposed to be boring, but if you've got a weird brain like Wink and me, those numbers mean things, show you the ebb and flow . . .' He coughed, looked at the trail beneath his trudging boots, then went on, 'Anyway, Wink enjoyed the extras too. Travel especially. BB sent him to Europe, South America, I think one project in India. Lots of places in the US too. Our paths crossed a few times a year, early on.'

They had reached a flatter area dominated by a tall limestone bluff with a creek burbling at its foot. The wind had erased most of the hoofprints but Wes spotted one on the lee side of a rock. He pointed at it and kept walking, saying, 'OK, but something happened, right? You said you hadn't heard from McGabben for years.'

'He quit the job. Went out west, started working for the state of California. I lost touch with him.'

'You quit sending him cards?'

'Didn't know where to send them.'

A gust of wind rattled the treetops. Wes said, 'But you knew he was working for California.'

'Because his department head told me she'd written letters of recommendation for him.'

'I see.' Sounded to Wes as though Mark and Wink had

stopped communicating with each other before Wink quit and moved away. But before he could follow up, something else caught his eye. 'Hey, what's this?'

A riderless gray horse tethered to a little tree swung his head around to watch them approach.

Twenty-Seven

Liv was cold. The heat from her straining muscles during the climb had kept her warm for a while, but it was going on forty-five minutes now that she'd been stranded on this ledge. She'd jogged in place for a few minutes and that helped, though her safety tether didn't allow much movement. The sun was near its highest point and that helped some too. But in the end she was stuck on an exposed rock face in below-freezing weather, where every puff of wind whisked away heat.

What if something had happened to Gabby? He'd seemed so competent and at home on the rock, but there were odd things about him. What did she really know about him? Not enough.

Well, OK, she knew he was a skilled climber. She'd seen him move on the rock, plus he'd invested in some useful gear. Those chocks and carabiners, the harness she was wearing, even the rope that had fallen had been professional quality gear. He'd said he'd climbed in the Rockies and the Andes, and she was ready to believe him. Chimborazo in Ecuador, he'd said.

She frowned for a moment. Had he brought up Ecuador? No, he'd mentioned the Andes; it was natural to talk about it. And she'd been curious about Corson, had asked if he knew him. He hadn't, but he'd been interested in talking about Ecuador, finding out what she knew about it. Wanted to know if her friends had been there too. He'd had quite a few questions about Mark, and about what the sheriff had asked her.

Natural to be curious about that, though. When you met strangers by chance and found yourself spending some time with them, you talked about external things – weather and sports and the latest headlines.

When you met strangers by chance . . .

High above in the intense blue sky, a jet left a white contrail. It was headed south. Damn, she wanted Elena! The minute she was off this cliff, she'd head straight for Cancun.

The howl of the wind seemed to be getting worse. Sometimes it sounded almost like words. Liv looked out across the treetops, saw the branches shaking. She hugged herself and wished Gabby would hurry up.

Maybe he'd had a heart attack or something. He wasn't all that young.

Maybe he'd never come back.

The weird thing about the gray horse was that there weren't any footprints around him. The wind had been at work; it was howling around them so that they had to yell sometimes, but Wes thought it was more than that. The only odd thing they'd seen in their hunt was somebody's rope on the far bank under the cliff, maybe brought down by the creek at high water and dumped there. But on this side where it mattered there was nothing. They'd taken a hard look at the ground between the creek and the woods, mostly skeletal brush and weedstalks on both sides of the trail. Their own prints showed up fine where the snow was sheltered. Wes remembered the story Marty had told about the footprints that led from the flaming cabin to the truck and disappeared.

Here, his guess was that someone had gone to the trouble of brushing the footprints to blur them and let the wind do the rest. Why? 'Mark,' he called, 'we better get a search party.'

Mark was more agitated than Wes had ever seen him. 'How can they help? There's no trail! Dammit, where is she?'

'They've got manpower. Tracking dogs. Rescue equipment.'

'Where is she?'

'C'mon, Mark.' Wes threw his arm around his old teammate's shoulders. 'Let's get some real help.'

'But why Liv? She's not involved!'

'Involved in what?' Wes asked, but Mark just shook his head, so he added, 'Maybe she just got off the horse to go relieve herself, and she got lost. Look, you could ride the horse up and call the sheriff, and I'll wait here in case she shows up.'

Mark didn't seem to hear him. 'Liv wasn't there! What would he want with her?'

'Who?' Wes asked.

'Just, if someone has her . . .' He stumbled toward the woods.

Wes realized that he'd better stay with Mark or they'd have two missing persons to search for. He grabbed Mark's elbow and yelled over the wind, 'We'll leave the horse in case she comes back. Now let's go, Mark. March!'

Once he got him moving, Mark was almost too quick, hurrying up the trail. Wes didn't want to have another heart attack and dropped behind.

He was worried about the things Mark wasn't telling him. Mark thought someone had Liv, even though she wasn't involved. Who had her? And what wasn't she involved in? And why wouldn't Mark tell him?

Liv eyed the rock: a lot less friendly than when she'd had a safety rope. But enough of playing it safe. It was time to start thinking of what to do if Gabby didn't return. She opened the locking carabiner on her harness, freed herself of the safety anchor and walked toward the narrower end of the ledge.

Halfway there she paused to study the rock. Two interesting things ahead. Toward the far end, where the ledge was maybe four inches wide, she could see the good holds Gabby had used to start his climb to the top. And yes, partway up there was a smooth section with nothing but an inch-wide fissure. He'd used fingers and that little improvised ladder to get up.

Damn. She could see exactly how to do it, but not without the equipment.

The second interesting thing was only five feet ahead. There was a vertical edge that hid a slight widening of the ledge behind it. Beneath her boots, the ledge was still a foot wide. Piece of cake, she told herself, but took off her glove and jammed her fingers into a convenient little pocket in the limestone to steady herself just in case.

She was right. Beyond the edge there was a hollow in the rock, a shallow cave maybe three feet high and only two feet deep. On one side was a camp stove, a bottle of fuel, and a gray sleeping bag, rolled up. Weird. Who the hell would be camping up here? Gabby? Why?

He'd told her he had an insulated pad. There it was, under the sleeping bag. She pulled it out, sat down, and leaned back into the hollow, hoping it would be warmer; but the wind still gusted past her face, so it didn't help much, and the thought of snuggling into a sleeping bag he'd slept in gave her the creeps. Liv stood up again, glanced across the treetops, and found that from this angle she could see the Luganos' barn clearly. She could see most of the house too. She could see a horse in the paddock – Arlene's horse Cricket, judging by the way she tossed her head. With binoculars she could probably see the white star on her forehead.

Binoculars.

And that stove and sleeping bag spoke of hours spent here.

When you met strangers by chance . . .

Had it really been by chance? She'd worked cases in Brooklyn, women threatened by stalkers who'd watch them from windows sometimes two streets away . . .

But that wasn't logical. How could he have known she'd be interested in climbing? And anyway, her problem wasn't that Gabby was forcing himself on her; it was that he hadn't come back. Looking down, she could still see the tangled rope down there on the creek bank, under more and more snow. He hadn't picked it up. What the hell was Gabby doing?

Settle down, Liv, she told herself, just check those possible escape routes in case he got hurt. She turned her attention back to the cliff.

Gabby had said they'd cross the rock somehow to that wide gash – chimney, he called it – and from here it looked like a good plan once they got there. At the wall in the gym she'd seen some people chimneying up a similarly shaped formation, basically walking their feet up one side of the two-foot gash while steadying themselves by pushing their backs against the other side.

But how had Gabby planned to get them to the chimney? In contrast to the nice set of holds he'd actually used to go higher, there were few between here and the gash, higher or lower. Plus there was ice. Maybe he'd realized that she was too new to manage his first plan, that it would make more sense to just lower her on a rope.

Liv looked across the treetops at the barn again. No humans in sight. If someone came out, she could wave her arms – hope they looked up at the cliff.

How often had she herself looked up at this cliff? Not often. It was just there, eternal and silvery, part of the beautiful backdrop of the Luganos' place.

Of course even if the Luganos looked up and saw her, what could they do? They didn't know how to climb so they couldn't—

There was a skittering sound to her right. Liv looked toward it, saw the knotted end of a rope. Two ends! A pebble bounced off the ledge eight feet from her, and here he came, smoothly rappelling down, landing light-footed.

'Hey, Gabby! At last! I was getting worried,' she babbled in a tidal wave of relief, starting toward him but pausing when he stopped unknotting the end of the rope to raise his palm to halt her.

'Rope's falling,' he said. 'Get back into that hollow.'

She looked up, puzzled, but obeyed. 'OK.'

'Didn't mean to worry you,' he said, walking to the wide end to clip one end of the new rope to the anchor Liv had abandoned. Then he gave the ascending pair of ropes a shake and began to pull on one, coiling it on the ledge next to his feet. In a moment his prediction came true and the second half of the rope fell down and off the ledge, hitting Gabby on the shoulder a couple of times, but he was ready for it. Liv saw that he was wearing a second harness, like the one he'd given her. Guess he'd needed it for the rappel down. There also seemed to be more hardware on his shoulder sling.

'Well, we've got plenty of rope now,' she said, watching him reel it up on to the coil on the ledge.

'Yeah, thought it'd be good to have the right gear,' he said, jerking a thumb at the chimney formation. 'That's farther away than I remembered.'

'Doesn't look easy,' she said. 'Would it be better to go back the way we came up? Or maybe rappel down, like what you just did?'

'Rappelling needs practice. Really, that chimney'll be easier once we get there, and if I set the nuts right there won't be a problem. Just let me catch my breath a little here.' He pulled the insulated pad closer, sat down on one end and began inspecting the rope he'd just coiled.

Liv made her way across the ledge to the other end of the

pad. 'OK. But I'm really anxious to get back. I'm missing an appointment right now.'

Marty had noticed the pull-off on the right side of Ridge Road near the top of the last switchback, leading into a grove of cedars. When her cellphone rang she pulled into it before answering, 'Hopkins.'

'Deputy Hopkins. I am Alejandro Gallegos.'

'Hi, Alejandro. What's up?'

'Oleevia Mann ees not here.'

Marty glanced at her watch. Near noon. 'Well, about three hours ago she told me she was leaving on a horseback ride. She probably got delayed.' She didn't say it was because Sheriff Pierce had come by to talk to them. But he'd been there an hour max. No reason they couldn't have had their ride, got back, gone to their eleven-thirty appointments.

Alejandro said, '*Sí*, yes, she call me den too. Say we meet for sure.'

'Yeah, it's strange. I'll keep an eye out for her. Where are you?'

'Same as before – Edna's Diner, American pie. I estay half hour, OK?'

'OK. She's probably on her way.' Marty frowned as she rang off. She wouldn't have thought Liv was so casual about appointments, especially since she was going to show Alejandro photos of the machete that had been involved in her father's death.

Marty dropped her phone back on the passenger seat and glanced around the cedar grove. The road – in fact, all of civilization – was invisible from here. Might as well leave the cruiser where it was. Didn't want to drive in and scare the so-called birds Stanni claimed to be feeding.

She radioed Grady that she'd parked half a block down from the Gordon sisters' residence, then got out, pulled her collar up against the wind, and hiked the short distance to the house. The tiretracks of the sisters' van and of her cruiser on its first visit were already being blurred by blowing snow. So were the bootprints of the sisters where they'd loaded their vehicle and climbed into it. Marty walked around the side of the house to the back door. Yes, there were traces of more bootprints going to and from the woods back there on the

Gordon Creek rim of the ridge. She followed the tracks.

About forty yards into the woods was a weathered wooden box about three feet square, maybe five long. On top was a bird feeder, a clear plastic cylinder filled with seed. Some seed had spilled into the metal dish that held the cylinder. Marty studied it a moment. No snow on top of the box, and a circular depression in the snow nearby. She moved the bird feeder off and placed it there. Perfect fit.

The wind yowled, tossed grains of snow into her eyes.

There was a padlock, but it wasn't closed. Marty lifted the lid of the box.

Inside, a bag of bird seed. Also peanut butter, jelly, a loaf of bread. Granola bars, chocolate bars. A blue blanket that cradled some funny-looking little plastic wedges with sturdy cables attached. Some webbing straps, coiled neatly. A dozen D-shaped metal rings, the straight side hinged. She picked one up. It resisted a little when she opened it, snapped shut when released. She thought she'd seen rescue guys using gear like this.

The box was lined with metal, rodent-proof. Along the side, a tarp and a gray blanket were rolled up. At the end of the roll, warm and woolly socks, surgical tape, a first-aid box.

Except for the seed and a couple of the food items, nothing here would interest birds. Might interest a winter camper. But Stanni and Eunie had a house. Why would they camp here? Why keep supplies out here?

She closed the box, replaced the bird feeder, looked around. In the noon sunlight she thought she saw something beside the box, next to an evergreen bush. A bootprint? Yes. Several of them, scuffed over but not only by wind. They were close to the bushes where they'd be hidden except when the sun was high. Marty followed the scuff marks. They led farther along the ridge. Ten feet from the box she paused, looking at a print that had only been half obliterated.

She knew that print.

She'd studied it carefully next to Zill's cabin, next to Zill's truck.

The murderer's bootprint.

Twenty-Eight

'Gabby, really, can we start soon? I'm already late to meet someone,' Liv pleaded.

'Sure,' he said, but she'd already heard that three times. He explained, 'It's just that as I get older it takes a little longer to catch my breath. You young folks don't know how lucky you are.'

Liv wasn't feeling very lucky at the moment. Of course, after being stranded on the ledge she was abjectly grateful that he'd come back, very aware of how much she depended on him. But she was cold and wanted to get off this ledge no matter how much fun it had been to get here. A couple of times she'd thought she heard voices on the wind, but she was probably mistaken: there was no one in sight below. She buried her nose against her knees again to warm it, giving Gabby a sidelong glance. He was sitting yoga-style on the end of the insulated pad, his clothes as gray as the rock, not looking the least bit out of breath. Not even looking that cold, she thought resentfully, but of course he'd been exercising more recently than she had. What the hell was he up to? He said, 'Sorry about your appointment. What's it about?'

'Just a student I met.' She didn't want to tell him about Alejandro. She also didn't want to get him mad.

'Thought you were finished with school,' he said. The wind was louder than ever and they both had to raise their voices.

'Yeah. I'm out in the real world now. If you count the law as real.' She tried a smile. 'Guess it's as real as the numbers you work with.'

'Guess so. Is he a law student?'

She opened her mouth to say no, an engineer, but found she didn't even want to give away that much. Alejandro was already in trouble with people like Don Foley just for being Latino and speaking with an accent. Who knew why Gabby wanted to know? So she said, 'I think he's an undergraduate who wants to study law.'

'Mmm. And the friends you're staying with? Is he a lawyer? Oh, sorry; you told me he was an economist.'

Stange how he kept turning the conversation back to Mark. She said, 'He's retired. How are you feeling? Caught your breath yet?'

The smoke-colored glasses turned toward her. She realized she'd never seen his eyes. But he was smiling pleasantly enough. 'Yeah, I should be good to go in a minute or two. What did your friend do before he retired?'

'I never really understood the work he did. International, like my father.'

'He must have made a lot of money if he can afford horses.'

That chime of unease was ringing in Liv again. Was this about money? Had she been kidnapped? She said, 'I think his money is pretty much tied up in the property.'

'Nice property. Corporations pay well, I hear.'

'Guess it depends on the job you do.'

'You got that right. You said your father was a corporate engineer. What kind of projects did he do?'

Liv said, 'Don't know exactly. Mostly power plants, I think.' He was staring at her again. The wind was wailing. She jumped to her feet, said, 'C'mon, really. It's time to go.'

He looked down at his knees, nodded, stood up. 'OK. Let's get you ready to belay me here. Where's the ATC?' He riffled through the carabiners and nuts that jangled at his waist, pulled out the little double tube that had helped him brake her fall before, began threading the rope through it.

At last! Relieved, Liv asked, 'What does ATC stand for?'

The smoky glasses looked at her and a smile twitched at his mouth. 'Air Traffic Controller,' he said.

Liv burst into helpless laughter.

Marty looked up from the familiar bootprint and squinted through the woods that lined the rim of the cliff. A gust of wind puffed a dust of snow from the branches and made the sunlit air sparkle for a moment. Wouldn't be long before the brushed trail and even the clear print here would be sprinkled over, invisible.

Meant it was still fresh now.

She walked forward carefully. The wind sighed, masking the light crunch of her footsteps. Once in a lull she thought she heard a woman's laugh. But it didn't happen again, or if it did the wind covered it.

She watched the brushed trail, but even more she watched the woods ahead. She didn't want to confront him without backup, just figure out where he was hiding before the trail was obliterated. Then she could call for backup and do the job right.

Every sense alert, she crept along the ridge top. Then she paused. Which way had he gone? The cedar ten feet ahead of her was very close to the rim, so he'd stay away from the cliff, right? Stay on the ridge side? But she couldn't see any sign of the trail. No bootprints, no brush marks. And there was something odd about the base of the cedar.

Marty crouched low behind a tangle of bare branches and peered at it. Didn't seem to be a structure. No. Now she could see that there was a sort of sling made of brown webbing around the cedar trunk, clipped together by a couple of those D-shaped rings that she'd seen in the wooden box. A second strap led from the D-rings over the edge of the cliff.

The wind dropped a moment and she heard voices. A woman was pleading – Liv? Could it be? '. . . start soon? Please? I've gotta get back.' And a male voice Marty didn't know said soothingly, 'Sure, just tie into this. What did the sheriff—' And then the wind picked up again.

Marty grabbed a thick root, clung to it as she wriggled flat on her stomach to the edge of the cliff to look down. Something moved a bit ahead of her, down the cliff side from where that cedar grew. She could just see the top edge of two heads, a shoulder. One head was the bright green of Liv Mann's hat. The other was the warm gray of the rock and she wouldn't have seen it except it moved.

She pushed herself away from the cliff edge, hurried back quietly along the narrow trail, broke into a run once she thought she was out of earshot. She punched her shoulder radio. 'Three-twenty-one,' she said.

Grady's welcome voice acknowledged and she said, 'Ten-thirty-five, ten-seventy-eight, ten-forty.' Major crime, need assistance, silence sirens.

Grady repeated her calls, asked, 'Ridge Road address?'

'Yeah, down the cliff behind it.'

'It'll take them twenty to thirty minutes.'

'Damn. Well, do your best.'

'Ten-four.'

She'd reached the cruiser and opened the trunk. She pulled out some fluorescent triangles and the old coil of rope they occasionally used to pull snowmobiles from ditches or cows from sinkholes, and ran back to the cliff edge, hanging the triangles on branches for the backup guys to follow when they came.

Twenty minutes was too long. Liv had sounded worried, not panicked, so she probably didn't know this rock-colored guy had killed her father. Also three ex-Marines who worked security. Whatever he'd done to them, small Liv wouldn't have a chance against it.

Marty reached the cedar with the webbing, hung on to the strap, looked down cautiously. The two seemed to be about four stories below her, still well above the faraway creek. They stood on a natural shelf of limestone. If Marty strained she could make out some words, the man saying, 'How come you're here? Talking to them? Does it have something to do with your father?' and Liv's wary reply, 'What do you mean?'

Marty was holding a strap that led from the belt of webbing around the cedar over the rim. She saw that a second tree a little farther along also had a belt and a strap leading over the edge. Below her, the two straps were clipped together by a pair of those metal D-links like the ones in that wooden box, forming a V that dangled over the cliff edge. Looked like a really sturdy attachment.

The man was saying, 'Your father died. Was it like this death? Is that why they're talking to you?'

'Maybe.'

'And they'd both been to Ecuador, you say.'

Marty realized that he'd learned a lot from Liv about the investigation. She finished knotting her old rope through the two D-links at the apex of the V and slung the coil over her shoulder so it wouldn't fall and alert the guy below. Then she grabbed it tight, and got the rope around one leg, and let herself over the edge.

Damn, this was hard on the arms. The rescue teams she'd seen had harnesses and lots of rope gear and teammates. She'd seen some solo acrobats in a circus once who used leg-wraps to steady themselves while sliding around on their ropes, but she couldn't figure out how to slide. The old rope was too tight around her leg, or else so loose it suddenly threw her entire weight on her arms. Finally she resigned herself to letting herself down hand over hand while walking her feet down the rock.

She peered down over her shoulder every few steps to see if they had noticed her, but they hadn't, probably because of the howl of the wind. Pretty soon her arms were so tired she hated to take even a second to look. It was easier to check her progress by glancing up. How the hell had they gotten to that ledge? Lucky backup was coming. They'd be able to get ladders or whatever . . .

Ouch. The rope had eaten through the palm of her right glove. She risked another peek down. She was about halfway, still two stories to go. But they weren't looking up yet.

With her teeth she managed to pull her glove partway off so a fresh part of the leather was against the rope, but it made her grip clumsy and she'd only gone a few feet farther when she glimpsed something to her left. Smoky glasses. A flash of metal. The rock-colored man was cutting through her rope.

Marty kicked furiously, grabbed at him.

Then she was falling.

211

Twenty-Nine

The *chaski* was about to fall. The stupid deputy had grabbed his knee and pulled his left foot from its hold, and he'd had to use his right foot to stamp on her shoulder until she slid down his leg and he kicked her off, so now he was dangling from one hard-crimped hand. Couldn't hold it long.

He could go back up to where he'd been, but there was no percentage in that. Her cruddy rope would be out of reach, and the only other way to get farther up that smooth section of the rock face was along the finger crack twenty feet to the right. And once he got up to the rim, he might find another deputy. No, down was better. At least he was rid of this deputy. When he'd glimpsed the uniform, he'd instinctively swarmed up the rock to cut away the problem, as he'd cut away that Ohio cop. His instincts were usually good.

He looked down to his left, saw that he'd remembered correctly. There'd been one jug-sized bump as he came up. Above it to the right, invisible from above but engraved in his muscle memory, was a two-inch pocket eroded into the limestone. He sighted on the jug, gave a gentle side push with his knee as he let go and then his left foot was solid on it, his right fingers sliding into the limestone pocket above it. Now he was only ten feet above the ledge.

He heard Liv's voice from below, faint through the wind sounds. 'Are you all right?'

He called, 'Yeah, be with you in a minute,' and wondered how much she'd seen. Liv Mann was a fine young woman. The Inca in her made her so much better than her father. He thought she'd been on the verge of telling him about Mark, had even felt a wisp of hope that she'd understand him the way May had. But, sensitive as she was, she wasn't yet ready to understand about the deputy. Maybe he could convince her that he'd seen the deputy's rope fraying, and gone up to help.

212

But he'd been too late and she'd bounced down the cliff to her death.

He looked down to his right to sight on the last hold before the ledge and froze, astonished. The deputy was lying on the ledge!

Was she dead? Liv was probing her unresponsive legs gently with her fingers. When she moved up to the left arm the deputy twitched. Liv, already anchored for the belay, unclipped the protection from her harness and attached it instead to the deputy's belt.

What had happened? He'd kicked her away from the rock, she should have cleared the ledge – oh. He remembered now: that last wild clutch at his ankle must have snugged her against the cliff, and if she'd plunged feet first, she'd hit the ledge, yes, and her legs and knees might absorb some of the shock of the short drop.

But she still would have been off-balance, should have fallen backward off the ledge. Mathematically speaking she should be gone. What was missing from the equation? There was nothing she could grab, except . . .

Except Liv, who'd been clipped solidly to an anchor he'd placed himself.

Well, there were variables in the world as well as constants, though in the end they were all subject to the same laws. He could solve this equation too. He moved smoothly, left hand down to the edge where his foot rested, right foot down to the little hold, and then just a hop to the ledge. He said, 'Her rope was old and frayed. I was too late to help.'

Liv looked at him an instant, big dark Inca eyes, before she said, 'I think she needs an ambulance. Do you have a cellphone?'

'No.'

'Can you go call for help?'

'I have a first-aid kit. Just a minute.' He didn't want to leave them together, although the deputy looked neutralized. But of course there might be another deputy up there. The problem with police was they worked together. How much time did he have?

He opened the first-aid kit. 'What does she need?'

'I'm still checking.' Liv was closing the deputy's coat again. 'No obvious broken bones, but I saw her bump her head, and

213

this gizmo on her shoulder is smashed, so she must have hit something.'

'Her radio.' The *chaski* was relieved. Must have happened when he stamped on her shoulder to get her off his leg. He added, 'Too bad. Phones are pretty unreliable in this landscape but the sheriff might have a good frequency. Maybe we could have called for help.'

'Maybe.' Liv's fingers were probing the deputy's curly brown hair now. In a moment she said, 'Here we go. Bump swelling up.'

'Let's see.' He leaned forward to touch the deputy's head. Liv didn't stop him, but she stiffened, watched him intently, and he realized he had a ways to go to regain her confidence.

But first, the crushed shoulder radio had reminded him of something else. As he straightened, he let his hand trail along the deputy's right side, unsnapped her holster, took out the gun.

'What are you doing?' Liv grabbed his arm with both hands.

'Don't want her to wake up all confused and do something harmful,' he explained, and jerked his arm free to drop the gun into his pack.

Liv nodded slowly. 'Good idea. What do you think we should do next?'

'Wait for her to wake up.'

'I still think you should go call someone for help.'

'Liv, look, if it's just that bump it shouldn't take long for her to wake up. Then we can see if there's anything serious – spinal injury or anything. We'll know what to tell the emergency team. Plus, she probably has a partner up there who's going to be checking anyway.'

'Right!' Liv stood up and yelled, 'Sheriff! Help! Down here!'

The *chaski* glanced at the route back to the lower ledge, the chocks still in place in case he had to retreat; then looked up to see if anyone would answer.

But the only response was the moan of the wind.

Marty's head throbbed, and her shoulder, and there was a sense of something wrong, something she had to do. She started to open her eyes, but a glare of blue sent a spike through her head and she closed them again. Then a shout, 'Sheriff! Help!'

Someone needed her help. Liv. Liv needed help. She tried opening her eyes a tiny bit, and this time her lashes screened out the worst of the glare. Yes, it was Liv standing above her, looking up at the blue glare, yelling, 'Down here!'

Next to Liv was the rock-colored man. Also looking up at the blue sky.

Nobody was looking at Marty. She was lying down. Lower than they were.

Then Liv glanced down at her and knelt suddenly, her hand brushing gently over Marty's eyes to close them again. Liv said very clearly, 'Nobody's answering up there, Gabby. If she has a partner he can't hear us. We need to go get help for her.'

'Let's give her a few more minutes to wake up,' said the rock man. 'If she can tell us what hurts we'll be much better off.'

Liv said, 'Look, Gabby, you've been great. Taught me some climbing, fetched us a new rope, went up to help Deputy Hopkins. But now she needs an ambulance, and you're delaying. I don't get it. All you've done is take her gun. Do you need to catch your breath again?'

Through the ache in her head Marty was getting a hazy picture. She could tell Liv was nervous about the man, but thought she could communicate with him. Liv wasn't tied up. But, Marty realized, if the rock-colored man – what had she called him? Gabby? – if he controlled whether or not she could get off the cliff, she was a captive all the same.

They both were.

Yet Liv was talking. And her words explained what was happening so that Marty could understand it. Like, backup hadn't arrived yet. And something about Marty's gun – damn! The man Gabby had taken her gun!

He was saying, 'I'm OK, but seriously, it's not easy getting an injured person off a ledge like this. I've done some Alpine rescue work and I know. So the more we can tell them about her condition the better.'

Liv objected, 'But the quicker they get here, the better, too!'

'Sure, if they've brought the right equipment. Otherwise they have to go back for it and it takes three times as long.'

Marty's memory was beginning to kick in. She'd been

215

tracking the bootprints of Zill's killer. She'd looked down, seen that man on a ledge on a cliff, and Liv with him. And she remembered starting down to help Liv.

After that it was all a haze.

Liv was saying, 'Yeah, I see, but what if she doesn't wake up?'

'Then we'll have to leave her and go for help.'

'Leave her alone here?'

'I need to get you away safely.'

Liv's fingers, still resting against Marty's cheek, began to tremble. His idea of getting away safely was not the same as Liv's. Marty realized how close to panic the other woman was. Time to give her a little help.

Always remembering who had the gun.

Right now, weakness was strength.

Marty moaned. Liv's hand stiffened and she said, 'She's waking up.'

Marty flexed her toes experimentally. Seemed to be bruised but in working order. And her arms – ouch! The left one shrieked protests into her aching brain. She rolled a little to her right to get her better arm underneath. Through half-open eyes she saw she was facing the rock face. Good thing she hadn't rolled the other way.

She managed to push herself into a sitting position. Didn't have to fake moaning because it seemed every part she tried to move was sore.

Even her butt, when she finally worked her way around to sit leaning against the rock.

Liv asked, 'How are you?'

'Feels like I fell off a roof,' Marty said. It was hard to make her tongue work. 'Did I?'

'Pretty much,' said the man called Gabby. 'I went up to help you because your rope was fraying. I was too late.'

Marty didn't move – just sat with half-opened eyes, letting herself look as miserable as she was. She couldn't remember what had happened, but she heard relief in Gabby's voice at her confusion, and knew he was lying. She said, 'Thanks for trying,' and looked around, blinking. 'So where are we?'

Liv said, 'A cliff along the border of the Luganos' property.'

Luganos? Well, yeah, that'd be about right, though Marty

hadn't realized they owned the whole stretch to the foot of Demon Ridge. She said, 'We're really high up. How did you guys get here?'

'Gabby's an expert rock climber, and I always wanted to try it,' Liv said. 'So he's giving me a climbing lesson.'

Gabby said, 'She's a natural. I think it's her Inca blood.'

So that's how he lured her up here. Marty said, 'Boy, I'm no natural. Guess French blood doesn't hack it. D'you know where my gun fell?'

Liv said quickly, 'Yeah, Gabby's got it in his pack.' She gestured at a gray cylinder tucked into a sort of niche three feet to Marty's right.

'Do you want it?' Gabby asked. He was standing next to the gray pack.

Marty shook her head. Of course she wanted it but she sure as hell didn't want his hand on that gun as he pretended to get it for her. She said, 'In a minute. What's this stuff?' She gestured at the D-rings that attached her to the straps.

'I clipped that to you in case you rolled the wrong way when you started waking up,' Liv said.

Marty looked at the drop from the ledge, at least double the distance to the rim up there, and nodded. 'Thanks. This strap thing is long enough for me to see if I can stand up, right?' The other end was behind her somewhere.

Liv said, 'Sure. You've got maybe five feet.'

Marty pointed at the edge. 'Not that direction! Well, here we go. Testing one two three.' She managed to get her legs under her, pushed up with the help of her good arm, finished with a lurch to her right but ended up standing. In fact her legs were pretty functional despite their complaints, but she'd added the lurch to get her a couple feet closer to her gun.

But the man was quick too, jumped to grab her elbow. 'You OK?'

'Yeah, thanks, just a little dizzy.' She looked him full in the face for an instant and memory stirred. Did she know him? The set of the jaw ... but she couldn't see his eyes behind the smoky glasses, couldn't see his ears because the gray cap was pulled down, couldn't quite remember.

From somewhere above her head she heard a faint report on the wind. Then another. Shots? Her backup, maybe? But what was there to shoot at?

The gray man had heard them too. She said, 'I better sit until my head settles down,' and thought she heard three more shots while she was talking. To keep him distracted she dropped suddenly, intending to land to the right again to be in reach of her gun in the pack. But he countered with a half-step toward it and a nudge of her elbow. She smiled at him and said, 'Thanks . . .' She started to say 'Gabby' and the penny dropped. 'You've been great, Mr McGabben.'

He took a surprised half-step back. Liv said, 'You know each other? He said he hadn't talked to the sheriff!'

Marty looked from one to the other. 'No, we haven't talked. But we were doing background work on your father's old friends from high school.'

Liv stared at McGabben. 'High school? You knew my father?'

Uh-oh, Marty thought, Liv didn't know that. Can she keep her cool?

But McGabben also looked stunned, and there was an angry twitch at the corner of his mouth.

Marty hoped he'd keep his cool too.

Thirty

L iv stared at Gabby. 'You knew my father?'
Gabby covered his hesitation by glancing sideways to lean his left shoulder against the cliff wall next to the niche, and part of Liv's mind, the part that wasn't contending with total confusion, noticed that Deputy Hopkins used the fraction of a second he looked away to slide a few inches closer to the gray pack. The deputy was the one who answered Liv: 'Yeah, Mr McGabben was in the high-school math club with your father.'

Liv met Deputy Hopkins's gray eyes for an instant and saw that it was not a ploy, it was true. Gabby – McGabben – had known Pops. God! So why had he pretended he hadn't? Had he lost track, was just catching up? Was he testing her? Or . . . Horrible possibilities shuffled through her mind and she almost blurted out an accusation, but Deputy Hopkins headed her off, suggesting in a calm voice, 'That's probably why he was interested in meeting you. Catching up after all these years.'

It steadied Liv and she beat down her outrage. Hell, she'd already worked out that this hadn't been a chance meeting, that he'd been spying on Mark's place, that he'd stranded her on purpose by kicking the rope off the ledge. She'd play along with Deputy Hopkins. Liv said, 'So that's why you were asking about him! I'm afraid I didn't answer your questions very well, I was so interested in learning how to climb.'

McGabben nodded. 'Yeah, climbing keeps you focused. Sorry I didn't say anything about high school. Long time ago.'

'That's true; when you're climbing you don't think about much else.' Liv wanted to scream questions about high school at him but managed a grin instead. 'He's brilliant, Deputy Hopkins.'

Deputy Hopkins also gave him a friendly smile. 'I believe it. But you don't live around here, do you?'

'No, I live out west.'

'So did you climb these cliffs when you were a kid?'

'I got into climbing later. Except I used to try to scale those quarry walls.'

'Wow, I never did that,' Deputy Hopkins said. 'When I went swimming I used the easy trails through the spall rocks.' She turned her head to look at Liv, her brown curls blowing in the icy wind. 'Liv, did your father tell you about our quarries?'

Liv didn't give a damn about the quarries; she wanted to know what this strange man could tell her about her father. She said, 'Pops said the quarries were real good swimming holes. Is that how you got to know him, Gabby?'

'More the math club,' he said.

Because he was looking edgy, Liv framed her next question carefully, offering him an explanation as Deputy Hopkins had done. 'Oh, hey, I didn't tell you the name of the friends I'm staying with. You must have known them from the math club too! Mark Lugano?'

He said, 'Mark. How about that.'

As though it had never occurred to him! Anger made Liv less cautious. She said, 'Strange, isn't it? Nichols County High School Math Club – and all three of you went to Ecuador. I mean, it's a great country and everything, but not that many Americans go there. What are the odds?'

There was a scowl behind the smoke-gray glasses that froze on her a moment and she was afraid she'd pushed too fast. But to his left Deputy Hopkins made what must have been a painful move for her, pushing herself to a standing position with her left arm and leg while holding out her right hand toward Gabby, saying, 'Give me a hand, Mr McGabben? I want to try standing up again.' And it distracted him as she grabbed his hand and pulled herself upright, smiling at him again. 'Yeah, it's better this time.'

'Good,' Gabby said curtly, and dropped her hand. They were both standing in front of the gray pack now.

Deputy Hopkins said, 'That's not so strange about Ecuador, Liv. A friend helped me get this job. I mean, they worked for different companies but Mark steered work to your father, right?'

'Well, that's true,' Liv said. 'You could say my father was there because Mark was there first.'

'How about you, Mr McGabben?' Deputy Hopkins turned to him cheerfully. 'Did Liv's father bring you to Ecuador? Or Mark Lugano?'

'I went to climb the Andes,' he said.

'Chimborazo,' Liv said. 'You told me to allow time to adapt to the altitude before a major climb. Do government book-keepers get long enough vacations? Or were you posted there?'

She couldn't see his eyes but it felt like he was glaring at her. Deputy Hopkins seemed alert too and raised a palm at Liv to wait, as though they were closing in on something, but Liv couldn't figure out what and mused aloud, 'You were telling me that sometimes big corporations do criminal things and that's why you quit. Did you quit Bielefeld Burke? Or Telmeck?'

And then she gasped as Gabby dove under Deputy Hopkins's arm, grabbed at the gray pack in the hollow. The deputy kicked at him furiously, pulling at the pack. She managed to shift it in Liv's direction. Liv jumped forward, pulled it out, and Deputy Hopkins gave two mighty backward kicks. The second sent it off the ledge. Liv watched it fall sickeningly down to the creek.

But when she looked back she saw it had all been for nothing.

Gabby was backing away toward the wide end of the ledge, out of reach of the tethered deputy.

And he held her gun.

By the time Wes came chugging up from the creek to the Luganos' house, his heart doing better than it would have five years ago, Mark had gone ahead and was already on the phone with the sheriff's office, Arlene hovering beside him. From Mark's end of the conversation Wes could tell that Grady was giving him the usual line about how in a free country it was OK for adults to go missing. He grabbed the receiver, said, 'Grady, Cochran here. Listen up.'

'Yes, sir.' That was always the thing about Grady: he responded well to authority. Not like Marty, who sometimes got stubborn. Although – Forget Marty. He said, 'Listen up, Grady, two things you should know. No, three. Number one,

Mark is right: there's a strong possibility that Liv Mann has been kidnapped by a killer. Two, Sheriff Pierce will have your head if he finds out you blew off an important citizen like Mark Lugano. Three, this call is from Mark, not from me. Got it?'

'Yes, sir.'

'Say, "Yes, sir, Mr Lugano."'

Grady did and Wes handed the receiver back to Mark. 'Give him directions and see if he can give you an estimated time of arrival.'

The news wasn't totally satisfactory. 'He said the closest people are twenty minutes away, and they're on another urgent call, so if it takes them time to wrap that up it may be longer.' Mark sank into a chair, face in hands.

Wes felt like doing the same thing. Instead he said to Arlene, 'Give Mark a Valium or something and then let us be. We have some talking to do.'

Marty leaned back against the cliff wall so she could watch McGabben to her right on the wider end of the ledge and still keep track of Liv on her left, who was staring in panic at the revolver in his hand.

He hadn't cocked it. That was good news.

But McGabben looked uncertain, which was bad news. She wished she could see his eyes behind those gray glasses. His body language said he was bewildered, not sure of the next step. Liv's question about quitting the corporation had upset him and he'd impulsively gone for the gun, abandoning whatever game plan he'd had before, a plan that had kept him mostly friendly and talking, and did not include killing them immediately. She wasn't sure what he wanted, though she had no doubt that he would kill: he'd already killed.

But only once with a gun. Only once that she knew about.

And he seemed to respect Liv.

So try to find out what he wanted. She licked her dry lips and said, 'I think you were right to quit, Mr McGabben.'

He muttered, 'You don't understand.'

Understanding. OK, maybe that was something he wanted. Marty said, 'That's true, but see, we weren't there. We don't know what was going on.'

'Horrible,' he said.

'Yeah, I believe you.' She didn't take her eyes from him

222

but gave a palm-down gesture at Liv to keep her clumsy questions to herself. Damn lawyers didn't know when to shut up. His mouth was working and Marty felt that emotionally he was in another place. Use it. She said gently, 'Sometimes we can't stop horrible things from happening.'

'I told them! I was the *chaski* and I told them! But they didn't pay attention. Until later – then they paid attention, all right. Then they understood.'

'But later was still too late,' she guessed. 'It was horrible.'

The wind moaned past them and took away his words, but Marty thought he had probably said 'Yeah', because his chin dipped in a nod.

She said, 'I'm beginning to understand a little. But I wasn't there.'

'Yeah.'

'Somebody died, right?'

'She died. She ran into the fire bleeding. And the children were screaming and they died.'

Pieces were sliding into place. Marty damped down a shudder and said, 'The school was burning.'

'They didn't listen to me.'

A freezing gust of wind whipped by and she stuck both hands in her pockets next to her papers. She said, 'You tried to stop them and they didn't listen.'

'I was the *chaski*. The messenger. She told me to explain why the villagers were protesting the loss of their land. It would ruin so many lives. But they didn't listen.'

'See, I wasn't there. I don't know why they didn't listen.'

He frowned at her. 'Because their bosses wanted it to be built, they said. The school had to be burned to show they were serious. They said they were sending a message.'

Liv had crept up very close behind her against the wall. Even though it hurt her left arm to reach back, Marty grabbed her hand. She couldn't look away from McGabben but she was afraid she knew what was coming and it would be hard on Liv. Marty said, 'They didn't listen to your message about saving lives. And when they sent their message to show they were serious, people died.'

'Yeah. Yeah, that's it.' He still held the gun but the safety was still on and the muzzle was drooping.

She said, 'You're helping me understand. She told you the

people's lives would be ruined and you should tell the company not to build the dam.'

Liv's hand twitched in Marty's but she stayed quiet. McGabben said, 'Yeah. May was good. She loved the children. They had Inca blood.'

Liv breathed, 'Oh,' and Marty wondered if her Inca blood was why Liv was still alive.

McGabben shifted his feet and the climbing gear on his shoulder sling jangled. He went on, 'She said I knew Ronnie Mann, he would listen to me. We were old friends from Indiana, right? So I went to Quito, where he was. But Ronnie said the whole country would benefit, and he showed me Mark's report. But it was garbage.'

'Garbage?'

'Electricity from that dam would only help a couple of companies; no one else could afford it. Mark fudged the conclusions. I showed Ronnie that all it would do was put Ecuador into debt; they couldn't pay back the loans to the international bankers.'

Marty kept her hold on Liv's hand. 'And what did Mr Mann say?'

'He said Telmeck was getting paid from those loans, and he was just the engineer, and anyway I was too late – he'd hired a security company to clear the site.'

Liv's hand was trembling in hers and Marty gave it a sympathetic warning squeeze as she said, 'I see. Mr Mann hired Armadillo.'

'Yeah, he knew Johnny Bowers, so he chose Armadillo.'

'To show the villagers that Telmeck was serious about building the dam.'

'Yeah. So I rushed back to tell her about Armadillo, but . . .' He bowed his head.

'Maybe they were already there,' Marty suggested.

'Yeah. We didn't know until we heard the explosion.'

'Yeah.' Marty was gripped by sadness.

'We ran toward the school. I was yelling to them to stop, but Zill had already thrown the grenade. Bowers told him to. They wouldn't listen to me.'

'That's horrible.'

'And she was running beside me; she said there were children inside. And we could hear them screaming.'

Marty said, 'Didn't they know there were children inside? I wasn't there, but it was a school. Didn't they know?'

'Bowers said it was after hours. It was supposed to be empty – he kept saying that: it was supposed to be empty.'

'But it wasn't.'

'They were practicing a play, she said. And she said, "We have to get them out!" They were screaming. And I started to go with her, but Zill and Bowers grabbed me, said there was white gasoline, it was hopeless. And she said, You're the *chaski*; tell them they're wrong!'

He stopped, swallowed, the gray glasses aimed down at her feet. Marty said, 'You told them, but they didn't stop.'

'No. And they tried to keep her from going in. Gene Elkins held up his machete, but she ran past it and he cut her.'

Liv said, 'But . . .' in a small voice.

Marty tugged her hand, hard, to shut her up, and said, 'She was bleeding but she went in anyway.'

He said, 'Back then I didn't know how to make them pay attention. Now I know how. Now they pay attention to her message.'

'I see,' Marty said, shaken by his ghastly story, by his ghastly vendetta. Behind her, Liv was sobbing.

He said, 'I have to finish the job. The message. You can't stop me. I'm the *chaski*. The messenger. The accountant.' And there was a click as he cocked the gun and again leveled it at Marty.

Fear was bitter in the back of her mouth. She ignored it and kept her voice gentle. 'I'm not stopping you. I wasn't there, but you explained so I could understand. I came to help, like May's sisters. They helped you.'

'No! They only gave supplies. I planned everything, I'm the *chaski*.'

'I understand. Can I give you a photo?'

'A photo?' He was confused, frowning.

'It helped me understand,' she said as she pulled out the notes in her right pocket, let go of Liv's hand and picked out the copy of the newspaper article. She held it up to him like a shield. 'Here she is in the picture.' She'd hoped to distract him and was gratified when he took off the gray glasses and squinted at the photo, hunger and grief on his face.

'May? It's May?'

'Yeah. And the Inca children. She loves the children.' Marty pushed the picture an inch closer to him. 'She's full of love. See the beautiful smile?'

He was riveted, took another step. Marty said, 'Look at her.'

He nodded, still staring at the lovely vivid face with the wild curls, and reached for the page. The gun dropped from his fingers and Marty kicked it off the ledge as she slowly laid the photo on the ledge, anchored it with a stone. She repeated gently, 'Look at her. What's her message?'

He said, 'Don't hurt the children.'

'That's right. She didn't want the children to be killed. She didn't want people to die. She loved people. She wanted justice. Look at her!'

He was staring at the photo and no longer seemed to notice her. *Can't see, just stares* played in her mind as she slid her hand into the niche where the sleeping bag and camp stove sat, picked up the bottle of fuel, and cracked him hard on the head.

He collapsed on top of the photo. She pulled his arms back and snapped on the handcuffs.

Liv was leaning back against the wall, weeping, her face in her hands. Marty nudged her. 'Help me lock him to this anchor.'

Liv made an effort, wiped her nose on her cuff, said in a snuffly voice, 'Wouldn't do any good. Those come out if you pull up instead of down.'

Good, she was functioning again, though it was bad news. Marty said, 'Well, he may wake up mad. And my backup is way overdue; something went wrong. Can you get us down from here?'

Liv said, 'No. But if you get me the gear he has on that shoulder sling, I can get us up.'

'Up's better anyway: my cruiser's there.' Marty stepped over to McGabben, still solidly out. She cut the sling with her knife and handed the gear to Liv. 'Let's go.'

Thirty-One

Liv felt shaken up, as though she'd just taken a bar exam or had a tooth extracted. A zillion questions were flapping ominously in her head like Hitchcock's birds. The story that Deputy Hopkins had pulled from Gabby had engaged her sympathy and indignation until she realized . . . well, better sort out that stuff later. At least Pops hadn't thrown the grenade. Right now, get off this damned wonderful cliff.

She looked dubiously at her belayer. Deputy Hopkins had never even done a gym wall, and her technique coming down that rope had looked really lousy in the glimpse Liv had before Gabby got up there and cut it. She'd looked strong, at least, though now her left shoulder was banged up and probably undependable. Liv had helped her put on Gabby's harness, given her a five-minute lesson in working carabiners one-handed and foot placement. She'd explained how to belay three times. She'd even gone up a few feet over the wider part of the ledge, set a chock and clipped the rope through the carabiner, and let go on purpose so the deputy could see what it would be like. Her reactions had been quick and she'd stopped Liv before her feet hit the ledge. Still, it was a long way from ideal.

Better than staying on the ledge with Gabby, though, because he'd wake up. While they were taking his gear, Liv removed his climbing shoes too and threw them down into the creek. Deputy Hopkins said, 'Can we tie him down somehow? For our safety and the guys' who come to pick him up. Don't know why they aren't here yet.'

They looped a sling of webbing under his arm and Liv anchored it to a chock beyond his lolling head, and then they stretched him out and attached one ankle to an anchor set in the opposite direction, so that moving toward either tightened the other one. But it was looser than Deputy Hopkins liked. 'Let's get out of here,' she said.

Liv finished taping the deputy's hands, especially the nasty rope burn on the right hand. 'Your part of the climb will be easier if you watch where I put my hands and feet,' Liv said. 'Correction: watch where I put them when I succeed in making the next move.'

'Gotcha.'

They were down at the narrow end of the ledge now, the deputy anchored to the rock. Liv checked the sling with the gear, the safety rope, made sure she had enough slack to move but not too much. Then she looked up at the rock, at the thin crack Gabby had used, flexed her fingers.

'Climbing,' she said.

'Climb away,' the deputy replied.

And then Liv was moving, remembering the beginning of Gabby's route clearly enough. Ten feet up there was a pocket and she figured out which chock would fit, oriented it carefully, tested it, and clipped the rope through its carabiner. 'Now if I fall, the rope will stop me about here,' she called down.

'I see.'

'Climbing.'

'Climb away.' The deputy's voice was almost lost in a gust of wind but the rope eased. Liv hoped they could hear each other when she was higher.

There was another good crack eight feet farther along, so she set another protective chock. Then came that little vertical slit. Right hand clinging to a nice waist-high three-inch pocket in the limestone, she set a chock low in the crack to hold the rope, then jammed her taped fingers up into the crack and moved her toe into the pocket where her hand had been. A gust of wind roared past. When it was quieter she shouted, 'I need more slack,' and the rope eased. She pulled a loop of it into her teeth, eyeballed the little edge to her left, got her toe on it and pushed. Hard to tell which was worse for her fingers, painfully jammed into the little crack – the chewing of the rough rock or the numbing cold or the weight of her body as she lifted it. But each inch gained brought triumphant joy.

OK, just over her head was the slight widening in the crack where Gabby had placed the chock for the ladder. Her first try was the wrong size and pulled out when she tested it. She had to keep hanging from her unhappy left fingers and cramped toes while she found a bigger chock, nudged it in, tugged on its carabiner. This one would hold. She fumbled the thin webbing ladder from her sling and clipped it on. 'Climbing!'

'Climb away!' came the deputy's voice, faint on the wind.

Steadying herself with fingers in the narrowing crack, Liv climbed to the top of the little ladder. Ten feet to go. She popped in a final protective chock and clipped the rope to it for the deputy's benefit, then found a bucket-sized foothold to her right, an eroded pocket for her left hand, and for her right hand – a root! She tested it and pulled herself to the top.

Woods. Snow. Freedom.

But there wasn't time to feel elated. When she looked down she saw Deputy Hopkins looking up at her, still alert on belay, and behind her she saw Gabby, finally awake, jerking at his tethers.

Liv stepped back from the rim to clip webbing straps around a tree, two more to attach her harness to the anchor and still allow her to reach the rim so she could see down. Then she began frantically pulling up the slack in the rope. She yelled, 'Belay off,' and once Deputy Hopkins had unclipped her ATC the rope moved faster. This must be a short pitch by climbing standards because there was sure a lot of extra rope. She threw it willy-nilly behind her, working as fast as she could.

Below her she saw the deputy look over her shoulder at Gabby bucking in his bonds. The deputy yelled, 'Climbing!' but Liv could see it wasn't safe yet. She shouted, 'Belay off!' and kept pulling the rope. She still had a ways to go, but as soon as she figured the deputy wouldn't trip on it she clipped it into the ATC on the belt of her harness and shouted, 'Climb away!'

Taking up the slack was a little slower working through the device, so the rope was still loose when Deputy Hopkins reached the first piece of protection. It took her a moment and Liv realized that one of her boots had slipped off one little foothold, but she got back on and fumbled at the carabiner until she got the gate opened and the rope free.

Ten feet below her, Gabby had figured out the weakness in his bonds. Belly down, he'd wriggled back toward his feet so there was some slack in the strap around his ankle. He was using the other foot to scrape at it. Damn – might just work.

Liv looked back at the deputy. She was taking a minute to

study the rock. When she moved she was definitely favoring her left arm. Liv was worried.

Especially since Gabby had pushed the tether off his ankle.

Deputy Hopkins was working with the carabiner at the bottom of the thin crack, trying to get the rope out so she could climb higher. This time she had to do it with her left hand and it looked to Liv like she was in pain. Finally it came free and she moved both hands into the crack up to her second finger joint, as Liv had done, and the toe of her boot up to the hold where her hand had just been.

But when she started to move her right hand higher in the crack, her left apparently couldn't manage that much of her weight. The deputy slid, scrabbling to hold on. Liv pulled the rope back hard from the ATC at the belt of her harness.

The jolt skidded her six inches forward as the weight hit the belt of her harness and transferred through it to the tree behind her. Somehow she kept the brake pulled tight, and the anchor straps held, and Gabby's good rope did its job, acting like a shock absorber. Liv could see Deputy Hopkins dangling safe below.

She could also see that Gabby's feet were free. He was on his knees now, still with hands cuffed behind him but able to move toward the other tether. He'd have that chock out in a minute.

And sitting in her harness, Deputy Hopkins was massaging her left arm.

Damn.

Mark Lugano waved off the pills Arlene brought him, and she looked at Wes with eyes so anxious that he wanted to tell her to take them herself. Instead he said, 'Maybe later, Arlene. Right now Mark is going to take me into his office and we're going to compare notes.'

'No! We should go down and look for Liv,' Mark said.

'We're going to do exactly that,' Wes told him, 'but not until you tell me what the hell I'm up against here.'

Mark was almost as tall as Wes and for a moment the tortured brown eyes stared into his, frightened and angry at once. Then he looked at the floor, said, 'C'mon,' and led the way into a book-lined office with comfortable leather chairs and a big modern desk.

As soon as the door closed, shutting out Arlene, Wes asked, 'How come you didn't take that pill? It's like you want to suffer.'

'Nobody wants to. Some deserve to,' Mark said.

'Does Liv Mann deserve to?'

'Oh, God, that's the problem, isn't it?' He slammed his fist on to the desk.

Wes pointed out the window toward the limestone cliff that cradled Mark's property. 'What's out there?' he asked. 'How does it involve Liv? If you give a damn about your friend Ronnie, tell me so we can fix it.'

Mark pulled something from his pocket, tossed it on the desk. A little gray string, looked like, with knots in it. Wes said, 'What's this?'

'My ticket to freedom,' Mark said. 'It's part of a *quipu*. The Incas in South America used it to keep accounts. This came in the mail, arrived the day Corson was killed.'

Wes stepped closer to the desk and inspected the knotted string. Mark went on, 'Ronnie Mann got one a week before he died. We'd both received something else in the mail, years before, a clipping about a guy who'd been killed in Ohio. Named Gene Elkins. I didn't know him but Ronnie recognized the name because he'd been in charge of a unit of Armadillo Security that – that –' Mark broke off, cleared his throat, said, 'Ronnie hired Armadillo to clear a site for a hydroelectric dam his company was building in Ecuador.'

Wes said, 'Not just bulldozing, right? You get a security operation, that means moving people out.'

'There were some villages along the river. The dam was going to flood them. But the villagers didn't want to leave, and the new president, Roldós, might back them up despite the signed contracts. So there was time pressure.'

'Even so, people move away when you pay them off, right?'

'Except they get paid pennies on the dollar of what the land is worth, in Latin America at least. Dammit, the villagers were right: the dam would ruin a lot of them and only a few people would benefit from the electricity. Plus Ecuadorean taxpayers are still paying off the huge loans that paid for that dam. It was a lousy deal. But that was my job: to peddle lousy deals.'

'You? How did you get into it?'

'My job was to work up the numbers. Real numbers, mostly,

but by tilting this or that you can always massage the projections. I was the one who convinced the Ecuadorean politicos that this dam would be great for the future. This was before President Roldós.' He snorted. 'I did my job well; I got money to the people I was supposed to. Ecuador took out loans to pay for the dam, so the international lenders got their interest and Ronnie's company got paid, and my company got paid, and the US construction contractors got paid, and the Ecuadorean politicos got paid, and fucking Armadillo Security got paid.'

'What did Armadillo do?'

Mark looked at him, hollow-eyed. 'Burned down a village school with eighteen kids and a nun inside.'

'Jesus!'

'I was long gone from the country. But Wink McGabben had been there with me, had gone back because he liked climbing the mountains, plus I think he had a thing for the nun. Ronnie told me later – it was right after we got the clipping about Gene Elkins's murder – he said that Wink tried to get him to stop the project, actually showed him how I'd cooked the results, but it was too late: Armadillo was already there. Ronnie went to the village the day after the school burned. He said three of the kids hadn't died yet. They were screaming and screaming.'

Wes could only shake his head.

Mark said in a low voice, staring at the *quipu* string, 'Ever since Ronnie told me that, I've heard those children. Every night. Screaming.' He looked up at Wes. 'Ronnie made me promise never to tell. He was worried about his family. The big-money guys can be secretive and ruthless. President Roldós died mysteriously a couple years later. Plus Ronnie's wife was from Ecuador; she'd take it hard. But I think she found out because she left him that same week. Then a few years later Ronnie got the *quipu* string and was killed.'

'And you didn't tell the cops?'

'I didn't want the cops to stop him.'

'Him. McGabben?'

'At the time I thought it was a villager hunting us down. Doesn't matter. I heard those kids screaming every night. I wanted my turn.'

'Your turn?'

'Catholics can't commit suicide.'

Wes understood suddenly the power McGabben had over Mark Lugano, their strange dance of vengeance and guilt over the years. 'OK, let's go,' he said gently. 'We don't want Liv on our conscience too.'

After the blinding pain in her shoulder and the terror of the fall, Marty found herself sitting almost comfortably in her harness, back to the cliff. Her whole left arm still hurt and her heart still pounded, but the landing had been much softer than she'd expected. She felt her shoulder gently. It was swelling, all right. Something was seriously torn in there, not broken, she thought. Well, hoped. She tested the arm again. Sideways, it hurt a lot. Raising it was almost impossible, so it was close to useless for the strenuous job ahead. Maybe she should get Liv to tie her right here and go for help. That'd take a long time, though; the houses on Ridge Road were few and far between, even if she found someone home. And there had been those shots. So maybe climbing was better.

Marty glanced sideways. Twenty feet to her left McGabben had freed his feet somehow and was shuffling along the ledge on his knees. Yes, climbing was definitely better.

She pushed herself around until her boots were against the cliff and looked for wrinkles in the rock. She found some possibilities and, with her hands on the rope and her shoulder shooting flames into her brain every time she steadied herself with her left hand, she pulled herself back to where she'd been when she fell. She got her good hand into the crack in the rock, yelled, 'Climbing,' and Liv took up the slack. She pushed and pulled herself up with feet and right hand, keeping the left on the rope just for balance because it sure as hell couldn't catch her weight.

And suddenly, like the answer to a prayer, the little ladder made of webbing appeared. She pulled herself up to it, got her left toe in the bottom rung, worked herself to a standing position and paused to catch her breath.

Down on the ledge below her, McGabben had pulled out both of the tethers but his hands were still cuffed behind him. He was looking up at her and started along the ledge in her direction, but partway there he paused and looked down at something white on the ground. May's photo. He knelt slowly before it.

Marty felt for the guy. She was going to lock him up, yeah, but the thought of those burning screaming children and the woman he obviously loved, dying that horrible death – yes, blinding rage at the people who caused it would be a very human response.

A cold-blooded fifteen-year vendetta, no. He had to be stopped.

So get moving, Hopkins.

She climbed to the top of the little ladder, checked over the last part of the rock, clenched her teeth against the pain and hauled herself up most of the final ten feet. When her right hand found a root near the top Liv grabbed her wrist and pulled hard to help as she scrambled over the rim.

Marty lay flat a moment, puffing, finally was able to gasp out, 'Hey, thanks.'

'Same to you.' But Liv looked subdued, unhappy.

Marty thought she knew why. She sat up, still panting. 'I want to say something about your father. He graduated before mine. But they overlapped a year.'

'Really?'

'They probably didn't know each other. Yours was a math whiz, mine was a jock and a couple of years behind.'

Liv's dark eyes were fastened on her. 'Your father – is he still alive?'

Marty got to her feet and walked to the rim of the cliff, looked down. McGabben was still there on the ledge. Kneeling, looked like. Still handcuffed. She turned back to Liv, moved a little closer because of the moan of the wind. 'No, he's not. He died when I was twelve. He drank too much, totalled his car. Burned to death.' She saw rather than heard the little catch in Liv's breath, and continued, 'It took a really long time to come to terms with it because I kind of worshipped him, you know? He was all those good male things: brave, protective, wise. I wanted to be like my dad.'

'Yeah.' Liv nodded. 'I know what you mean.'

Marty started unbuckling her harness. 'My mother kept saying my dad's crash was not a simple DWI. Everyone thought she was nuts, including me for a while. But just this week I found out she might have been right. It confirms what

I figured out over the years. My mother was also brave and protective and wise. I can try to be that way in her honor too.'

There was a blast of wind. Liv stepped out of her harness and flung it to the ground. 'Your mother didn't run off and leave you when you were fifteen.'

'No. Maybe if she had, I'd be too mad to go ask her what really happened. Or maybe not.' Marty tossed her harness down too. 'Right now let's go to my cruiser and radio the guys to come pick up McGabben. Then I want to compare notes with you.'

'Yeah.'

They left the ropes and harnesses in a tumble and hurried through the windy woods toward the cruiser. They passed the place where Marty had tied the old rope from her cruiser trunk and she shuddered. Beyond it, she could see that, as she'd expected, the wind had obliterated her bootprints as well as McGabben's. That's why she had . . . 'Hey,' Marty said, stopping abruptly.

'What's wrong?' Liv asked.

'My triangles! Highway warning markers. I hung them in the trees so my backup could find where I'd gone over the rim. Where'd they go?'

No wonder the guys hadn't found her – although once McGabben had her gun, backup wouldn't have been much help anyway. With her radio gone she'd had no way of telling them it wasn't a routine rescue operation. McGabben could have picked them off as they came down.

But where the hell were the triangles?

Liv was looking around for them. 'The wind?' she suggested.

'I oriented them for that,' Marty said. 'Still, what else could it be?'

The answer appeared as they emerged from the woods. From behind the evergreen bush near the weathered wooden supply box stepped ex-Deputy Don Foley. He held a Police Special in his hand.

He seemed startled to see Liv, but that lasted only an instant, and the look he gave Marty was pure triumph. 'Caught you this time, Hopkins!' he said.

Thirty-Two

A snarl of bad thoughts was choking Liv – fears that Gabby would come after her, ghastly imaginings of her father's death and Corson's, shudders at the school burning long ago, new confusion about why her mother had left and, worst of all, a sense that Pops was an impostor, that her beloved father had helped set all these nightmares in motion and had never said a word about it.

The sight of Foley's gun snapped her back into the present. Also bad.

Deputy Hopkins was saying, 'Hey, Don, take it easy!' Her hands in her torn gloves were held elbow-high, palm-out in the classic surrender position. Liv was about to scream, 'What are you doing?' but Deputy Hopkins seemed wiser, so she bit back her outrage and put her hands up too.

Foley said, 'Don't worry, Olivia, I've got her under control now. Hopkins, lean against the tree, legs apart – you know the drill.'

Liv realized she remained the good girl in Foley's system, tried to figure how to use that as he patted down the deputy. He was frowning, said, 'Hopkins, where's your sidearm?'

'Fell down the cliff.'

Liv said timidly, 'I don't understand, Mr Foley.'

'I know, she's probably spun you some story, how you should come along with her.'

'No, it was . . . ' But Deputy Hopkins gave her head a tiny shake and Liv shut up.

Foley said, 'See, I knew something was up. I heard that there was an alert out for you.'

'There was?' Liv was surprised.

'Yep. And I knew where Deputy Hopkins was—'

'Because you're the guy who's been following me around, aren't you?' Deputy Hopkins nodded at a dark-green car parked at the side of the road just beyond a little gray-shingled house.

'Somebody better keep track of you,' Foley snapped. 'I knew you'd turn up saying you'd found Olivia and all the TV people would swarm all over you. And meanwhile nobody's finding Zill's killer.'

Still leaning against the tree, Deputy Hopkins said, 'Don, look, Zill's killer is handcuffed back there. If you just call the sheriff – shoot, call the TV people too – you can have all the credit you want. Olivia will tell the story.'

Foley laughed. 'You see how she twists everything around! Trying to trick me into going into those woods. Look, Olivia, it's getting cold; why don't you get in my car out of the wind? I'll drive you back to town.'

'But Mr Foley ...' Liv glanced helplessly at Deputy Hopkins, who gave a tiny gesture with her chin toward the car. OK, she was right: no sense both of them wrangling with a guy who'd gone bonkers. *Olivia will tell the story* – that was what Deputy Hopkins wanted. He'd drive her back, then she could spread the word. She said, 'Well, you're right, it is cold. Thanks, Mr Foley,' and headed for the car.

When she reached the passenger door she glanced back. He'd moved a little, still keeping Deputy Hopkins immobilized but able to see Liv too. She waved at him cheerily, opened the passenger door and got in.

And felt trapped. She just couldn't deal with another nutty male with a gun right now. Liv lay face down across the seat, opened the driver's door just a little, very quietly. Then she belly-wriggled through the door, sliding out on to the road. She nudged the door closed but didn't slam it. Still keeping low, she crawled straight across the road and down the far bank. Steep over here too, though nothing like the cliff.

How soon would Foley notice she wasn't in the car?

She saw a knoll that the wind had cleared of snow, went down to it because it wouldn't show her footprints. Would he think she'd gone right or left?

He'd think that, being female, she'd pick the easiest way and go down. Liv went up instead, paralleling the road but keeping to the bare windswept places as long as she could. As soon as she was safely away, she'd speed to the nearest phone. Wherever it was.

And until this was all over, she wouldn't try to figure out what she thought about what Pops had done. She was ashamed how relieved putting it off made her feel.

Wes and Mark had taken a horseblanket down to where Blueberry still stood stamping because they'd decided that if Liv had been wounded they might need the animal for transport. Deputy Neal arrived a few minutes later, and Deputy Mason shortly after that. He nodded at Wes.

'I hear you were on another emergency call,' Wes said.

'Yes, sir, funny one. Hopkins called in urgent but when we got up there nothing was going on and Foley told us she'd left already.'

'Well, she figures she can take care of herself,' Wes said. It troubled him that it was Foley who'd told Mason nothing was happening, but if she said she didn't want his help, damned if he'd offer it. He said, 'Let's find Olivia Mann.'

They developed a search grid with the gray horse at the center and began working it.

Marty asked, 'Can I straighten up?'

'Hands where I can see 'em,' Foley said. 'Now walk toward the house.'

She held her hands open at elbow level, trying to ignore the painful throbs in her left shoulder with each step, and asked Foley, 'So what do you want me to do now?'

'Nothing. Stop.'

She was about eight feet from the back of the house. She said, 'Good, 'cause I'm tired and I haven't had lunch.'

He leaned against the corner of the house, gun still steady on her. 'You figured the TV people would be wining and dining you, huh?'

'No, I hoped backup would be here and I could have my lunch break.' There was a little flash of triumph in his eyes and Marty added, 'How'd you talk them into leaving? They're reliable guys.'

He smiled. 'You hid your cruiser. I knew you were plotting some kind of crazy story to make you look good.'

'OK, they couldn't see my cruiser, but they'd see the safety triangles. So you hid them, right? And made up some story.'

'Didn't have to make anything up! I said you'd left. That's

238

true. I said you'd get around to notifying them in your own good time. That's true too.'

'And they just walked away?'

'Mason poked around the backyard a minute,' Foley admitted, and Marty gave Bobby Mason points for believing her call. Foley went on, 'But when the Lugano call came in he left.'

'What Lugano call?'

'The bulletin on Ms Mann missing from the Luganos' place.'

'So why are you doing this? You want credit for finding her?'

'I want you to shut up! I want to get you out of the sheriff's way so he can find the guy who killed my buddies!' His jaw was working and Marty realized that this wasn't just his old anger at an uppity female. The man was full of grief for his murdered friends. And maybe full of fear that he'd be next. He'd focused all of it on her.

She said gently, 'But see—'

'Shut up, Hopkins.' He waggled the muzzle of the gun at her, and she shut up.

The *chaski* was very cold from sitting immobile for so long. Behind him, one handcuffed hand clutched the photo of May that the woman deputy had given him. He was troubled, not clear yet on what to do. The deputy had said, 'Look at her!' and he'd tried, but something about May's face seemed to freeze his mind, and he'd stare at her but couldn't see her. Maybe he'd never really seen her before. It was as though somehow he'd overlooked an important number in the equation.

So instead he'd watched Mark Lugano and the others walk around searching the ground, seldom glancing up, and when they did, missing his immobile gray form against the rock. They didn't pay much attention to the cliff or even the cliff side of the creek. They didn't find the rope, now snow-covered and on the wrong side of the water. They did find his gray knapsack with his dinner and clean clothes and binoculars and spare fuel. No climbing gear in it – that was all on the sling Liv had taken up with her. When there was a lull in the wind he heard the deputies down there talking about careless campers, shaking their heads.

The thing that got them most excited was when they found the woman deputy's gun in the creek.

Finally the searchers finished working their grid and moved on to do another one deeper in the woods, and it was safe to move. He made sure no one was left behind, then stood carefully. It was harder to balance with his hands locked behind him, and harder to find his things when he had to grope for them without being able to see them. But by kneeling and reaching behind him, he unrolled his down-filled sleeping bag, got out the boots he'd tucked into the roll when he'd first descended the rock this morning, got his feet into them for warmth.

With the help of his teeth, he draped his sleeping bag around him.

They'd send people to arrest him, take him off the rock. He should be planning how to fight them, how to use them for his escape.

But he still held the photo of May that the woman deputy had given him. 'Look at her!' she'd told him, but when he did his mind couldn't move. May was smiling in the picture, yet she didn't seem the warm happy May he remembered from Ecuador. She'd been inspiring – unattainable, of course, in any carnal sense because she had devoted her life to spiritual things; but that was good: he'd always craved purity. And she was eager to hear what he could tell her about the Incas, about the battles of the Inca fire god and the rain god, about *quipus* and Inca mathematics. She in turn had taught him about the pride of the villagers in their history and in their future, their children. He'd brought her medicine for the dysentery the children had, and she was delighted. She'd said he was her *chaski*, the messenger who must carry the message that would help the Inca villagers, and help her. And he had vowed within himself to serve her and be true.

Where was that May? This photo showed a sad, human May, who thought he hadn't understood her message. It frightened him and froze his soul.

After a while Marty broke the silence and tried another tack. 'Must be after three o'clock,' she said. 'I haven't had lunch and neither has Olivia.'

Foley glanced briefly across at his Crown Vic. A little troubled frown shadowed his round face. Foley seemed to have some respect for Liv. Marty realized that his plan, whatever it was, hadn't taken her into account. She remembered what Coach had told her, back when he was still speaking to her: 'It never crossed my mind to put Foley in charge of anything important.'

Not a consoling thought at the moment, when Foley had put himself in charge of her life, and Liv's. She had the sense that he wasn't planning to kill her, though of course that could change if he got too upset. So she didn't push too hard, said only, 'Well, guess Olivia will just have to wait too.'

'No.' Foley came to a decision. 'We'll just tie you up here. I'll take Olivia back down, keep you out of the sheriff's way for a few hours and let him make some progress on finding the bastard that killed Zill and Sarge.' He choked up a moment, confirming Marty's hunch that the man was grieving, striking blindly at her because his buddies were dead. He coughed and went on, 'Let's go to your cruiser. You've got a rope in your trunk, right?'

'Don, it's tied to a tree back there in the woods.'

Anger flashed in his eyes and he might have struck her except he'd been trained not to get too close to a suspect who might lash out. He said, 'Quit trying to get me back there! I know how close it is to the edge of the cliff. You'd like to give me a push, wouldn't you? Oughta do it to you.'

'And then tell Olivia and the sheriff it was an accident – see if they believe you.'

'I told you to go to your cruiser!'

She obeyed, starting down the road toward the pull-off where she'd stowed her vehicle. He limped behind her with the gun, but even so it was good to be moving after he'd made her stand in the wind for so long. As they passed Foley's Crown Vic, parked roadside in front of the house, she wondered what Liv was thinking about this fiasco. Not that she could see Liv through the glare of reflected branches on the windows.

They arrived at the pull-off where she'd left her cruiser. The first thing she noticed was two flat tires. Dammit, he'd shot them out. Even worse, she saw a hole in the driver's side window. He'd shot out her radio too.

So much for Plan A. Foley had made sure she wouldn't be leaving the scene in her cruiser.

Liv was cold and exhausted. It seemed that she'd been stumbling through these scrubby woods over rough snow for hours. Maybe she had. The sun was lower now so that must be west. Meant she was going south. Not that knowing her direction was any help. She didn't know where town was, or roads, or telephones.

But she had to keep going. To find someone to arrest Gabby, to help Deputy Hopkins. To save herself.

She'd been keeping away from higher ground because she was afraid of being seen, and in the shallow gullies there was too much brush to see far. But maybe if she went downhill she'd hit a road or something.

She'd stopped to pee once and it had been terrifying, thinking that Gabby or Foley might show up at any instant when she was so alone and vulnerable and hobbled by her own clothes. Even on nasty streets in Brooklyn there were always lots of people and only a few of them were toughs, so the others would help you out and you'd have a chance.

Though, to be honest, she felt nervous about the toilets in those neighborhoods too. At least here in the snowy woods she wasn't likely to catch hepatitis. She giggled, startling herself with the sound, and went downhill.

Thirty-Three

Ignoring the panic that was starting to bubble within her, Marty stared at the remains of her cruiser radio. And cellphone, dammit – he'd even shot the cellphone on the passenger seat! Those were the shots she'd heard while she was on the ledge. Not her backup running into trouble, but Foley taking out her cruiser.

Now it was up to Liv to get help when he'd driven her to town.

Foley snapped, 'Quit mooning. Unlock the trunk.'

Don't snap back at an idiot with a gun. Marty took a deep breath. 'Don, you took my keys when you patted me down.'

'Oh, yeah. Well, lean against the cruiser.'

She obeyed. Foley unlocked her trunk, watching her every minute except for quick glances into the trunk. Finally he said, 'So where's the rope?'

'Like I said, I took it out earlier. It's tied to a tree in the woods.'

'Shit.'

Marty said, 'You know that old box where we met you? There were some straps in it.'

He glared at her suspiciously. 'Why are you telling me this?'

'There's bread and peanut butter too. I was hoping you'd have a heart, let me eat lunch once you get me tied up.'

He scowled a moment but didn't seem to come up with any better ideas; finally said curtly, 'Move.' They trudged back past his car. The driver's door hadn't quite latched, she noticed. And a quick partial glimpse of the inside showed no sign of Liv. She began to feel uneasy. Had she run away?

Better go to Plan C, risky as it was. They passed the Gordon sisters' shingled house and finally reached the wooden box behind it. 'Want me to open the box?' she asked, starting to move toward it.

He responded as she expected. 'No way! You stand right where you are!' Keeping his gun on her, he limped to the box. As he started to tug at the top she took a couple of tiny shuffling steps sideways, just enough so he had to move his head a little to look from the box to her. She waited. He got the box open, fumbled inside it while watching her. She heard a carabiner clink against the steel lining of the box but she was watching him and the gun. He glanced at it, looked back at her, muttered, 'What is this stuff?'

She shrugged, ignored the pain. 'Some kind of camping gear, I thought.'

He glanced in again. The muzzle of the gun wavered a fraction. In that instant, Marty dove, hit her good shoulder hard against his gimpy leg. He fired but he was falling sideways and her momentum shoved her under his arm so the shots stayed wide. Before he could catch himself she drove her knee into his crotch. The firing stopped and she stomped his wrist to the ground, twisted the gun from his fingers, leaped back out of reach and yelled, 'Face down, Foley!'

He'd gone pale from the crotch-kick and was lying as though stunned. She fished the webbing straps from the box left-handed, shoved him over face down with her boot, then dropped the gun into her holster. She knotted the straps around his wrists, patted him down. A knife, his car keys, her cruiser keys, extra ammo. No phone, dammit. She left him his wallet.

He was cursing her now. She ignored him, lassoed the ankle of his good leg with the last webbing strap and pulled it up behind him, tied it to his wrist bonds. If he managed to stand up now he'd have to hop on his bad knee. She started to give him an extra kick for good measure but she reminded herself that the idiot was trying to avenge his dead buddies and her anger notched down.

'I'll send someone to check on you when I get back to the station,' she said, and picked up McGabben's bread and peanut butter from the box. They could use a snack as they drove to the station.

But, as she'd feared, when she reached the Crown Vic, Liv wasn't there.

Wes didn't like it that they'd found nothing in their careful search for Liv Mann. They finished working their third grid and trooped into the Luganos' big garage to regroup. Arlene Lugano brought out coffee, her forehead furrowed with worry.

Wes also didn't like it that Bobby Mason seemed uneasy about Hopkins. In Wes's opinion Mason was a good deputy. He hadn't been as good a shot as Sims or Foley, not as smart as Hopkins, but he was solid in all departments and had good instincts. He watched Mason radioing back to the station, then turned to Mark Lugano. 'Mark, you know McGabben. Where would he take her?'

Mark came back to earth from whatever deep despair was occupying him. 'Wes, I haven't seen the guy for years. And I never could figure him out, except if you asked him a math question he could answer it.'

'What about the terrain? Where else is there?'

'I thought we covered everything. And there wasn't a trace.'

Wes nodded gloomily. 'The few things we found were real close to the gray horse. I can't figure it either. Listen, can I make a call? Gotta tell the wife I'll be late.'

Shirley wasn't back yet from Indianapolis, but he left her a message. He also made sure his second-in-command had shown up at Asphodel Springs. Then he returned to the garage.

Bobby Mason was coming in from his cruiser. 'Sheriff says he's putting in a call to the state for a canine unit. Rescue dog. Mrs Lugano, do you have a piece of clothing of Miz Mann's? Don't touch it, he says – might confuse the dog – but know where it is.'

Arlene looked happy to have something to do. 'There must be things in her suitcase. That's a wonderful idea. Will the sheriff be coming too?'

'Yeah, says it'll be about an hour; he's still got a couple things to do. He's been calling the detectives in Staten Island and Indianapolis to see if they have any traces of this McGabben.'

Wes knew it would soon be time for him to leave. Couldn't stay here and have Chuck Pierce cutting him down, and he couldn't see how he could help further. Hopkins's message needed looking into, but the ungrateful idiot had told him to stay off her case. So he pulled Mason aside. 'If you get a chance, tell Pierce to check into what Hopkins thinks she's up to.'

'Yes, sir, already did,' Mason replied.

Mark Lugano had unrolled a map of his property on the garage floor. Wes joined them to try to figure out where Liv could have gone.

The *chaski* had forgotten whether the cold had started outside or inside. The wind was cold, yes, but his brain seemed too cold to think. For years he'd worked to deliver May's message, to make the criminals understand what they had done, and he'd believed that he'd done his work well. But now when he looked at her he couldn't remember what she had really said. Had he spent his life delivering the wrong . . .

No, it was just too cold to think. He had some soup – that's what he needed. He'd boil a little water. It would be tricky, working behind his back, but he'd done it a million times, sometimes while hanging in his harness from an anchor set in a rock wall halfway up a volcano. Just take it step by step.

The *chaski* dropped his sleeping bag from where he'd draped it over his shoulders, pushed it carefully into the hollow with his boot so it wouldn't fall. The wind moaned past his shoulders. The soup was prepackaged in a cup – just add hot water. By moving both arms sideways he was able to confirm that his lighter was in his pocket. He looked carefully at the stove. Have to attach the bottle of fuel to the hose that came from the stove. Where was his fuel? Oh, there was the bottle, out there on the ledge. He went to it, turned his back, knelt, picked it up, took it back to the little hollow in the rock.

He looked carefully at where everything was in the hollow. Again he turned his back, knelt, began fastening the fuel bottle to the flexible hose that went to the stove. Push it on – oops, almost tipped the stove over. Hard to work behind your back. Try again. Push it on to the hose gently – there, that felt right. Flip the wire clamp closed to seal it. Find the pump handle. Hold the bottle with one hand, work the pump handle with the other to build up pressure inside the bottle. Lucky the pump handle was only six inches long, so even handcuffed he could build up pressure. There, the resistance felt right. Open the . . .

A loud hiss, droplets hitting his wrist. Uh-oh. Wasn't sealed.

The pressurized fuel sprayed out past the stove. Lucky he hadn't lit it yet.

What had gone wrong? The *chaski* made his cold brain focus. Finally he realized that the clamp worked only from one side. Because he was working behind his back he'd mistaken left for right and the clamp had jammed against the bottle instead of closing properly.

OK, start again. Push the bottle on to the hose – there. Clamp it. This time make sure it's right. Yes. Start pumping again. OK, done. Open the stove's valve – done. This time the hiss sounded familiar as fuel entered the stove's reservoir. Now take the lighter from the pocket – yes. Click it—

Whoa! A flash of light! What happened?

And heat. Too much heat. Automatically his singed fingers shut off the valve, but that wasn't it. The smell of burning hair – no, not hair, down! His sleeping bag had caught fire!

He jumped to his feet, stumbled, righted himself, began stamping on his sleeping bag. The nylon cover was melting, but the fluffy down was blazing. The flames were angry, grew higher, and he realized that fuel had sprayed on to the bag when the clamp had failed. And now the fire was reaching for his clothes.

He aimed carefully, swiftly kicked the burning bag out toward the creek. It was so light. He hoped the wind wouldn't blow it back at him. Instead, it wafted the bag across the stream to snag on the bare branches of a bush in the weedy section of the far bank.

But flames had caught his clothes. The *chaski* pushed off his pants and kicked them from the ledge, then managed to roll on his burning jacket and extinguish the flames. His skin hurt; it would blister, but he'd survived worse. He looked out and was surprised to see that the flames from the sleeping bag were spreading, running through the brush.

He wondered if Mark Lugano was still in the woods. Maybe this was to be his pyre. Carefully, the *chaski* unscrewed the pump from the half-full fuel bottle, placed it open at the edge of the ledge, then kicked it in a long arc toward the far side of the creek. When it landed he was rewarded with a beautiful burst of flame.

The *chaski* moved a few feet down the ledge to the pad and sat down to watch the burning of Mark's woods. It would take a while. Trees had not yet caught, but the winter-dry weeds and brush were good kindling, and licking flames were already toasting the trunks of saplings. They would soon be ready to burn.

Marty looked around Foley's car, spotted the open door and the scuffed snow across the road. So she'd run away. Damn. She couldn't really blame Liv for wanting to scoot, but she hoped she hadn't gone far. She called 'Liv?' a couple of times, but heard no response. She took off her ragged right glove and was surprised to see her hand still taped from the climb up the cliff. She grabbed a piece of bread from McGabben's loaf, tossed the rest of the loaf with the peanut butter into the passenger seat and locked the Crown Vic.

Then she followed the scuffed snow down the bank out of sight of Foley's vehicle as far as a windswept patch. No tracks visible here. Marty sighed, made sure her collar was up as far as it would go, and started a wide circle through the snow to see where the exit track would be.

It was almost ten minutes later that she found it, all the way around on the uphill side. She followed Liv's bootprints along the hillside, occasionally calling 'Liv?' into the icy breeze.

There was no answer.

Before long she came to another windswept patch. She went straight across, looking for the track to continue, but Liv hadn't made it easy. She hadn't gone very far down the side of the ridge and Marty thought that might be her next move, but when she finally found Liv's tracks they were heading uphill again. Was she going back up to Ridge Road? No, looked like Liv had turned at the next small windswept patch. Now she was angling down toward the White River where Sullivan Creek joined it. Nobody much lived in the area, just old Lester Holtz who could barely keep up his scruffy farm.

Marty looked at her watch. She'd been tracking Liv half an hour, had still received no answer to her yells. And on the other side of Demon Ridge, if Don Foley was telling the truth, searchers with better equipment were hunting for Liv in the wrong place.

She turned abruptly up to the road. She'd drive down to the station, get the searchers over here to find Liv, send people to collect McGabben and Foley. Pick up Chrissie at the bakery and go home.

Marty reached Ridge Road and started trotting along it toward Foley's car.

Thirty-Four

L iv stumbled down an icy, weed-infested gully. She had to hurry, to get help for Deputy Hopkins, to get someone to arrest Gabby. But she didn't seem to be getting anywhere. This hillside was nowhere near as steep as the cliff she'd climbed so proudly on the other side of the ridge, but it was not easy going. On this south-facing side the snow had melted a little and refrozen on the uneven surface, so it was slicker than the wind-dried cliff. Hard for a tired woman to keep her footing. Adding to her worries were exhaustion and hunger and soon thirst because she'd finished the last of her water an hour ago.

She skidded again. What she really wanted was something tropical, maybe with rum. In Cancun. Tropical drink, tropical heat, Elena – that's what she was thirsty for.

Her route down had brought her briefly to the top of a stony outcrop, clearly the same silver-buff stone as the cliff on the other side. She'd taken a quick look at the terrain before heading for cover again. There was a big river and a valley down there, much easier countryside than this hillside, more like Mark and Arlene's. She hoped there was a road down there too.

She'd gone a long way without seeing a house or even a trail. Higher up she'd passed a couple of trees with old signs saying 'Posted', so somebody must own this hillside; but then even those signs disappeared. Well, it was so steep here it was useless land, she thought, focused on her footing. It probably served chiefly as a boundary, like the creek and cliff on the other—

A sudden sharp explosion of noise. Liv gasped, jumped back, realized it was a dog barking a few feet away. Black-and-white collie type, running back and forth in front of her, yapping in a frenzy.

Back and forth because there was an old wire-mesh fence between them.

An old rusty wire-mesh fence topped by a nasty string of barbed wire.

She took a deep breath. Neither fence nor collie seemed very welcoming, but they were definitely signs of human beings not too far away. The fence might lead to a house or a road. Not that she could see either one from here. The gully had widened into a sort of dip, so she was still too low to see.

Should she go right or left? West or east?

The collie, she noticed, glanced east after each burst of barking.

She didn't especially want to meet the dog up close, but maybe its home was to the east, or its master, or at least a road.

Liv turned east.

The god of fire was showing off. The *chaski* watched fascinated as flames ran up saplings, turning them into torches, while smoke billowed from the underbrush. The god of rain was not going to join in today. The sky was still deep blue, although the sun was very low. Once it was down, the blaze would be glorious.

The flames danced and occasionally he could hear a distant cracking as a branch fell, but most of the noise was still from the wind. It was pushing the fire now, making it bigger, joining the game of the gods. He could see shapes in the flames sometimes, maybe aspects of the fire god.

Despite the blaze below, despite the insulated pad he sat on, he was cold. The flames had eaten away the back of his jacket before he rolled on them to put out the fire, and now his jacket hung loose on his handcuffed arms and the wind hit his blistered back. He couldn't feel any warmth from the flames below. He couldn't smell the smoke either. The wind seemed to be cleaning the cliff, pushing the fire away, pushing the heat away. It was almost like watching the show through a window, his nose pressed to the glass. Look but don't touch. Like May.

He wondered if Mark Lugano had repented, if he was burning yet. Then a wraith in the fire took shape, smiling sadly at him, her hair a mass of curls, writhing like snakes, like flames. It had been so long since he'd seen her.

'May?' he called. 'Did I do the right thing? I wanted to do the right thing.'

It was hard to hear her because the wind still howled and his brain was cold, but finally he made out the words: 'My message was justice. Not vengeance. Goodbye, Wink.'

She flickered into smoke, into nothing.

Wink pushed away the pad and stretched out on the cold rock and felt his tears freezing.

Marty had almost reached Foley's Crown Vic when she slowed. A cruiser was creeping up the road, the driver peering at the dark-green car, at the Gordons' house, at her. Sheriff Pierce.

Marty waved, trotted to the cruiser.

'Hopkins! What the hell is going on here?'

'OK, sir, uh . . .' Where to start? She said, 'Number one, Liv Mann is down there on the hillside, White River side of the ridge. Maybe lost. Last seen going the general direction of Lester Holtz's farm.'

Pierce keyed dispatch. 'Fourteen here, Sims. Tell Mason to move the search operation to the area of the Lester Holtz farm – know where it is? . . . Ten-four.' He frowned at Marty. 'Why didn't you call it in, Hopkins?'

'My radio's disabled, sir. Number two—'

He looked at the remnants of the shoulder radio. 'Disabled? Both?'

'Uh, yes, sir. Number two, Zill Corson's killer—'

'How'd you break both – what? The killer?'

'Yes, sir; he's handcuffed. We left him stranded on a ledge. Gordon Creek side of this ridge.'

'You're kidding.'

'No, sir. He's a rock climber.'

'Our apeman! Christ.' Pierce called Sims again. 'Who you talking to at Lugano's? Adams? Good, tell him to get someone to check out the cliff by Gordon Creek – whereabouts?' He raised white eyebrows at Marty.

'There's a gray backpack and some climbing shoes and, um, my gun, all fell off the ledge, sir, into the creek. The ledge is about two-thirds of the way up from where they fell. He's dressed in gray – real hard to spot him unless he moves.'

He nodded, relayed the information, added that the guy was

252

dangerous, keyed off. Then his eyes narrowed. 'Your gun fell off the ledge, you say. What's that?' He nodded at her holster.

This was going to be the worst. Marty said, 'It's Mr Foley's, sir. I had to stop him.'

'Stop him? What do you mean?' He jumped out of the car.

'Not shoot, sir; I just tied him up. He was, um, interfering.'

'Interfering?'

'Pulled a gun on us, sir.' She gestured at her holster.

'Where the hell did you put him?'

'Behind the house, sir. I left him there and went to look for Miz Mann.'

'Let's take a look.' The sheriff ran toward the house. Marty followed, wondering if this was her last day on the job. Wondering why smoke was smudging the sky beyond the cliff. Then she had to focus on Don Foley. He'd wriggled about half the way back toward the house.

Pierce said, 'Don! What the hell is happening here?'

Foley looked up. 'Chuck! That bitch attacked me!'

'Take it easy, Don. Why did she attack you?'

'Get me untied, Chuck.'

'OK, take it easy. Why did she attack you?' Pierce moved around, reached down for the straps tying Foley's ankle to his wrists.

'No reason. Probably she wanted to get the credit for finding Olivia.'

'You mean Olivia Mann?'

'Yeah, I told Olivia to wait in my car and then this bitch attacked me.'

Foley's good leg straightened. Pierce said, 'There, got one knot. But the others are tough. Here, I'll help you up.'

With a lot of grunting and help from both the sheriff and Marty lifting his elbows, Foley regained his feet. He glared at Marty, said to Pierce, 'You oughta arrest her!'

Sheriff Pierce looked at Marty, at Foley, and said, 'Don, we'll get this straightened out. But we've got a couple different stories here. And right now Hopkins is on the team and you're not, so I gotta go with her.' He gave Foley a nudge. 'C'mon, let's go back and take a seat until we get this straightened out.'

Foley obeyed, a stunned look on his face.

Marty was stunned too. Had he said that – 'Hopkins is on the team'?

They walked back to the vehicles, slowed by Foley's limp. He started for his own car but Pierce said, 'Over here, Don, just for now,' and pushed him toward his cruiser. As they reached the door the radio came to life.

'Mason's got Ms Mann,' Sims reported. 'Near the gate of old Lester's farm. And if you're still on Ridge Road, sir, Ms Mann says Hopkins is being held there at gunpoint.'

Don Foley sagged and got into the back seat without a murmur.

Pierce slammed the door, looked at Marty. 'Hopkins, this case is getting too big for Howie Culp. I want you to take charge of the national side, liaise with the FBI.'

'Yes, sir!'

'Coordinate with Culp, of course, and—'

He was interrupted by another crackle from the radio.

'We got a complication, sir,' Sims said. 'Can't check out that cliff yet. Forest fire.'

Wes helped Ray Bramer heave the sapling from the firebreak. Bramer and the other firemen were going to try to save the woods to the southwest but had given up on the hillside toward Gordon Creek and the cliff. So they were chopping a long firebreak to protect the Lugano house and barn and were nearing the end. Bramer paused, wiped his brow. 'This one got going really fast. Are you sure you guys didn't notice anything while you were searching?'

Wes shook his head. 'Nope. Didn't even see a cigarette.'

Bramer frowned. 'It'd take more than that. Mason said something about finding camping supplies. That white gas they use? Whoosh.'

'Could be,' Wes said.

'We're about done here,' Bramer said. 'I gotta go join the guys closer to the fire. Can you round up the volunteers and take them on back to the house? I'll send up a guy to monitor this firebreak.'

'OK. I'll collect the volunteers and you guys tell us what you need.'

As they reached the garage, he saw Pierce's cruiser turning into the drive. Wes decided he'd just make a pit stop and then get back out there to help away from the sheriff.

Inside, Shirley and Arlene waylaid him with trays of

sandwiches. Wes gave Shirley a kiss. 'What are you doing here?'

'I heard about the fire on the car radio coming back. At home I got your message that you were here, and I figured you could all use some chicken salad.'

'And you were right, as usual.' He picked up a sandwich.

She added in a lower tone, 'There was a message from Agent Jessup too. Said he'd send the details to Pierce, but the fingerprints checked out.'

Damn. So it was true: Rusty LaForte had been the first victim in that other string of killings! He'd seen the Klan burglar in the parking lot, started off to tell Wes, and got gunned off the road. Marty's mother had been right, all those years ago. Shoulda listened.

Sheriff Pierce was outside, talking to firefighters. Wes pulled Mark aside. Despite his singed hair and sad expression, Mark was something of a hero at the moment. When Adams had come panting back to report the fire, Mark had disappeared. Twenty minutes later Blueberry, his eyes wild and tail frizzed, had come charging out of the woods. Sooty-faced Mark clung fast to his back, not yet in control but soothing the animal, getting him pointed toward the barn. Wes hadn't had a chance to talk to him for an hour. He said, 'Mark, good work saving the horse.'

Mark just shrugged and Wes got suspicious. 'Look, I gotta go in a minute. Don't want to get in Sheriff Pierce's way. But you know you scared Arlene half to death when you ran off into the woods. She said you told her you were going to die in a fire.'

Mark looked at the floor. Wes exploded, 'Christ, man, that was your plan, wasn't it? You know, on the job we get these cases every now and then. Guys who are down on their luck, or their girlfriend walked out or something. Can't face life. So they get themselves drunk and disorderly, threaten the deputies who show up, try to force them to shoot them dead. We call it suicide by cop. Is that what you're doing? Making this nutcase kill you because you feel bad? In my book, it's suicide all the same.'

Mark looked at him with stricken eyes. 'Maybe so. I couldn't do it. I heard the horse screaming like those – those – I couldn't let him burn.'

'Well, that's a good sign.' Wes shook his head. 'Look, I don't know what kind of God you have, but mine gives other ways for atonement besides dying. Maybe God's telling you he doesn't want you yet; he wants you to do something here on earth. Like the twelve-step thing, you know: talk to the people you hurt, try to make things right.' He paused, thinking. 'You paid May Gordon's family way too much for this property, right? That's a start. Can't you do something for those Ecuador kids too? Anyway, think about it.' He turned to the two women who were approaching. 'Hey, Arlene, coffee's just what I need! Thanks. And is this Olivia?'

Mark looked up, grabbed the young woman's hands. 'Liv! Oh, God, I'm so glad to see you!'

She was pretty, tan, scuffed from head to toe, and very serious. She glanced up at Wes, seemed to dismiss him as irrelevant, and looked back at Mark. 'We have to talk about that dam in Ecuador. And the kids and the nun.'

Mark's smile disappeared. 'Where did you hear that?'

'Up on the cliff. McGabben told Deputy Hopkins and me. I've got to know the rest!'

Mark still hesitated and Wes cleared his throat. 'Mark, this is one of the people you hurt. Tell her about it, and figure out how to make things right.'

Mark gave a slow nod, almost of relief, and the two started toward his office. Wes sipped his coffee, wondering where Hopkins and McGabben were now.

Thirty-Five

'You gonna be all right?' asked Barbara, the corrections officer. Most of the deputies were still helping at the fire, so Sheriff Pierce had detailed her to drive Marty up to her stranded cruiser and help change the tires. It was a nasty job on this dark, icy ridge, but Barbara had thrown her considerable brawn into it and they'd finished the job quickly. Marty had been nervous about turning the ignition, worried that her flashlight check of the engine and underside might have missed some further mischief Foley had done, but apparently the idiot had been telling the truth and only wanted to delay her. So except for the radio and bullet damage to the window and upholstery, the cruiser was fine.

'Yeah, Barbara, I'm good to go. Thanks,' Marty told her.

'You can drive one-handed?'

'Hey, I've had plenty of practice drinking coffee on patrol. Anyway, the sheriff says I'm to go straight to the hospital to have the shoulder looked at. No high-speed chases tonight.'

'OK.' Barbara glanced across the ridge, where billowing smoke was underlit by the flames far below. 'That's some fire they've got going. Maybe the snow will help.'

'Snow?'

Barbara waved a gloved hand at the west. Sure enough, a soft mass of clouds was approaching, barely lit by the rising moon on the opposite horizon. 'See you back at the jail,' Barbara said before slamming her door and driving off into the dark moaning wind.

OK, thought Marty, no high-speed chases, and straight to the hospital – almost. She locked the cruiser and hiked up the road to Stanni and Eunie's.

Silhouetted against the grim orange smoke billowing from the gorge behind it, the little house was dark, but Marty had glimpsed the clown-face van parked in front of it once more.

Holding her left elbow to soften the painful jarring of her swollen shoulder as she walked, she passed the van and crunched through the snow beside the house. The smoke haze intensified as she approached the gorge. She didn't use her flashlight, instead let her eyes get accustomed to the play of dim light in the clouded air, the warm dull reflected glow from the fire below and the cool hazy gleams from the low moon on her right.

Stanni and Eunie were standing near the rim looking down at the flaming woods, one occasionally murmuring into the other's ear. Far below them, the fire was still going strong, clouds of smoke rolling up. It would be hours before there would be enough visibility for the climbers and the helicopter backup they'd need to move a dangerous felon from the ledge. But no need to mention any of that now. She said, 'Hi.'

They turned to look at her. Eunie said, 'Hi, Marty.'

Stanni said, 'Quite a fire.'

'Sure is,' Marty agreed. 'Um, I'm not here to arrest you, but Sheriff Pierce will send someone soon. You should be thinking about a lawyer.'

No shocked exclamations. Stanni asked calmly, 'Why?'

'We caught the guy who killed your sister's killers.'

'We don't know anything about that,' Stanni said.

'Wrong answer, Stanni. He's the guy who rigged the ropes for your bluebird act. Now, he said you didn't kill anyone, you just got supplies for him. But that's assisting a criminal, maybe four years in jail.'

There was a brief pause. Stanni said, 'Your shoulder's hurt. Did he do that?'

'Yeah. Are you OK for money for a lawyer?'

Stanni was silent, but after a moment Eunie said, 'We've still got some Lugano money from the land sale.'

'OK, get yourself a good one and it'll go better. Your sister wouldn't want you in jail for long.'

Stanni said, 'You've gotta be pissed that we helped him – didn't turn him over to you. Why are you warning us?'

Good question. How could you weigh Maudie Corson's tears, Liv Mann's pain, against the grief of those Ecuadorean mothers, of these two sisters? The sorrows of souls caught in the crossfire of others who shouldn't be shooting in the first place? Marty said, 'Number one, May shouldn't have died

258

the way she did. She devoted her life to justice and caring, and I want to honor her. Number two, vengeance is a dumb way to run the world. It gets in the way of justice.'

There was another brief pause. There was a catch in Stanni's voice when she said, 'OK.'

Marty hiked back down to Foley's Crown Vic. The loaf of bread and the peanut-butter jar were still on the passenger seat. The jar no doubt had Stanni's and McGabben's prints on it as well as hers, so she put it into an evidence bag and took it to her cruiser. Then she headed for the hospital.

Liv had returned to the floral splendor of the Limestone Motel. The little slicked-back FBI agent had had a fit when he'd arrived at the Luganos' to find her talking to Mark. She'd heard his tinny voice outside Mark's office door. 'They're witnesses, k-k-keep them apart!'

Sheriff Pierce, sounding frayed, had replied, 'They're friends. She's been staying here, Agent Jessup.'

Liv needed to digest what Mark had been telling her, anyway. She'd said, 'OK, Mark, with your connections and my legal background, maybe we can help those villagers. I better go, but one word of advice: don't talk to Jessup without your lawyer.' Then she'd opened the door with a big smile, introduced herself, and suggested, 'Why don't I go back to the motel, Agent Jessup? You guys are dealing with a fire and a serial killer here; I'm just in the way. I'll be at the Limestone Motel.'

'Good idea, ma'am, I'll c-c-call as soon as we're finished here.'

'Mark, take care of yourself; you need some rest just like me.'

But she was still unrested and unwashed. At the motel she'd done nothing but drop her suitcase and pull off her scuffed boots before sitting on the edge of the bed to call Elena.

They got off to a bad start. Elena squawked, 'Where have you been? I know your damn cellphone won't work in the country but there's other phones. Why the hell didn't you—'

'Um, number one, I'm fine, don't worry, and number two—'

'So you're fine, great, that sure makes up for all the hours I've been tearing out my hair! What's number two?'

'It's that you were right to be worried. I was scared as hell.'

'Livvy! What happened?'

For half an hour Liv had been trying to explain everything. After a couple of skeptical outbursts Elena had shut up and let her explain, except to question the climbing. 'What do you mean, you want to do it again?'

'Not with him, silly, with you. It's just indescribable, how strong and alive it makes you feel.'

'Cool. Let's do it. So what happened next?'

Liv shrugged out of her parka and lay back on the flowery stripes of the bedspread, looking out a crack in the curtains at falling snow as she finished her account. There was a pause. Suddenly nervous, she asked, 'So, what do you think?'

'I think you legal types are way too competitive,' Elena said, and Liv could almost see her little crooked grin. 'Here I was, feeling sorry for you in dull old Indiana while I was having a great adventure hiking in the jungles of macho Mexico. And you totally outdo me!'

Liv smiled back at the phone. 'You haven't seen macho until you've seen Indiana. Not the place for you and me. Except there's this one terrific woman deputy.'

'Is she hot?' Suspicion in her tone.

Liv laughed. 'No blips on the gaydar. But you know what would be hot? You in that Stetson.'

'I'll see what I can do. How long before you get here?'

'Don't know how long the FBI interview will take. Sometime tomorrow, I hope.'

'Can't hear you; your phone's starting to fail.'

Liv repeated clearly, 'Tomorrow, don't know when.'

'Let me know and I'll meet you. This vacation sure got clobbered.'

'Yeah.'

'But not wasted. You had to find out.'

She understood. Liv felt a rush of gratitude. 'Elena, you're super.'

'Well, of course! But next time I'm going along with you. Because now you'll want to connect with your mom, right?'

'That's what the deputy said too,' Liv said slowly, remembering those gray eyes on hers, the clear Hoosier voice explaining how she too had wanted to be like her dad, and only slowly figured out that her mom had been wise and brave

260

too. Liv shook her head. 'But after all this time hating Mama, I can't just, you know . . .'

Elena sounded serious now. 'You gotta remember, your mom got swallowed up in something much bigger than you knew. Telmeck might have retaliated, financially or worse. I think both your parents were trying to protect you.'

'From the truth?'

'Look,' said sensible Elena, 'if you'd gone with your mom to Ecuador when she left, she might've told you. But you chose to stick with your papa. Probably broke her heart, but she knew you were having a rough time too. Now, your father maybe earned his bucks as a tool of the evil empire but he tried to be a good dad, right? So your mom, being wise, decided not to rat him out.'

'You're right!' Liv was amazed she hadn't figured it out.

'Of course I am. Listen, you're fading out. Better recharge your phone while I go buy a hat. Love ya, Livvy; see you tomorrow.'

Liv smiled at the phone, plugged it in to recharge, and dozed off still unshowered, thinking of Stetsons.

Wes watched through the window in the Lugano garage door as the FBI helicopter touched down, its rotors kicking up a second snowstorm. The chopper was landing on the vast front lawn of the Lugano place because Arlene had refused to allow it to land in the back near the barn. 'The horses are so upset already,' she'd almost screamed, and when Shirley had put a protective arm around her and scowled at Agent Jessup, he'd shifted the landing to the front. Wes sympathized with Arlene, who looked shocked and haggard because her forest was burning, because her husband had called a lawyer and was being questioned by the FBI, because the world as she'd known it was gone.

They'd had to wait for hours to collect McGabben. At first it was because smoke from the fire had pushed visibility down to nothing. Then around ten p.m. the firemen had finally caught a break when the snowstorm blew in. The wind that had been their enemy now brought sleet and heavy snow and the fire shrank back from it. Wes had plodded back to the Lugano garage with the firemen and volunteers, all of them exhausted but hopeful that the worst was over. He stood back while the younger guys went for Shirley and Arlene's sandwiches and coffee. The FBI team that Jessup had called in sat in a corner, waiting for the snow to stop. No one said it out loud but everyone was worried that McGabben would escape, even though Sheriff Pierce reported that Hopkins had stranded the guy on a ledge in handcuffs. People thought he might somehow elude them again. That fire was not a coincidence.

The rotors stopped. Wes could see that they were maneuvering a stretcher out of the chopper. He counted the good guys as they jumped down. Yeah, there was most of the team. And the last guy, the pilot, was in the door now, so the stretcher had to be McGabben.

Doc Altmann's car had been waiting in the driveway for twenty minutes. Now Wes saw Doc get out, and someone else from the cruiser behind. Hopkins, her arm in a sling. They walked together to look at the stretcher, inspected it. Hopkins nodded, said something, and turned away, looking very tired. Doc stayed, talking to the FBI team. Wes decided he needed another coffee.

A few minutes later Hopkins came into the garage and headed straight for the sandwich table. She was scuffed up and had that sling, but she looked eager enough at the sight of the sandwiches.

Wes pretended he hadn't seen her.

When he glanced back a minute later she was gone.

But Shirley wasn't. She came up to him frowning. 'What happened with you and Marty, Champ? She shows up and you get your thundercloud look, and she doesn't even say hi to you.'

'Nothing happened.'

'Champ!'

'I offered her a job, that's all. And she said she didn't need me any more, go to hell. Right in front of Pierce she said that!'

Shirley fixed him with a stare that let him know he wasn't getting off the hook. 'You offered her a job in front of her boss? What were you thinking of? And she said no. What were her exact words?'

'What does it matter?'

'It matters.'

The bitter scene replayed in his mind. 'She said, *I'm on*

262

Sheriff Pierce's team now, and I'm gonna play my position.'

Shirley smiled. 'Hey, Champ, you won!'

Wes frowned. 'Shirl, you're a nut.'

'Oh, yeah? Who taught Marty about teamwork? Who taught her to play her position? You march right over there, Champ, and make things right.' Shirley picked up the empty sandwich tray and headed toward the kitchen.

Make things right. As though you ever could. Yet he'd told Mark to do just that.

Wes looked across the garage to where Marty was chewing on her sandwich, caught her glancing furtively at him. Hell, he oughta tell her that her mother had been right about her father's death, and that it had already been avenged.

He took a deep breath and started across to give it a try.

Marty tried to be quiet coming in at four-thirty in the morning, but Chrissie, wearing an oversize Pearl Jam sweatshirt as a nightie, popped into the kitchen while she was still taking off her jacket. So much for the few minutes she'd hoped to have alone with Romey, unwinding. She eased her sling back on and Chrissie asked, 'Hey, Mom, what happened to your arm?'

'The bad guy stomped on my shoulder. How come you're up?'

'I heard your car.'

'You hear too much. I wish you'd listen to a lot more of your music; they say it'll make you deaf.'

Chrissie grinned. 'OK. Did you arrest that bad guy?'

'Sort of. But he died before we could lock him up.' She saw her daughter's dark eyes widen, filled with questions, and said, 'Let's fix some hot chocolate, OK? Romey said he'd come over.'

Chrissie headed to the cabinet for the chocolate. 'Are you going to marry Romey?'

'Probably. Do you think it's a good idea?' Marty asked warily.

Her daughter shrugged. 'It's OK. He's pretty cool for an old guy.'

'Yeah, I tried for a young cute one, but nobody in Pearl Jam would have me.'

'Mom!' Chrissie punched her in the arm. The good arm, but it still hurt.

Didn't matter, the kid had answered an important question.

Marty said, 'Hey, my arm's useless; stir the milk, OK?'

Chrissie stirred, hot chocolate being one of her specialties. 'So tell!'

Marty told the story, brushing lightly over the dangers on the ledge, giving only enough detail to account for her damaged shoulder and bruises. 'It was strange. When I showed him that picture of the nun, it's like he really saw her for the first time. Realized that the woman in his mind was not the real one. It stunned him.'

Chrissie turned down the flame, stirred some more. 'Weird. Then what?'

Marty went on, moving quickly to the fire and the Feds. 'So of course, they called in the FBI to pick him up. Helicopters, sharpshooters.'

'The FBI? Cool!' Chrissie said.

'Yeah. But they couldn't go get him until the fire was out, and by then it was snowing a lot and that held them up too.'

'Was he covered with snow when they got him?' Chrissie asked.

'No, there was a lot of wind on that ledge.' Marty shivered, remembering. 'It was really cold, but the wind blew the snow off. Even so the guys in the FBI chopper didn't see him the first time. They had good searchlights but there was still some snow falling and I think they focused on the wrong ledge.'

'Don't they have like heat sensors?'

'Yeah, but those kind of went berserk with the hotspots from the fire below, plus McGabben wasn't giving off much heat.'

There was a thump from outside. 'Is that Romey?' Chrissie asked, lifting the saucepan from the flame.

Marty stepped to the back door, pushed the curtain aside, looked out at the porch. She said slowly, 'No, not yet.'

Her daughter took three mugs from the shelf. 'So was the bad guy already dead?'

'Probably. They took another pass about three a.m. when the snow had stopped, and finally spotted him lying there. He'd been on that cold windy ledge for twelve hours, and his warm clothes had burned. He died of exposure, Doc Altmann says.' She took a deep breath but Chrissie's dark eyes demanded more. 'Of course the FBI didn't know for sure he was dead, so they had snipers in the helicopter aim at him while they lowered two armed guys from the ridge. But he was completely frozen.' She shuddered.

'Did you have to look at him?' Chrissie was very still now.

'Yeah, I had to identify him as the guy who'd threatened us on the ledge.'

'Did you want to puke?'

Marty knew it wasn't a flippant question. Knew she had to be honest. She said, 'He didn't look as bad as the body you saw when you puked. But it was bad. His eyes were open. It was like that song you play, Chrissie. He could just stare, he couldn't see.'

Chrissie nodded solemnly.

There was a tap on the door. Marty opened it and Romey stepped in, glanced at the sling, brushed her cheek gently with his fingers, then turned to Chrissie. 'Do I smell chocolate?'

'Yeah, there's a mug for you.'

'Good. What's that on the porch?'

Marty said, 'Someone just dropped it by. Can you bring it in? My arm's useless for a couple weeks. Chrissie, don't put the mugs on the table yet.'

Romey brought it in, a big box-shape wrapped in furniture padding, and placed it on the kitchen table. Chrissie helped move the padding aside and frowned at the glass walls in puzzlement. 'It's empty! Just branches.'

Marty said, 'It's not empty. Look hard.'

Romey pulled off the note taped to one side, handed it to Marty. They read it together: 'Heading for new horizons. Take good care of Pythia.' Romey looked at Marty, mouthed *The sisters?* and she nodded.

Chrissie squealed, 'I see it! A snake! Can I keep it?'

Marty nodded. 'Yeah, but keep her in your room. Don't want to give Aunt Vonnie a heart attack.'

'She's beautiful! Where'd she come from?'

'Can't say.' Marty took Romey's hand, smiled at her daughter, at the snake, happy to be home. 'Maybe from the god of science projects. Let's have that chocolate.'